DAUGHTER
OF
WINTER
AND
TWILIGHT

HELEN CORCORAN grew up in Cork, Ireland, dreaming of scheming queens and dashing lady knights. After graduating from Trinity College, Dublin, she worked as a bookseller for over a decade. She lives in Dublin, writing fantasy novels and haunting coffee shops in search of the perfect latte. Her first novel, *Queen of Coin and Whispers,* is also published by The O'Brien Press.

DAUGHTER OF WINTER AND TWILIGHT

HELEN CORCORAN

THE O'BRIEN PRESS
DUBLIN

First published 2023 by
The O'Brien Press Ltd,
12 Terenure Road East, Rathgar,
Dublin 6, D06 HD27 Ireland.

Tel: +353 1 4923333; Fax: +353 1 4922777
E-mail: books@obrien.ie
Website: obrien.ie

The O'Brien Press is a member of Publishing Ireland.
ISBN: 978-178849-370-3
Text © copyright Helen Corcoran 2023
The moral rights of the author have been asserted.
Copyright for typesetting, layout, editing, design © The O'Brien Press Ltd
Design and layout by Emma Byrne
Cover design by Emma Byrne
Map and family trees pp8-11 by Bex Sheridan
All rights reserved.

1 3 5 7 8 6 4 2
23 25 27 26 24

Printed and bound by Norhaven Paperback A/S, Denmark
The paper in this book is produced using pulp from managed forests

Daughter of Winter and Twilight receives
financial assistance from the Arts Council

Published in

For Gabbie, without
whom this book would
still be languishing on
Chapter Four.

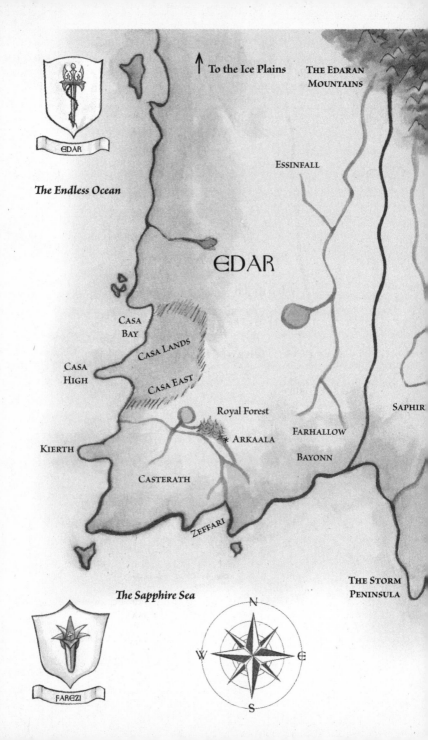

EDAR

To the Ice Plains

THE EDARAN MOUNTAINS

ESSINFALL

The Endless Ocean

CASA BAY

CASA LANDS

CASA HIGH

CASA EAST

Royal Forest

★ ARKAALA

SAPHIR

FARHALLOW

KIERTH

BAYONN

CASTERATH

ZEFFARI

The Sapphire Sea

THE STORM PENINSULA

EDAR

FAREZI

N

W   E

S

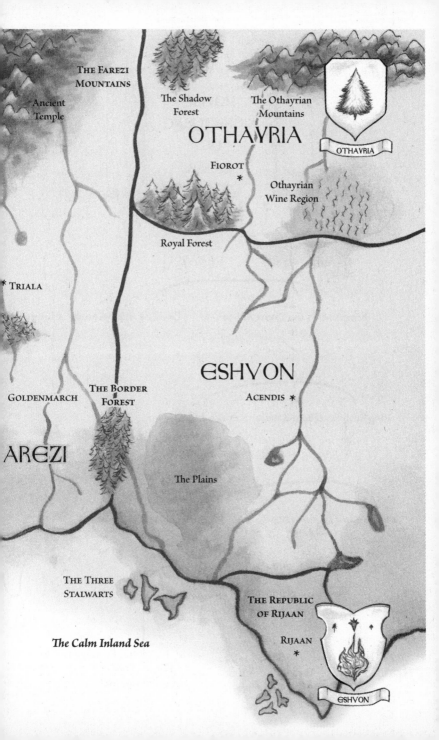

HOUSE
SIONBOURNE
OF
GOAR

(noble ancestors)

King Anderrs II = Queen Aldara   Lord Erik = Queen Firelle of Farezi

King Ruan II = Queen Katarin   Prince Aelfred

King Erwan = Queen Jienne   Prince Artur = Lady Issabel

Queen Aurelia IV = Queen Xania

Princess Emri
(once of Farezi)

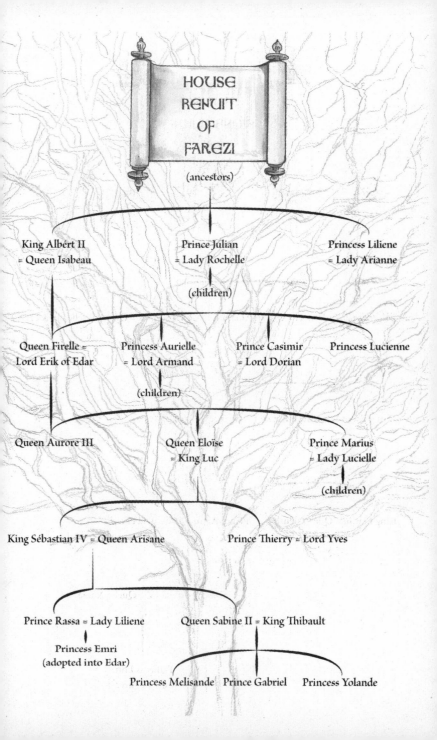

HOUSE RENUIT OF FAREZI

(ancestors)

King Albért II = Queen Isabeau   Prince Julian = Lady Rochelle   Princess Liliene = Lady Arianne

(children)

Queen Firelle = Lord Erik of Edar   Princess Aurielle = Lord Armand   Prince Casimir = Lord Dorian   Princess Lucienne

(children)

Queen Aurore III   Queen Eloïse = King Luc   Prince Marius = Lady Lucielle

(children)

King Sébastian IV = Queen Arisane   Prince Thierry = Lord Yves

Prince Rassa = Lady Liliene   Queen Sabine II = King Thibault

Princess Emri
(adopted into Edar)

Princess Melisande   Prince Gabriel   Princess Yolande

O nce, there is a tree.

A tree of life.

It isn't the tree of its kind, for there are many in history, referenced in scribbles on the margins of sagas, a background detail, a bit player in epics and wars and romances. But it's the tree of life in this particular land, on this particular continent, in this particular part of the world, and so it is the most important one.

The tree of life is, simultaneously, budding, blooming, fading, and bare – a tree in all stages of life at once. Its roots, deep, deep down in the dark of the world, are touched by the magic that is the source of all things.

People believed, once, that the tree bore fruit, and that magic passed to those who consumed it. But if they did, they didn't overcome the limits of their mortality to become legend.

Instead, a woman boasts that she will cut the tree down and take the power for herself.

This detail, in and of itself, is not so remarkable. Almost every country, every culture, has such a person. Someone who may become beloved or reviled, a hero or a tragedy (both, sometimes, when the winters are especially miserable, and people need to hear about someone else making poor choices to feel better about their own).

The woman, forced to make good on her boast, undertakes the quest. She traverses many miles, fulfils the obligatory slaying of monsters – as expected of an adventurer – and eventually faces the tree of all life with a trustworthy axe in her hand.

And the tree devours her.

...a sparse Treasury, frayed international diplomacy, and an inefficient government headed by a politician as corrupt as the royal Court were only some of the problems faced by Queen Aurelia IV upon taking the throne. However, even at nineteen, she showed early signs of the indomitable will of House Sionbourne during her first year of rule, and later contemporary accounts now agree that her temporary downfall, through the usurpation of her throne by Prince Rassa of Farezi, was the result of political treason rather than proof of the weak character already evidenced in her predecessor.

Queen Aurelia IV, alongside her wife, Queen Xania I, became known as the first of Edar's Great Queens. Their marriage and joint rule are considered the foundation that ushered in a Golden Age for their adopted daughter and heir, Princess Emri, once of Farezi and daughter of Prince Rassa himself...

— excerpt from *Stewards of the North: A History of the House of Sionbourne and the Creation of Modern Edar* (Third Edition)

History will note the achievements of Queen Aurelia IV, who grimly returned to power following the – shall we say *unusual?* – circumstances of the usurper's sudden death. In the four years since, the Sionbourne Queen, who will perhaps one day be known as *great*, has already shown a startling level of determination in dragging Edar out of its backwater state. (Incredible, what one can achieve when one no longer fears dying at the hands of one's own Head of Government *and* royal cousin.)

History will note Her Majesty's political and cultural achievements, but today *we* are more concerned with the great romance that she chose over her royal duty. Others may consider this beneath a monarch's dignity, but it's now widely known that Miss Xania Bayonn – once Queen Aurelia's spymaster and soon to be wife – courted treason to find her in Farezi, refusing to believe that she had willingly abdicated in favour of Prince Rassa, a rescue fraught with considerable peril and an uncertain outcome.

History will note Queen Aurelia's achievements. But today we celebrate a woman marrying into House Sionbourne with a determined will all her own.

— excerpt from a society page published during the fifth year of Queen Aurelia IV's reign, upon her marriage to Queen Xania I

16

SPRING

ONE

Sometimes I was convinced that Edar would have benefited from fewer men being in power. Probably because I was descended from a particularly useless one: Lord Erik.

He was the only sibling of King Anderrs II, first monarch of House Sionbourne. Anderrs, after taking Edar by force from a weak ruler, had privately fretted over Erik's ambition now that he was so close – and yet so far – from the throne.

The solution was swift and resolute: he would be married abroad. The new Edaran King did not have to look far: Farezi, their closest neighbour and closest enemy, had a future Queen in need of a husband. Erik would have a throne, and peace would be secured between the two countries for another few decades.

Lord Erik: my great-great-grandfather. The blood link between the countries of my birth and future.

It was ridiculous to stare at a portrait of a man from generations ago, trying to find a shred of resemblance. I knew this, and yet I couldn't stop, following each brushstroke, trying to find any familiarity in his thin face and dissatisfied expression.

My reasons, secret and never voiced to anyone, were especially pitiful. It would be kinder to find something in a bitter man whose story had faded into history, since so many noted my resemblance to my usurper birth father.

Sometimes, when I looked in the mirror, it was all I could see, too.

The bells tolled the hour, a familiar sound that shaped my morning, my day, my life…

…and I was officially late.

I swore under my breath, the curses harsh between my teeth, and glared at the faint cracks across Lord Erik's face. 'This is all your fault,' I informed him, then turned, picked up my skirts, and bolted down the length of the portrait gallery.

At the entrance, I switched to a brisk walk: a princess never ran in public. And I was almost eighteen, no longer able to get away with rushing anywhere.

Spring had arrived with surprisingly good weather that hinted towards a glorious summer. Sunlight poured in through the windows, smooth and butter-soft. The trees were already thick with buds close to opening. I loved spring best: a fresh start for everyone, a chance to put aside the poor humour that had built up over the colder months and try again.

Meetings with Isra, my parents' spymaster, were unpleasant at the best of times. Everyone assumed they were tense, clandestine affairs, but the position mostly meant a lot of paperwork, while the intelligence agents tried to stay alive and safe. During my first official meeting with Isra, I'd made a joke from nerves; she'd chosen to be offended, and our dynamic had never recovered.

At the royal wing, I nodded at the guards by the entrance and asked after their children.

Princess Isra of Eshvon, Duchess Casterath, kept three offices in different parts of the palace. I only knew of two; her private one, hidden deep in the secret passages within the walls, was still a mystery to me. I wasn't offended: I was an heir still being trained, and unlike the spymasters before her, Isra had decided to be open about her position. There were risks. Today, I'd been summoned to her semi-public office in the royal wing. It was better than being summoned to my parents' study, where she usually berated me in their presence.

Years ago, after deciding to stay in Edar, Isra had been removed from the Eshvon succession, stripped of the privilege that her titles granted her. Unofficially, it was an etiquette nightmare – foreign royals didn't stick around unless they married in – and Mother had swiftly made her Duchess of Casterath, a vacant southern estate that had reverted back to the Crown.

Even so, I knew from cautious eavesdropping that Isra still missed Eshvon. The doors of her office were stamped with Edar's rose briar wrapped around a sword, the Casterath coat-of-arms, *and* the stylised Eshvon pomegranate. Isra might be employed in Edar's service, but she never let anyone forget where she came from.

I knocked and entered, smiling at her forever unruffled secretary, who bowed and tilted her head for me to go through, then quietly closed the inner doors behind me.

The walls were the golden shade of a perfect autumn day, the floorboards buffed and polished. Isra's desk and the seating area by the fireplace were muffled by thick rugs spun in yellow, orange, and brown, with splashes of red. One wall was taken up by maps of the continent: Edar and our neighbours, and the countries further north and east. Notes and scribbles were pinned to the maps, written in a code I was still learning to decipher quickly. The wall to her left was taken up by a large window, cracked open to let in a breeze. Every other scrap of wall was filled with floor to ceiling bookcases.

It was a cheery room. I often suspected Isra had decorated it as such to fool people into lowering their guard.

She was at her desk, head bent as her pen moved steadily across paper. Ink: formal correspondence then. For initial decryption, she worked in pencil to burn afterwards.

Out of everyone in my parents' private circle, Isra was the only one I interacted with solely as princess and never as myself. Isra took her role as Whispers, the royal spymaster, seriously. And the older I got, the more she seemed to consider me a headache. It was a source of contention between her and my parents, who remained firm that as royal heirs went, I could be much worse.

'Good afternoon, Your Grace,' I said.

She glanced up and raised an elegant eyebrow. 'Your Highness

– you're late.' Despite her dry tone, she inclined her head.

From what the Court said, Isra's beauty had only sharpened over time. Her thick, dark hair was only beginning to show hints of grey and silver. Her brown skin was still free of the stress of her position. One of her few tells was a sort of weariness around the eyes.

She gestured towards the seating area by the fireplace, where the game board was already set up. As Isra rose from her desk, I dropped into my usual chair.

'An unavoidable detainment, I'm afraid,' I said, soaking my voice with casual brightness. I knew better than to elaborate. Isra had limited sympathy for worries she considered out of my control.

She took her seat, eyeing me with a calmness that I'd learned to dread.

The board was set up for an Eshvoni game that when loosely translated into Edaran was called Root and Fang. The board layout was similar to chess. Each player had five main pieces, carved into mythological creatures, under their control as an army. The game combined logic and strategy (root) and war (fang). The goal was to strengthen one's own army, while destroying the other, helped or hindered by cards that affected attacks and defences to be unleashed and discarded at will.

While the game was better (and rowdier) with several players, Isra and I had played together weekly for years, and I was nowhere near beating her swiftly. I'd only progressed to winning in the last year, but my victories were laboured and slow.

She sipped her drink, gaze flickering across the board, then scooped up the dice. A cold smile before she turned the hourglass with her other hand, and the game began.

As we dealt cards and considered our strategies, Isra drilled me on various poisons. All my food was tested before I ate or drank it, as was my parents'. During her first year as Queen, even before her coronation, Mother had narrowly avoided a blatant poisoning attempt. She had a healthy fear of poison, against herself and those she loved, and it was a key area of my education that Isra and I always took seriously.

For years, we had gone over poison after poison, their smell and taste. Whether they could be detected or not, what the antidotes were, if any. With some of the common ones, she'd decided I would ingest them in small amounts, building a tolerance over years. With others, it was too dangerous, so I simply had to arm myself with the knowledge and hope.

I'd had a reprieve on poison examinations for the last few months, but during our last meeting, I'd missed a non-fatal one that she'd lined my glass with, and suffered not only a night of my body trying to relieve itself of my insides, but Isra deciding I'd become dependent on my poison-taster. To no one's surprise, she'd promptly revoked my reprieve from surprise tests like this one.

When the drilling was done, Isra eyed the discard pile and

remarked, 'I heard the most fascinating thing today, Your Highness.'

Inwardly, I frowned at my poor hand of cards. 'I'm intrigued, Your Grace.'

'Mmm. Apparently the Court – and your parents – vastly underestimated your affections for the Admiral's nephew.' As Isra played a card that prevented me from using force and discarding anything for two turns, I scowled.

'You were the one who said there was a new leak in my ladies,' I said, deciding to build a hand that would bulk up my defences. 'So I let some drips out.'

Disbelief flickered across Isra's face. 'And who, precisely, would believe *for a moment* that you've been nurturing a secret passion for Micah of Casa East?'

I smiled grimly. 'Florette Sigrath.'

Florette had been elevated to my ladies as a reconciliation gesture between my parents and her family, who'd remained neutral when Rassa, my birth father, had usurped the throne. We weren't particularly close, though I enjoyed her singing and noted her true feelings and opinions whenever she slipped up and revealed them. But until Isra had said at our last meeting that she'd suspected at least one new turncoat, and I'd dutifully spread different strands of false information amongst my ladies, she'd shown no sign of being a spy, efficient or otherwise.

I suppose that was the point.

'How did the rumour get back to you?' I asked.

'She had tea with Lady Mizyr's eldest daughter. At the third invitation, she could no longer hold her tongue about what you'd said in her presence. Unfortunately for Lady Sigrath, most of the Mizyr staff is also within my employ – including the maid serving their tea.'

Most people would probably consider the amount of people Isra had followed or spied upon to be excessive. Those same people probably wouldn't have survived as Whispers for almost twenty years.

The Sigrath and Mizyr families had no marriage history nor extended ties. Neither were they political allies, and they certainly weren't publicly civil. To call the Mizyr unpopular was an understatement. They'd thrown their support wholeheartedly behind Rassa when he'd taken the throne. After his death, they'd not only refused to recant their poor judgment, but thrown their weight into criticising my parents' reign.

'I didn't think Florette was so... *silly*.' I spoke slowly, still trying to discern the pattern. Florette and I weren't exactly friends. I was polite to all my ladies, but the majority had accepted the position for political reasons and future royal favour. Even so, it still hurt a little that she'd visited a family who loathed my parents.

'The eldest Mizyr is unattached,' I continued, 'as is her brother. But neither is favourable for marriage, especially since the Sigrath family has only recently regained their standing.' I worked my jaw, a piece of the puzzle snapping into place. 'Florette is acting alone.'

'Very good.' Isra poured fresh cordial and nudged a glass towards me. 'I agree. After taking a decade to recover their prior, *modest* standing, the Sigrath would be fools to throw it away. Consider: Florette is unhappy that you're keeping her at a respectful distance, and the Mizyr need fresh blood since they are anathema at Court.'

Another puzzle piece clicked into place. The picture partially revealed made me sigh. 'She's their new spy.'

'Precisely.' Isra's expression turned hard. 'My understanding is that the Mizyr, before their disgrace, wasn't a particularly bad family to marry into. Not until they threw their lot in with *him*.' She seldom acknowledged Rassa's existence, but when it was unavoidable, she refused to call him by name. From what I'd heard, they had loathed each other, and his death hadn't changed her feelings. 'I imagine they've fed Florette sweet poison about their star being on the rise again.'

'Through me?'

Isra drummed her fingers against the table. 'They've been pushing for your marriage. If you marry from outside Edar, they'll want to get in early to gain favour.'

'Hence why Florette warned them about Micah.'

'If you marry within the Court, particularly from a family who stood by the Crown, they'll regain little.'

My eventual marriage was a matter of endless speculation. My parents both ruled in their own right, so I wouldn't inherit until both were dead or otherwise unable to reign: a future I wasn't eager to face. Gaining a crown wasn't worth losing them. Not now, not ever. I was probably the only royal heir who felt like this – for most, being next in line was an endless waiting game.

Now it was my turn for disbelief. 'And they believed Florette so easily?'

'Perhaps,' Isra said. 'In other countries, being one of the royal ladies is a mark of esteem. But your mother's first set were mostly spies, and yours aren't much better. This country,' she muttered. 'Almost twenty years, and it still baffles me.'

'So I winnow Florette out?'

'No.' Isra smiled, slow and sharp. 'Let her trip up again.'

'You want me to feed her more false information?'

'We haven't flushed out informants in your ladies for over a year. I expect your methods to have improved.'

When I was younger, I'd memorised all the noble families, from the barons in the lower ranks up to the dukes and duchesses, the highest and closest to the Crown. I'd learned their histories and their mistakes. I'd deciphered the alliances not only tied together by blood and marriage, but through noble handshakes; loans; a whispered word in the right ear.

Mother hated Root and Fang, preferring the less fashionable but, to her, more reliable game of chess. Yet to me, Court seemed like an elaborate chess board. Every courtier could potentially advance my power or end up needing to be swept aside. Mother had wanted me to have an easier time than she'd had as princess, but she also believed in preparing for the worst. And the worst was that some people would only ever see me as a usurper's daughter, who should never have been made heir. So it was my responsibility to know those courtiers better than they knew me.

'If it were me,' I said, rolling the dice between my fingers, 'I would have stopped Florette from speaking while we were being served.' Being careful of what I said around others had been drummed into me since childhood. 'And I certainly would have reconsidered her suitability as a spy.'

Isra looked disgusted. 'Her career won't be illustrious. She's a means to an end, or the Mizyr are especially desperate. Likely both.'

The hurt at Florette's silliness, already fading, was fully extinguished by a wave of pettiness. She might be trying to work against me, but at least she wouldn't be *good* at it.

My mood only turned worse when, with a flourish, Isra played her hand and destroyed my griffin and winged horse, neatly scuppering any chance I had of winning.

For as long as I could remember, a spark of pettiness had lingered inside me. I wasn't entirely certain what, or who, had shaped it, but not even my parents' love could smother it. Instead, I used it to prove people wrong – to be better, smarter, *sharper* – no matter what they secretly thought of me.

I couldn't be motivated by spite forever. I knew that.

But as I studied Isra's winning hand, I knew spite worked for now.

TWO

Later that afternoon, I was informed that my parents' meetings would stretch late into the evening, and they wouldn't be dining with me. We no longer ate with the Court, except for banquets and other state occasions, and my grandparents and aunt were all away. I didn't really want to eat alone, so I asked Rialla and Micah if they would join me.

Micah arrived first, brandishing a bouquet almost threateningly at me. 'It appears I've been horribly remiss at showing my great esteem and affection for you during our courtship,' he said, a smile tugging at his mouth. 'Please, take these blooms and pretend I'm good enough at poetry to flatter you against them.'

Trying not to laugh, I relieved him of his floral burden.

'Please,' a voice said from behind him, 'spare us from your poetry.'

He stepped aside to reveal Rialla, who raised an eyebrow and held up her empty hands. 'Are we celebrating something?' she asked. 'Or are you finally telling me about the courtship I've been hitherto oblivious to?'

I handed her the flowers, succumbing to the laughter bubbling in my throat. 'Please, accept these as an insufficient token of apology.' In a more normal voice, I added, 'There's no court-ship, as you well know.'

Rialla shut the door and, turning back, caught my gaze. 'Oh, I do, Your Highness. Very much so.' For a moment, I stood rooted to the spot, my stomach twisting as I flushed. I hadn't so much as walked into the trap as tripped head-first.

I'd *had* something close to a courtship with a friend... but not with Micah.

Sensing the atmospheric tipping point, he coughed, then asked what was for dinner. 'I'm positively famished!' he declared, too brightly, slipping into the role he'd taken on since Midwinter: trying to dissipate the tension that arose when Rialla and I navigated... whatever we now were to each other.

'The food is here,' I said, trying to metaphorically pull myself together by laughing. 'Come, before it gets cold.'

My rooms were close to my parents' suite. I'd made them as light and airy as the space allowed, with bright tapestries on the walls, pale furniture, and elegant green and white drapes. We settled around the table, passing dishes and pouring wine, and the awkward moment faded. We'd all known each other for so long that the familiar habits of our friendship always reas-serted themselves, no matter the strange new territory between us. And tension could never last long around Micah.

Every day I secretly thanked Diana of Casa High, the Royal Admiral and Micah's aunt, for all but dumping him into my presence. Micah, seven years old, with his family's blue eyes and a shock of black curls, had taken my measure and gravely asked if I could climb trees.

I could not, but he'd patiently taught me, and I'd never once fallen out of one.

'So,' he said, after swiping the last of the green beans and crunching a mouthful in satisfaction, 'are you going to explain why I felt obliged to bring you flowers?'

I dragged the last of a sauce-soaked vegetable skin across my plate and resisted a sigh. 'Politics. I can't tell you. If it works, you'll find out.'

When my meetings with Isra had started, she'd stressed that anything we discussed could only be trusted to a handful of people: us, my parents, and Matthias, their advisor and oldest friend. Everyone else, no matter how close they were, should be considered potentially suspect. It was compounded by the fact that I was a princess, but my parents ruled; it was not done for me to play political games without keeping them informed. Everything would gradually change once I gained my majority, and officially took on further responsibilities. But this was the agreement for now.

However: Micah was the nephew of the Royal Admiral, one of the most feared women in the country, and Rialla's aunt was the Master of Coin's successor. They both had brains, frequently used them, and recognised a false lure when it was dangled before them.

Micah opened his mouth, whether to argue or otherwise press the issue, but Rialla gently squeezed his arm. She knew all too well the myriad threads of power woven between my parents, their advisors, and me.

Taking the opening, I added glibly, 'I appreciate the flowers, but must regretfully decline your affections.'

He snorted, choosing humour over irritation.

If there was anyone who'd be an ideal Consort, it was Micah. But we'd never thought of each other that way, even though I knew he was a good choice for a stable marriage. A few others had attempted cautious flirtations, including Lady Cira, who had liked me more than she'd liked being at Court, and Lord Hisham, a budding poet, whose cheerful company I'd enjoyed until his uncertain family arrangement had turned into an all-too-certain betrothal contract. But it was Rialla, tall and sharp-tongued, yet somehow romantic, who'd truly turned my head, a slow process that still seemed to have happened all at once.

And what a disaster it had turned out to be.

No, that was unfair: it had ended as well as it could, under the circumstances. I'd plastered on the regal mask I'd so often scorned Mother for hiding behind, and acted like nothing had changed, while inside my heart had struggled to mend the cracks splintered within.

'Emri?'

I blinked, suddenly aware I was staring into space, my fork held in mid-air. An uneasy glance flickered between Rialla and Micah; I coughed and dredged up a smile. As always, I hid the upset away, shoved it down so it would only resurface when I was alone, and it was safe.

'Sorry,' I said. 'I was… thinking.'

'A dangerous pastime,' Micah teased, but with little effort.

I rallied before the sweet course, while Micah gossiped about who his aunt had decided could – and more importantly *couldn't* – return to the family estate for the summer gathering. Rialla grumbled about her parents sitting her down, once again, to fret about her *lack of ambition*. I managed to avoid snorting; Micah did not. Rialla was many things, but not lacking in ambition. She and her parents simply disagreed on the acceptable paths upon which to direct said ambition.

But I couldn't stop myself from turning the problem of Florette Sigrath and the Mizyr around in my mind, nor ignore my resurgent uneasiness around Rialla. My contributions to the conversation once again petered away, and I only snapped out of my thoughts when Micah tipped the last of the wine into my glass.

'Apologies,' I said, as he suggested, 'If you'd prefer to be alone, we can leave?'

We fell into an awkward silence.

When Rialla pressed her hand against his arm again, he caught her in a hard stare. They engaged in a silent battle of wills, as I focused on chewing a rose cream to nothing.

Three was an awkward number of friends when two fell for each other. Rialla was fond of Micah, but I was closer to him. He was unenthusiastic about any sort of romance, whether because he couldn't be bothered with the fuss, or was already aware of his place in his family's marital strategies.

When Rialla and I had succumbed to our year-long tension, we weren't sure whether to tell him. But the next day after our first kiss, he'd simply known something had changed. He'd tried to accept it good-naturedly, though fear that he would be cast aside clung to his easy smiles. He'd had no reason to worry: I had so few close friends that I wasn't willing to discard one for romance, and Rialla had agreed.

But now that Rialla's feelings for me had changed, so had her friendship with Micah. She didn't exactly pull... rank was the wrong word, but the closest to what it felt like. When she did, I liked it about as much as Micah – not very much. The implication of possessiveness sat sour in my stomach. Micah didn't know me any less than Rialla now did; she just knew different parts of me.

Yet they must have been more concerned about me than I realised, because Micah acceded the battle of wills with only a little poor grace. Still, he finished his dessert and wine before he left, smiling and bowing with a flourish, reiterating his *great esteem and affection* for me at the door.

My laughter faded, along with my smile, as I returned to Rialla.

'You shouldn't have done that,' I said. 'It's not fair on him, and it's not like you had the right to pull... pull – *former romantic rank*.'

It didn't matter how well I was taught, how delicately the chains of ruling and duty were impressed upon me. Deep down, I'd convinced myself that it would be different for me, obsessed as I was with Rialla's kiss, the scent of her hair, the angle of her jaw, the brush of her cool fingers against my neck. I'd have a love match like my parents, who had endured assassins, abdication, treason, and desperation to be together. What Rialla felt for me was surely as strong as what Mama felt for Mother, what had given her the strength to marry a Queen and rule a country.

It was not. And though I could hardly admit it to myself, I couldn't blame Rialla.

It was different when you married into royalty. Especially since Mama ruled in her own right, a much different responsibility to prior Consorts. Whoever had the misfortune – some days that's all it felt like – to marry me would shoulder an immense shared burden, depending on the political situation I'd eventually inherit. A lot of pressure even for another royal, never mind a courtier.

'Was it Florette Sigrath?' Rialla asked, smoothing away a flicker of irritation. 'She's been talking about Micah incessantly. He was becoming worried the Sigrath had lost the run of themselves and were considering him for a betrothal.'

I scoffed. 'As if the Admiral would consider them for a moment.' The Casa family not only had a long and glorious naval history, but were also impeccably loyal to the Crown. The Sigrath may have regained a little royal favour, but they were nowhere close to marrying into a lineage like Micah's.

'Well, was it?' Rialla repeated.

I'd forgotten how piercing her gaze was when she devoted her undivided attention on someone. I'd also forgotten that, even though I was forbidden from sharing anything from Isra's meetings, it didn't stop Rialla and Micah from drawing their own conclusions.

I shrugged, an elegant action that wouldn't fool her for a moment. 'Your guess is as good as mine.'

Rialla narrowed her eyes, that flicker of resentment rippling over her face again. 'You'll have to trust us eventually.' *Don't I, at least, warrant your trust by now?* lingered, unspoken, between us.

'It's not a matter of trust,' I snapped. 'My parents rule, not me.' I was usually good – certainly better than I was today – at controlling my temper around her. But Rialla poked at a wound, whereas Micah tried to soothe it. Together, they were usually a good balance for me, but Rialla and I had upset it all.

She fixed me with that sharp gaze again. The lamplight highlighted the russet tints in her brown hair. 'They rule for now,' she said. 'And you'll be eighteen in a few months. You can't keep putting off gathering your own allies. Isra won't be around forever to serve you.'

My face turned into my coldest regal mask. 'Your concern is

noted, Lady Rialla, but was not requested.'

Maybe that was our problem, really. I'd fooled myself into believing that a relationship between us could last, even though I was a royal heir. And perhaps Rialla had fooled herself into believing that by loving me, it would bring her closer to the centre of things, that she could handle the delicate balancing act of ruling. And even though she'd realised the reality of our future together and had rejected it, maybe part of her still wanted to be close to power.

I'll have to watch Rialla, I realised bleakly, *as closely as the rest of my ladies.*

Like Mother, Isra was often right, but unlike her, she was rarely kind with my feelings. And just as I needed Mother's firm kindness, I also needed Isra's brutal practicality. Court would devour me, otherwise – even those who cared for me.

THREE

During my early years in Edar, the word *Goldenmarch* lingered in my wake: a whisper, a curse, a warning.

I soon pretended not to hear it, for no one met my eyes if I reacted. Goldenmarch: the estate of the Farezi heir, given to them in trust when they came of age. Known for its orchards and good hunting, the sun never seemed to set there.

When I was twelve, eavesdropping outside a gathering with Rialla, I finally learned why Goldenmarch followed me like a stain in my shadow.

When Rassa usurped the throne, this was where he'd had Mother hidden, drugged and afraid. Every speck of colour had been erased on the estate in favour of endless white. The light in her room was never extinguished. The servants and guards didn't speak. Her food was limited and bland, enough to keep her alive and little else.

It didn't take long for Mother's mind to unspool.

It took much longer to weave it back together.

The Court skittered around the words *torture of the mind*, but that didn't change what it was.

After we overheard it all, Rialla couldn't look me in the eye, and I feared I'd lost her. At the time, befriending children of the high nobility was a slow, painful process – a stark distinction to the courtesy and etiquette their families publicly showed me. Politeness and friendship are not the same.

As the daughter of a Farezi prince, I should have been raised in Goldenmarch, but it was shuttered and abandoned, as disgraced as my family. Instead, I was raised in Saphirun, the estate of my grandmother, the Dowager Queen Arisane. I remembered little, as if my mind had abandoned the hazy memories as soon as I arrived in Edar, but I did remember that Princess Melisande, my older cousin, who had taken my place as the Farezi heir, had soon joined me at Saphirun.

The estate derived its name from the large river that cut through it, eventually joining with others to wash out into the southern sea. The manor was a monster of grey and white brick, centuries of architectural styles meshed into repairs and improvements. But inside, you could believe you were drifting upon the sea, each room and corridor decorated or highlighted in different shades of blue.

At the time I hadn't thought about there being so much blue. Farezi's banners were green and gold. So much blue, part of Edar's royal colours, made little sense in a Farezi royal estate. But I found out later, after I arrived in Edar, that the estate had been gifted to Lord Erik upon his marriage, which he'd decorated in blue to remind every visitor of *his* lineage, and been maintained as such for over a century mostly from a perverse sense of amusement.

Three days after my meeting with Isra, my eyes snapped open to blackness. It was too close to the darkness in my nightmares, shadows pooling around me in a locked, shuttered room; a dream that had haunted me since childhood. In my scramble to light a candle, I almost toppled out of bed.

My chest heaved, as I sucked in air and forced it out with a strength that hurt. I stuffed my knuckles into my mouth, bit down. In out, in out, in and out, in and out. In and out. Slowly – more painful than the teeth marks on my hand – my breathing calmed.

Sinking back onto the pillows, I followed the candlelight and shadows dancing across the ceiling. The dark could always be conquered. Always be driven back. Night could never fully outwit the dawn.

I closed my eyes. Pressed the heels of my hands against my eyes until spots of colours burst. I hadn't had nightmares like this in years. If I managed to get back to sleep, I'd *probably* be all right when the servants arrived to start my day. But my eyes were wide open, my heart still unsteady, and both had chased away drowsiness.

I ground out a curse and flung off my blankets.

The halls were quiet, save for the patrolling guards. It felt embarrassing to be wandering around so late – or so early, depending on how you considered it.

While the halls were bright enough that a candle was unnecessary, the portrait gallery was dim. With windows only near the doors, my light was pitiful against the shadows.

My heart pounded again as bits of the dream flashed in my mind: that cursed room where I was curled up tight on the bed, and I couldn't cry because *she* always knew when I did –

No. I shook my head hard enough for my curls to bounce against my neck. I was almost eighteen years old. My childhood nightmares could no longer have this power over me. I wouldn't allow it.

Even without the feeble candle, I could still have easily found my way to the portrait; I'd been here so often, my feet knew the precise number of steps.

Lord Erik gazed down at me. The flickering light heightened his dissatisfaction.

'This is all your fault,' I informed him bitterly, as always. 'You and your damn brother.'

Blaming a dead man's portrait wouldn't actually change anything. But saying it aloud make me feel calmer. A little weight off my shoulders was better than none.

And it was true. If Anderrs hadn't feared his brother's ambition and married him off to Farezi, the distant blood link wouldn't have meant that Rassa was Mother's heir until she had a child. He might still have overreached, but it would have been more blatant – a hostile takeover that no one could ignore.

Without these two *stupid* men, I might also not have been born, but I also wouldn't have been a disgraced princess, forever caught between my history and the family who loved me.

'Emri?'

I jumped, snapping my head to the left. 'Mother!'

She stood a few paces away, holding her own candle. Queen Aurelia IV and I didn't look alike. She was pale, her face thin, her eyes the stormy grey common to House Sionbourne. Her long brown hair was twisted into the braid she wore to bed.

But sometimes, when I practised a presentation for a tutor in the mirror, I caught my mouth moving like hers, or a familiar steely glint in my eye. We didn't look alike, but we were similar in the ways that made a family.

She came closer, a thick blue robe trailing behind her. 'Couldn't sleep?' Her face brightened with a smile, but when she noticed the portrait I stood before, her eyebrows shot up. 'Ah, Lord Erik.' She gestured behind her. 'As it happens, I came to scowl at Anderrs.'

As the lesser brother, with few achievements beyond his marriage – Anderrs had decreed his children be granted royal titles, but refused to grant the same to his brother – Lord Erik's painting was insignificantly placed. The official portrait of King Anderrs II with his Consort was further down, near the centre of the gallery. Where Erik was dissatisfied and weak, Anderrs and his wife were grim, almost ferociously proud, the generation that had turned

Sionbourne into a royal house. The old emblem, a stylised snow-flake, was still used in the heir's coat of arms.

We gazed at the first Sionbourne King in silence. Mother's eyebrows were drawn together in a frown, a hard set to her mouth.

'You couldn't sleep either?' I finally asked.

The old worry pricked in my chest. The worst of Mother's recovery after Goldenmarch had happened before I'd arrived in Edar. I'd only learned about it years later. With the help of her family and the physicians, and her own tattered will, she'd faced the nightmares, the flashbacks, the nights of poor sleep. The days she could barely stand food, or daylight, or darkness – whatever obstacle her mind dragged up from its lingering terror.

I often suspected Arisane had resented me because she couldn't do anything to *him*. She wasn't particularly religious, but dese-crating even Rassa's traitor bones would have been unforgivable. So her eye had turned to me and seen him, and our course was set.

If she could have resurrected Rassa, as our darkest myths hinted was once possible when the gods walked the land, she'd have given him a slow death. My parents would have probably fought her for the chance to do it themselves.

Sometimes, I wondered if I could do it. If I hated him enough, with all the agony he'd caused so many people, to kill him. If doing so would haunt me for the rest of my life.

Mother blinked, as if I'd disturbed her from deep thoughts –

now I knew how my friends felt around me – and I waited for her familiar smile before she brushed my concern away. Instead, she remained pensive.

'Come,' she said, gesturing towards a bench. 'Sit with me.'

My parents, much as I loved them, often gave themselves away. When Mama was annoyed with me, she tapped her pen against the blotter in a certain pattern. They usually shared a particular glance when I was in the process of being gently managed. And before delivering bad news, Mother always said, 'Sit with me.'

I tidied my robe, set my candle down, and braced myself.

Mother didn't speak immediately, allowing the silence to deepen. She'd been a careful child, Matthias had once told me, a consequence of navigating a hostile Court. But some of her habits had begun as coping methods after Goldenmarch: one being steady breathing. It stopped the panic before it gripped her, kept her from spiralling during moments of great stress. I hadn't seen Mother in the midst of an attack in years, but that didn't mean they didn't happen behind closed doors.

But being cautious didn't mean she was afraid.

'You're eighteen in autumn,' she finally said. 'Midwinter will be different this year.'

I nodded. Midwinter's longest night was one of Edar's most important celebrations. It was the closest thing we still had to religion. My parents held a ball each year, and danced as Lady Winter and her companions, Twilight and Night. They traditionally switched between Lady Winter and Twilight, with a favoured courtier taking the role of Night.

This year, marking my formal introduction, I would attend as Night. While the old myths mostly claimed a romantic connection between all three, the stories also held roots of deep loyalty and devotion. And my parents and I could definitely honour the old gods in that respect, for family was loyalty and devotion in ways that had nothing to do with birth and blood.

'Has something changed?' I asked.

Mother pressed her lips together, then said, 'Farezi intends to recall their diplomat. As a gesture of goodwill, their Queen has suggested that Princess Melisande accompany the replacement for an extended visit over winter.'

I stiffened; I couldn't help it. 'I see.'

When Queen Aurelia IV reclaimed her throne, my birth mother returned to Farezi pregnant; another of Rassa's pawns. He'd needed an heir to secure his reign; she was lovestruck and had ignored the worst parts of him. Nevertheless, my grandparents were pressured to abdicate following Rassa's actions. Aunt Sabine was suddenly Queen, a position which she'd only been half-heartedly trained for. She could easily have resented me for everything I symbolised.

Both she and Mother had become monarchs in the shadows of arrogant men. It was probably why Mother had insisted on building cordial relations between them, despite Rassa's treachery, recognising the position my aunt was in. And unlike Rassa, Queen Sabine had accepted peace while Farezi struggled to rebuild its dignity.

Mother studied me with a raised eyebrow. 'Do you?' When I glanced away, she continued, 'You'll be expected to spend time with Melisande. You're not just cousins, but heirs of neighbouring countries. But we can set limits: no small gatherings, for example.'

I swallowed, and gripped the edges of the bench hard enough to hurt. 'I know this is important, that the shadow of… *his* visit will linger while Melisande is here. I won't make things harder than necessary.' Against Mother's silence, I attempted a smile. 'The least I can do is be civil to my cousin.'

Mother didn't immediately reply, and it took more restraint than I expected not to squirm under her thoughtful gaze. 'We'll discuss it further with you tomorrow,' she said at last. 'You should try and get back to sleep.'

As we headed back towards the door, we passed Mother's coronation portrait. My parents had one each where they posed alone, and one together. Further down, we had an official family portrait, painted a year into my life here.

I'd be sitting for another once I came of age, decked in regalia. Privately, it felt like a waste of time and money, but my parents wanted an official record of me as daughter and heir – in paper, responsibility, and paintings – to solidify my legitimacy.

My gaze lingered on the old throne in her coronation portrait, turned it over in my mind.

Before we separated, Mother grasped my shoulders in the reassuringly firm grip she always deployed when I was unsettled, but needed steadiness rather than comfort. 'All will be well,' she said, kissing me on the forehead. It was what she and Mama always said when things were difficult at Court, or political discussions had collapsed into shambles, or they faced unexpected rains or underperforming harvests. When everything threatened to overwhelm, they reminded each other that hard times must be endured, but would always end.

I returned her smile and watched her walk back towards the royal wing, shadowed by two guards, and counted my heartbeats until the doors closed behind her. Then I turned and headed in the opposite direction. If the guards were exasperated at my refusal to sleep, they were too well trained to show it.

In the throne room, my candle was an even poorer defence against the shadows as I started the long walk towards the dais. A large standard hung from the ceiling; the royal sigil emblazoned in silver upon dark blue: a crown above a rose briar twisting around a sword.

When King Anderrs II took the Edaran crown, one of his first actions was to burn the rotting wooden throne of the deposed ruler. Such was his hatred of it that he'd delayed his coronation – a dangerous decision considering his unstable position – and ordered a new one built.

The civil war he'd unleashed was one of the few times Edar had tried to rip itself apart while not under colonial rule. Every weapon taken from the battlefield dead was melted and reforged into a beautiful, deadly throne in the shape of a rose: Edar's symbol.

In Mother's coronation portrait, the seat and back of the throne were shaped like large petals, worn smooth over decades. Vines of thorns and leaves, sharp and begging for blood, had looped around the armrests, skulked behind her feet, and loomed over her head. It was a brutal warning to everyone in her family, passed down with the crown: power was intoxicating and a delight, but one could never let their guard down around thorns.

Mother had hated that throne as much as her great-grandfather had hated the one he'd replaced. When she married Mama, years after her coronation, she'd ordered the throne melted down. Two new ones were commissioned, marble and gilt-edged, which my parents stood before in their shared portrait. The thrones were linked by a winter rose, forged from the old steel, painted in the royal colours of blue and silver.

And the thorns winding around the edges were just as sharp, if a more subtle threat.

I stopped at the steps leading to the dais, gazing up at the thrones. While Mother had changed the laws so Mama could rule in her own right, they were not absolute. I was not obliged to make my future spouse a ruling monarch instead of a Consort.

My parents were the first to rule from dual thrones. It was seen as an enlightened gesture, the most modern thing Edar had done in centuries. (By the standard of monarchs, at least; Rijaan, the republic to the south-east, considered all its neighbours unenlightened and about thirty years behind, culturally.)

I wasn't sure if I wanted to rule from dual thrones. My path to power was difficult enough, compared to other heirs, without sharing it. But my parents supported each other through immense responsibilities and workloads. They'd done so much together: opened schools, balanced the Parliament, kept the nobles who'd betrayed or undermined them cowed, stabilised the Treasury and banks. We had the best roads in almost fifty years.

But my parents had also made extraordinary choices for each other. My odds of finding someone similar were abysmal.

Every day, my parents showed me what it was to be a good Queen.

I only wished I knew whether I'd be able to follow their example.

FOUR

I slept for a while longer, but not well.

After the maid opened my drapes, but before she coaxed the fire back to life, I begged for coffee. The liquid scorched down my throat, the familiar smell a balm, but my mind was still fixed on an irrefutable fact: Melisande would be here by winter.

It didn't matter that it was months away: my brain dithered as if she were arriving next week.

I closed my eyes. Tightened my hands around the cup, the porcelain smooth and warm against my fingers. Breathe in. Breathe out. In. Out. Each breath was like a wave in my mind, a gentle push and pull, soothing my frightened thoughts, the tension in my stomach and muscles. Slowly, slowly, I returned to myself.

I opened my eyes, then got out of bed.

Being freshly washed and dressed was armour in itself. It was essential to present a neat, calm façade to the world, no matter what was happening in my head. As I stepped into the hall, I shoved away all thoughts of Melisande and began running through my mental list for the day.

The tactic lasted until I approached the breakfast room, where my parents' voices drifted through the open door, brittle and tense.

I stopped.

A common myth around their marriage was that they never argued. Absolutely untrue. They were strategic about it, with several rules about losing their tempers that I was also expected to follow:

1) Never allow resentment to fester. ('Better to tackle a thread of annoyance before it's woven into a tapestry of complaints.')

2) Never argue before or during a meal. ('Everything is always worse when you're hungry.')

3) Never sleep on an unfinished argument. ('One person will have calmed down after sleep. The other will absolutely *not* have calmed down.')

And yet it was breakfast, and while it didn't seem like they were properly fighting, they were definitely rising to the occasion.

'We were supposed to tell her together!' Mama – Queen Xania – seethed. Her temper had a wicked flare, and Rialla could just about match her for holding a grudge, but it was always worse when she was trying to contain her anger: it scalded rather than burned.

'I hardly expected to find her in the portrait gallery in the middle of the night! It ... it felt kinder to tell her then, rather than us springing it on her this morning.' Mother sounded tired, unsurprisingly, but her words were hesitant, tinged with something close to defeat. I recognised it: the hopelessness of being part of the legacy of foolish and arrogant men, and having to repeatedly face the consequences of it.

'I don—'t like this,' Mama said.

'Emri and Melisande haven't seen each other in years; it makes sense for them to meet again as heirs. Sabine has shown us nothing but good faith, especially since she's sending *her* daughter to *us*.'

Silence fell, stretching out long enough that I could have walked in and reasonably pretended I hadn't overheard anything. Then, just as I was about to move, Mama said, 'Sabine may be acting in good faith, but I don't trust whoever will accompany Melisande.'

'You think Arisane will interfere?'

My blood pounded in my ears, a faint beat that grew to a steady throb.

'Naturally. She'll likely send *him*.'

Mother made a sound awfully close to a hiss.

'He's kept in touch, after all,' Mama said, 'since we returned from Farezi.'

Sweat broke out under my arms. The conversation had turned private, to things my parents didn't speak of around me. Everything I knew about Rassa overthrowing Mother, and Mama fleeing to Farezi with Matthias to find her, was mostly picked up through careful gossip. There were some things that deserved to stay between my parents, even if it involved Arisane. *Especially* if it did.

Just as I was about to sneak back down the corridor so I could loudly re-approach, Mama called, 'Emri, stop lurking at the door, or learn to hide your footsteps better.'

I flinched, then slunk in.

My parents faced each other across a battlefield of plates strewn with crumbs and smears of butter, cream, and jam. Mother gripped her coffee cup in a white-knuckled hand, as Mama stirred her tea with deliberate slowness.

I curtseyed before the table – as a family, we kept a simpler protocol in private, but this felt like a situation where I was the princess and not just their daughter. 'I didn't mean to eavesdrop,' I said, resisting the urge to be sheepish. They were, after all, the ones who'd argued near an open door.

Mother rubbed her right eyebrow, which meant a headache threatened. 'We shouldn't have been speaking about it in here, anyway.'

Mama sighed. 'The news is already spreading around Court, I imagine. I'd be more afraid if it *wasn't*.'

She was the parent who looked most like me. But when someone drew closer, they'd spot the differences: her black curls were tighter than mine, her skin a deeper shade of brown. I could only dream of one day mimicking her sharp gaze. While Mother pinned people with a cold, probing look, Mama's displeasure was viciously precise, like a honed blade.

'If you're going to eavesdrop—' Mama began.

'Remember the sounds you don't make, not just the ones you hide,' I finished wearily, dropping into my chair. 'Don't tell Isra. She'll have me trailing people again for a month.'

Before Isra, Mama had been the Whispers, Mother's first spymaster. They'd met when Mama had unintentionally put herself forward for the job, an explanation which presented more questions than it answered, judging from their smiles when it was mentioned.

At my age, Mother was almost Queen and Mama was working in the Treasury. They'd grown up during the old King's reign when Edar was gripped by lethargy and political instability. Logically, my upbringing was calmer because I'd grown up in a more stable country. Even so, it still felt like I'd never come close to their achievements.

'Did you manage to get back to sleep?' Mother asked, calmly pouring my tea, as if their argument were a figment of my imagination.

'For a while, yes.' *Badly*, I added in my mind.

Mama sighed again. 'Please, it's too early for polite waffle. Now that you know Melisande is coming here – well, I'm not in favour of it, but we can hardly refuse, unless you want to still be dealing with the upset when *you're* Queen.'

'I'd prefer not,' I said dryly.

A ghost of a smile curled her lips. 'As Lia said last night, I agree there should be conditions. Isra will have Melisande watched while she's here, along with everyone in the retinue.'

Including the mysterious *him*, whoever he was, if he came on Arisane's command. I knew better than to ask: if my parents didn't mention someone by name, even between themselves, there was a good reason for it.

'If you don't want to be alone with her' – alone, in royal terms, meant any kind of engagement devoid of courtiers – 'that will, of course, be arranged.' Despite Mama's steady voice, a muscle flexed in her jaw. My parents were careful to only show the polite respect expected in their dealings with Farezi. In private, however, they didn't hide their lingering dislike concerning the past.

Her unhappiness gave me the courage to ask something I otherwise wouldn't have dared: 'Why do you think Arisane will try to interfere?'

As my parents exchanged a look, the lingering uneasiness from my nightmare crawled over me.

'Arisane didn't take her loss of power well,' Mama said, reluctantly. 'I met her when I was in Farezi. Back then, well – I didn't see the potential for her bitterness.'

'I imagine you had more pressing concerns,' I said softly, as Mother reached across the table to grip her hand with a sad smile. Her eyes were tight, her expression hard, and I had to look away.

'She made an… *impression*,' Mama said. 'And we have unfinished business. This would be a prime opportunity for her to bypass official channels to address it with correspondence sent through the retinue.'

The way Mama said *unfinished business* made me shift in my seat. I'd always assumed Mama's longstanding irritation with Farezi was because of their failure to contain Rassa's ambitions, the consequences of which had forced her and Matthias to handle it themselves. Now, far too many years later, I wondered if her lingering anger was because of deeper grievances.

I glanced between them. 'I'm not afraid of Arisane,' I said, though I knew that wasn't the point. 'She's a Dowager Queen on the fringes of society. She has no power anymore. Her bitterness drove away all her old allies.'

'Not all of them,' Mama said. As she gazed into the distance, something terrible flickered across her face. She swallowed and abruptly shook her head. 'Sabine may send Melisande to us with good intentions – and indeed, Melisande may share them – but we can't assume the same of everyone travelling with her. I don't want to frighten you, but it will be a difficult few months. I have no doubt that some in the retinue will be reporting back on you.'

'Of course,' I said, unable to hide my bitterness. 'I'm living proof of the family's disgrace, after all. They've never forgotten that.'

To my surprise, Mama flinched. 'You are our daughter. We love you. Melisande will not be allowed to forget those things, nor that you are our heir and thus her equal in rank. If Arisane seeks to reassert herself, it will be towards us, not you.'

No, I thought, but kept silent. Whatever past grievances they shared, Arisane surely also had unfinished business with me. She needed to see – needed to know – what kind of person I'd become, now that I was heir to the throne that her son had briefly stolen.

I clenched my hands into fists underneath the table, and blurted out, 'I can write to her.' At my parents' shared astonishment, I clarified, 'To Melisande. Resume our old correspondence, try and build a rapport before she arrives. If Arisane wishes to upset things, that will make it more difficult.'

Mama frowned. She exchanged another glance with Mother, who looked equally unhappy. The royal cogs moved between them, a lightning-quick, silent communication they'd honed over years.

It made sense.

Melisande and I had stopped writing years ago. I couldn't remember who had stopped replying first, but we'd dropped the correspondence with unacknowledged mutual relief.

And now I'd pick up a pen again, not only to bridge the last six years, but to try and glean who Melisande now was, what kind of person she'd grown into. I'd have to be slow, careful, with inane chatter and observations about the weather and all the entertainments we were planning for her.

Just like an ideal courtier. I'd write as a confident princess and heir, who knew her place as she recognised Melisande's, and was thoroughly unthreatened by her and our past.

I'd play the part Isra had spent years training me for.

FIVE

'Well, what would *you* say to her?'

Tufts of cloud drifted above us through an eggshell blue sky. I sucked in a deep breath and held it for a moment, my heartbeat throbbing in my ears. Grass rustled, as Micah shifted his arms to better support his head and neck.

'I'm not really sure,' he confessed. 'I probably wouldn't write, even though it would mean several people yelling at me. They wouldn't really mean it, though.'

I scowled up at the sky. 'It's easy to say *I'll just write*, but then I actually have to… do it.'

My grim determination had only lasted a few minutes after breakfast. As I walked through the halls, hopelessness had crept over me like a riptide, until I was caught and drowning. I'd sent a message to my linguistics tutor, pleading an afternoon reschedule, and then found Micah mired in his monthly expenses, all too happy to abandon his receipts for a walk in the gardens.

He'd been so happy, he'd even let me thump him in the arm after he gravely remarked, 'I'll remind you that a walk *could* inflame the rumours of our courtship.'

We'd strolled towards the lawns by the north-western palace

wall, on a hill that overlooked the royal forest beyond the city walls. I'd glared at the dark smear in the distance, then dropped onto the grass and all the words had simply poured out of me.

'But don't Queen Aurelia and Queen Sabine exchange annual correspondence—'

'Just let me be annoyed for *one* moment, Micah!'

Nevertheless, he was right. Mother and Aunt Sabine sent yearly letters, ostensibly filled with Midwinter greetings and bland enquiries about our families. It was how Farezi was *officially* updated on me, whatever their spies reported back, but I had the impression there was a lot more said between the lines.

'It's going to be so embarrassing.' I wriggled, trying to find a more comfortable position. '*Dear Cousin,*' I recited in a mocking tone, '*I hope the weather is well and winter wasn't too harsh. I look forward to your coming visit, even though I haven't forgiven you for—*'

I barely caught myself.

—for never standing up to Arisane hovered on my tongue, almost spoken so it couldn't be taken back.

Where had that come from?

I'd hesitated too long. But Micah – likely through a great bout of self-preservation after realising we were on the precipice of a sensitive topic – said, 'They're surely not sending Melisande here to consider her marriage prospects?' He sounded a bit frightened, and little wonder: his family was ranked high enough to be considered for royalty.

'No. She'll marry within Farezi. No one in Edar will marry into Farezi royalty for another generation or so. Besides,' I added, unable to resist teasing him, 'your family is old, but their long naval history wasn't always legitimate. Several of your ancestors likely plundered Farezi's southern coast. You won't even be on the potential list, I promise.'

Micah sniffed. 'There's no need to insult necessary duty.'

I gave him a solid five heartbeats of silence before I started laughing.

But his concern wasn't unreasonable. Queen Sabine had married young – a love match, apparently – and Melisande was born two years later. It was probably why Rassa had been sent to woo Mother; as the heir, he should have married first, with children swiftly encouraged.

Most had expected Melisande to be pressured into marriage just as quickly. I'd heard conflicting rumours about the delay: that Queen Sabine was in no hurry for her to marry; that Melisande was reluctant. It shouldn't have mattered, really, but the Melisande I vaguely remembered was a stickler for duty and rules. If she was digging her heels in about marriage, something had changed.

Also unsurprising, since we hadn't seen each other for fourteen years.

Which led back to my current problem.

'So.' I hauled myself up to a sitting position. 'What do I say to her? What do you and your cousins talk about in letters? Court gossip? Naval training? Pirating—'

Micah sighed. 'Privateers, Emri. The family has *privateers*, never pirates.'

I rolled my eyes. '*Privateering*.' The only difference between being a pirate and a privateer was my parents' approval, something the Admiral had strong opinions about. The topic was the fastest way to make Mother grind her teeth.

'How long has it been since either of you wrote?' he asked, sitting up.

'Six years, give or take a few months.'

Micah ran a hand through his thick curls. 'All right. Give her the barest bones about yourself, picked clean of everything but polite slivers of information. And ask for a full update on everything that's happened to her.'

I stared. 'She won't waste that much ink and paper.'

'Of course not. If she's even a half decent courtier, never mind a princess, she'll know you're making her do most of the work, while giving her nothing in return.' He shrugged. 'The Farezi Court's awful, but they all surely love to boast about themselves. Even if it's mostly lies.'

I frowned. 'That's… that's brilliant, actually.'

Micah shrugged again, but looked pleased. 'It's what I do when I can't put off writing to Great-Aunt Vareen anymore. She doesn't actually want to hear about me. She just wants to talk about herself. And it's *all* bad news.'

'Wait. Isn't she the one who's dying?'

He snorted. 'She's been at Lady Death's door for the last fifteen years. I reckon the Lady has been ignoring her knocks.'

Dearest Cousin,

Spring came early this year, so I assume the same can be said for Farezi. If my memory serves correctly, faint as it is by now, you've left Court for Saphirun. Travel is still a bit slow here – the North's snows are still deliberating whether they wish to fully melt, and we've had a few late storms that bogged down the roads – but the palace is slowly emptying out, and it already feels easier to breathe here.

~~Why am I bothering, it's not like any of this is interesting to you?~~

If I were a better courtier, perhaps, I'd have opened with the required flattery and waffle as to why I'm writing for the first time in six years. The simple truth is Their Majesties informed me you're visiting us next winter, and I was a great disappointment for letting our correspondence lapse.

To be fair, this is not especially high-ranked in all the ways I'm occasionally a disappointment. The diplomats would probably wince at that last line, but they were not raised by the Dowager Queen Arisane and so do not fully grasp the depths of disappointment one can sink to.

I decided to be a disappointment to *you* by opening with the weather.

~~...I better make sure Isra doesn't intercept this~~

It's a letter, why is this so difficult

I've done this before

Dearest Cousin,

Spring came early this year. What a relief! I'm hoping the same happened in Farezi, and you're reading this at Saphirun.

My parents, Their Majesties, have informed me you'll be viiting us later this year. As I'm well aware of what it feels like to come to Edar as a stranger, I hope to renew our correspondence so that when you arrive, you will have ~~someone forced to tolerate you~~ one friend here, at least.

Forgive me for opening with the weather. It was a necessary obstacle to overcome. As your cousin, I wish to know all your news from the last few years.

~~Was it easier for you, after I left~~

~~Or did Grandmother become worse~~

I can't do this.

Though it's either get the letter out, or endure another lecture from Isra after she's finished seething at me.

I'd prefer the seething, to be honest.

Dearest Cousin,

Spring has come early this year. Such a relief! I hope the same is true for Farezi, and you are free of Court and reading this at Saphirun.

My parents, Their Majesties, have informed me that you will be visiting us later this year. I hope to renew our correspondence so that when you arrive, you will have a friend here.

Forgive me for opening with the weather. It was a necessary obstacle to overcome.

Since it *has* been six years, I should have been a better courtier and opened with the necessary flattery and waffle. However, I have limited tolerance for such things.

To strengthen our bonds of familial connection (I have some reserves of poeticism, I suppose), it would be in both our interests to have more than a passing familiarity with each other. If any significant matters have occurred in the last six years, I would be most obliged if you would inform me. I'm not especially picky.

Your humble cousin,

Emri

SUMMER

Third Month of Summer,

Nineteenth Year in the reign of Queen Aurelia IV and her Queen, Xania

Dear Micah,

I know, I should have sent this letter *weeks* ago, especially since your first missive arrived promptly from Casa High. The Admiral may fault you on many things, but never your dedication to correspondence.

Why am I talking to you like this, like we're acquaintances and not friends

The weather's been wonderful since we arrived ~~you know this, you're a few days away on horseback, not in a different country~~ and the visit is just what my parents needed. Mama and Aunt Zola have been on their best behaviour around Grandmama Kierth, and only one breakfast has descended into a lecture so far. I've spent most of my time with Grandpapa Kierth. We spent an entire week helping to pick his experimental strawberry crops, though I think we ate more than we were supposed to...

I hope your sister is well, and she was given leave from the Navy to visit. If she's still there when this arrives, tell her I knew that promotion would always be hers.

The neighbours have kept to the unspoken arrangement and sent greetings but no invitations nor calling cards. ~~Though apparently Lord Alec Ash tried to orchestrate a visit without his parents' knowledge because he thinks I'm actually marrying you, and I want to throttle Fi~~

I've spent a lot of time walking and reading, and trying to make my paintings look less... like ones I've painted, with little success. The painting, that is, not the walking and reading.

I'm so lonely

I don't want the summer to be over, too much is going to change and I'm not ready I'm not ready

Dear Rialla,

I think for the first time since we've known each other, this will be the summer where I'm worse at sending letters than you. In my defence, we've had no visitors, as expected, so there hasn't been much to write about, other than the usual.

~~Grandmama Kierth's left knee has been giving her trouble, and Grandpapa Kierth's hair is suddenly more white than grey. Aunt Zola drank too much wine and I overheard her and Mama worrying about them~~

Grandpapa Kierth's strawberry experiments were a success. They've turned some into jam, and he's promised to bring some back to Court so I can share it with you and Micah. I've tried to improve my painting, but I remain dismal at perspective and any sort of flair.

It's been quiet ~~I'm so sad~~

Luci was asking about you. ~~I think they found out what happened last winter.~~ After breakfast, I usually go outside and read where they're working, and bring food to share during their break. ~~We overheard two maids gossiping about my potential marriage to Prince Theobilt of Othayria, and I can't escape marriage talk even in Kierth.~~
~~Kierth is supposed to be SAFE.~~

I don't know what to say to you anymore
I don't know how to pretend to be what I used to be around you

Too much is changing, and you were supposed to be beside me so it would be easier.

SIX

'Emri?'

I looked up from my desk, pressing my hands over the unsent letters to Micah and Rialla – all partially written and, inevitably, given up on – that I'd been brooding over. 'Yes, Mama?'

She stood at the doorway to my bedroom, a light cloak folded over her arms. 'I was hoping you'd join me on a walk.'

I'd already stood up. 'Of course,' I said, gathering the pages to stuff them into a compartment and lock it, trying to remember where my own cloak was.

As spring had shed her neat layers, heat had accompanied summer with the force of a hammer striking an anvil, until the capital's atmosphere had resembled a blacksmith's forge. The Court emptied out, as the last of the nobles with estates or invitations to visit them had finally departed. Towards the end of summer, my parents and I had left for the west coast to spend a month with my Kierth grandparents and Aunt Zola.

Every year, I looked forward to our summer visits to family, whether to Kierth or Grandmother Sionbourne's estate. For a month, my parents slept well, free of meetings and Parliament, the veil of exhaustion temporarily lifted from their faces, while I had a reprieve from Court. For a month, I was with people who loved me, who saw me for who I was and not where I'd come from.

The days had stretched out, belonging to Kierth's rolling lawns and fields, to the sea crashing against the cliffs and beach. Because we accepted no invitations nor visitors, it was the one month where we had privacy, a stretch of time to remember who we actually were when free from intrigue.

But this year my worries had followed me from the capital, discovered the cracks in Kierth's familiar safety, and slipped through to cling to me throughout our stay.

A guard followed us outside at a discreet distance, holding what I suspected was a basket of food, strongly implying that there would also be A Talk during this walk. My suspicion only increased when I realised Mama was leisurely guiding me towards the cliffs.

The family rule was that no one – absolutely no one, heedless of rank or crown – went to the cliffs alone. The drop was too sudden and steep, the waves too harsh. Help would come too slow, whether death came from the impact of the fall or the waves bashing you against the rocks. My parents often rode out there together, while I generally avoided it. But it was one of the few places on the estate where it was difficult to be overheard; the wind had stripped away everything over the centuries, and Grandpapa Kierth considered it a lost cause to replant anything that close to the sea.

Most of our talk was easy, retouching on familiar topics: Micah, Rialla, my time spent with Grandpapa Kierth, how the harvest was faring. Grandmama Kierth and Aunt Zola were deeply involved in my new wardrobe for my formal introduction to Court and the season that would follow; every seamstress fitting had been scheduled and double-checked. Mother was disappointed that Matthias – Baron Farhallow, their oldest friend – and his husband hadn't been able to join us at Kierth this year, but was trying not to show it.

But I knew the true purpose of Mama's idle conversation was coming. And when we settled a respectable distance from the cliff edge, but still with a commanding view of the sea and the horizon, she began the gentle manoeuvres.

'Lia is worried about you,' she said, examining a thick slice of bread smeared with a soft pale cheese studded with herbs. 'As am I.'

'I'm fine—' I began automatically, then stopped at the look Mama sliced towards me.

She held my gaze for a long moment, then took a bite of the bread and chewed pointedly. When she gestured at the basket, I sighed and rummaged for something to eat. The guard had even brought a bottle of cordial and two small cups.

'Lord Martain' – Mama and Aunt Zola loved their stepfather, but always referred to Grandpapa Kierth by his name – 'also feels you have not entirely been yourself since we arrived.'

Gripping the basket so tightly that the weave dug into my skin, I thought about how much time I'd spent with him over the last month and couldn't help a brief stab of betrayal, then immediate shame. Grandpapa wouldn't admit such a thing to my parents unless he was truly concerned.

'I...'

Mama waited. She poured us both cordial and sipped hers as she finished the bread, then considered a block of harder cheese. As I pondered my own bread, thinking furiously, Mama asked the guard what he would like to eat. No one could cross the fields towards us without being seen, or scale the cliffs without difficulty, so the biggest threat was us tumbling over the edge and into the sea, an onerous task when we were several feet away, absorbed in eating and a painful family discussion.

And if he would have to pretend not to listen, he might as well eat during it.

'I... I'm scared,' I finally admitted. 'I haven't... everything is changing and feels wrong, and when we return after the summer, I won't be in control of anything.'

Without any warning, I burst into tears.

Rialla and I hadn't managed to properly smooth things over before her family had left Court for the country, which perhaps accounted for her not having written (though she usually never wrote, preferring to tell us everything over three hours on our first evening back together) and certainly accounted for my worthless attempts at letters.

'Would you prefer a hug or to scream?' Mama asked.

I wiped my eyes. 'A hug for now, please.'

'Keep the screaming in mind,' she said, scooting over to wrap her arms around me, enveloping me in the warm reassuring presence that had, when I was a child, seemed invincible. 'This is an ideal place for it, and you're not the first in the family to scream at the sea.'

When my tears had reduced to sniffles, she pulled back and handed me a handkerchief. After considering my face, she reached into a pocket for a second one, which had the intended effect of making me laugh, wetly.

We lapsed into silence, as the waves raged against the cliffs and the wind raged at everything, the atmosphere softened by the warmth and salt tang on the air. I sucked it deep into my lungs, as Mama waited for me to speak.

Sunlight glimmered over her dress, picked out the embroidery on her bodice and sleeves, and warmed her brown skin. In the years since our family portrait, the strain of rule had marked itself upon my parents: delicate lines around their eyes and mouth, and a weariness in their gaze when they were deep in thought. They'd married when they were only a few years older than me. Sometimes I forgot they'd borne so much responsibility for so long.

'How have you and Mother stayed in love?'

She blinked. 'Now there's a question.'

I shrugged awkwardly. 'I just… everyone considers it an epic romance—'

'Everyone who doesn't know us well,' Mama interrupted.

'—but… you're both so… so…'

'Lacking in grand romantic gestures?'

I flushed, and Mama laughed. 'Well, it wasn't a normal courtship. I was her spymaster. She was supposed to marry a prince. Then she abdicated, and I committed treason to find her. I think we used up our grand romantic gestures too young. Nothing could come close after all that.'

My parents' love story was so famous, poets had spun ballads and songs about it. But as I'd grown older, the romance of it all had worn away. In Mother's weary eyes and the hard set of Mama's mouth, I saw the choices they *didn't* talk about. They didn't permit anyone at Court to perform those ballads. So few people ever seemed to notice the love story's shadow.

'Things fell apart between us before she abdicated,' Mama added thoughtfully. 'Only a few people know, mind you, and it's in none of the songs.'

'You forswore each other?' I asked, startled.

'Yes, but not that dramatically. Lia was expected to marry for an heir, and I was too low-ranked for her. Rassa had manipulated her into a corner until all she had left were poor and worse choices. And I – I couldn't support her in those. So we ended it. I was still her Whispers, but nothing else, and we were both miserable.'

I perked up, though it seemed a terrible reaction to their pain. They'd rejected each other, but still managed to reconcile. It *was* possible. 'How did you fix things?'

'Well – abdication and treason, as I said. When you're willing to do such things out of love, it implies you'll probably outlast the smaller problems.'

My shoulders slumped. 'I'm not sure I could do that without being disinherited.'

'Finding a new heir would be inconvenient,' Mama agreed.

Her gaze turned distant. 'We didn't know if we could fix things between us. Lia was so traumatised after Goldenmarch… but I couldn't abandon her. Not after everything we'd been through. It took years, but she found her way back to herself and to me. And she made me her equal upon marriage. We'd weathered possibly the worst thing that could happen to us – of course, then you arrived, and the new worst thing was something terrible ever happening to *you* – so I knew we could rule together.'

'Should I be thrilled that I rank so high on your list of worries?'

'Yes,' Mama said dryly, and returned my smile.

But the scale of what they'd gone through, compared to my much smaller concerns, only made me feel worse. My jaw began to ache from clenching my teeth. The curdling in my stomach turned to a roiling burn that charged up my throat.

'We… Luci and I…' I forced the words out through the burning. 'We overheard a *discussion* about my impending marriage to Prince Theobilt.'

Mama went still. 'Nothing has been settled or agreed for a betrothal. We would tell you if anything had. You know this.'

I did. For several years, my parents had been seriously considering Prince Theobilt of Othayria, a match approved both by his uncle, Prince Aubrey, and Isra, who considered Othayria the best of my marriage options, politically. By all accounts, Prince Theobilt was agreeable and had been raised with the expectation that he would be marrying into *my* family, and so would be supporting me as Queen and not grasping for power through our marriage.

And yet – the realisation hit like a blow to my stomach – I'd still acted on my feelings for Rialla, heedless of complications and naïvely certain that they could be worked around.

If things had ended worse between Rialla and me, how vulnerable I'd left my family. How silly I'd been, threatening an alliance with a country that still keenly remembered Mother's rejection of Prince Aubrey.

It had been such a nice day, the morning I'd heard the gossip. I'd gone outside to read after breakfast, as usual, tracking Luci down in the garden they were working in. Our companionable quiet was broken only when Luci had stopped for a break; I shared my food, as they updated me on everything I'd missed since our last visit. Luci was only two years older than me; I'd known them for as long as I'd been coming here, and we always slipped back into an easy friendship.

And then we'd overheard the two maids as they'd passed down a path outside the garden, unaware of my presence behind the large hedge that hid me from view.

Until now, I'd always been safe from speculation at Kierth; the staff was well aware that Grandmama despised gossip in general. But now, it seemed, such speculation would follow me everywhere until I finally married, or was officially betrothed at least.

When Isra had discovered my relationship with Rialla, I'd expected a summons to be shouted at. Instead, I'd faced my Kierth grandparents, who had explained the political reasoning behind their reactions when they'd first learned that Mama had fallen for her Queen, how they had respected her feelings, but were terribly aware of her vulnerable position if they were publicly discovered. Unwilling to force me into anything after learning about Rialla, my parents had dampened their interest in Prince Theobilt, claiming they wanted to wait until I was older to secure a betrothal, even though Othayria had begun to signal overtures. But when Rialla had backed away, discussions had resumed again during the last few months.

After last winter, I'd turned that conversation with my grandparents over in my mind, convinced that everyone else's concerns were the reason Rialla had pulled away from me. But now, the truth unfurled before me like a dark flower in the midst of brighter blossoms.

Even if her family had disapproved – a reasonable reaction, since being a royal's lover complicated a courtier's life – Rialla knew her own mind. If she'd felt we had a future, she would have fought for it, no matter the poor odds. It had been *her* decision to admit that she didn't want her life to involve a throne, no one else's.

But I still hated that she'd made it.

'I hate it!' I burst out. 'I hate that I'm almost eighteen and everything is changing, and all I can *still* think about is Rialla deciding I wasn't enough. It's been *months*, and it still hurts.' It felt like a sliver of glass in my palm where the skin had grown over. I couldn't see it, but I could feel it if I hit my hand against something. 'I have more important things to worry about than *feeling sad*.'

'Grief takes time to heal, Emri,' Mama pointed out. 'This has changed you both. You need to relearn how to be around each other again.'

'She's from an esteemed family,' I muttered. 'How could she not realise what she was getting into?' As if I hadn't let myself daydream of a future with Rialla, deliberately ignoring the realities of my future.

'Emri, need I remind you that I fell in love with a Queen?'

'Oh. Yes.'

Mama propped her chin on her palm. 'I understand what you're feeling, but I can't understand how it affects you.' She raised her eyebrows. 'But I won't continue this conversation if you're so convinced that your parents could *never* understand what you're going through.'

I groaned. 'I wish things were easier.'

'As do I,' Mama muttered. The change in her tone hinted that her sympathy was edging towards irritation.

As I flung her a sheepish smile, she coughed and pulled a small, wrapped box from one of her pockets. 'An early birthday gift,' she said, holding it out. 'We'd planned to give it to you back at the palace, but we brought it with us in case an opportunity presented itself, and well…'

The box was slim and surprisingly heavy, wrapped in blue and silver paper.

Something flickered across Mama's face, too swift for me to decipher. She shifted on the grass. 'Open it, please.'

I unwrapped the paper carefully. The box was simple dark wood. A pen lay upon crushed dark blue velvet, black and marbled with a gold sheen. A small rose overlaid the larger part of the nib.

I sucked in a breath at the weight and elegance.

'Hold the nib away from you,' Mama said, 'and twist the gold band between the barrel and the nib. Don't drop it.'

I followed her instructions, frowning, then yelped as a needle shot out from underneath the nib, thin and wickedly sharp. 'Is this—'

'Poison,' she interrupted, as if she wanted this part over with as quickly as possible. 'A cylinder within the barrel holds the poison. It won't corrode, so you needn't worry about hurting yourself. Lia and I each have one, as do Matthias and Isra. They're a family tradition, of sorts. We'll have inner pockets sewn into your clothing, so you can reach it without drawing attention.'

This was a way to protect myself if I was ever in a dangerous situation. Secret and safe, hidden upon my person with no one the wiser. If things were truly lost, and I had no access to a dagger or other weapon, it was a way for me to kill.

As if she could sense the turn of my thoughts, Mama leaned forward. 'I need not clarify the dire situations where a pen full of poison is your best defence. Be careful about wielding it. And don't tell anyone – including Rialla and Micah. Knowledge leaks, as you know. We don't need the Court to turn indignant about the ways in which we protect ourselves.'

'If this is a family tradition,' I asked slowly, 'then why isn't Mother here?'

Mama stiffened. If I hadn't been so close to her, I probably wouldn't have noticed. 'Her first gift to me was a similar pen,' she said. 'Before Goldenmarch, and long before we had an inkling of a future together. We decided I should give this to you, as I once had cause to use mine.'

I opened my mouth to demand further details, but something dark, almost ugly, twisted her face, and the words died in my throat.

Instead, I turned the pen over between my fingers, careful of the poison band. At last, I hefted the weight and said, 'Thank you. I promise I won't pull it on a courtier.'

'I'd appreciate that,' Mama said, her mouth twitching. She pulled me into a hug, careful of the pen. 'I don't think the Court would be pleased if you went around pulling a poison pen on those who displeased you.' She paused, and her mouth twitched again. 'Perhaps Isra would be.'

As I laughed, Mama's expression turned thoughtful. 'You should observe Melisande when she arrives. Marrying into Farezi royalty is unpopular these days, but I suspect she's well versed in Court games.'

The mention of Melisande only made my heart sink. But Mama was right. The Farezi Court had always been notoriously cut-throat in jostling for power, and Queen Sabine had only moderately improved that aspect of its character.

No matter how much I prepared, Melisande would be more than a match for me in manipulation and intrigue.

AUTUMN

SEVEN

Back in spring, the year had stretched out, bright and glorious, and the responsibilities attached to my birthday and Melisande's visit had seemed far away. Now, as the carriage rumbled back towards the capital, our visit to Kierth over, they loomed unpleasantly close.

For all of the pomp around it, my eighteenth birthday was a quiet affair spent with my parents and our family, who'd returned to Court for the social season. My parents had suggested a larger gathering, but I'd refused.

Mother officially made me Duchess Sionbourne, the title traditionally held by the heir once they came of age (though she had become Queen instead), and which Grandmother Sionbourne now held as Dowager.

Micah and Rialla returned to Court with their families a few days later, and we had our own celebration together.

While we waited for Rialla, Micah regaled me, with much sarcasm and extravagant hand gestures, about his summer with his relatives. But when she came through the door, I knew immediately by her expression that something wasn't right.

Even so, Rialla acted as if nothing was wrong, slipping into her sardonic manner as she teased Micah. But her posture remained stiff, and her gaze never lingered on me long, flickering away as if she'd noticed something embarrassing or distasteful.

I held a glass of cordial tight enough to break, and smiled as if nothing was wrong. The familiar wave of loneliness from Kierth tugged at me, just as it had when I was with my family, even Grandpapa Kierth, or walking through the gardens, or out riding with Aunt Zola.

I'm so lonely, I'd written to Micah, the letter unsent and eventually burned to ashes. The words were gone, but the feeling had remained. I'd hoped this evening would be quiet and comfortable, a chance for us all to catch up and indulge in harmless gossip. How foolish of me.

As Rialla came to the end of a story I'd lost track of early on, I glanced at Micah and found him watching me. Even though a faint smile tugged his mouth at Rialla's story, a crease between his eyebrows betrayed his awareness of the strange atmosphere between us.

She finished; an uncomfortable silence descended, into which I flung myself with as much social aplomb as I could muster. Micah laughed when I mentioned an amusing anecdote from one of his letters, about his aunt eviscerating a cousin over breakfast after they'd made the unfortunate choice to question one of her decisions.

When I paused to take a breath, Rialla said, 'Yes, well, at least

Micah *bothered to write* over the summer.'

This time, the silence turned ghastly.

'I… I'm certain Emri had the best intentions of writing,' Micah finally ventured. His cheeks had turned bright red, and he looked as if he wished to be somewhere, anywhere else, once it was far away from here.

I thought of everything I'd attempted to tell them on the half-scribbled pages I'd fed into the fire. The jars of strawberry jam sitting on the nearby sideboard from Grandpapa, which I'd planned to give Micah and Rialla just before they left. Of Lord Alec's thwarted foolishness, how much it had irritated my parents, and how Aunt Zola had laughed herself sick about it when they weren't in the room.

How I'd sat beside Mama near the cliffs and cried while a guard stood nearby and pretended not to hear.

None of it had fitted on paper, not like it used to. The words had sputtered in my pen, stuck fast in the ink, pathetic and ill-judged.

What hurt even more was how Rialla had brought it up: sharp and pointed, the unpleasantness made worse because she *knew* it would hurt. It wasn't like her.

Well, it wasn't like her – *before*.

Before she'd ended things between us. Before she made her choice, and then sometimes seemed to regret it, but now it was too late to take any of it back.

She couldn't just expect me to hold out my arms with a warm smile, as if nothing had happened. As if her gentle, terrible words from last winter hadn't felt like the rug being pulled out from under me. She couldn't admit her regret, and I couldn't admit how foolish I felt, and so we circled each other, gripping the broken shards of our friendship and lashing out when they bit into our palms and made us bleed.

We hadn't seen each other in months, and already I was spiralling back into obsession, exactly as I'd told Mama on the cliffs.

Micah, eternal peacemaker and sensitive to the shards of friendship he crunched over, said, 'Rialla, I don't think—'

I swallowed the rest of the cordial, then slammed the glass down hard enough that he winced.

'Micah,' I said with deadly softness, 'please excuse us.'

He eyed me, then swept a bow and turned for the door. He and Rialla locked gazes as he brushed by her, his annoyance sharp against her grim resignation.

Fool, his expression said.

As the door shut after him, she said, 'Emri, I didn't—'

'You've said quite enough.'

Bewilderment rippled across her face, quickly replaced by a courtier's smooth mask.

I was tired: of feeling stupid, of the hurt neither of us could truly acknowledge, the awkwardness we kept subjecting Micah to. It was a miracle he hadn't given up on us both.

'You haven't written to Micah and me during for the summer *for years*,' I said, trying to dampen the rage that swirled in my stomach, roared up my chest and throat, and threatened to spill over into my voice. 'If you noticed my lack of letters, it still didn't concern you enough to write to *me*.' I'd spent the summer miserable, still caught up in the wretchedness of our broken friendship, and now that we were finally together again, we hadn't even managed to last an evening before returning to prickly discomfort.

Rialla swallowed. Her expression softened with guilt, but she kept her chin up. She paced across the room, flexing her fingers, her skirts sweeping around her. She was over a head taller than me – almost everyone was taller than me, it was infuriating – and I kept my distance so I wouldn't have to look up at her if we started properly yelling. This wasn't really about us not writing letters, of course it wasn't, but there was a good chance that Rialla's pride would force her to dig her heels in instead of admitting what was actually wrong.

At some point, I'd folded my arms, a flimsy protection against my upset. Even with Rialla and Micah, some instincts still went deep, and now they were stirring:

To beg for someone to speak was weakness.

To make a sound, when ordered to silence, was to face punishment.

To expect unconditional love was foolish.

Arisane hadn't tolerated weakness, nor mistakes, and never foolishness.

'Did something happen?' Rialla abruptly demanded, spinning on her heel to pin me with a glare. 'Something you didn't want to tell us? Is that why you didn't write?'

There was a strange tone in her voice, something that I'd have considered *unsettled* in anyone else. But Rialla didn't waver, and she was never unsettled. Whether she was icily formal, or coyly sly, or intent on losing her temper, she was always assured in her reasoning. You couldn't survive at Court – couldn't survive as my oldest friend and senior lady-in-waiting – without that kind of confidence.

Even when she broke my heart, Rialla knew what she was doing.

And I suspected I knew exactly why she was doubting now. For as long as the three of us had been capable of half-decent correspondence, Micah and I had sent letters while we were apart during the summer, and Rialla read everything we sent. That was how it had been for years, up until summer last year.

And then winter had happened. And during our first proper separation since then, I hadn't written. I'd scratched words on paper, and all of them had been useless, all worthless. And Rialla, who somehow hadn't expected this to happen the moment I had a chance to brood alone, didn't know how to handle it.

And I didn't know how to explain.

'Whatever has happened,' Rialla tried again, 'we'll understand. *I'll* understand.' We lapsed into another silence, before she added in a small voice, 'Once you would have told me anything, even in a letter.'

She was right. Once, I wouldn't have thought twice about telling her and Micah almost everything. They were my twin stalwarts at Court, my most trusted companions outside my family. I hadn't told them everything, of course. But we'd all shared enough that I was convinced, as we grew older, our bonds would never buckle.

'Once,' I agreed, my arms still tightly folded. 'But we're not children anymore.'

The change had crept up slowly, as if suddenly a pattern hidden in a design had become clear. I could have blamed Isra – it would have been easy to blame her – who'd spent the last few years hammering a sense of secrecy into me. I wasn't privy to all the decisions my parents made as rulers, but they discussed them with me as they saw fit. Mother feared that should something happen to them, I would be left on the throne as young and inexperienced as she'd once been, and was determined to prevent such a possibility.

And Rialla and Micah surely also kept secrets from me. And eventually, as we grew older, there would be other things they wouldn't tell me, in letter or in person, shaped by their responsibilities. They would take on positions of power and authority, perhaps even marry, and our friendship would become that between a future monarch and her subjects.

Of Micah's ability to weather the change, I had no doubt. He was Diana's bright hope for Court, as his younger sister was considered a future star in the Navy. I would have said the same for Rialla, before we'd fallen for each other and then destroyed everything.

Maybe my feelings were mirrored upon my face, for Rialla whispered, 'How do we fix this?'

The fire crackled behind us, highlighting the glimmers of flame within her brown hair. Her eyes were dark pools reflecting the light, and as we gazed at each other, her expression began to crumple.

'I don't know.' It was the truest and most terrible thing I'd said to her in a long time. 'And I wish to be alone.'

For a moment, I feared she would cry. She hadn't cried even when she'd ended our relationship, her expression practically carved from marble as my heart had splintered. The last time I'd seen her in tears, she'd half-fallen, half-flung herself out of a tree, and they were mostly angry ones. Now, there was no trace of fury, and I couldn't bear it if she cried.

With visible strain, she gathered herself and curtseyed. 'Your Highness,' she said, her chin held high, and turned for the door.

After she left, I didn't move for a long time. Instead, my ears pounded, and all I could focus on was the sensation of my chest rising and falling as I took deep breaths. I didn't remember staggering to the nearest chair, but suddenly I was there. Tremors buckled up and down my body.

I buried my face in my hands and surrendered myself to tears.

EIGHT

As autumn deepened, the social season began in earnest. And all the changes I'd feared swept in alongside it.

I'd known this would happen. But the reality was still unpleasant, as invitations to dances and evening gatherings began to pile up. I wasn't expected to attend them all – a royal should be choosy about where she graced with her presence – but the prospect of a heightened social calendar still wasn't thrilling.

It was different for others, especially those also debuting into society. For them, dinners and dances, the theatre and the opera, musical recitals, were all moving pieces in the marriage game, if they chose to play, a chance to be seen and flirt and consider their prospects. My presence was mostly a symbol of royal favour and, hopefully, if I were lucky, a chance to have decent conversations.

But first, this year's debuts had to be presented to my parents. And also, ironically, to me for the first time, though my own formal presentation to Court would be two weeks later during the Harvest Ball.

The event turned out to be much quicker and simpler than I'd expected. Under earlier monarchs, debuting was an elaborate affair of anxious parents and nervous young courtiers. After

Mother had sat through her first presentation as Queen, she'd proposed streamlining the affair and, braced for resistance, was instead surprised at how eagerly her changes were supported.

Old-fashioned wigs were abolished. White was no longer the established colour. Now, Edar's newest generation of marriageable courtiers was presented only to the royal family. A welcome relief from the old torture of waiting hours to face not only the monarchs, but all the esteemed senior courtiers more than ready to note the slightest error.

This year's crop was smaller – few wanted their children to debut alongside the heir, especially when her royal cousin would also be visiting – but it still took me barely ten minutes to realise why my parents suffered through this every year with weary resignation: an endless parade of new courtiers, to which we were required to smile and incline our heads. My parents occasionally bestowed compliments or remarks, to the terrified delight of the recipients. All the while, I felt like I was turning to stone from boredom, even as my royal mask remained firmly in place.

The one time it almost slipped was during Rialla's turn.

As she was announced and ascended the steps in an elegant cloud of copper silk to sink into a deep curtsey, I resisted the urge to swallow. This was the closest we'd been since my disastrous birthday. The sunlight made her hair and dress gleam; her usual sharp perfume teased my nostrils. I forced my posture to stay ramrod straight, my expression calm.

Rialla lowered her head demurely, perhaps sensing Mother's scrutiny. Mama pressed a hand upon hers in gentle warning, and said, 'Lady Rialla, please rise. You are a credit to your family, to whom we owe a great debt for their long years of Treasury service.'

Her eyes sparkled, inviting Rialla to smile, which led to a ripple of laughter through the crowd. Mama's financial puns had likely been deliberate, given her history there, and a delicate jest towards the considerable power Rialla's family wielded within the Treasury.

As Rialla glanced at me, I smiled faintly, easier now that Mama had lightened the mood. As much as it all still hurt, allowing my disaster of a personal life to influence Rialla's public debut would be *extremely* petty. I'd also be in significant trouble with Their Majesties behind closed doors.

So I smiled, both as a princess and a friend, and let Rialla have her moment. My genial expression didn't falter for a single heartbeat.

When my parents finally nodded a subtle dismissal, Rialla curtseyed again and backed down the steps with just as much grace as she'd climbed them.

Once the last presentation was done, the atmosphere briefly collapsed into shared relief, then buoyed as servants circled the room with trays of cordial and finger food. Those who'd crumbled under pressure (one young lady, unable to hold in a nervous sob, and a young man, who'd stumbled and almost landed on Mama's skirts) made discreet exits with their families.

We gazed upon the mingling crowd, and older courtiers occasionally broke out of the fray to approach. My parents' responses varied from coolly professional to warm, depending on who they were, and the topics ranged from the success of the debut presentation to state matters.

One especially tedious conversation centred around new fishing quotas, which would have been pertinent in an actual meeting, but not at this exact moment. In my head, I started to count down until we could leave, and I could only imagine Mother was truly desperate when she politely cut off the conversation to beckon Rialla and her mother forward, who'd been patiently waiting by the steps.

As they rose from their curtsies, we greeted them, and I added to Rialla: 'You were impeccable, of course.'

She returned my smile blandly. 'Practice, Your Highness.'

Despite her neutral smile, something twinged in my chest, sharp and quick, at her insolent tone. My parents stiffened, as Rialla's mother froze. I'd thought here at least, in a public setting, we'd be able to – no, *required to* – put an acceptable façade over our feelings. But apparently that only extended to me.

'For such a brief moment,' Mother remarked into the tense silence, 'it's astonishing how much practice is actually needed.'

As Rialla's mother metaphorically grabbed the topic with both hands and much relief, she and my parents veered into a discussion about the expectations of debuting versus the experience, while Rialla and I remained silent witnesses to the conversation.

I paid careful attention to Lady Amarié, Rialla's mother. Apart from that tense moment, she was calm and elegant, as always. Rialla had eventually admitted that her mother was unhappy that we'd fallen for each other, but too clever to let it show around my parents and me. She wouldn't have encouraged Rialla to act like this.

That made sense: a close friendship with royalty usually led to stronger favour and influence. It was why so many tried to get their daughters recommended to join my ladies. Lady Amarié might not have wanted Rialla to marry me, but she also didn't want every thread of goodwill broken between us.

I snapped out of my miserable thoughts when Mama said, 'Emri, why don't you and Lady Rialla mingle for a while?' The request was about as subtle as a hammer, and it trapped us both neatly. Especially Rialla, whose mother would later gut her in private if she protested a Queen's polite order.

'Of course, Mama,' I said, as Rialla curtseyed.

The conversations around us – buzzing, rippling, interspersed with bursts of laughter – drifted towards the throne room's vaulted ceilings. Gazes followed us as we drifted through the crowd. Everyone preened in their best clothing, the fabrics rustling and swishing, their smiles and eyes as bright as the light gleaming upon their jewels. Amid bows and curtseys, I grabbed the first glass of cordial that came my way. Rialla stayed silent, her gaze fixed on the middle-distance.

I raised the glass to my lips to hide my mouth. 'People will speculate if you don't say something,' I murmured. 'Do you really want the rest of my ladies vying for your position if they think we've fallen out?'

For something so simple in theory, the cutthroat power divisions between my ladies put most social climbers in Court to shame. As my senior lady-in-waiting, Rialla wielded the most influence and had no qualms about putting overconfident newcomers swiftly in their place.

If the others suspected, even for a moment, that we were no longer close, it would turn into a metaphorical bloodbath.

Rialla putting on such a poor show was laughable and highly ironic, since we *had* managed to keep our relationship secret from my ladies and the Court. It was Isra's ironbound condition to the relationship continuing, agreed by my parents. Mother had been careful with romance when she was younger, since she'd been expected to marry for duty before she and Mama had crossed paths, and had cautioned for me to be equally so.

Rialla, to my surprise, had also agreed. She'd claimed it was because she didn't want an inevitable fuss to explode if everyone knew we were together. Now, it looked like a warning sign that I'd unintentionally ignored – one which my parents and Isra likely hadn't. Or perhaps it had slowly dawned on Rialla that, as Mama had realised long before, loving a royal wasn't simple. Maybe that was why Isra and my parents weren't surprised when they learned she'd backed away from her feelings.

'You wouldn't find it entertaining to watch them try and take my place?' Rialla replied, her voice just as soft and irritated. Despite our barbed conversation, something in me flared as her eyes glittered. She raised her chin almost in challenge, daring me to contradict her.

For a long, inadvisable moment, I wanted to kiss her.

I hadn't actually wanted to do so in months. Every time I'd looked at her, all I remembered was the feeling of my ribs cracking around my heart (metaphorically: dramatics didn't give me the ability to perfectly align my body with my emotions, more's the pity).

But maybe enough time had finally passed. Or maybe it was simply because we were in public, having to twist our mutual hurt and resentment into something more beneficial. Apart from our families, we weren't really among friends. With her glittering eyes and haughty expression, she looked more like the Rialla I'd fallen for, and not the one who'd broken my heart.

She drained the rest of her glass, taking another after summoning a servant with an imperious tilt of her head. 'Let us play the game, then,' she said, her eyes still glittering. 'The sooner we do, the sooner we can leave.'

So we resumed moving through the crowd. Rialla, beginning to look and sound more like herself, teetered close to mildly insulting those she disliked, but never descended to anything that couldn't plausibly be denied.

Here was where I slipped firmly into the guise of Her Royal Highness, Princess Emri of Edar. I smiled and complimented and retorted wittily, all while noting what people *didn't* say, or what they actually meant, sifting through delicate insinuations within supposedly careless remarks. The Edaran Court was no longer the vipers' nest from when my parents were young, but power was a constant desire. Everyone wanted some, even if it meant playing the long game with a princess who likely wouldn't inherit for decades.

After a while, I started to feel reasonably entertained. My parents were also showing signs of preparing to leave, which meant I could also soon excuse myself...

...when Florette Sigrath appeared before me.

Rialla's expression brightened, like a cat unsheathing her claws. Her insults were, potentially, about to turn into things that could *not* be plausibly denied.

I hadn't deliberately avoided Florette, who had come to support her younger sister. But unlike practically everyone else here – including her sister, whose guileless enthusiasm was apparently genuine – Florette seemed reluctant to approach me. It almost felt like our mutual wariness was a test of some kind.

A ridiculous test, since other sharp-eyed courtiers would have already noticed that Florette was avoiding me. She'd never had a choice to stay away.

'Your Highness.' Florette curtseyed, and added, 'Lady Rialla – your presentation was wonderful. Your mother must have been overjoyed.'

Before Rialla could reply, I said, 'Lady Florette. Your sister did your family proud.'

Florette's mouth twisted into a sardonic smile, before she said the expected response: 'Practice.'

Here was the thing: under normal circumstances, Florette was a perfectly well-brought-up noble daughter. Her blonde hair and ice-blue eyes were acceptable, as Court judged these things, even though her gaze flickered constantly, as if she were trying to memorise everything happening around her all at once. This habit fed into an assumption of a sly character, which meant people, for better or worse, tended to keep her at arm's length.

Rialla considered her a weather-vane: liable to shift allegiance however the wind blew. Truthfully, I felt the same, but was still polite to Florette. Weather-vane she may be, but I would remain the direction she kept returning to.

We lapsed into a silence that I had no intention of breaking. *Quiet*, Mother had impressed upon me from a young age, *is a monarch's greatest weapon. Those who cannot bear silence will rush to fill it, and they will always let something slip that they intended to keep secret*. So I sipped my cordial, smiled blandly, and waited for Florette to crack, if Rialla didn't goad her into doing so first.

The crack was neat and easy.

'Your Highness must have precious little good feeling towards the Ashes,' Florette remarked, aiming for nonchalance, but unable to hide the eager note in her voice. 'Lord Alec, especially, considering his actions. Arriving at the Kierth estate without permission or an invitation! The presumption!'

If you didn't know Rialla well, you wouldn't have caught her stiffening, how she briefly tightened her fingers around her glass stem. Her expression was still bright, but her eyes sharpened upon Florette as she carefully didn't look at me. I could practically see her reconsidering our argument. Was this why I hadn't written? Was this what I hadn't told her about?

As for Florette… well, Isra would be happy about the unintentional trap she'd flung herself into. No matter her ambition, Florette would always be ill-matched for intrigue. Even so, ambition was more dangerous when driven by foolishness.

I met Florette's gaze, affecting polite confusion. 'I'm afraid you've been somewhat misinformed, Lady Florette. Lord Alec *did* try and visit, despite my parents' longstanding wish that we not be disturbed while visiting Kierth. However, his parents got wind of his intentions and put a swift stop to them. I believe the Duke and Duchess thought it wise for him to remain in the country for the season, rather than returning with them to Court.'

A wise decision on the part of Lord and Lady Ash, who'd been obliged to send their apologies to my parents when a rumour of Lord Alec's aborted plan had drifted to Kierth. Mother's reply – curtly polite and rewritten three times on Mama's insistence – noted that while Their Majesties appreciated their apologies, they should perhaps teach their heir to understand a royal request. Upon their return to Court, the Ashes had carefully avoided my parents, but their son's foolishness hadn't leaked into gossip.

Until now.

Still congenially baffled, I continued, 'I must admit, it was all a bit *odd*. Lord Alec was mistakenly told that Lord Micah planned to ask for my hand. Utter nonsense, of course, though I value Lord Micah's friendship highly.' I raised an eyebrow, quite flawlessly I thought, and – still holding Florette's gaze – added, 'If I were Lord Alec, I'd be *highly* wroth with whoever told him such incorrect speculation.'

She almost held her nerve. Almost.

We both knew I was alluding to her. I'd been careful in what lies I'd divulged around each of my ladies. But now, as a flush blotched her cheeks, Florette was likely realising that she was the only one who'd *acted* upon this seed of false information.

'Indeed. How foolish of them,' she forced out, and promptly excused herself. Most would have considered her swift exit to border on rudeness.

Before I could feel anything (triumph, annoyance, or both),

Rialla slipped her arm through my elbow and dug her fingernails in. 'What, I beg of you, was *that* about?' she hissed close to my ear, lips barely moving, her expression still pleasant.

I hesitated.

Isra had always been clear: everything involving the Whispers was to remain private, even from Rialla and Micah. But Florette had fallen into my trap partly because Micah had (unintentionally) fanned the rumours of his supposed intentions towards me months ago – just enough to be useful, but not so strongly that his family had to get involved. In matters like these, he was a better courtier than Rialla, who was sometimes so convinced of her own cleverness that she missed the subtleties.

But people were still cautious around her. Rialla came from an old, powerful family, and her belief in herself was almost unshakeable. It was better to have her as an ally than an enemy. And I needed that loyalty and unshakeable belief, especially with Melisande soon to arrive, who'd grown up in a Court far more vicious and unstable than ours.

I sighed. It was always easier to beg forgiveness than ask permission. And for all her power, all her responsibility, Isra didn't know what it was like to live in my unusual position. A beloved daughter and heir, haunted by the shadows of Goldenmarch, entangled in the repercussions of decisions from years ago.

And Rialla was right: I'd need to start gathering my own allies sooner rather than later. Isra was my parents' spymaster, but I couldn't assume she'd live long enough to be mine when I became Queen.

The decision was easy, when broken down by logic.

'Let's go back to my rooms once my parents have left,' I murmured, careful to move my lips as little as possible. 'It's safer to explain there.'

Dear Cousin,

How unexpected to hear from you. The circumstances surrounding my upcoming visit notwithstanding, the significant lapse in our communication did not lead me to assume that it would be resurrected before my arrival.

To overcome my own necessary obstacle concerning the weather: the usual spring storms were not so strong this year, so I made good time to Saphirun where, indeed, your letter awaited me. Most of the staff is still here from when we were children, just older now. They were pleased to know you remain alive and well – I admit I assumed the latter from your rather flippant tone.

As for my continued existence, you may conjecture similar from this missive.

Her Majesty, my mother, sends her regards.

Your cousin,

Princess Melisande

NINE

Melisande's letter arrived a week after the Harvest Ball, my own formal entry into society.

I reread it once, twice, my frown deepening. It was the perfect courtier's response, with just a touch of politely bared teeth, and gave me absolutely nothing to work with. She'd not only seen through my ploy, but refused to entertain it.

I refolded the letter with vicious precision. She'd be here within a few weeks, right before the autumn rains turned bitter. If this was the game she wished to play, winter would be long and cold, but that was her choice.

Now that I had debuted and Melisande's visit was imminent, my parents and Isra had made it abundantly clear that not only was I expected to make a good impression, but to also show Melisande that I was her equal. I pretended to take it all in stride, but soon forgot what it felt like not to have a stomach filled with fretting butterflies, their delicate wings trembling against my insides.

The days sped by faster than I wanted. Since my hazy memories of a sharp-tongued, rigid girl had been proven correct by her letter, I knew exactly what to expect during Melisande's introduction to my parents. She wouldn't address them as she had me, especially since her survival instincts had been honed by the Farezi Court, but she surely wouldn't be able to fully hide her sharp edges; I looked forward to seeing how they hurt her.

The morning of her arrival, the butterflies in my stomach hardened into a mesh of dread. When I was suitably dressed, I picked up a novel I was halfway through, then a historical brick about the First Empire that sank into myths and speculation, but neither held my attention. I finally gave up and stared out the window, mired in a sense of impending doom, my chin propped on a clenched fist, until the summons came.

My parents were waiting in the throne room, dressed in formal regalia, and I took my usual place beside Mother's throne. As Melisande's introduction to Court could potentially be fraught, people's memories being long when it came to Rassa's treason, she and the new ambassador would first meet us privately. She was only a little later than expected, due to an unexpected downpour flooding parts of the primary eastern road.

'Finally,' Mama said, as we arranged ourselves, 'a royal that doesn't want to impress by showing up early and annoying everyone. I like her already.'

I stayed quiet. Every time my parents had mentioned Melisande during the last few weeks, I'd kept my replies neutral or swiftly changed the subject. They knew full well what I was doing, if not *why*, but I felt it better to remain cautious since I wasn't certain how I'd actually feel until Melisande arrived.

When we were ready, Mother gestured, and the doors were flung open.

'Her Royal Highness, Crown Princess Melisande of Farezi!'

When we were young, Melisande was already taller than me. Now, she was about Mother's height, perhaps even taller. She glided towards us in green velvet with full underskirts of gold silk: Farezi's royal colours. While Mother usually wore blue and silver, a habit from her first year as Queen, Mama preferred not to wear the royal colours unless making a point, and I was not yet obliged to sport them until I became Queen. (Mother often told me to enjoy a varied wardrobe while I still could.) Even though it made sense for Melisande to wear her country's colours, this being a diplomatic visit, it made me feel lesser in comparison, as if I were a child playing at being princess.

The top half of her hair was pulled back in a smooth knot, held in place by a gold pin studded with emerald shards; the rest fell in black waves down her back. Like Arisane and Sabine, she had the family's thick-lashed hazel eyes, lightly accentuated with kohl, and her pale skin was powdered luminously smooth. Her mouth was stained red and naturally pursed. But the sparkle in her gaze, the poise of her long neck and posture – that was all simply her.

Melisande paused at the steps leading to the dais, flicked her skirts into place, and sank into a deep curtsey. Precisely the right depth for a princess giving courtesy to royalty, not an inch more nor less. My etiquette teacher would have wept from delight.

Moments trickled by, until Mother said, 'Your Highness, please rise. We are honoured by your presence.'

'The honour is mine, Your Majesties.' Her gaze flickered towards me, and she added, 'And Your Highness, of course.' Her voice was low and rich, her accent spiking the ends of her sentences. Had I sounded like that when I'd first arrived here?

I inclined my head, not yet trusting myself to speak. Surely I wasn't the only one sensing a tense undercurrent beneath our civilised veneer, the ghosts of a usurper's greed, his ambition and cruelty, lingering in the room? It was a neat juxtaposition: two women who had been dragged into Rassa's schemes against two of the younger generation, all of us having suffered the consequences of his actions.

My parents and Melisande settled into the polite act of diplomacy: they exchanged pleasantries and enquired about her journey; Melisande offered personal correspondence from Queen Sabine, gesturing the ambassador and his husband forward to segue into their introductions. No ambassador in foreign lands truly had an easy time of it, but he seemed shrewd in his calmness, his husband was charming, and it was anyone's guess if they'd make an impact after Melisande left in spring.

I should have been following the intersecting strands of the conversations, an attentive expression plastered on my face even if I wasn't contributing much. Instead, my thoughts spun like water down a drain. I couldn't understand the churning in my stomach, or why I clutched my hands together behind my back, until Mama laughed at some wry remark of Melisande's that I had only half-caught.

Then I realised: I was afraid my parents would like her, as would Rialla, Micah, and even my own ladies. They would look at her and see how I lacked in comparison, and they would automatically prefer her.

It was a child's fear. Melisande hadn't been here a full hour yet, and she was already dredging up the worst parts of me from Saphirun, even if I didn't fully understand them.

How was I to survive this – survive *her* – until spring?

An emphasis on my name jerked me out of my gloomy thoughts. With a flush of cold awareness, I realised that for the first time in years, I had lost track of a conversation in public: unthinkable for a royal. Should I respond, and likely reveal my embarrassing lapse in attention? Or attempt a remark to fish for the topic, which could possibly result in the same mortification, or—

'Emri is already deep in thought,' Mother said before I could reply, smoothing over the awkward moment, 'on how best to entertain you during your time with Us.'

My cheeks scorched, as I barely kept a flinch in check at Mother's use of the royal We. A gentle rebuke for me and a subtle show of power towards Melisande.

'I look forward to it,' Melisande said, gravely earnest. 'My mother so wished to visit Edar when she was younger, but marriage and… later responsibilities took precedent.' I could only admire her delicate sidestep over Rassa.

Then she glanced at me. We met each other's gazes: heirs and cousins, with the diplomatic future of two countries resting on our shoulders. And for a moment, from one blink to the next, her courtier's mask faltered, and she looked at me with something very close to worry.

And I knew:

Melisande no longer acted like the girl I vaguely remembered from our childhood, too aware that she was next in line for a throne that was never meant to be hers. In that, she and Mother were similar. But she still kept that little girl close, deep inside, a shadow within a shadow. And from the worry in her eyes, Melisande also remembered everything that had happened in Saphirun. She had been just that little bit older for the memories to stick, but she didn't know how much *I* remembered… and it made her afraid.

I stood beside my parents' thrones and straightened my shoulders. With Melisande's fear, I held more power between us than I'd realised. But it depended on how I would wield it.

TEN

The Court was absolutely unprepared for Melisande. For her bright eyes, pursed mouth, and glorious hair. For her self-confidence.

Yes, she was the Farezi heir, set to inherit a throne tarnished by treason, but Melisande met people wearing armour of a beaming smile, witty conversation, sharp observations, and an assured stride. As the weeks went on, I watched her face the older factions of Court, who judged her, and the younger courtiers, who judged her based on their parents' influence and yet also wanted to be her. Or simply just *wanted* her.

She faced their polite barbs and retorts, then flicked the insults away with practised ease, like how Grandmother Sionbourne popped the oysters she was fond of.

I would have laughed for days, if I'd found it the least bit amusing. Instead, I spent most of my time seething at the Court's shock and surprise, annoyed enough to clench my teeth until my jaw ached.

'If I've noticed you've been sulking since Princess Melisande arrived,' Micah remarked one day, after I trounced him at chess and couldn't even gloat, 'then your parents definitely have.' When

I fixed him with a glare, he shrugged. 'I'm just saying that they *will* ambush you with an *I'm not angry, just disappointed* lecture.' His warning niggled like food trapped between my back teeth.

Like me, Melisande was trained to memorise names, faces, and important details, and was already using this to win people over. Melisande was fluent in Edaran, with only traces of her own accent, and educated to high standards of languages, history, and mathematics. I'm sure if we'd wanted, we could have sat down and compared notes on our respective tax legislation. She also enjoyed reading, hunting, cards, dancing, and was proficient at the harpsichord.

If we hadn't been related, I still would have hated her.

I sighed. Micah didn't push, unlike Rialla, but he didn't let something go when sufficiently annoyed. 'She's just... so highly accomplished.'

'She's three years older than you,' he pointed out.

'And three years from now, I'll still be nowhere near her equal.'

Micah frowned, beginning to reset his side of the board. 'It's not a race, Emri. The crown isn't a prize you can win from her.'

'It *feels* like a race,' I muttered. Even though said race was likely all in my own head.

The old Farezi King had strained relationships between his neighbours to the point where Farezinne marriages for Edaran noble children had become significantly unpopular when my parents were younger. In the aftermath of Rassa's treachery, my parents had strengthened their alliances with Othayria and Eshvon, while Farezi had floundered. Not even my adoption had helped much to soften its disgrace.

Now, Queen Sabine wanted to rebuild the old alliance. And if that meant Melisande had to smile and charm and compliment everyone from dawn to dusk, she would. I'd been so focused on my parents' expectations for me, I'd forgotten that this trip was also a test for her.

We looked up at a polite cough. Melisande stood beside our table, holding two steaming cups. 'My apologies for interrupting, but…'

I plastered good humour over my face and gestured at the empty chair she was hovering by. 'Cousin! Please, join us.'

Melisande flashed a smile, the scent of spiced cider in the air. As she nudged a cup towards me, she said, 'I've been reliably informed that this is one of your favourites.'

My eyebrows jumped up. 'Oh?'

Melisande tilted her head. 'By the member of your ladies who always looks like she wishes to stab me.'

Rialla sat at a nearby table with three others. She was pretending to be deeply involved in a card game, but the tense jut of her eyebrows and clenched jaw gave her away. She appeared to be winning the game… and also close to making the other three cry.

Upon first meeting Melisande, Rialla had recognised an indomitable will equal to hers and despised her on sight. It didn't matter that it made things difficult for me. It didn't matter that her own family likely berated her in private, as her dislike of Melisande also reflected poorly upon them. Rialla continued to avoid her, teetering on unforgivable rudeness, but it only seemed to heighten my cousin's amusement.

Micah's general life policy was to be friendly to everyone, while keeping his true feelings limited to a handful of trusted people, so he sighed and went to save the three ladies from Rialla, since he couldn't save her from herself.

Melisande slid into his vacated seat, and studied the board with apparently genuine enthusiasm. 'Do you play chess much?'

'Only when I'm annoyed.' As much as Mother enjoyed playing with me, irritation at my poor humour usually meant she finished every game wanting to whack the board over my head. 'I prefer Root and Fang.' Since Melisande disliked it, it was one game I knew we'd never play together.

A sly smile curled her mouth. 'Why ever would you be annoyed?' she asked, her eyes gleaming as she picked up her cider. 'The day is bright, the hall is warm; you have a good drink, and everyone is in fine spirits.'

Because I loathe every moment you are here, I thought. I knew better than to say it, of course, though my ability to hide my true feelings seemed to crumble around her.

I leaned back, holding eye contact. 'Nothing,' I said, in the flattest tone possible. 'I have absolutely no reason to be annoyed.'

The games hall was a large room, its arched ceiling marking it as part of the palace's newer construction (newer, in royal architectural terms, meaning built in the last century). We were surrounded by courtiers our own age, who were either flirting, politely insulting each other (or both, in some cases), or simply whiling away the afternoon. Later, this would become the domain of the older courtiers, the gambling becoming more serious, while the younger set drifted in search of other entertainment.

I missed my old routines. When I wasn't at the mercy of Isra or my tutors, or with Rialla and Micah, I'd preferred reading and trying, yet again, to improve my sketching. Micah and I had often spent hours together with novels and a bottle of wine in companionable silence.

My ladies, truthfully, didn't know how to react to the changes that had accompanied Melisande's arrival. I now actually spent a considerable amount of time with them every day, and I genuinely liked some of them. But they'd known I preferred my own company and had accepted it since, in turn, I mostly left them to their own devices and pecking order. I only stepped in when their intrigues grew too sharp, or their insular friendships turned cruel towards others.

Now, my continued presence – and Melisande's – upset their own routines, since we outranked them all. It even curbed Rialla's terrifying grip over the rest of my ladies, which only increased her disgruntlement. And if they'd taken my generally hands-off approach for granted, they no longer did when faced with Melisande, who, though charming, had kept firm control over her own ladies-in-waiting.

'You're too lenient with them,' she'd told me once, after they'd all left for the evening, 'so they treat you with less respect. They'd turn on you in a moment if it gained them something.'

'Rialla wouldn't,' I'd said absently, then grimaced.

Melisande went still – she'd caught my reaction and no doubt folded it away for later contemplation – but then she'd eye-rolled and flung out some meaningless retort.

I'd found myself smiling, despite everything, and struggled against the wave of shame that rose during these moments. Sometimes I didn't know what was worse: my reasonably clouded judgment of her, or the realisation that if we hadn't spent our childhoods together, if my wavering, treacherous memories of Saphirun and Arisane didn't loom between us, we'd likely be fond acquaintances. We'd have sent better letters to each other, at least.

Now, Melisande lounged back, her legs crossed, to finish her cider and consider me.

'Tomorrow,' she pronounced. 'We should take the horses out into the forest.'

'You want to go riding?'

She shrugged. 'Mother takes her horses seriously.'

Melisande had arrived almost a month ago, on the cusp of autumn turning into early winter. The Farezi Court took hunting as seriously as its Queen took her horses, but my parents didn't care for it, much to Melisande's disappointment. I probably did owe her a trip out before the weather fully turned.

'Very well,' I said. 'Be up early. We'll make a morning of it.'

I'd assumed, uncharitably, that Melisande was the sort of courtier who survived on late nights and later mornings. She'd promptly won my parents' approval by never drinking to excess in public (a longstanding family rule: alcohol led to loose tongues and lost secrets) and keeping to a sleep schedule, though I suspected it was less her usual routine and more her adapting to ours.

Because of my uncharitable inclinations, I wasn't prepared for her response. Her eyes lit up, and guilt immediately withered my skin. When considering daily activities, I hadn't really considered what she enjoyed. It was simply easier to suggest things that involved my ladies as a social buffer.

But I had to stop assuming the worst of her. So I hesitated, then added, 'Just us and a groom or two.' Before Melisande could respond, I glanced down at the chessboard. 'I presume you play more than just when you're feeling annoyed?'

Her smile turned sly once more. 'My dear cousin,' she said, 'I can thrash you with absolutely no effort.'

She wasn't lying.

ELEVEN

The next morning dawned bright and clear. The cloudless sky stretched out in a glorious swathe of blue.

Melisande was already in the stables when I arrived, greeting her mare, Lis, and chatting to a stable hand. I paused, taken aback. The Melisande I remembered had certainly acknowledged servants, and been as kind as her demeanour allowed, but little more. In her letter, she'd mentioned the servants from our childhood in Saphirun, but I'd assumed it was a feeble attempt at nostalgia, not a hint that in this, too, she had changed.

My own horse, Briar, was brought out, saddled and ready. I scratched the top of the stripe on his forehead, smiling. Rialla adored him, for they shared a similar spiky personality, while Micah, who had what he claimed was a sensible fear of horses, insisted Briar could smell said fear and taunted him.

Micah had an overactive imagination and needed to bribe my horse better.

Mounting up, I took a deep breath and let it out slowly, as Briar shook his head and snorted, settling under me. Melisande and the two grooms accompanying us followed my cue, and we headed out at a brisk walk that shifted into a trot. The morning was dry and pleasant, everyone was in good spirits, and I didn't feel a drop of guilt for being away from the palace for several hours.

The forest sprawled out to the north-west beyond the city walls. While my parents didn't enjoy hunting, they organised a large one annually in their name, and courtiers regularly used the forest trails.

Melisande was an excellent rider – better than me, though I'd never admit it – and for the first few miles into the forest, we drifted in comfortable silence.

Pale sunlight did its best to glimmer through the treetops. Birdsong trilled and whistled around us. The horses swished their tails, and I lulled myself with the sounds of hoofbeats and the grooms' quiet conversation. The roads and trails were also used by merchants and other travellers, so were regularly maintained and suitable for even the most nervous rider. I trusted Briar, I trusted the trail, and for the first time in months, my thoughts didn't trouble me.

The need for alertness returned when we swerved off the road and into one of my favourite trails that led north. Further upstream, the river cut in two. The one in the trail cut through the city and towards the docks, while the other continued south until it eventually emptied into the sea. It all looked better in summer, but if Melisande had truly wanted beautiful horseback rides, she should have arrived at a better time of year.

She finally broke the silence, starting with the last orchestral recital she'd attended in Triala, the Farezinne capital, before leaving for Saphirun and from there to Edar. It had been dominated by a harpist taking the country by storm, and the birdsong this morning reminded her of the music.

Unlike some of Melisande's other interests, this one I could converse about with reasonable confidence. Mother played the pianoforte with the competence expected of a royal, and both Mama and Aunt Zola played the viola. I had tried to, until Mama had gently suggested that while I certainly appreciated music, being proficient didn't appear to be within my skillset. Since I came attached with a crown and a country, my lack of musicality would thankfully be the least of my suitors' concerns.

As we made our way deeper into the forest, the trees crowded closer, and the deepening shade made me glad of my gloves and riding cloak. Our conversation drifted into literature: novels, plays, histories and manifestos. She was aghast at the amount of history I was expected to read, while I couldn't understand how she loved poetry so much and suggested Micah as an interested party if she wanted a proper conversation about it.

'He has no designs on a throne,' I said, getting the obvious out of the way, even though Micah would be mortified if he could hear us. But he'd be even more humiliated if they struck up what he thought was a genuine conversation about poetry, while she thought it was the start of a flirtation.

Melisande snorted. 'He need not fear. I seek no husband.'

Rialla, my parents, and sheer habit made me automatically reply: 'Then a wife?'

She paused for too long, which said more than it didn't. 'No one would think it a fair bargain to marry into my family right now,' she finally said. 'Even if we're royal.'

There was little I could say to that. If my parents hadn't brought me into the Edaran succession through adoption, I would have likely remained forgotten in Saphirun. Certainly no one in Farezi would have wanted to marry Rassa's disgraced daughter. I wasn't sure if anyone wanted to marry me as the Edaran heir, either, but that was my parents' problem.

As the silence lengthened, I realised that Melisande had inadvertently opened an opportunity for us to talk about deeper matters. But I wasn't sure I wanted to. For all that we were related, and had the ramifications of other peoples' mistakes dumped upon us, when I looked at her, I saw a young woman that Arisane had likely shaped and influenced for years after I'd left. No matter how beautifully she smiled, no matter how easily she spoke, I still couldn't trust her.

Of course, there were also two grooms behind us, far enough away to give the illusion of privacy, but close enough to overhear if we weren't careful.

So I let the silence linger and stretch. Melisande offered no further conversation, and I almost thought I'd imagined the easy moment between us.

While the trees still pressed close to the trail, the birdsong and rustling undergrowth were joined by a new sound: gurgling water.

'We can stop for a bit,' I said. 'Eat something and give the horses a rest.'

Melisande smiled. 'As Your Highness wishes.'

The title was technically correct, but unlike other times, where it felt more sarcastic, this time Melisande sounded almost like she was gently teasing. In public, we greeted each other by title, but discarded them for the rest of our conversations, referring to each other by name or *Cousin*, in recognition of our family ties and the affectionate moniker used by royalty across borders.

The clearing was a waypoint upon the trail, with a pleasing view of the river in summer. When I was younger and here with Rialla and Micah, we'd wade in up to our knees, the silt and mud cool between our toes. It was deep enough to swim where it curved further along, but still treacherous with a sudden drop in the riverbed.

The grooms had a fire going in short order, and retrieved water to boil and mix with coffee. Melisande and I had both stopped by the kitchens on our way to the stables, so we pooled our provisions. The cooks had been ambitious, giving us a fruit pie each. We divided one between the four of us, while I suggested the other be shared out to the morning's stable hands.

'We won't be hungry, at least,' Melisande remarked. On her

second day here, she had reportedly risen early to find the kitchens and befriend the cooks. Isra had been disgusted at such a show of good sense.

But we had apparently also reached the limits of her kindness, or perhaps Melisande had finally decided to forego pretence as to why we'd ridden out today. Whatever it was, the grooms picked up the change from amiable noble to haughty princess and moved further down the riverbank.

I took a long swallow of coffee. 'Shall we keep waffling like good courtiers, or just get to the point?'

'I have a letter from your birth mother,' Melisande said.

The coffee turned sour upon my tongue.

Arisane had despised my birth mother, Lady Liliene, for what she considered her 'innate weakness'. She'd had the decency never to say it to me directly; I'd overheard the staff during my birth mother's sole visit to Saphirun, though I hadn't understood it at the time.

Unlike Arisane and Rassa, whose family connections I'd discarded, I couldn't do the same to Liliene. Arisane would never be my grandmother, and I'd never acknowledge Rassa as my father. But even though I had parents who loved me, Lady Liliene remained a fragile scar upon my heart. I didn't feel the same about her as I did for Mother or Mama... but she still had a place in my history.

Out of all my Farezi family, she had never been disappointed by my existence.

Lady Liliene was still, technically, a Dowager Queen of Edar. There was not a little debate on the subject, most of it academic and safely out of earshot of the monarchs. While her marriage to Rassa had been legal, her right to the Dowager title was murky. Rassa had coerced Mother into abdicating, then had her kidnapped. His usurping of the Edaran throne was legally shaky, and he'd had even less right to do it under international law.

For her part, Lady Liliene had never used the title. For Their Majesties' part, they were reluctant to strip it from her, especially since they'd adopted me, but Court and political pressure meant that she would never be welcome in Edar. I suspected they regretted caving in to the pressure: they had never wanted to cut me off from my Farezinne family, especially not my birth mother.

'I noticed that you only refer to Grandmother by her name,' Melisande said. 'And Rassa, that one time someone was foolish enough to mention him. I wondered, but well – he's wiped from the family record, and…' She hesitated before curling her right hand into a fist: an unconscious action, perhaps. 'Grandmother never gave you – either of us, really – much reason to love her.'

My lingering memory of Lady Liliene was her perfume and trembling smile. The rest was vague, much like my memories of Arisane and Saphirun.

She loved me. I think. No, I knew it. She'd worn regret like a widow's veil, and her sorrow had stifled the room. But she had knelt, so she was at my eye level, and whispered that she was my mother and very happy to finally meet me again. When she held out her arms, I'd stepped into them unthinkingly. She'd shivered only a little while hugging me, and tried to muffle her weeping against my hair.

Arisane had hated my birth mother, as she loathed all weakness in others – because she feared it in herself, I'd finally realised many years later. But Queen Sabine had tried her best, in allowing Lady Liliene to visit. Perhaps. In my birth mother, Arisane had seen the disgrace they'd brought upon themselves, while Sabine was plagued with guilt for a victim of Rassa's who was forever linked to the family.

Before she'd met him, Lady Liliene had been a rising star at Court with great potential, a beauty with a delicate presence. I was an astonishing reflection of her: the same tumbling curls, shining dark eyes, and warm brown skin, but with the royal family's thick eyelashes and sharp bone structure.

A few months after my birth, I was sent to Arisane in Saphirun, and Lady Liliene withdrew to the reluctant welcome of her family in the country. Queen Sabine had given her an annual allowance and an inadequate apology for her life having been destroyed, never mind that they'd also taken her only child away from her. But when the adoption was finalised with Edar, Sabine had called Arisane's bluff by allowing Lady Liliene to come to Saphirun and say goodbye to me.

She had been kind, and heartbroken, and abandoned. I had desperately wanted to make her smile and also flee from her radiating despair.

If Sabine hadn't sent me to Arisane and Saphirun, if Lady Liliene had fought harder not to lose me, perhaps things would have been different.

If was an unspoken wish, never proven true.

I had never seen Lady Liliene again. We had never exchanged letters. The ambassadors never brought any messages from her. My parents had never forbidden me from contacting her – they'd broached the subject many times, but the history between them all was horrifically fraught, and nothing had ever been decided.

I met Melisande's gaze. 'I'd like the letter, please.'

She nodded and handed me an envelope. There was no sly grin, no witty retort nor mocking look. Melisande had always known she would eventually return to her mother at Court, while I would never return to Lady Liliene.

We sank into silence again, this one strained. I was suddenly glad that Melisande had forced the grooms to give us some distance. Draining my coffee, while wishing it were something stronger, I stared at the treetops reaching vainly towards the sky. 'So we're finally talking about it all – Saphirun? Arisane? I wondered how long we'd manage to avoid it.'

Melisande stared into her cup, as if she too wished it held something stronger. 'We did well to last this long. But you were never going to talk about Grandmother, or Saphirun, or anything else from our past inside the palace, where people could so easily interrupt or overhear us. So I decided we had to go outside.'

The forest was the most secluded place we could have this conversation. There was no danger of my parents overhearing us, or a courtier interrupting with some frivolity. But did I want to do this? Dredge up memories and pain that I'd buried deep years ago? My birth family was my terrible keystone, the core of my past, and it had followed me like a hidden shadow since I'd left Farezi.

I tilted my head further back. 'I hate you sometimes.'

'I deserve it,' Melisande said, her calmness surprising me. 'I was terrible to you.'

'The night they told me you were visiting,' I said, the words spilling from me, because if I paused or hesitated or thought too hard, I'd stop speaking, return to the palace, and never again spend a moment in Melisande's company, which would be inconvenient for diplomatic purposes, 'the nightmares came back. I dreamed of being locked in a shuttered room.'

The same dream every time: alone in a shuttered, locked room, bereft of even a candle. Alone, with only the shadows pooling deeper around me and no way out. Even beside the tumble of water, sheltered under trees in golden autumn sunlight, my skin shuddered and crawled from the memory.

Melisande stiffened; her mouth pressed into a thin line until her lips were as white as her face. If this nightmare – this *memory* – made little sense to me, now, after so many years, it was familiar to her.

But she didn't explain. I didn't speak for several moments, my right hand wrapped against my left wrist; my pulse skittered against my fingers. 'What did Arisane do,' I finally ventured, hating the softness, the *weakness*, in my voice, 'after I left?'

Melisande's eyes darkened as they filled with ghosts. She smiled: a true, bitter curl of lips, nothing like the teasing moue she reserved for courtiers. 'Everything she threatened you with. Threats I suspect that you, thankfully, don't remember well.'

For a moment, a crystalline heartbeat, the promise of eternity between one breath and the next, we almost did what Melisande had intended: discuss our shared pain and resentment frankly and honestly. I opened my mouth and it was in my throat, all ready to be spoken into the crisp air:

What did she do to you?

But you're the *heir*—

You're the ideal princess, the perfect courtier—

Why would she punish *you*?

Did you meet her at Saphirun, before continuing on to Edar? Speak to her? Could you even deign to be in the same room as her?

Instead Melisande took a sharp breath and shook her head, as if brushing away the lapse in composure like mist caught in her hair. 'Of course, we both blame Arisane,' she said, affecting a casual air, 'when she's only partly at fault. Your mama agreed all too readily to her plan to depose Rassa.' Her mouth twisted, showing her teeth, as if she were a she-wolf baring fangs in warning. 'I never discovered if my mother knew about their plot. I could never bring myself to ask. Better to always wonder, then know she sent us to live with someone who arranged her son's murder when he could no longer be contained.'

My pulse roared in my ears. I should have already wiped any hint of expression from my face, stilled myself, so I wouldn't betray anything that could be used against me. But I couldn't. In my head, there was the sensation of several puzzle pieces finally slotting into place, revealing the reasons for my past, the consequences of my childhood that I'd always suspected but could never figure out *why*.

My voice betrayed me. 'Mama?'

When she said *your mama*, did she mean—

The brief glimpse of the she-wolf in Melisande died, and she somehow turned even paler.

'You didn't know,' she whispered. 'They never told you.'

'Told me *what*?' This time it was my turn to bare fangs. '*Explain.*'

Melisande closed her eyes, as if she could take back the words she'd tossed out to avoid her own pain. 'When they found Queen Aurelia in Farezi, Arisane offered your mama the means to kill Rassa. If she did, but never admitted that Arisane had helped her,

Farezi would support Queen Aurelia in retaking her throne.

'Queen Xania agreed. And Arisane gave her the poison to kill Rassa.'

Once, there is a woman.

And she is dying.

She knows this like she knows that she needs air to breathe, water and food to live, movement to keep her body limber.

She knows this like she knows a blade must be kept sharp to be useful.

The moment her axe touches the tree of all life, the air shudders around her. Her ears fill with a low, crackling roar, like roots slowly ripped from the ground.

A blink, and she is trapped within the trunk, pressure above, below, all around, her eyes wide in the endless dark.

She does not cry out. She will not cry out.

A low laugh echoes, caresses inside her skull. **Heroes are brave. And always foolish**. A sigh, much like the sound of grave dirt being overturned, with a crackle like flames devouring kindling. A dangerous thing, the meeting of fire and wood.

The voice is ancient. The pressure builds. Her ears throb. The magic surrounding her is old, very old, and it cares little for the petty wishes of mortals.

This is what she gets for her folly. This is what she gets for her boast.

You are unworthy. A faint thread of scorn.

What an inglorious death, trapped within a tree, slowly squeezed to death.

A long pause. **Regret.**

She waits. Her pulse jumps and skitters and pounds.

There is a choice.

She waits. She waits, and the magic presses against her, and for all she knows the entire world outside has died while she is trapped here. No scrap of light, and only the ancient, crackling voice.

A mortal death, doomed to be forgotten. Or immortality. But there is a price.

Of course there is. In all the stories, there is always a choice. And a price.

She is, perhaps, being flippant about the situation: trapped within a magical tree, at the mercy of an ancient power that is stronger than anything she has faced thus far. But for all her faults, the woman knows herself. If she does not try to think, does not try to reason with herself, she will scream until her mind shatters and she loses all sense of herself.

What is the price?

Your mortal life. Your soul. You will crave the endless devotion of mortals – and if it is lost, so shall you be. A god cannot exist without worship.

A god.

She instinctively recoils – give up her life? Her soul? She had wanted to find adventure, infamy – to be remembered. Part of her, that loves others even when she desires more, chafes at the restraints placed upon her by life and duties, insists that even immortality is not worth the loss of those things. But... but being a god.

Gods are always remembered.

Do I serve you?

Another dry chuckle. **I will be your creator. You will always remember me.**

She thinks. Thinks, even though the magic keeps pressing against her juddering heart. Her thoughts are splintered, jagged – soul, immortality, devotion, infamy – and really, there is no choice. She came to cut down the tree and take its power for herself, and she failed. She went on a quest to do great deeds and be remembered long after her death.

A god is immortal.

A god is always remembered.

Yes.

Very well.

Before she can form another thought, or consider the wisdom of her decision, the magic claws through her.

The sensation of being trapped within a snowstorm, huddled on the ground, each snowflake a gentle kiss of death. Tree roots wrap around her heart, pin it in place for branches to grow, nourished by her blood to twine around her bones,

meld into her muscles, twist under her skin before breaking
free to stretch around her head.

And she screams.

TWELVE

Mama. Arisane. *Poison.*

Everything blurred after that.

I blinked, and suddenly I was back in the palace, standing in my receiving room, still in my riding clothes. The fire crackled. A servant hovered nearby, ready to take my cloak, and asked if I would be having lunch alone. From her tone, this wasn't the first time she'd asked me.

Melisande had somehow got me back on my horse, and had the grooms pack up and lead us back to the palace stables. I'd clearly gone from there to the royal wing, but there was no sign of her. I almost asked the servant if Melisande had accompanied me here, then bit my tongue. All I needed was speculation that I was losing my memory or wits.

I couldn't remember if we'd said anything else about Mama and Rassa. If I'd screamed at her, if she'd shouted back, if the grooms had actually overheard anything. When I tried, there was a low hum in my memory, like a nest of bees slowly growing to anger.

Did Mother know what Mama had done? She'd been traumatised when they returned to Edar, tormented day and night by what had happened in Goldenmarch, not considered in good enough health to be told of Rassa's death until weeks later. The country had been held together by the combined efforts of Grandmother Sionbourne, the Admiral, and the Master of Coin. Mama and Matthias hadn't even really been involved, since the Court and Parliament had wasted weeks debating if Rassa declaring them traitors still mattered now that he was dead.

Officially, his heart had given out, but no one had really believed it. The servant who'd found him had lost his good sense and babbled *poison* to half the Farezi entourage. That servant had recanted his story swiftly, I abruptly remembered, and nothing more was ever heard from him. Now, I recognised Arisane's shadow all over the situation. Farezi hadn't even pretended outrage when Rassa's body was returned, the general consensus being that they had no grounds since their son had unlawfully disposed of a ruling monarch, then had her abducted and tortured.

Logically, I knew why it had been kept quiet – the consequences between Farezi and Edar could be dire, especially if both royal families had kept the truth secret. And the more people who knew, the more chances that loose talk could explode into public knowledge.

And people died *all the time*. Not as much now as during the old King's reign, when people had barely flickered an eyelid at so many people succumbing to a swift, deadly 'illness', but people still plotted and schemed, despite my parents' best efforts.

But in my gut and heart and the part of me where I now suspected that Saphirun had dug deep, I despised that Mama had kept this from me. That she'd left me in a position where I'd learned about it from someone I couldn't trust even a little. Though Mama surely hadn't suspected that *Melisande* would be the one to tell me, since it implicated Arisane as much as Mama, and potentially implicated Queen Sabine in turn.

I took a deep breath, tried to examine this argument with the care it deserved, but I couldn't stop trembling, my palms pressed to my temples, gritting my teeth against the harsh truth slamming against my skull:

In conspiring with Arisane to kill Rassa, Mama had unintentionally orchestrated my terrible childhood, which I would later be rescued from with the adoption. Yet she couldn't have known that. Lady Liliene's pregnancy had only been truly confirmed after Rassa's death.

I was in a chair near the fire, my cloak discarded, but still in my riding clothes, wishing I'd thought to ask for a hot drink, when Melisande entered the room, the servant rushing at her heels.

'My apologies, Your Highness,' the servant – what was her name? I never forgot a name – babbled, wringing her hands. What expression was I wearing? None of the staff ever feared me. 'I couldn't stop Her Royal Highness, she insisted—'

'Leave us,' I said softly. I'd meant to be kind, but it came out flat, and the servant practically fled the room.

A strange tinge lingered on Melisande's skin. Oddly, this was what convinced me that she hadn't cradled this secret like a dagger in the dark, waiting for the right moment to lash out. She thought I'd known, that my parents had already shared one of their biggest secrets with me, the consequences of which affected two countries, their royal families, and the current and future diplomatic relations between them.

For the first time, Melisande seemed foolish to me; almost naïve.

Because no matter my bewilderment, no matter my outrage, righteous or not, if I had been in Mama's position, there was a good chance I would have made the same choice. Kept my silence. Kept my terrible secret.

How had Mama lived with this for so long? When she looked at me, and saw the features I shared with Rassa, was I always a reminder of what she'd done?

I gestured carelessly at the chair opposite me. Melisande sat, still looking ill and uncertain.

'I wish you'd never come here,' I said.

She rubbed her eyes. 'I'm sorry. I… I thought we were circling around this, as we were with Grandmother and Saphirun and – and my cowardice.'

I wanted to snarl *This is not a game*, but that was exactly what royal Courts were like. People's lives and secrets and hopes: all pieces on the chessboard, ways for others to jostle for power. It would have been natural for Melisande to consider it a game piece being toyed between us.

I straightened, pulled back my shoulders, and finally looked at her properly. 'Who told you? Arisane or Queen Sabine?'

'Mother,' she said. 'Grandmother never would have. When I came of age, Mother inducted me into the family secrets, so to speak.' Her elegant smile was mirthless. 'She sat me down and told me all the things I needed to know, for fear she'd die suddenly or be murdered. I was finally old enough that she trusted me to put the repercussions into context.'

The part of me trained ruthlessly by Isra stirred at the phrase *family secrets*, but Melisande was too canny to let anything else slip – not just because of the consequences of this particular secret, but because no matter our blood ties, we were still heirs to different countries. We would always have our own interests at heart.

'Does Aunt Sabine mourn him?' The distinction between *Queen* and *Aunt* was subtle, but Melisande tilted her head; she'd noticed.

'No.' Melisande sighed and crossed her legs. 'From what I've heard – mostly through gossip – Mother and Rassa never liked each other. My parents were a practical love match, and sometimes I think she married young and had me to humiliate Rassa. As the heir, *he* should have married first to secure his own succession, but he rebuffed every suitable bride.' Her lips curled. 'Of course, now we know why: his sights were set on Edar, probably groomed by Grandfather, long may he *not* rest peacefully. Rassa didn't visit after I was born. I never met him before he left for Edar.'

And died lingered, unspoken, between us.

'He did the most damage to the family reputation since our ancestors brought down the old Empire,' Melisande continued flatly. 'So, no, Mother does not mourn him.'

The ensuing silence felt different. The sun was almost at noon peak, filling the room. I always enjoyed winter sunlight, the way it bloomed across paper and turned reading into a mystical experience. Now the brightness felt like a mockery of our terrible conversation.

After a while, Melisande asked, 'What will you do with this?' She made a good show of a courtier's effortless mask, but couldn't fully hide her uneasiness. Beneath the bland question, I caught the truth: *will you confront your mama? Will you tell your parents I was the one who told you?*

I blinked. For all my reeling astonishment, for all that I'd focused on what this meant for my family, for *me*, I hadn't fully considered how much this was a catastrophic mistake for Melisande.

'I don't know, *dear cousin*,' I finally said, because it was the truth and I needed time to think. My focus wasn't on the upper hand I'd now gained against her, but what might happen if I confronted Mama. If she denied it, would I have to go to Mother? What if she didn't know and refused to believe me, so assuredly certain of Mama's goodness? How would this affect us as a family? How would it fracture us?

But if Mama didn't deny it, and admitted it was all true – what would that mean for us? How could I trust her again, if this was the kind of secret she'd kept my entire life? And once she knew that *I* knew, would she always watch me through the eyes of a spymaster instead of a parent, viewing me not as a daughter, but a potential threat?

WINTER

THIRTEEN

A week after Melisande told me the truth about Mama and Rassa, I woke to a hard, bright frost over the city. Overnight, Arkaala's paths and streets were transformed into treachery. Waiting for hot water, and shivering under my thick morning robe, I blew my breath on the window, tracing over the ice pattern bursts on the cold glass. Edaran winters had been harsh for decades. My parents had never experienced a mild one in their lifetimes, but a shift had truly become apparent a few years before Mother took the throne. There had been five winters during her reign which were considered the harshest in living memory.

The weather reflected my mood: bleak, almost numb.

But in front of everyone else, including my parents, I performed my duties and social obligations with poise and deft skill. My conversations were light and brisk, focused on the shallow topics expected at gatherings and dinner parties. I attended new plays, an opera, a recital by a soprano making her debut, all the rage at Court. At each one, my smile remained fixed, and to each one Melisande accompanied me. No one could suspect there was even a hint of friction between us.

Truthfully, now I realised how accomplished a courtier she

was. Keeping up the façade was slowly taking its toll on me, but if she hadn't told me about Mama poisoning Rassa, I'd never have thought for a moment that anything was troubling her.

In private, when we were stuck together in the carriage, a faint veneer of exhaustion rippled over Melisande. Her hazel eyes dimmed, her mane of dark hair seemed to wilt, and she looked like she wanted nothing more than to sleep for the next decade. But in public, she shone like a Midwinter star, as if she could take on the role of Twilight without needing any costume.

Despite their initial reluctance, the Court was slowly falling under her spell, entranced by the double act we made as the polished, witty princesses. But alone, we had nothing to say to each other. If we tried, our words crumbled into the yawning chasm that stretched between us, bridged only by our terrible secret.

And as we drew closer to the Midwinter Ball, I wasn't sure how much longer I could keep it to myself.

After lunch on Midwinter, the household threw themselves into getting my parents and myself ready for the evening's ball. This year, Mother was attending as Lady Winter, Mama as Twilight (since their marriage, they swapped the roles each year), while I would be introduced in the guise of Night.

Until I became Queen, I would always be given the role of Night when it wasn't gifted to a favourite of my parents, or a courtier being moved upon the chessboard of Court politics. As a result, I'd grown up feeling a strange sort of attachment to the god, despite my nightmares about the dark.

Night was part of the Edaran triumvirate, but lacked the closeness of Lady Winter and Twilight. The story went that the night had grown too powerful without a god to hold dominion over it, so Lady Winter and Twilight had created a binding force together. A god whose reach was as vast as the sky itself, worshipped beyond borders, yet bound by the Eshvoni goddess of the day, with whom Night had an eternal, resentful alliance.

I steeped in a bath, politely interrupted by a servant before I nodded off, lulled by the warmth and steam. My curls were washed and brushed through until they were slippery and sleek, then carefully combed and shaped, held in place by a glittering diamond and obsidian headpiece.

Traditionally, dances between Lady Winter and her companions, Twilight and Night, opened the ball. But when we'd discussed our costumes months ago, my parents had dryly said they didn't expect me to dance with them, so they would open the ball themselves, then present me to the Court. Once I mingled, and accepted a dance from at least one ambassador and three others who were not Rialla nor Micah, the rest of the night was mine to spend as I pleased.

I had firm plans to hide in a corner with Micah and people-watch.

Come to think of it, no wonder people assumed we'd eventually marry.

The servants helped me into a long tunic-style dress of thin dark silk, glimmering with silver thread at the hems and collar, with old-fashioned dagged sleeves. The seamstress had split the folds for ease of movement and to reveal the elegant black trousers and dancing shoes I wore underneath. They pinned a short crushed-velvet mantle to my shoulders, as deep as a starless night, which I could remove when I inevitably overheated in the ballroom. My necklace was simple: a large piece of obsidian set in silver.

Firelight splashed over the walls, catching the embroidery. When I was ready, we stood before the looking glass and admired my reflection. Candle flames reflected in my eyes, as light washed over my face and the silk.

A sharp rap on the doors proceeded Isra sweeping in, flicking her hand in a silent command. As the room emptied out, I made an exaggerated bow. 'Do I meet your standards, Your Grace?'

Her gaze seared over me. 'Acceptable, Your Highness.' No admiration in her expression, only brutal satisfaction that I wouldn't shame Their Majesties. Nevertheless, her mouth curled in a faint smile. 'Perhaps you'll bring tunic dresses back into fashion. The Court might embrace something sensible for once.'

'I'll do my best.'

She hadn't come here to critique my outfit: that was my parents' concern. No, for her to arrive and dismiss the staff (who wouldn't be listening at the door; others had tried in Isra's early years as spymaster and paid dearly when they were discovered) meant she wasn't here simply to wish me luck.

'You need to wear a dagger tonight,' Isra said. Other courtiers – perhaps even other royals, like Melisande – would have been offended at her bluntness, but to me, it was a relief. If Isra was still her usual irritated self, then she was cautious about whatever rumours had brought her here, not fearful.

Even so–

'I can't. Not tonight.' At her narrowed eyes, I shook my head. 'No one is allowed weapons, hidden or not. If it was discovered that I wore a dagger, there would be justifiable uproar.' Every noble was thoroughly searched, no matter their lofty dignity, before the banquet after the opening dances of the ball.

Even so, my parents never went anywhere without the poison pens hidden in their clothing – my own family secret, I suppose. It was a matter of self-defence, not a weapon for attack. If a monarch ever wielded a weapon against a noble for any other reason, the consequences were civil war. Monarchs and their nobles all shared an unsteady balance of power. The slightest overreach from either side could threaten everyone.

Unlike my parents, I was still getting used to remembering the pen, but then, they'd had years to make it a habit–

Oh.

I met Isra's gaze. 'I can't wear a dagger, and I won't. It would be a terrible precedent, but the outfit also wasn't designed to hide one.' I gestured at the tight upper sleeves which trailed from my elbows and the equally tailored trousers: nowhere to hide a scabbard. When Isra opened her mouth to argue, I held up a hand. '*However.* The seamstress inserted the pocket for the poison pen, as she does now for all my clothing. Would that satisfy you?'

Isra frowned thoughtfully. I could practically see her flicking through potential scenarios in her mind, considering how much time poison would buy me if the nearest guards were all cut down. Not enough, compared to a dagger, but this would be a heavily guarded event. If the worst happened, and all that could keep me alive was the threat of poison, Isra would have far more to worry about.

'Very well,' she said with a decisive nod. 'A pair of guards are assigned to you for the night, though they'll blend in with the others. If you leave the banquet or ballroom, they will follow.' She didn't need to add *or answer to me*. It was assumed.

It wasn't that Isra was more frightening as Whispers than as Duchess Casterath. She was frightening as both, just in different ways.

'You mean this is the one time everyone would prefer me to stay in a corner with Micah?'

She didn't smile in response.

A twinge of uneasiness quivered in my chest. 'What's going on? Is it to do with Florette Sigrath and the Mizyr?'

She shook her head. 'Not as far as I'm aware. But I believe

there's a reasonable chance you're in danger. I've had reports from some of my agents abroad.' A muscle flexed in her jaw. 'Since the autumn equinox, the younger Othayrian and Eshvon heirs have been… under threat. No attempts made, from what my agents know' – which could mean someone had tried and failed, since no royal family *admitted* to failed assassination attempts – 'but tensions are high in both Courts, and religious unrest has been spreading from their capitals.'

'Religious unrest?'

Isra sniffed. 'Public demonstrations declaring that everyone, including royals, has strayed from Aestia's true purpose for us, and that is why the country declines. Because without pure faith, they insist magic can never return. The usual nonsense, we've seen it all before.'

But if she wasn't concerned about it, she wouldn't be telling me any of this.

Once, centuries and centuries ago, during the First Empire when gods had supposedly walked the land, magic had also existed. Seasonal power, derived from each country's patron god. But as the First Empire had crumbled, religious faith had also dwindled, and magic had slowly died out until it was nothing more than stories within myths about the gods.

Edar didn't hold with religion anymore, apart from Midwinter celebrations involving Lady Winter, but that was more because it was tradition than genuine worship. Farezi still believed a little in

La Dame des Fleurs, a spring goddess considered Lady Winter's counterpart, but with no real expectation that she could affect their lives.

Othayria and Eshvon refused to abandon all faith, as Edar had done; their faith was more sincere than Farezi's. Of the two, Eshvon's was stronger: the royals still believed themselves the living voice of Aestia, and most Eshvoni believed that only through loyal faith could magic return.

I eyed Isra. 'You surely don't believe that magic will return one day.' She'd always seemed too *practical* to believe in such things.

She snorted. 'Of course not. The rest of my family all believe – though deep down, I suspect Mother would abandon religion in a heartbeat if any god laid claim over her right to rule. What little belief I entertained couldn't survive after living in Edar for so long.'

I hesitated, as something she'd said earlier dawned on me. 'The younger Eshvon heir is…'

'My niece, yes,' Isra said flatly. 'But she's a clever girl. The family would expect no less.'

Isra's oldest sister was next to inherit the Eshvon throne – only Queens ruled, their princes used for marital gain – with her oldest daughter next in the succession. Isra's niece was born after she'd decided to stay in Edar, so they had never met. Isra had received a portrait, but since she was now another country's spymaster, contact was discouraged.

Her expression tightened. 'She'll be fine. Even so, faith can cause people to do strange things, or question what they always considered unshakeable truth. If there's one thing Edar got right, it was abandoning the entire business.'

The details of how that had exactly happened were thin: few written accounts existed, and none really made sense, more legend than logic. We still had a religious order, of sorts, but they were limited in scope and power and resembled little of the mythical record. They were mostly considered harmless, a sanctuary for those hopelessly nostalgic for a time that had, perhaps, never existed, who otherwise struggled to find a place in the world. They weren't even involved in most Midwinter celebrations beyond their own, which they spent together in private.

Speaking of Midwinter celebrations–

'We'll be late, Your Grace,' I said. 'I'll wear my pen, and do nothing reckless, and make sure my guards can see me at all times until I retire for the night.' Just as well I'd no intentions of a grand Midwinter seduction: nothing like a pair of shadows to kill a sense of romance. 'Will that satisfy you?'

'Nothing ever fully satisfies me, Your Highness,' Isra replied. 'But thank you for treating my concerns with respect.'

Frankly, I wouldn't dare do otherwise.

After she left, I checked myself one last time in the looking-glass, the deadly pen safely hidden away, before leaving to meet my parents in the ballroom's antechamber.

Two things niggled at me:

Something connected to La Dame des Fleurs, something obvious, but just out of reach no matter how I strained to pin the memory.

These changes had also started at the turn of autumn into winter. Just after Melisande had arrived here.

It was probably a coincidence. She was *far* too modern and sophisticated to believe in the gods, even if she said all the right things about them, as expected of a Farezi royal.

But in all the myths I'd read, there were no coincidences.

FOURTEEN

My parents were waiting in the antechamber, impeccably dressed as always.

Midwinter was important to them. They had danced together during Mother's first Midwinter as Queen, already in love and conscious that Mother had to marry another for duty.

Mother smiled, and I gripped her hands tightly, grinning despite myself. She had been born for this role, in more ways than one. Even when Edar had a ruling King, Midwinter always belonged to his Queen, who celebrated by dressing as Lady Winter. The design varied, but always in shades of white, cream, or silver, defined by stark branches: the goddess's symbol in her founding myth.

With such limitations, it was always a challenge to design a new dress every year. My parents usually chose a new seamstress, young or unknown and ambitious, reasoning that to dress royalty was a coup for a burgeoning career.

This year, Mother's dress flowed in iridescent silver, the fabric rippling and gleaming as if trapped under sunlit water. An open ruff began at the edges of her low neckline, rising to encircle her neck and head: stiff lace patterned with jagged winter-bare branches outlined in black and dark blue thread and studded with sapphire and diamond shards. The Midwinter tiara rested easily upon her head.

Mama was dressed as Twilight, the same as her first dance with Mother so many years ago. Her bodice was twilight on the brink of night, fading to a glorious deep blue-black at the hems. Diamonds studded the gown from shoulders and bodice right down to the hem, a sky full of glittering stars. Traditionally, those attending the ball as Twilight or Night wore no crown or head-piece, but Mother had changed the tradition after marrying. As Twilight, Mama wore a diadem decorated with silver stars across her brow, polished until it glowed.

As they stood together you could believe they were Lady Winter and Twilight returned.

'You'll be fine,' Mama said, pressing her palm gently against my cheek, as if my expression betrayed my worries. 'You look wonderful, my dear.'

Once again, as it had for weeks, the sight of her so close brought a jolt to my chest. She was still Mama, still Queen Xania, who had heralded a period of steady change with her marriage. But now I looked at her, and all I could think about was the price she had paid for saving Mother, for marrying her, for becoming Queen – for safety and security.

The price she had paid and carried for so many years. And the consequences her actions had wrought for me.

She quirked an eyebrow. 'Are you that nervous? You really *will* be fine.'

I blinked, realising I'd been staring at her, and forced myself to smile. 'Of course I will.'

To the servants, we must have looked the perfect image of a royal family: two loving Queens and devoted mothers, and the self-assured, elegant daughter they were raising so well to continue their legacy.

The potential moment was here, and it would be so easy. Feign a bout of nerves, perhaps even the fear of a churning stomach, and my parents would clear the room in moments to talk me down. It wouldn't matter that I hadn't experienced public fright like this before: Midwinter was one of the most important nights in the year. The first one, I'd been told, was always the worst, but every Midwinter had to surpass the previous. For royalty, Midwinter was less an act of worship than one of extravagance.

The room would be empty, and I could finally say it aloud, the terrible secret that had pushed and pulled between Melisande and me for weeks. It would exist beyond my own tortured mind, and…

And…

And I would break my mothers' hearts.

For me to admit everything, right before we put on a show for the Court, who would scrutinise our every expression and move, for me to release all the hurt, pain, and rage simmering within me for weeks – I'd never be able to hide it. And though my parents were long accustomed to hiding their feelings in public, I wasn't sure they could pull this off, either.

Never mind how Mama would react – to my feelings, or that I knew the truth of what she had done in exchange for Arisane's aid.

And I wasn't ready to see any of that, really. Because once I said it, there was no taking it back.

So I held their hands, smiled, and let the potential moment drift away.

Once they were ready, the candles in the antechamber were dimmed until there was more shadow than light. Mama tucked her hand into Mother's elbow and, as a booming voice announced them, they swept into the ballroom to loud cheering.

As they danced, I waited in the antechamber, watching them spin in pale and dark fabrics, glittering and beautiful and danger-ous. Lady Winter and Twilight, celebrating the Longest Night, the height of her powers and season. Nineteen years ago, they had danced like this. So in love that Mother had abdicated to protect Mama, who had fled to Farezi, hunted as a traitor, to save her.

It was the stuff of ballads and epics, the foundation for a legend that would probably outlive them, no matter what else they achieved during their reign. As they twirled around each other, resembling a gale rising to its full strength, it felt almost like there was real magic in the air: cold, brutal, and magnificent.

In the myths, magic was a privilege. And the stronger the power, the harsher the price.

The dance ended with a roar of applause and cheering. My parents, stunning in their finery, linked their hands and smiled at the crowd.

The servants ushered me towards the doors, fussing at my clothing for any last wrinkles. Fear suddenly hammered in my ears, as my parents turned in graceful unison and gestured for me to step out.

My name and title were bellowed out, and I walked into a wall of noise. No matter my fear, my legs knew what they were doing, and I stood between my parents in dark silk, obsidian, and diamonds, my head held high. Succumbing to a strange instinct, I abandoned the bow I'd practised and instead swept an old-fashioned one, my arms flung out on either side.

I straightened and took a deep breath, my ears still ringing.

'Well judged,' Mother whispered in my ear.

As the noise lowered, someone struck a bell, indicating that the banquet hall was about to open. The nobles began to shuffle into rank. My parents squeezed my arms one last time, then indicated for me to follow them into position at the front. Mother moved away first, leaving Mama and I together.

It was probably the only moment I'd be alone with her all night.

When she relaxed her grip on my arms, already taking a step away, I grabbed her wrists and forced her still.

'Emri?' Puzzlement filled her dark eyes.

If I didn't say it now, I'd never be able to. The knowledge would rot within me, infection spreading until it killed everything good in me.

I leaned in, my mouth close to her ear. And soft enough that only she could hear, I asked, 'Did you kill Rassa on Arisane's orders?'

FIFTEEN

Mama stiffened.

For a moment, I thought I'd spoken too quietly, and she was waiting for me to release her. Then she murmured, 'Not here. I will summon you.'

I froze. There was no immediate confusion nor denial in her words, no accompanying baffled look. It meant Melisande hadn't lied: what she'd told me *had* happened, or something like it, and further explanations were necessary.

Mama had been involved in Rassa's death. And so had Arisane.

She flexed her hands, a silent command to let her go, before the moment between us turned odd. Mother glanced over, still pleased and oblivious.

Something flickered across Mama's face, too quickly for me to decipher. Then she turned and followed after Mother.

Now I'd see how well we kept our royal masks in place.

I remembered nothing of the food, though I'm sure it was splendid, and I drank more wine than was advisable. Foolish of me: seated at Mother's left, it caught her attention during the third course, and she subtly indicated for the servants to slow in refilling my glass. I knew better than to protest: never losing control by drinking to excess in public was a strict rule. My head was already beginning to swim, my vision stretching at the edges: potentially dangerous since we were at the high table, in full view of everyone seated below us.

Mama, at her right and conversing with Melisande, didn't look at me once.

By the final course, I felt vaguely ill, the air turned nauseous from spun sugar, flavoured ices, candied fruits, tart curds, and thick custards: only a selection of the desserts on offer. This was my favourite course, and I couldn't even enjoy it after trying to curb my upset with wine.

Matthias, Baron Farhallow, my parents' oldest friend and my uncle in all the ways that mattered, sat at my left. To my relief, he and Mother kept a conversation running around me, which I occasionally contributed to while trying to work through my plate and sober up. I was in no fit state to dance, and if I tried, there was a genuinely terrifying chance that I would vomit on my unfortunate partner, which would keep the Court gossiping for days.

Not to mention how my parents would react – after they stopped being furious. And *Isra*. I nearly threw up at the mere thought.

After I'd had a few bites of a custard, Mother closed her fingers around my spoon. 'I don't think that's a good idea, hmm?' she said, her lips barely moving. 'We'll have them keep a portion aside for when you can enjoy it more.' She glanced at me. 'It's frankly more than you deserve. *What is going on?*'

I took a slow, trembling breath. 'I liked the wine too much, that's all.' I struggled to keep my expression under control, bleakly aware of the misery awaiting me tomorrow. 'I should know better, I'm sorry.'

'You don't show your appreciation for a vintage by drinking it all in *one night*,' she hissed.

'And if you do,' Matthias quipped, giving up the pretence that he wasn't eavesdropping, 'it's something you only do once,' and drained his glass with a jaunty flick of the wrist.

Mother looked close to rolling her eyes. 'You're old enough to be a better role model.'

He tilted his head towards me. 'To that stubborn terror? Hardly.'

A headache started behind my left eye.

Mother sighed. 'Switch to cider. And retire early. You'll need sleep.'

'I'm sorry,' I said miserably.

She cracked a brief sympathetic smile. 'As Matthias said: everyone does this once at a banquet and learns their lesson.'

When the meal was finally over, Melisande and I followed my parents back into the ballroom, the nobles trailing behind us. She eyed me. 'Another cider, then get your easiest dance over with immediately, if you can stomach it. It'll buy you time before your essential ones.'

I glared.

'I overindulged at one of my first banquets. You do it—'

'Once, and never again,' I finished sourly. 'I've been informed. Repeatedly.'

Melisande's lips twitched. 'If you like, I can stay with you.'

'I mean this as politely as possible,' I said, 'but absolutely not. Go and dance and flirt, and whatever else you do at these things, and make everyone forget there are two princesses here.'

I should have been furious at Melisande: she was the one who had indirectly caused me to confront Mama, which had then led to my drinking too much. But I felt too ill and exhausted – much like she'd looked during the weeks when the truth was trapped between us – and I was disgustingly grateful for her amused kindness.

She didn't move for a long moment, until I looked up at her, startled. 'We'll discuss why you did this some other time,' she said, then strode away before I could reply, the light catching in her hair.

Moving to the ballroom only helped for a little while. Soon, as predicted, the room began to heat up, and the terrace doors to the surrounding gardens were flung open. It was a bitter night, the heart of Midwinter, but the cold eased the stifling air, and a brisk stroll outside would help revive flagging spirits as the night progressed. And possibly help me sober up, though it was too soon for me to run into the gardens and hide. But it seemed preferable to hiding in my room, watching the ceiling lazily spin above me.

My easiest dance would be with Micah, if I could find him. He wouldn't make conversation, and even though he was my friend, his family rank would still satisfy those who kept track of whom royalty favoured at events. But as my gaze swept across the nearest swathe of courtiers, a tall figure in russet velvet stopped and bowed before me.

'Your Highness,' said Lady Frida, the Othayrian ambassador, in a low, rich voice. 'I believe you shall be indulging me with a dance tonight.'

I returned their smile. Truthfully, I liked this ambassador, and my parents complained about them the least, but a dance with a diplomat certainly wasn't 'easy'. If I wasn't on guard, I could potentially slip up if they tried digging for information while we danced. The headache had solidified at my temples, strained against my skull, a powerful reminder that I was absolutely *not* at my best.

But I had no choice. And if I managed to pull this off without embarrassing myself (any further), perhaps Mother would yell less at me tomorrow.

Unless Mama summons me tonight, I thought uneasily. It was extremely likely, if she'd realised that I'd drank too much during the dinner. She'd be in a stronger position with a clear head, easily able to contain me if I lost control of my emotions.

Lady Frida was an excellent dancer, as expected from an Othayrian Countess. Their skirts whispered across the floor, their grip light but assured. Our conversation was pleasant – mostly about music, of which the Countess was particularly fond. I didn't even have to think too much about my answers; a relief, since halfway through the dance my headache started to keep time with the steps.

When it was finally over, I went in search of Micah. The night was in full swing: courtiers resplendent in velvets and silks. Their voices spun around me as they chattered, laughed, and debated each other. As time wore on, they'd splinter off into the smaller rooms nearby for deeper conversations, embraces, or spirited arguments.

As expected, my parents were surrounded by a clutch of courtiers, mostly people they actually liked or tolerated. One didn't progress their ambitions by flattering the monarchs these days, not like during the old King's reign, but good will and recommendations still took people far.

Melisande was also within a group of admirers. She glittered in a lethal sort of way. Surrounded by people mostly dressed in white, blue, and black, the traditional Midwinter shades, she wore Farezi's colours: a sleeveless gold and green silk brocade jacket, the shade of a forest falling into shadow, complimented by billowing shirt sleeves and dark trousers. In front, her jacket stopped at the waist, but turned into a tailored fall of silk at the back, which spun around her as she moved. Her boot heels were so sharp, I had no idea how she hadn't broken an ankle yet.

Of the courtiers around our age, her mere existence broke half their hearts, and she confused and flustered the rest. But she was coy with her flirtations, preferring ladies who blushed but still met her gaze, traded sleek barbs with lingering eye contact.

I eventually discovered Micah on a sofa squashed into a corner, protecting a platter of fruit and two cups of cider. I'd promised him a dance later, as had Rialla, so he could truthfully tell his mother that he'd danced with *someone*. Whether I could actually go through with it now remained to be seen.

When I settled beside him, he was also watching Melisande, but his fascination appeared abstract, like he was carefully memorising everything so he could describe it later in a letter.

I sipped the cider. 'Do you think I'll ever be like that?'

'No. It's probably for the best. There's at least five people here who've admitted they'd gladly let her step on them.' He considered. 'I imagine it would hurt with those heels. Her sense of balance must be extraordinary.'

I choked on my drink. 'How... how do *you* know that?'

'Oh, I overheard it,' he said. 'They're all talking about her. Court hasn't lost their heads like this in years. I wish Aunt Diana were here, she'd love it.'

'She'd hate Melisande.'

'Absolutely,' he said. 'But she'd enjoy the fuss even while hating her.'

I worked my way cautiously through the chilled fruit. Court functions were always easier when I could spend them with Micah. Though now that we were older, those times were dwindling. Melisande stunning everyone was a blessing in disguise: as Night, I should have been dancing more. The lack of people approaching me made me suspect Mother had taken reluctant pity upon me and subtly dissuaded others.

Being around Micah was comforting and easy, and once again, I wished marrying him was a good idea. But if Rialla had balked at the idea of a future leading to the throne, Micah had sworn off it while still practically in the cradle.

Still: 'Are you absolutely, positively certain we couldn't make a marriage work—'

He laughed. 'I'm not marrying you.'

I sighed. 'It wouldn't be *all* frustration and diplomacy, you know.'

He raised his eyebrows, then glanced towards my parents. Mother was deep in discussion with a politician, while Mama was politely listening to Lady Frida.

'What do you want in a marriage, then?' I asked, taking two fresh cups of cider from a passing servant. Every time I asked, he gave me a different answer. They weren't especially outlandish, more bittersweet reminders that the expectations for his marriage – should he agree to one – were far different to mine.

He contemplated his cider, until I reminded him that it would turn cold.

'A third library,' he finally said.

I froze with my cup against my mouth. 'That's a good one, actually.'

'Don't get ideas.'

I laughed, then stopped when his gaze turned serious.

'You won't need marriage to keep me in your life,' he said. 'You're my friend. I don't always like Court, but I love *you*. And this will be your domain someday. It's the necessary evil of being your friend.'

I gulped a mouthful of cider, but it did little against the lump swelling in my throat. My eyes burned with the possibility of tears. For a moment, the blooming wave of affection within me even seemed to make my head hurt less.

'Thank you,' I whispered.

He nudged me, smiling. 'Please don't cry. You're not supposed to in public, and the rumours about us will start again.'

I snorted, just before a servant appeared at my side. 'Your Highness. Her Majesty, Queen Xania, wishes to speak with you privately. Please follow me.'

SIXTEEN

Mama was waiting in a small library near the ballroom. The door quietly clicked shut behind me. For a moment, I didn't move, conscious of my pounding head and loud breathing. My hands had turned clammy. The candlelight wasn't strong enough for the room, leaving shadows to pool in the corners.

She sat in a chair, her back straight, her hands folded upon her lap. Her skirts draped around her like spilled ink.

'Sit, Emri,' she said, and gestured to the chair opposite hers.

If I'd expected kindness, or a display of overwhelming emotion, I was disappointed. Her voice was calm, her demeanour steady, similar to when she was asked to settle a dispute. Right now I was, essentially, a problem to be dealt with.

When I sat, I made to mimic and mock her regal bearing. If she noticed, she gave no indication.

'I presume Melisande told you.' A statement, not a question.

'She didn't think it was a secret.' When Mama made a disbelieving sound, I snapped, 'She was told when she came of age! If I had been, I would have assumed the same of her.'

Mama sighed. 'That is reasonable.' She took a deep breath through her nose. 'We should have anticipated this, but we didn't think either of you would talk about Rassa.'

'This isn't just about Rassa,' I said, my tongue smarting around his name. 'This is also about *you* and Arisane.'

'Your grandmother—'

'*Arisane.*' The response snarled from me before I could stop it.

Mama tapped a fingernail against an armrest. The candle-light reflected in her eyes, turning them eerily bright. Beneath her serene veneer, I suspected she was thinking furiously, flicking between memories of my childhood, slotting pieces that hadn't previously fitted into the puzzle of my history.

'If Arisane were to speak of our agreement,' she said, apparently coming to a decision on how she would handle this, 'she would say that she had offered me a choice. That is incorrect. There was never truly a choice, only something that had to be followed through.'

I scoffed. 'Easy to say when it was years ago.'

Her expression abruptly turned cold. I suddenly knew how she appeared to courtiers when they displeased her. 'If you think I have ever forgotten what I did – with Arisane's blessing and her poison – then you must think me foolish indeed.'

'Because I'm the living reminder of what Rassa did,' I said bitterly.

'No,' Mama said. 'Lia is.'

Shame welled up inside me, thick and hot. I had the sudden overwhelming urge to cry, for Mother and myself, and quelled it with a ruthlessness I usually reserved for thoughts of Saphirun. I couldn't appear weak now. If I did, Mama would find it too easy to brush all this aside.

'Why didn't you tell me?' I asked, trying to approach this from another angle. 'Did you ever intend to?'

Mama shifted in her seat. 'Eventually. Not while Melisande was here. If this visit was a success, and things stabilised between our countries, we intended to tell you when you'd settled into your duties as heir. Things had already changed enough for you this year.'

'Who else knows?' I asked.

It was easy to say, *We intended to tell you when you were ready*, but would that time have ever come? Would they have kept putting it off, using excuse after excuse, until one day I was Queen? And if relations soured between us, Melisande would have been able to leverage this against me, something fundamental about our history, of which I would have known nothing.

Mama pressed a fingertip against the groove between her eyebrows. 'Lia and myself. Matthias. Arisane, Sabine, and Melisande. Arisane's then-spymaster. Isra, when she became our Whispers. The Farezi King was not told, and neither was Sabine's husband.'

'And now me.'

'And now you.' She didn't sound disappointed or angry. Mostly just tired. 'I have never forgotten it, but sometimes I can stop thinking about it, for a while. I had to help Lia, then we had to rule, and then we had to learn how to be your parents. There was enough to worry about, without remembering a cruel, selfish man willing to do anything to get what he wanted.'

'Why did *you* have to kill him?' I asked. 'There were other ways: let Farezi deal with him, exile—'

'You were born after Goldenmarch,' she interrupted. 'Even our families can't fully understand that place. Matthias can, but only because he was there when we found Lia. And even we can't fully understand what she went through.

'It broke her. Every physical injury was self-inflicted. No one at Goldenmarch laid a hand upon her. But everything they did was the kind of injury you couldn't see. Her sense of self, her dignity, her confidence, her belief in others – they stripped that from her, bit by bit, in silence and endless white. Even now, your mother isn't the same as the Lia I once knew. That person is gone forever.'

Mama closed her eyes, a vein rising at her temple. 'Her hands were bloody when we found her. She'd clawed at the shutters and pounded the walls, screamed until her voice broke. She wrote in her blood. Begging someone to find her, begging for help, mourning all her failures.'

My eyes scalded with the threat of tears again, but this time they were all for Mother. These were the details that had always been brushed over. Her captivity had been alluded to, but never described.

'If Rassa had appeared in that doorway,' Mama continued,

'while I held Lia as she wept and screamed, I would have killed him. No weapon needed. I'd have ripped his throat out with my teeth, if need be, and Matthias would have helped me.'

Her eyes snapped open, and I glimpsed a shadow of what she must have been as Mother's Whispers. Calculating and ruthless, braiding secrets and rumours into a deceitful web.

'While I was Lia's spymaster,' she said, 'Rassa was the only person I killed myself. I have no doubt my agents killed to keep themselves safe, but that is the dreadful cruelty of being Whispers. You keep the monarch safe by employing others to do your dirty work. You can never become attached.'

I presumed she meant to her agents, yet I said, 'But you fell in love.'

'I did.' She lapsed into silence again. 'Until I saw Lia in Goldenmarch, I wasn't certain about killing Rassa. I'd thought about it. While we searched for her, I obsessed over whether Lia was still alive, or if he had ordered her death. And when I wasn't thinking about that, I worried that even if we found her, we wouldn't get the throne back if he'd already turned the country against her. And when I couldn't sleep, I worried that Rassa had killed my entire family.'

The images loomed in my mind: Grandmama and Grandpapa Kierth, Aunt Zola, all kneeling before the executioner's block because Mama had refused to accept Rassa as King. I swallowed against the bile scorching up my throat.

'But when I found Lia,' Mama said, soft and lethal, 'I knew. Even if she became Queen again, we'd never be able to live easy. Rassa hadn't accepted her rightful rule; there was no chance he'd accept it after having his taste of power ripped away. And it was widely suspected that he'd plotted with his father, which meant Farezi could never be trusted, especially if they kept Rassa in the succession. Lia would always be afraid. And I wouldn't let her – let *us* – be afraid for the rest of her days.

'So he had to die. And Arisane offered her bargain… and the poison.'

I held my fingers against my lips, breath warm, as a wisp of memory resurfaced. 'The poison pen. You gave it to me because you'd once used yours. That was what you said.'

'Not in the way you think,' she said. 'And the pen was always meant to be yours.'

'You poisoned him.'

'Poisoning him was a *kindness* compared to the death I wanted for him.' The words ground out of her. 'He might have been in Edar, wearing Lia's crown and trying to dismantle everything she'd accomplished, but make no mistake: everything she went through in Goldenmarch was on his orders.' She shook her head. 'I love you, Emri, but I will not tell you the specifics. No one knows them, not even Lia. I killed him; that is enough. Some things are mine to haunt myself with.'

I pressed my hands flat to my thighs, fingers splayed until they hurt. I'd once wondered if I'd have been able to kill Rassa, if doing so would haunt me for the rest of my life. Now I sat before someone who had weighed that choice and acted upon it, and I still had no real answer for myself.

Since Melisande had told me the truth about Mama and Rassa, I'd spent hours wrestling through my spiralling thoughts and churning emotions, trying to pinpoint why this was such a shock. When I was growing up, I'd known that Rassa had been murdered – *everyone* had known he was murdered – and his memory reviled by my parents *and* my family in Farezi. I'd wondered who in my family would have killed him if they'd had the chance.

When my parents were younger, courtiers had died all the time.

But none of the consequences of those deaths, unlike Rassa's, had directly affected me.

'Did you ever think, once, about what would happen *later*?' At Mama's disbelieving look – when had she *not* thought about what would happen after Rassa's death? – I clarified, soft and vicious: 'What would happen to *me*?'

She went statue-still. Only the shadows of the wavering candlelight moved. She suddenly let out a harsh breath, her shoulders sagging, as if she could no longer bear the weight of her years-long secret. 'This was also why we never told you,' she admitted. 'My own selfishness, I should stress: Lia wanted you to know. We argued about it.'

Too many suspicions suddenly made a great deal of sense.

'You knew,' I said bleakly. 'You knew how I grew up in Saphirun. All those nightmares I only half-understood and remembered… and you pretended it had never happened.'

'We *suspected*,' Mama replied sharply. 'We never could get a proper answer out of Sabine about your childhood, probably because if she acknowledged how Arisane had raised you, she'd have to admit she left her own daughter in the same situation.

'All of Isra's spies failed. Those she got into Saphirun's staff were always ferreted out, fast, but then, Arisane hadn't held onto power for so long by being trusting.'

My mind whirled, as I tried to remember any staff who hadn't stayed long. But even if I'd noticed them, they wouldn't have been kind to me – that would have been too suspicious.

Mama scrubbed her face. 'You were an anxious child, always desperate to please, terrified we would punish you for the slightest mistake or misstep. You screamed if you were left in the dark, so we had to keep a lamp in your room until you were seven. It was so bad that Lia relapsed into nightmares about Goldenmarch, though we hid that from you.'

I remembered hardly any of this, but it explained so much. And I had been so self-righteous, in my own way, about Mother's struggles to recover from her own horrors. I slapped my hand back over my mouth, but this time I couldn't stop a sob.

Mama's eyes gleamed with unshed tears. 'I'm not telling you this to make you feel worse. We couldn't ask you about Saphirun, or Arisane or Melisande. You were a *child*. How could we dredge up what your mind was so clearly trying to protect you from?' She let out a choked laugh. 'Every day we had to remind Isra that she couldn't orchestrate Arisane's murder, she was so furious. We thought it better if we just... helped you as best we could, and loved you, and convinced you our affections wouldn't go away if you made a mistake.' She pressed her fingers over her trembling mouth. 'We didn't know what else to *do*.'

'Saphirun was a nightmare,' I choked out. 'It was— Arisane—'

But I couldn't say it. No matter the memories tightly leashed inside me, no matter that they were trying to resurface from Melisande's arrival, no matter my suspicions about my childhood, I couldn't say anything. To admit any of it, say it aloud, meant that I couldn't take any of it back. Mama would have irrevocable proof, no longer bound by speculation, assumptions, and suspicions.

I didn't want her to know. The consequences of her decisions had already rebounded on me. Even though I knew she loved me, that there was nothing she wouldn't do to keep me safe, her knowing the truth about my childhood in Saphirun still felt like giving her power over me.

Mama rose and knelt by my chair, reaching out for my hands. 'Emri.' Warmth was spreading down my cheeks as I wept in earnest. 'Emri, please, this wasn't how I wanted you to find out. I love you. You are my daughter, and I would kill to keep you safe.'

If Mother had said this, I would have laughed and scoffed at her dramatics. But knowing that Mama had actually killed, and it had led to my misery at Saphirun, it felt less like a promise and more an insult. Mama, Arisane, Queen Sabine – they had all abandoned Lady Liliene and me. Left us to shame and loneliness. They had failed us, and I was simply expected to understand and accept it.

I wrenched my hands out of Mama's grip. Wiped my tears and glared at her, suddenly relieved that the servants had used so little face powder tonight.

'Would you do it again?' I asked. 'If you had the chance, would you kill Rassa again?'

Mama's arms fell back to her sides. Her gaze turned distant, but I couldn't tell what she was thinking. What she was remembering, what decisions she was reconsidering.

Deep down, I already knew the answer.

'Yes,' she finally said. 'I would, if it kept Lia and my family safe. I always knew when I became her Whispers that I would likely have to kill.'

She cupped my cheek. I wanted to close my eyes, but if I did the tears would begin again. I wanted to jerk away from her touch, but I couldn't find the energy. All my strength was gone. Even my rage was collapsing into embers, leaving me to wallow in exhaustion.

The sadness in Mama's eyes made me feel like my heart was close to breaking. I wanted her to hug me and make it all disappear – the rage and grief and fear, my memories and nightmares – no matter how much my trust in her was now in tatters. But I knew she couldn't.

I was too old to believe that my parents could fix everything.

'But if I'd known Arisane would punish you for her fall from power,' Mama added, 'I would have requested that Lady Liliene stay in Edar. I would have kept you here, where it was safe.'

That was the flaw of hindsight. It couldn't fix what had already come to pass.

It couldn't change Saphirun.

SEVENTEEN

I should have done what I wanted to do after dancing with the Othayrian ambassador: gone back to my rooms and straight to bed.

Instead, after fleeing from Mama, I found myself outside on a terrace near the ballroom. It hadn't felt that cold inside thanks to the crush of bodies, but now I shivered, pulling the velvet mantle closer around my shoulders. The night sky stretched overhead, scattered with stars. The new moon was beginning to shift towards the beginning of a waxing crescent, still a long ways from being full. But even when it couldn't be seen, the moon was always there, a stalwart comfort.

My teeth ached as I gulped in the frigid air. I ignored the pain, filling my lungs again and again, as if the icy scorch could burn away the conversation with Mama. The ache in my head had eased a little after leaving the ballroom, but the high emotions and crying had made it worse again, a deep throb across my forehead.

I headed down the steps towards the nearest garden, gripping my upper arms to keep my fingers under the velvet. It was deserted due to the hard frost; those who needed relief from the heat were sticking mostly to the terraces.

My thoughts swirled. Something had irrevocably changed between Mama and me; between both my parents and me. Nothing would be the same after this, even if we patched over the damage. I'd look at Mama, and see a former Whispers who had killed, so driven by love and her convictions that she'd spared little thought to those affected by the consequences of her actions.

But that surely wasn't giving her enough credit. She'd been eighteen and desperate. There was no certainty that Mother would retake the throne, never mind that they would end up married and adopting me. And even if they'd suspected Arisane's cruelty, there was no way to confirm it. After Rassa's murder, relations had deteriorated between the two countries; being a foreign spy had included an astonishingly poor life expectancy. Isra had struggled to gain any useful information during that time, never mind any truth about my childhood. And as Mama had pointed out, Sabine had little to gain by being honest, since she would be judged for leaving Melisande in Saphirun, too.

And it wasn't Mama's responsibility that Arisane had reacted to her loss of power by punishing me.

I rubbed my face and hissed out a breath through cold lips. I didn't *want* to be reasonable. I wanted to cradle my rage close to keep me warm.

'Emri?'

I closed my eyes in resignation. 'Melisande.' I tried to keep my voice neutral, but knew I'd failed at the brief pause in her footsteps before she resumed walking towards me.

'I know you've drunk too much, but being out here isn't going to help if you catch cold.'

I shrugged. 'I'll be fine.' Brave words considering I could no longer feel my hands or the tip of my nose.

'Liar,' Melisande chided me almost jovially as she nudged me, then held out a tiny glass. 'Is this recipe secret? I really want to bring it back home, but not if it turns into a diplomatic incident.'

The ice liquor we drank at Midwinter celebrations was clear and frost-cold. A swallow burned all the way down, sharp and swift; the effect was slow but brutal. Too much, and someone would stand up and suddenly find the world spinning around them.

The very sight made my stomach lurch. 'You should drink mine.'

'Suit yourself.' Melisande tossed back my glass, but sipped her own more sedately.

My eyes narrowed. 'How many have you had?'

Melisande laughed. 'Don't worry, I know my limits.' I could have read *unlike you* in her tone, but she was too relaxed and spoke almost fondly.

'That's what everyone thinks when they try the ice liquor for the first time,' I said. 'It always proves them wrong.'

'Well, in that case, tomorrow we can share our misery together.'

I looked down; she'd changed into boots with a more sensible heel. 'Did your footwear defeat you?'

Melisande snorted, most unladylike, before downing the rest of her drink. 'They're the most impractical things I own. I wore them mostly to terrify people.'

'Well, they were magnificent, and you succeeded.' I toyed with another meaningless compliment, but didn't have the energy for it. 'How did you not trip? Can you teach me?'

'Maybe.' Melisande pretended to study her glass, flicking out her tongue to catch the last drop, then sighed. 'Did something happen? You're not yourself.'

I wanted to laugh. With the secret out and Mama aware of what I knew, I felt the most like myself in weeks, even if it was accompanied by self-loathing. 'I told Mama I knew the truth about Rassa's death. She didn't deny it.'

Melisande stiffened, then slowly glanced around to check we weren't being overheard. Despite Isra's threats, the guards hadn't followed me out of the ballroom when Mama had summoned me, nor had they realised I'd cut back outside. I'd have to tell her tomorrow, even if it meant they'd suddenly be unemployed. When Melisande turned back, her eyes were very large.

'She knew you told me,' I said, shrugging.

Melisande swallowed, suddenly looking like she regretted those glasses of liquor. 'Do you—'

'How foolish you both are. So wrapped up in the demise of a

cruel man driven by circumstances you will never truly understand. In this, he achieved his greatest wish: to be remembered
beyond death.'

I whirled as Florette Sigrath slipped from the shadows behind
us. She hadn't been invited tonight, nor had any of her family.
Her gown was pale green, patterned in yellow and white flowers
with silver-grey leaves: spring colours, never in fashion this time
of year. Her hair was pinned up, her face framed by delicate curls,
but there was something strange about her expression.

No sign of anyone from the Mizyr, but my shoulders were up,
and no matter how I tried, I couldn't get them down. Where were
the damn guards? Should I scream? That would bring them – and
my parents, and every courtier here – running, and what if I was
overreacting? It was *Florette*.

And she is a spy, a voice whispered in my mind. *She may not wish
you ill, but she has never wished you well.*

Melisande frowned in baffled disdain. 'And you are…?'

I put myself between them before I realised I was even moving.
'You forget yourself, Lady Sigrath.' She gazed at me, her
expression still odd, and I was acutely aware of my hidden poison
pen. How much time would I need to get it out and twist the
needle if she lunged at me?

Florette smiled, an unsettling curve of her mouth. 'No, *Your
Highness*. You do.' She spoke my title with scorn, her eyes cold as
she came closer. 'You both forget yourself, in fact, but the Farezi

royal blood is most lacking these days. How disappointing.'

Melisande moved to stand beside me. Her eyes had narrowed, and two spots of colour bloomed high on her cheeks. 'Who— you *dare*—'

She cut off as shadows rippled on the grass near Florette, twisting and arching into the vague shape of people. Their eyes were scorching pits of bright blue and green. They were a mass of writhing shadows – except for clawed hands, which appeared viciously sharp.

My heart started hammering behind my ribs. Melisande stepped back. They were absolutely, irrevocably not real. They couldn't be. Shadows didn't move of their own accord. They didn't have flames for eyes.

'Lady Sigrath, what is going on?' Inwardly, I was proud that my voice didn't shake. I sounded authoritative, unflustered, as if I saw shadows moving independently every day. 'This is…'

Impossible, I wanted to say.

Instead, I let my instincts take over.

When my clothing was first adjusted to fit the poison pen, my parents made me practise getting it out every day. Isra and Matthias took it a step further, surprising me to see if I could free it under duress. Again and again, I had yanked at the loose threads to release the pocket, tightened my grip on the barrel, twisted the band to snap out the needle.

I'd resented them all, but now I thanked them in my head,

before my mind blurred and I moved. My hand went under one of the tunic folds at my right hip to the pocket sewn underneath, the pen light enough, compared to a dagger, not to upset the drape of silk. My nails ripped at the threads and the pen thumped into my palm, reassuringly solid.

As I twisted the band, I was almost upon Florette. Time slowed around us. I adjusted my grip on the pen, the needle now free, positioning it so I could drive the point into her neck. Florette's gaze locked on mine. Her hair moved in a breeze I couldn't feel, her expression unnervingly calm.

'*Emri!*' Melisande's scream sounded distant, faint, but my stomach still dropped.

At her scream, however, Florette's calm faltered. A ripple snapped in the air, like the change in a room when a thick curtain was pulled back to reveal morning light. The end of Melisande's scream turned piercingly clear.

A moment of tense silence. Then uproar from inside the ballroom.

The guards were loyal. But once Melisande and I had gone outside, had the ripple in the air shielded us from everyone else – perhaps by whatever had created the shadows around Florette?

Magic, I thought. This was all magic. Somehow. There was no other explanation, logical or otherwise.

I skidded around Florette, still somehow moving, trying to get behind her so she couldn't grab me. Dig my fingers into her hair, tilt her neck, and sink the needle in. Simple. I'd practised with a blunt empty nib on Isra and Matthias for weeks now.

Florette moved with me, dizzily fast, and grabbed my wrists. Her grip was strong, stunningly so, and she ground my bones between her fingers.

I yelped. The pen dropped to the ground.

Florette's eyes bored into mine, and there was no trace of her usual anxious, flickering gaze. Her blonde hair suddenly seemed a deeper colour. Her irises glowed, and for a moment they were no longer light blue, but the shade of new spring leaves.

'Interesting,' she said, a strange echo to her words. 'I always knew there was more to you than the cautious, poised princess.'

'Who *are* you?' Whoever she was, it wasn't Florette Sigrath. At least not the façade she wore at Court.

She smiled again, still unsettling. 'Now it finally begins.'

For a moment, the scent of flowers rose around us, delicate and sweet. The warmth of a spring sun cascaded over me – never enough to win against the lingering chill, but a hopeful sign of better times to come.

Then, still holding my wrists, she dragged me around and flung me at Melisande.

While I'd launched myself towards Florette, the shadows had closed in on Melisande, who eyed them warily, a dagger ready in each hand. (Unlike me, she'd clearly not argued against Isra's instructions to arm herself tonight, no matter how it would look for a foreign royal.) She gasped, but had no time to brace before I crashed into her.

My head smashed into her chin; her pained wheeze cut off as her teeth snapped together.

We toppled back into a pool of spinning shadows.

I tumbled head over heels in the dark, flickers of light twisting around me. Wind howled in my ears, snatched the scream from my lungs, and I fell down, down, down.

When I finally managed to take a breath, it felt like snowflakes and ice streamed down my throat, sharp and cruel. The cold filled me, raced along my bones, wrapped around my heart.

The darkness swallowed my vision.

EIGHTEEN

When I came to, I genuinely thought my head had cracked open.

My skull throbbed, as bursts of light exploded across my eyes. A gentle sort of agony. I shifted, trying to get my left arm under me, and whimpered. My teeth hurt, but a quick tongue swipe revealed no gaps nor blood. I'd never fallen down the stairs, but this was what it probably felt like, my body marking each place that had hit against something.

I finally managed to push myself up. My head swam, nausea ricocheted through my insides, and for a terrifying moment I thought I was about to vomit. I took a long breath through my nose, counted to three, and let it out through my mouth. Each time, the nausea slowed, though the pain remained.

When I was sitting up, I opened my eyes cautiously. The light in the room shifted in strange patterns. The cold ground felt odd under me. I peered down, squinting. I knew what it was, but my brain creaked as it struggled to spit out the word.

Mosaic.

That was it.

How had I ended up somewhere with a mosaic? There were

a handful in Edar, usually in ruins believed to date back to the First Empire: the earliest temples, according to the stories. Most of the First Empire architecture had crumbled away through the many centuries. Some fragments remained in the oldest parts of Arkaala, ghostly echoes of courtyards and street patterns long absorbed and built over until most people had no idea what they were looking at. I only knew this much because Micah had tried to pull me into his dabbling interest with little success.

I rose unsteadily, still squinting, but the mosaic pattern was smudged and dark. It was probably decipherable in better light, or – confirmed by a glance at my hands and trousers – when not covered by centuries of dust and grime.

A mosaic on the ground was best viewed from above. I tilted my head back, searching for a higher floor or balcony, or even steps, but everything above was lost to darkness.

It all came back in a rush.

Florette. Melisande. The shadows. Falling, falling, falling.

What had *happened*? One moment I was in the gardens, then suddenly Florette was there, looking and behaving strangely, commanding shadows and smelling like spring flowers. Her eyes had changed colour...

No. It was the wine, that was all, compounded by my fragile mental state after confronting Mama–

Mama. Everyone had heard the end of Melisande's scream. Had they seen us disappear? Did they know what had happened, where we were?

As much as I didn't want to believe that I'd witnessed *magic*, my body, mind, and senses couldn't all be wrong. And there was no denying that I was standing in a room, on top of a mosaic, filthy and in pain and with absolutely no idea where I was or how to get out.

Well. Standing here doing nothing wasn't going to help me.

I turned in a slow half-circle and stopped, suddenly confronted with the reason for the wavering light.

A circular stained-glass window – the largest I'd ever seen – dominated the wall behind me. It was so tall that the intricate details were lost to the overall picture: an immense tree, divided into the seasons. The sky arched above the highest branches, while its roots reached towards darkness in the earth below. The tree was budding in spring, bright in full summer finery, robed in the decaying colours of autumn, and stark winter bare, like the branches on every Midwinter dress.

I knew little about stained glass, really, but enough to recognise that this window was exquisite. Not only in the amount of colour, but in the tiny details of leaf and bark and root. Mother adored stained glass, and would have happily sat beneath this one to study it for hours.

I frowned. Squeezed my eyes shut. Opened them again. My vision kept drifting in and out, as if trying to find a hidden pattern within a design. Something seemed subtly *off* because…

because…

The stained glass…

The tree in the stained glass was *moving*.

The tree branches waved, as if caught in a light breeze. The leaves rippled like jewels sealed under glass. The tree budded, bloomed, died, and was reborn, tossed and trapped within the endless cycle of the seasons. Light glowed through the window, the tree's movement making it ripple around the room.

I walked closer, then glanced behind me. The light caught at parts of the mosaic, but not enough to reveal the design. I held out my own hands, barely able to discern their shape.

Only my breathing broke the eerie quiet, as I stood in the flickering light of an unnatural window.

Then: a crinkle of skirts, like the snapping of twigs and branches underfoot. Swishing, whispering, dragging.

My skin crawled. My hands turned cold, as if I'd plunged them into frigid water, the fingertips taking on a dusky hue. I let out a breath, and it drifted away in a puff of cloud.

The room filled with the snap and crackle of spreading frost. If there was proper light, I knew, somehow, that I'd see the patterns forming that I usually found on my windows in bitter mornings.

I closed my eyes, but that only made the footsteps and trail-ing skirts louder. A sob trembled in my throat, but I couldn't let it out, driven by ancient instincts that said to fear the dark and predators. Whoever was coming closer, I could not let them hear my fear.

They can already hear your heartbeat, a scornful voice hissed in my head. *A sob is no better nor worse. They already know you're afraid.*

I couldn't turn around.

I had to.

If I were about to die, I would see who planned to kill me.

As I turned, a figure appeared out of the shadows.

My heartbeat veered from a staccato beat to full revolt, as if it were trying to bash itself against my ribs.

A blink, and I was on my knees in the dirt, shuddering.

The figure stopped to study me. In the gloom, she shone like moonlight upon fresh snow, her skin ghastly white. She was taller than anyone I'd ever met, taller than it was possible to be. Her gown gleamed like diamonds in water, the folds moving in a breeze I couldn't feel. It spilled from her shoulders and pooled around the floor; the dragging sound. Her hands were delicate, though they ended in dark claws, as if she'd dipped her fingertips in ink.

Her long, straight hair fell down her back until it reached the ground, shining like a raven's wing. She held herself oddly, as if trying to mimic a mortal stance but unable to hide a simmering rage.

But her eyes…

Her *eyes.*

The last hints of twilight before the sky succumbed to night.

No whites, no pupils. They were full of stars – endless: growing, burning, dying, over and over again. I looked into her eyes and glimpsed eternity.

Her glowing skin was marred by branches, bulging against the surface of her skin, twining towards her wrists. They burst through her shoulders and the nape of her neck, arching up and around her head like a monstrous ruff, adding to her height.

Every Midwinter dress had branches on it.

Her symbol.

In the oldest part of the palace, there was a small room called the Little Church, full of stained-glass windows. Mother went there to think and be alone: only Mama, myself, Matthias, and Isra knew to look for her there, as a last resort. The three largest windows depicted Lady Winter, Twilight, and Night. I'd always known they weren't genuine representations – hardly any records of the First Empire remained, never mind accurate portraits of the gods – but Mother had almost burst with pride when she took me to see the windows for the first time.

'We are built from what they represent,' she'd told me. 'The harsh cruelty and mercy they embody. *Undying pride and unyielding strength.* If you believe in yourself, my dear, you can weather anything as Queen: the disputes, the lonely nights, the terrible decisions.'

In her window, Lady Winter had looked nothing like the god now before me, who seemed to reflect all cruelty and little mercy.

'So,' she said, her voice echoing with howling wolves, the sweep of snow across the land, shattering ice, 'you are the heir.'

A scream had been building at the back of my throat, caught between a keen and a wail, and now it ripped free. Already on my knees, I toppled forward onto my palms, lowered my head until my forehead pressed against the dirt. I shut my eyes, but the magnificent splendour of Lady Winter shone against my eyelids, scorched into my memory.

I didn't know if I was trying to worship or beg for mercy.

NINETEEN

Moments passed, or maybe hours, days, while I pressed my face into the dirt, pinned by the starry gaze of a goddess. My breath panted in my ears; my heartbeat drummed in my bones, pounded against my ribs, too fast, too loud–

'Rise. Mortal you may be, but no worm to writhe against the ground.'

That terrible voice, echoing of wolves and the sweep of icy death.

My arms trembled as I forced myself back up to a kneeling position. But when I lifted my face, my gaze shied away, as if I instinctively knew I couldn't look upon Lady Winter for long, not without my mind splintering.

I swallowed. Loud in the silence, for a goddess had no need of air. Forced in a breath – *one, two, three* – let it out – *one, two, three* – tried to coax my gibbering mind into a poor semblance of order.

'Forgive me, my lady,' I finally said, and somehow the words came out calm, 'but I do not know how to address you, beyond the myths, and they may be insult veiled under the guise of truth.' The formal, stylised speech of *Her Royal Highness, Princess Emri* came easily, drilled into me over years, and I hid behind it with no small amount of terrified relief.

None of my etiquette lessons had covered meeting a god.

We'd have to remedy that.

A bubble of laughter swelled in my throat, tainted by hysteria, and I swallowed hard against it.

While I still couldn't fully look upon Lady Winter, I angled my face to catch brief glimpses: the snowfall-flicker of her gown, the dark claw tips of her right hand, the sleek fall of her raven hair. Her gaze pressed upon me like water closing over my head before it dragged me to the depths. Magic crawled over my skin like a creeping frost.

A shudder wracked through me.

'Lady of the Snows,' she said, 'Keeper of the Forests and Deep Lakes, She Who Commands the Frozen Paths.'

The myths only referred to her as Lady Winter, which seemed inadequate in the face of such grand titles.

I opened my mouth. Then, thinking better, I closed it again.

'But I suppose *my lady* will suffice,' she added, with something nearly akin to humour.

I was foolish enough to hope it meant there was kindness within her cold heart. But it lowered my odds of dying from terror, so I didn't question the assumption too deeply.

'My lady,' I repeated, pressing my palms against the cold ground and lowering my head again.

A little calmer, my gaze hidden from her, I thought furiously.

In myths, the mortals who faced gods were heroes or their chosen, or both. But I had been deceived and brought here against my will – along with Melisande, I suddenly remembered, my heart starting to hammer again: *where is she? is she alive?* – so I had my doubts about being a hero. And if I were a god's chosen, I wasn't especially certain that, in this particular instance, it was a blessing.

But I wouldn't know anything unless I asked.

I settled my weight back onto my heels. Keeping my gaze adjacent to Lady Winter, I asked, 'If this unworthy servant may request a boon of clarity as to why I'm here?'

The stories always had people talking like this, though the moment the words left my mouth, I worried it was a stylistic affliction of the authors, and not how one should acknowledge oneself to the patron goddess of one's country.

'Stop talking like you're in a saga,' Lady Winter replied. The temperature abruptly plummeted; displeasure, I realised, my shoulders tightening as if I'd been doused with icy water. 'I have no use for such florid language. Spare that for La Dame des Fleurs.'

Of course a goddess such as Lady Winter, known for a demeanour similar to the frozen landscapes of her domain, would dislike such flattery. I closed my eyes, steeling myself, and tried again.

'Why am I here? How could a lady of my parents' court – who seemed little more than an inefficient spy – summon shadows and fling me through them? Magic died out well over a thousand years ago.'

A laugh of cracking ice and the *shush* of snow toppling from evergreens to the ground. 'Finally. There is the child with the wits to be Queen.'

I automatically bristled at being called a child, but, really, compared to a goddess whose beginning was lost to time, what else could I be?

Instead, I ground out, 'My lady.' Then, before common sense could stop me, I added, 'This unworthy servant is honoured that she is finally having the correct reaction to facing divinity.'

A long pause, during which I suspected Lady Winter was considering freezing my voice in my throat.

Then: 'Dormant. Not dead.'

'I... I beg your pardon?' When in doubt, always cede back to manners.

'The magic was dormant,' she repeated, with seething patience, 'not dead. Never dead. It merely waited for those who still believed or returned to the faith.'

Words failed me. It took me several moments to realise it didn't matter anyway because my mouth had dropped open.

'There never was magic,' I finally sputtered, common sense failing me yet again. 'It was all just stories to explain away luck and stupid decisions!'

But if magic had never existed, then how to explain the goddess standing before me? Gods and magic and faith had always been intertwined. And when belief in the gods had faltered, seeped away like cliff faces against the hammering seas, so too had magic, fading like a half-remembered dream in daylight.

And it wasn't just in Edar. The stories were all across the continent, even in Rijaan, where they considered themselves above such fanciful things. A story of loss cosseted within cultural enlightenment. If enough people, in enough countries, across a wide enough stretch of land, accepted the same idea – surely that meant there was a seed of truth within it?

Lady Winter simply waited, as if my whirling thoughts were plain upon my face.

'Oh,' I said meekly.

Nothing, and no one – not my parents nor Isra – could have prepared me for this.

I had been trained to eventually rule a country, to survive Court intrigue, to balance people's wants against the country's needs. Not to face gods and magic.

But here I was, even if I didn't know *where* I was.

'Why am I here?' I repeated. Folded my hands on my lap, squared my shoulders, focused on a particular flurry on Lady Winter's gown. 'I am only the Edaran heir. My parents are the rulers, and Mother is of Northern lineage. If anyone would be especially gratified to learn of your... reappearance, and seek your grace, it would be her.'

Truthfully, if there was any moment that would shake Mother's elegant calm, it would be this, but if almost twenty years of ruling had taught her anything, it was surely how to gracefully (and swiftly) recover from an unexpected shock. Such as the return of a goddess long believed myth.

'I wield no power in my own right, not yet,' I finished, and silently added, *Hopefully not for a long time*.

'You are young,' Lady Winter said. 'A ruler to be shaped.'

Until now, I would have considered my most frightening memories to consist of half-remembered nightmares from Saphirun and my shared past with Melisande. All the ways I was a disappointment, a reminder of Rassa's stubbornness and Lady Liliene's weakness. A symbol of Arisane's own downfall. Unwanted and unloved.

It all paled to a goddess describing me as malleable.

I'd been a pawn for so much of my life. My conception to solidify Rassa's claim to the throne; my birth a problem to be solved within the Farezi royal family. Even Mother had used the Edaran thread in my heritage to persuade Court and Parliament, even the Edaran people, that I would be a suitable heir.

I was a symbol of future power to some, an obstacle to others. Even Rialla, whom I thought had loved me, could only see me as a future Queen.

To be a princess was to be a chess piece; to be an heir was to be manipulated with the utmost care. To be Queen was to manipulate everyone while pretending otherwise.

I would not be *shaped*, even by a goddess, not as a princess nor Queen.

Gritting my teeth, I dragged myself up, briefly regretting my trousers because they couldn't hide my shaking knees. Once standing, I forced myself to stay up, even as instinct shrieked that I should be on my knees in the dirt, as befitted one facing a goddess.

A goddess who wanted to manipulate me. An oddly mortal sentiment.

But then, the gods had faded because devotion towards them had dwindled, so perhaps mortal sentiments were derived from godly ones.

'With greatest respect, *my lady*' – without meaning to, I turned the honorific into a hiss – 'I will be manipulated by no one, god nor mortal. Force does not breed loyalty, only resentment and rage.'

The temperature plummeted again, but this time I was ready, shoulders hunching against the cold. But despite the shivering, and my chattering teeth – the overwhelming impulse to *kneel* – I stayed upright.

A low rumble started from the shadowy walls, a distant roar like the avalanches Mother said were common further north, where the Edaran mountains stretched east to meet their Farezi counterparts.

'We forgot so easily the foolishness of mortals,' Lady Winter said, her soft words belayed by the strengthening roar. 'The weakness of those lacking in faith.'

We.

My stomach jolted, propelling my heart into my throat.

Of course. Of course. If Lady Winter stood before me, then so too did the others exist: Twilight and Night, her ever-loyal companions.

'Such foolishness must be promptly dealt with,' she continued, still soft, still deadly.

Where am I? I wanted to scream, but once again, I demanded, 'Why am I here?' Thrice asked and no true answer given.

Moments trickled by, the roar gradually sinking back into the walls. I kept my gaze on Lady Winter's gown, tried to keep my breathing steady, and waited for an answer. If she kept diverting to another topic, then I would simply ask, again and again: *Why am I here?*

'A challenge,' she finally said, and there was no rumble in this reply, no freezing winds nor howling wolves. 'A bargain. Your loyalty tested against your future.'

Challenge. Bargain. Tested.

Words belonging to a story. A saga. A legend.

I was once more in the position of hero, someone offered challenges and bargains by the gods. But there had always been a hidden trap in the stories, and it had never ended well for them – the very reason heroes were remembered. Their honourable sacrifices… made tragically young.

My eyebrows jutted together as I worried my bottom lip between my teeth, then cast the matter of a trap temporarily aside. Perhaps it wasn't that Lady Winter was reluctant to answer, but that I wasn't asking the right questions.

I raised my head and shifted my gaze a little closer to her. 'What must I do to win my freedom?'

In answer, Lady Winter *flared*.

Light bloomed across her skin, scorched from her dress, pierced my eyes with a brightness no mortal could withstand for long. I squeezed my eyes shut, sunspots popping against my vision, as a scream ripped from my throat.

But this time I didn't fall. This time I didn't cower.

At last – moments? hours? days? – the light started to fade. When I finally dared to open my eyes, the light now flickered around Lady Winter like rippling coals, no longer a divine brightness. My eyes still smarted, but it felt more like being out in the midday sun without shade. A bearable, *mortal* sensation.

'I suppose I can only expect stubbornness from someone of Northern heritage,' Lady Winter said, her voice prickling. 'It always was a defining trait of your ancestors.'

When Mother was faced with a difficult courtier, her usual response was silence. Most people could not abide quiet, she always told me, and raced to fill it. Even I, who should know better, often succumbed to the tactic.

Lady Winter had used it on me, while my mind had grappled with the realities of gods and magic. Now it was my turn to try and wield it against her.

I interlaced my fingers, tight enough to hurt, steadied myself... and waited.

If the truth of gods and magic and religion stretched across the continent, then I was a thread within a larger pattern. In all likelihood, I was indeed a pawn for the gods. But I had been brought here against my will, to a shadowy place that seemed a divine prison, and so whether I was a thread or pawn, Lady Winter appeared to need me.

And I suspected I had finally asked the right question.

She stretched out her hand with those lethal dark claws, twisted her fingers, and the image of a tree shimmered between us, much like the one in the stained glass behind me. 'When belief faded, so did our power.' The summer richness began to fade, gaps showing on the branches as leaves fell, slow at first, shading from green to red, brown, and withering yellow. 'Our strength dwindled. At first the offerings grew indifferent, then fewer. As our priests and priestesses died, fewer acolytes waited to replace them. Our temples fell to neglect, then ruin.'

I glanced at the dirt-ridden mosaic beneath my boots.

'At first we were not unduly concerned,' Lady Winter continued. Her voice took on an echoing cadence. 'Faith has always swelled and ebbed. Devotion thrives in war and hardship, swiftly cast aside for petty concerns during peace and prosperity. So it has always been, and so we thought again. And as always, mortals once more destroyed their peace for war. But this time they did not beseech us for aid, for luck nor miracles. The Empire fell, but the lands were fractured, borders redrawn through alliances and the victors' spoils. And the costs were high. Lives lost that could have been avoided through spies guided by Twilight. Sieges could have been broken faster with Night's protection. Armies destroyed by my bitter winds and snows.'

For all her grand descriptions, the sorrow dripping from her words, the reality behind her tale was not so glorious. People had died, so many, so needlessly, because Lady Winter and her companions had not felt sufficiently *worshipped* to give aid. Mortals defending their families, their homes, the descendants of those who had turned from religion – all left to die and rot for decisions made long before they were born.

How cruel. How cold. How befitting a goddess with frost wrapped around her heart.

'But we were not beseeched,' Lady Winter continued, oblivious to my horror, 'and so our gifts were not bestowed. We faded, banished, bound to our oldest temples, where the last worshippers remained.' Rage rippled across Lady Winter's face, the stars in her eyes glowing as if about to die. 'We faded into legend, pitiful shades of ourselves. Only the last faint cries of the faithful kept us from disappearing entirely.'

'But what happened when the sickness came?' I asked. 'The plagues? The famines?'

She raised her eyebrows.

I was suddenly grateful for Mother insisting that history be part of my education, even when some of the tomes were dry as dust. 'Worse things always come after war. When the Second Empire collapsed, Othayria's harvest was already lost when the fighting ended, and the next failed. Several plagues bounced between Edar and Farezi for nearly five years. Eshvon narrowly avoided civil war. So when the First Empire crumpled, surely people remembered you, and prayed?'

A long silence. Unease pricked my heart.

'We would not be remembered as a last resort,' Lady Winter finally said, and unease turned my stomach into a yawning hole.

As they had turned from her, so had Lady Winter turned from mortals when they had desperately needed her aid. No food, no medicine, no cures. No hope. She had left them to starve and die, those not already rotting in graves.

I swallowed. Tears scorched in my eyes, but it was nothing compared to the rage burning up my throat. 'You blame us for your shadow existence, but no wonder you became nothing more than stories! No wonder Edar turned against religion! When people needed you – you abandoned them! Why expect anyone to try and believe, when their prayers did nothing? Faith means little when you have to bury your children, when you have to decide between feeding yourself or your child, or what will happen if you starve and they're left alone. Faith is useless when the rest of your family is *dead*.'

My voice rose with every sentence, jagged with fury, words tripping over each other. 'You're nothing more than a monster craving adoration, coveting the trappings of divinity without mercy nor love. Why would anyone want to believe in such a cowardly and selfish god?'

I knew I'd gone too far, fuelled by my own terror and anger, by everything ugly inside me that I feared had been shaped, long ago, by Arisane and Saphirun. The temperature dropped so swift, so sharp, that I blinked and the mosaic on the floor was suddenly hidden beneath a thick layer of ice. But none of it could be unsaid.

I took a deep breath. 'Why would I accept a challenge from someone like *you*?'

Wind howled through the cavern, painful with the promise of snow. I staggered, but kept my footing, despite my chattering teeth and my body spasming in revolt.

'I will tolerate stubbornness from someone of Northern lineage,' Lady Winter said in a lethal whisper, 'but never insolence.'

I blinked, and suddenly I couldn't move, body and limbs frozen in place. As Lady Winter approached, her skirts swishing and dragging over the ground, my gaze travelled from her deadly claws up her arms, tracing the branches under her skin before they erupted at her shoulders, arching around her head.

I had been caught by the shimmer and blaze of her, forgetting the darker aspects, the parts of her that people had twisted into embroidery on a dress to make them seem less frightening.

My eyes watered, unable to blink or look away as the god drew closer.

'If you refuse the bargain, reject the challenge,' she hissed, my chin gripped in her lethal claws, 'then by the end, you will wish for death because I will not grant it to you.'

I trembled – inside, because I could not move – and screamed – inside, because I could not speak – and waited for her to continue because I could do nothing else.

'This is the oldest temple in the country you call Farezi,' she said. 'This is where we fled, as our power waned, and this is where we were trapped, kept in existence by the devotion of those few who still followed us, and their children, and those whose faith eventually led them here. Regaining our strength and power, slowly, so slowly, with each passing year. Also aided' – and here Lady Winter smiled, a wicked curl of lip and teeth – 'by the Midwinter celebrations invoking us. Pitiful as they are, they helped us regain our strength.'

Once, before Farezi had created a Second Empire, Lady Winter was Edar's patron goddess, from the mountains of the far north to the southern port cities. But Farezi's influence had spread throughout the south and capital, including legends about *their* patron goddess, La Dame des Fleurs.

While trying to gather an army to take the crown, King Anderrs II had stressed his Northern heritage as proof of his suitability to rule; before they were royal, House Sionbourne was one of the oldest noble families in the North, their bloodline stretching back centuries through several branches of the family tree. It was why most of our modern traditions, including Midwinter, were so important – they were all Northern, unquestioningly *Edaran*, and free of Farezi's influence.

Every time my parents, and all the Edaran Queens before them, had danced as Lady Winter, she had taken strength from the celebrations because they were, technically, remembrance – and worship.

All these centuries, Lady Winter had bided her time, waiting to break free of this prison as patiently as her nature would allow, while we unknowingly provided the means for her to do so.

'Here is your task: prove yourself worthy as heir and my Chosen by escaping the temple alongside the other mortals also trapped here. Do so before the last full moon of winter, and I will support the reigning Queens – and *you*, when your time comes.' Something ugly crawled across her gaze like a smear of shadow. 'Royal blood, divine-blessed. Monarchs have gone to war for less.'

I knew then: she despised us. My parents. Me. All mortals. She despised us, but needed our faith and our adoration to maintain her power and true existence. And to be adored, even a god needed to hide how much they hated us.

I hadn't realised, until now, how much power there was in being hated, and how terrifying it was. Arisane's rage; the resentment towards me in the darker corners of Court during the early years after my arrival; the terrible childhood I had shared with Melisande: all of it a wisp compared to Lady Winter's contempt.

But even though I was at a disadvantage – I had, literally, been brought here against my will, and had no way out beyond my own means and cleverness – I was the daughter of two Queens, and I would not be so easily cowed.

She released my chin, shattering the frozen grip on me at the same time. I wrenched back, my mouth curling in a snarl.

'And if I refuse?' I raised my face as I spoke, and this time I did what every instinct in me had screamed against: I gazed upon Lady Winter in her full divine glory.

Before I had been unprepared; now, she knew it was deliberate.

The light flared, so strong and sudden that I *had* to squeeze my eyes shut, a scream whirling up my throat. The light scorched against my eyelids. I forced myself to keep standing – barely, admittedly, but I wouldn't – would *not* – give in to my shaking legs.

She was a god, but not yet powerful enough to free herself from this temple. I needed to get out of here… but she needed me because I was the future. I was young – *malleable*, as she'd implied – and it would be far easier if I believed before my parents became aware of Lady Winter's existence. The gods would be remembered long beyond my parents' reign if I were their chosen, their mortal voice.

So, for now, if I had to drag myself and Melisande through the temple – and whoever else was unfortunate enough to be involved in this cursèd challenge – I'd do it with only a healthy fear of gods. No matter how much respect I was supposed to show Edar's patron goddess, I wouldn't let Lady Winter terrify me further to satisfy her capricious nature.

Or so I told myself. So I hoped.

In the stories, those who defied the gods didn't enjoy long lifespans to witness the consequences of their actions. Or, as I now knew, the consequences could erupt generations later.

'So,' Lady Winter said, her voice a crackle of breaking ice, 'you appear to need more incentive than merely your life and the safety of those you love. What a pity. I had such hopes for you, that I would not have to resort to the old ways.'

'You need us,' I hissed, bristling before I could stop myself. 'You need our faith. You need us to convince the people of your return.'

Her eyes glowed, and she loomed above me. 'I have never had need of the unworthy.'

Before I could take another breath, before I could rethink my moment of defiance, Lady Winter stretched out her hand again, but this time the ink-dark claws plunged into my chest, slipped through my ribs, and wrapped around my heart.

No, I thought. *No, I need that. It's mine.*

But there was no breath, and I could not speak. And there was no pain, only a numbing cold, as Lady Winter's hand withdrew, red and bloody, steaming with my beating heart.

'So was the bargain,' she crooned, voice silky with the cadence of myth and legend, 'and here is the price. Win freedom, and retrieve your heart. Protect those you love by gaining my support. Fail, and be damned with the shadow of a life half-lived.'

Tears hissed in my eyes, hot where the void in my chest prickled with frost. *No,* I thought, but the sob was trapped in my throat, strangled by the breath I could not take. *No.*

'Fail, and you will live. I am not so cruel, despite what the stories claim.' The burning light faded enough for me to see her without further agony. Her expression was cold and empty, as devoid of feeling as dark water that drowned those in its depths. 'For you to die would mean having to shape another to the throne, and I can't imagine *Their Majesties'* – she spat the title – 'would take your death so kindly. To dispose of you would mean such effort upon my resurrection. So you will live… and walk through your reign with the steps of my choosing, your legacy shaped to my whims.'

The stars within Lady Winter's eyes glowed, spun with the terrible future awaiting me if I didn't win the bargain. 'As with you, so for your children and their children: each generation bound by your failure. Loyalty is bitter-won through force – but if not adoration, I will accept your obedience.'

O nce, there is a princess.

And a goddess ripped out her heart to seal a bargain.

But the bargains seldom end well.

For the mortals, that is.

TWENTY

Mercifully, just as I gave in to the threat of tears, Lady Winter summoned shadows and sent me plummeting through them.

I landed hard; a yelp snuffed out in a grunt of pain. For a moment I could only lie there, dimly aware of raised voices nearby as they were abruptly silenced, trying to breathe around tears and calculate the extent of my injuries.

But even crying didn't feel right. The heat still scalded down my cheeks, prickled at the back of my nose and down my throat, but now there was only the cold stretch of hoarfrost where once my heart had been. The emotions were still there – terror, loss, *she took my heart* – but an icy veil had drifted over them, a brittle layer I had no idea how to get rid of.

Bruises most definitely; sharper pain in my hands and legs where I'd taken most of the impact. I shifted gingerly, still summoning the courage to rise, and there was no answering flare of a potential broken bone. Good. One less thing to worry about on top of… well, everything else that I had no choice but to worry about.

Struggling to breathe through my crying-induced blocked

nose, I tried to coax my limbs to move.

Footsteps pounded towards me, reverberating through the ground against my ear and cheek. 'Emri? *Emri!* Are you all right—'

Melisande: her voice high and furious, wavering with uncertainty. Never in my life, not once, had I been so relieved to hear her. All I'd needed was to be kidnapped by a trapped goddess, then forced into a bargain sealed with her ripping out my heart, and Melisande was suddenly one of my favourite people in the world.

I could absolutely never tell her.

She fell to her knees beside me, hands pressing gently against my head and upper back. 'Can you move? You landed so hard through the ceiling – I can't believe I even said that, never mind that it makes *sense* – and she wouldn't tell me where you were—'

I opened my mouth, and let out a pained squeak that toppled into a sharp groan.

Melisande swore calmly. 'Don't just stand there,' she snapped at someone else. 'Help me try to safely move her, or go and find someone who *will* help.'

A rustle of robes, then someone said, coolly, 'You may be a Princess of Farezi, but I'd caution you to remember that your family's dominion is uncertain here.' As Melisande let out a sound remarkably like an enraged cat, the person added, stepping closer to my other side, 'Nevertheless, my vows state that aid must be given to all in a holy place.'

Gloved hands rested on my hair, and the person spoke in a low voice, instructing me to move slowly, testing for any broken bones. I could have told her that I'd already done this careful check, but all my focus remained on the bone-jarring pain colliding with delayed exhaustion. It wasn't just meeting Lady Winter that was catching up with me, nor the consequences of her terrible bargain – *my heart, my heart, my heart* – but the last few weeks and months: Melisande's arrival, the truth about Mama killing Rassa, the burden of my future and past, all the changes that were seeping into my life.

I was so *tired*.

Slowly, as my body protested and I clamped my lips shut against the worst of the whimpers and pained gasps, Melisande and the other person helped me to my knees. The world spun – no surprise, really, and I would never, *ever* again drink so much and eat so little – and I swallowed, hoping the sudden nausea wasn't a warning sign. But it settled after another few breaths, and I silently thanked my body for its continued cooperation.

I was in another cavern, larger than the one where I'd faced Lady Winter, this time without a stained-glass window. Pillars stretched away on either side, shimmering in a familiar way that tugged at my memory. Light flickered from torches on the walls, but there was no smell of smoke. The room was mostly illuminated by an icy light streaking through a circular hole in the ceiling. I squinted, but it didn't resemble natural light. More magic, probably.

Each breath filled my lungs with a sharp burn, oddly pleasing, similar to when I took a walk during an icy morning. Usually with Mother, who loved that time best and could no longer convince Mama to accompany her.

A wave of loss and homesickness welled up inside me, again muted, forcing my gaze down to my grimy trousers. Were my parents safe? Did they know what had happened, where I was? I had no answers, and was no longer in Edar from what Lady Winter had said, so there was no point indulging my worries. Not yet, at least.

'Emri?' Melisande touched my arm hesitantly, and I glanced towards her. 'What happened? I won't ask are you all right because, well, I don't think either of us—'

A snort, and Melisande glared at the person at my other side, eyes lit with a caustic fury. 'If your so-called goddess has hurt her, I don't think you understand the *furious royal power* that will land on you like a blacksmith's entire inventory—'

'I'm alive,' I interrupted. 'No blacksmith's inventory necessary.' I couldn't truthfully say I wasn't hurt, considering my general state, and after Lady Winter took—'

The ice in my chest burned and throbbed. I swallowed, though it did nothing to help.

Apart from when she'd told me the truth about Mama killing Rassa, Melisande had never appeared less than impeccable outside her bedroom door. On my worst days, when I wanted to pick at my resentment like a healing scratch, I was certain she woke up without a strand of hair out of place.

But now, like mine, her face and clothing were smeared with grime and dirt. Dust coated her hair in a mockery of the powder they'd used during the reign of Mother's grandfather, spilling down her back in bedraggled waves. But what caught me was the wild look in her eyes, a breath away from terror and a sidestep close to panic. A flash of relief wiped it away – yes, I was alive, if probably not looking my best, no more than her – and she made a movement, as if about to crush me into a hug, before she caught herself. Her expression flickered between too many emotions, with not enough time to neaten them. She probably wouldn't have reacted sensibly around Lady Winter, either.

After a moment, I added, 'I'm also thrilled you're alive.'

Her mouth twitched in the beginnings of a smile, before the other person enquired, 'Am I now free from a blacksmith's inventory being metaphorically dumped on my head?' The voice was soft, steady, but the arch tone was unmistakable.

Melisande clenched her teeth – I didn't know she indulged in such a bad habit, fascinating – as I turned my head to finally look at whoever had succeeded in so effectively irritating her.

A woman knelt at my other side. Her long, high-collared light blue robe, edged in white, looked reassuringly thick, and I eyed both it and her gloves enviously. She raised her chin, her expression firm as she met my gaze. Her brown eyes were large and thickly-lashed, and showed no fear. Some of her dark brown hair peeked out in thick ringlets from underneath a snug hood. Her skin was pale, but her face was blotchy with cold, especially her cheeks and nose, no matter her more suitable attire. She slipped her gloved hands into her sleeves and bowed. 'Your Highness.'

I hesitated, then bowed in return. What was… *who* was this?

Edar's current religious order was a modern affair, with only the dregs of worship. While they had a place on the Council, the Church mostly kept to themselves, occasionally becoming a political beast when a sticking point arose between the monarchy and the government. Most courtiers would have last seen the Arch-Bishop, the highest member, when she crowned Mama, but her robes were nothing like the woman's before me, whom I sincerely doubted I should address as a bishop.

The panic had returned to tickle at the back of my mind, but I refused to indulge it. After the terrifying visage of Lady Winter, the appearance of an apparently mortal woman shouldn't have felt terrifying. But none of this made sense. Other countries still worshipped, unlike Edar, but no one still lived in the old mountain temples. They were too bleak, too difficult to get to for a populace prone to a weaker devotion.

This was far larger than Florette Sigrath and her strange shadows.

'I'm afraid I don't know how to address you,' I admitted, swallowing hard against the hysterics building in my throat. 'But thank you for helping Melisande.'

I flexed my fingers, wincing against the cold stiffness. I was *not* suitably dressed for a mountain temple that was likely tucked away up in Northern Farezi. The maps of the continent during the First Empire were long rotted and lost, but there was long-standing speculation that Northern Edar and Northern Farezi had once been its own country, a predominately mountainous one, before the Empire fell and the boundaries were remade. Lady Winter, diminished in the wake of fading belief, wouldn't have fled to the south, the domain of La Dame des Fleurs.

To be more logical, it also never got this cold in the south, as Mama was quick to remind us. And the other woman had referred to Melisande being a princess and her family's dominion.

The woman bowed again. 'I am Aren, an acolyte of this temple and devoted to Lady Winter of the Snows; Keeper of the Forests and Deep Lakes; She Who—'

'–Commands the Frozen Paths,' I finished softly in unison.

Something flared in Aren's eyes, swiftly extinguished, while Melisande frowned at me.

'Then you have borne witness,' Aren said.

'Unfortunately,' I replied.

The corners of Aren's mouth flickered, but I couldn't tell whether in amusement or disapproval. 'I am but a lowly acolyte in training for sacred orders. Please address me as such, should there be any need to address me at all.'

The stark difference between her polite deference now, compared to her dry mockery towards Melisande, was not lost on either of us. Melisande opened her mouth, but stayed resentfully silent after I grasped her arm and squeezed.

We needed answers, not to mention proper clothing and food. Not an enraged acolyte for the sake of Melisande's pride. Not so lowly, no matter what she insisted, considering Aren had information that we desperately needed.

I thought back to how I'd goaded Lady Winter and flinched against an uncomfortable flash of self-awareness.

'Acolyte Aren,' I said, infusing my voice with as much humble respect as possible, 'may we request aid from you – clothing? food? – for the tasks ahead? I'm afraid I was not given... information on specific details.'

Namely, how we were to get out of the temple – out of the *mountain* – without proper clothing and food. I had no idea how large the mountain was, nor how intricate the temple within it, but I didn't doubt the poor odds Melisande and I would face even surviving the night without proper provisions and warmth.

'What tasks?' Melisande demanded, clenching her teeth when neither Aren nor I responded.

I avoided her narrowed eyes. Melisande was acting too normally to have faced a god, even lesser ones like Twilight or Night, and if she hadn't faced Lady Winter, considering her poor attitude towards Aren, she likely had no idea of the terrible danger we faced.

I would be kind enough to tell her in private.

Aren gave me a measuring look, as if she knew *exactly* whom I'd met and what bargain I'd been forced to accept, but said nothing.

'*What tasks?*' Melisande repeated, an unsteady note rising in her voice. I had the sudden horrifying suspicion that her rudeness towards Aren was a way to hide the true depths of her terror, and that she was absolutely not handling any of this well. She'd practically told me: *She wouldn't tell me where you were.*

But I had to stay calm. One of us had to, or all would be lost before it even started.

Aren glared at Melisande, who returned it sourly. 'Please, follow me,' she said, and rose in a smooth motion, her robe settling around her.

As we fell into step behind her, I glared at Melisande, who had the good grace to look ashamed at her behaviour. We needed all the help we could get, and once Melisande knew what was actually going on, she wouldn't take it well.

We followed Aren beyond the strange circular streak of icy light, which rippled up from a round pool. I stopped to peer in and found no bottom, only endless clear blue reflecting the light. My breath caught as I glanced up, squinting against the brightness, just able to make out that the circular hole in the ceiling was the exact same shape as the pool. A hum radiated from the light; a shudder wracked through me. My gaze unfocused, unable to stand the brightness for long, and it seemed to resemble gleaming sunlight upon fresh snow.

All unnatural.

Magic.

'I would not linger here, Your Highness.' I jerked, twisting to find Aren and Melisande watching me. Aren's expression was cautious, while Melisande looked as unnerved as me. It didn't suit her. 'Not when you are unused to the power of the gods.'

Power.

I thought I'd known power. My parents were living symbols of command, the gilt of their clothing and crowns and thrones a counterpoint to the daily stubbornness of duty and negotiation, all for people they would mostly never meet face to face. I thought I'd known the power I represented as a living symbol of reparation between two countries, even the delicate balance of alliances and favour-dealing that existed between my ladies and me.

The Queens were the heart of Edar, their ministers and government the minds and nerves that helped fulfil their purpose. The people were its bones: enduring, strong, able to weather and repair and continue living.

But against gods, my parents would be gouged, the government destroyed, and everyone else ground into submission.

What I had thought of as power was a candle flame against the roaring flame of the gods.

But without our faith, they were nothing. As mortals, we held a different kind of power, but it was power, nonetheless.

One last thoughtful glance at the pool and the rippling light, and I turned to rejoin Melisande and Aren, trying to keep my expression calm while I thought furiously. I could practically feel my mind creaking back into life, a familiar sensation from when I'd wrestled with the demands of Isra and my tutors. For the first time since I'd been told of Melisande's impending visit, I felt more like myself.

If I could think, then all wasn't lost. Lady Winter could take my heart, but she had not robbed me of my mind and so didn't fully control me yet.

Melisande eyed me warily, and I worked harder at my calm expression.

We entered a smaller, brighter room on the other side of the cavern. It was fractionally warmer, but the sudden heat made Melisande and I both gasp. Aren beckoned us over to a long table, groaning under piles of clothing, a large steaming pot, and an assortment of smaller plates and bowls that I hoped involved food.

'You are requested to refresh yourselves and change into clothing more suitable for our surroundings,' Aren said. 'We have provided basic provisions for your... travels.'

'Travels?' Melisande repeated, her irritation tainted by the confusion she couldn't hide. '*What* is going on?'

Aren flicked a meaningful glance towards me. When I remained silent, she said, 'I suggest you tell her, Your Highness. A god's will should be carried out with all due haste.'

Melisande choked on air.

I frowned, as something at the back of my mind clicked together. 'Wait. How do you know we're both princesses?'

'I will wait outside,' Aren said, ignoring my question, 'for you to be clean and decent. Once you have eaten, I will unlock the path for you, and guide you for the beginning.'

'Beginning of *what*?' Melisande demanded, her voice twisted with thorns, but Aren ignored her, too, and left me alone to face Melisande's furious bafflement.

TWENTY-ONE

'You agreed to *what*?'

Theoretically I'd known Melisande could shout – she'd definitely done it when we were children – but like every well-trained princess, she didn't show her temper in public. But now her fury raged, wrenched low from her throat. She drew herself up to her not inconsiderable height, eyes flashing, as her hair loomed around her.

'Agreement implies I had a choice,' I said coolly, meeting her flame with stern composure. 'I did not.'

The ice in my chest, where my heart had once been, throbbed in agreement.

Melisande's eyes glinted in warning. 'Tell me *precisely* what you agreed to, since I appear to be involved against my will.'

'*I* didn't involve you,' I shot back. Even now, Isra's training warred within me. Instinct cautioned me against revealing too much, while my common sense, much exhausted and battered from my encounter with Lady Winter, felt she needed to know everything. If we worked together, we had a better chance of actually getting out of here, alongside whoever else was misfortunate enough to be trapped here.

'Lady Winter is imprisoned here,' I repeated, 'as are Twilight and Night, most likely. She presented me with a challenge: I've to escape the mountain, with you and the others trapped here, by the last full moon of winter. If we do, upon her resurrection, she will support my parents' rule, and mine in turn. And if we don't...' I trailed off, unwilling – unable – to explain it all again.

Lady Winter refuting my parents' rule upon her return. My becoming her puppet Queen, controlled by her fury and will. And my heart...

The frost burned in my chest again. Melisande didn't need to know *everything*.

'But why am *I* involved?' she muttered, beginning to pace. 'My Edaran ancestry is practically a thread in the family tree at this point.'

Yet that thread had been enough to solidify my legitimacy as Mother's heir.

I sighed, dragging a hand over my face. 'This temple is in Northern Farezi. She must have been worshipped here before the First Empire fell. Also, we're cousins, and thanks to Rassa, our families are linked closer than Lord Erik's marriage ever managed.'

'But-but-*but*—' Melisande spluttered. Her indignation was somewhat lessened by her clutching a scrap of cloth in one hand and a lump of weathered soap in the other.

'Wash your face,' I said. 'You need it.'

She scowled, ignoring the dripping cloth. 'Emri. You made a *bargain with a goddess.*'

'Yes. And I'd prefer to never do it again. If you're not going to wash, move over before the water goes cold.'

All things considered, Melisande appeared to be taking the realisation that we were in the mountains of Farezi, trapped in an ancient temple with Lady Winter and her devoted, relatively better than I'd expected. Lady Winter, with whom I'd made a bargain.

Relatively better, however, meant she was a breath away from succumbing to hysterics, so I suspected she hadn't yet fully grasped our dire situation, clinging instead to her upset that my agreement was also upon her behalf.

Melisande stood there, still holding onto the cloth, her face twitching. Silence stretched thin between us, and her eyes tightened with fear. She might not be acknowledging the truth of our situation, but she wasn't oblivious – merely keeping it at arm's length so she could dredge up courage for what lay ahead.

'What was she like?' Melisande finally asked.

I held my hand out for the cloth, standing and gesturing for her to take my place on the bench. I dipped it in the water, wrung it out, then started carefully dabbing at the smudged kohl around her eyes. Hazel eyes, shot through with specks of gold. So like her mother's eyes; Arisane's eyes; Rassa's eyes.

While I... I had my mother's eyes.

For a few moments, we simply breathed, and I tried to put into words what didn't seem possible to explain. What mortal description could do justice to a goddess?

'Like the stories,' I said, 'and worse. Cold. Hard. Cruel.'

The scrape of her skirts as they dragged across the ground. The branches bulging under her snow-pale skin, twisted around her bones and muscle, bursting free to frame her in a horrendous ruff.

'There is no mercy in her,' I continued, 'not now. She is angry – so angry. The people turned from her, and there was just enough faith to keep her in existence and trapped here. And now… now her power has been growing steadily enough that she intends to return.' Satisfied that I'd got Melisande's eyes as clean as possible, I lathered the cloth with soap and started on the rest of her face.

She shut her eyes against the sting. 'If she's a goddess without mercy,' she managed around my firm rubbing, 'then why would anyone have faith in her at all?'

I shrugged, then remembered she couldn't see it. 'Northern Edar is hard,' I said slowly. 'The oldest families retain that hardness, noble and common. During harsh winters, they're often cut off from the rest of the country for months. Most of the nobles return to their estates to help their people through the dark months, so they're not always popular families to marry into. I imagine it's the same in Northern Farezi.' Mother didn't spend as much time in the North as she used to, but she'd spent winters there while growing up to learn how to manage an estate before she became Queen. That hardness was still in her, though she claimed the capital had softened her over the years.

Melisande snorted. 'We're a longstanding southern family, remember? When was the last time someone from Northern Farezi married in? Four generations ago… six?'

I stiffened; I couldn't help it. 'Do you honestly think Arisane imparted any sense of family pride before I was adopted?' I regretted the harshness, but only a little. Melisande was old enough to have reconsidered our years together in Saphirun.

Her eyes snapped open. 'I-I'm sorry,' she muttered. 'Not for what she did, because it's not my place to apologise for her, but that I keep… forgetting.'

'That I was treated as a traitor's daughter?' I asked bitterly. 'Come now, how else should I have been?'

'You weren't even born until after his death! It was cruel of her,' Melisande said. 'Far crueller than anything Lady Winter could do.'

Hoarfrost prickled around my ribs. 'Arisane wasn't any worse than Lady Winter. Just different in her cruelty.'

After that, Melisande retreated to her thoughts while I focused on scrubbing her face as best I could. Scentless torchlight flickered against the smoothened walls. We were in a small room in a mountain, devoid of all luxuries, there was no denying that, but compared to everything I'd experienced here so far, the room felt oddly pleasant and safe. An illusion, but I clung to it anyway, for as long as it would last.

We exchanged places. As Melisande started on my face, trying not to get soap in my eyes – I'd forgotten to do my own before I added it to the water – she found her voice again.

'I know the records are vague and mostly lost, but the First Empire properly fell after one last battle between Edar and Farezi, or whatever they were then. The borders were redrawn, and Lady Winter seems to have lost one of her oldest places of worship. Maybe that's also why I'm here. She's still angry.'

'It's possible,' I agreed.

More than possible, considering the depths of Lady Winter's bitterness. A god had eternity to nurse a grudge. And considering what I knew of Northern Edarans, even if the borders had been redrawn, the Northern Farezi would have been loath to give up their gods. Worship had likely continued in secret, especially if the temple was difficult to get to.

Her deep frown suddenly reminded me of Mother turning a problem around in her mind, breaking it down to figure out how to resolve it. Homesickness hit me like a wave, my chest burning as if I'd swallowed salt water. Melisande paused, startled, then continued with my face when I shook my head and refused to elaborate.

'I think that's the best I can do until we properly bathe,' she finally said, lowering the cloth and eyeing me critically. 'If that ever happens. We should eat. I don't think that acolyte has much patience.'

And neither would Lady Winter.

'So we just have to pass… trials, or whatever else she'll decide to fling at us, find the others trapped here, and work with them to get out of the mountain before the last full moon of winter,' Melisande said, punctuating her sentence by shoving a large hunk of cheese into her mouth and chewing. She swallowed and added in a brightly forced tone, 'That doesn't sound difficult.'

'Yes, because that's how all trials were in the stories,' I said flatly. 'Not difficult.'

'I don't suppose there's a book of myths in those provisions?'

'If only. Do you remember many stories?'

'Not many useful ones.' Melisande took a bite of day-old bread slathered in a tart jam. 'Most of what I know is trickster stuff concerning La Dame des Fleurs. Lady Winter's really only acknowledged up north, but we thought it was more tradition than true worship, and there's no consistent remembrance like your Midwinter celebrations. I never even heard of an old temple up here, and yet' – she spread her arms to encompass the room, still holding the bread – 'here we are.'

'But why here? Lady Winter is still *Edar's* goddess now, even if the borders were different a thousand years ago.' I poured the last of the oversteeped tea, grateful for the warmth even if the tea was so bitter it made me wince. 'There are villages further north in Edar, well below our side of the mountains. They usually keep to themselves, but they write to Mother every decade or so, mostly to remind her they're still alive and occasionally for aid. There were surely ancient temples up there for Lady Winter to flee to.'

Melisande shrugged. 'Maybe this temple is older. Maybe the worship here never faltered, small as it was. Maybe you should ask Lady Winter.'

Yes. Because that would end well.

The provisions were basic, but they felt akin to a miracle, considering we had nothing except our ball clothing and Melisande's remaining dagger. The clothing was equally simple, but the layers were sturdy and warm, sensible enough that it gave me hope – fragile, absurd hope – that between it and the provisions, we might actually survive and succeed. After we changed, the shudders wracking us from our unsuitable clothing finally began to subside. After a bittersweet moment, I left the filthy, tattered remains of my Night costume on the bench. No need to come face to face with Night and have them take offence at the ruined clothing that was supposed to be in their honour.

Melisande stared wistfully at her extremely-impractical-for-a-mountain boots, then slung a pack over her shoulders and sighed. 'All right. Let's go, before the acolyte becomes even more obnoxious.'

Aren was waiting, impressively still, her gloved hands tucked into her robe sleeves. If she'd heard us discussing her, she gave no sign. She eyed our new attire and packs, then nodded, apparently satisfied that if we died in this endeavour, it wouldn't be because she hadn't done her bit. 'Follow me.'

We returned to the large cavern with the pool and rippling light, but Aren veered towards a different wall. From a distance, it seemed smooth, but as we drew closer, the rough, uneven surface became clearer. The light made veins in the rock flare brightly; I flicked through my memory, trying to remember what mining Farezi was known for. Sapphire, perhaps, since this temple was in honour of Lady Winter? Maybe this place had started as a mine, then been converted into a temple. In uncertain times, seams of precious stones would be secure income, perhaps more useful than faith in the divine.

Aren paused before the seam, then pulled off her right glove and pressed her fingertips against it. She closed her eyes; for a long moment, nothing happened.

Then a rumble echoed from the wall, juddered in my bones and teeth.

Melisande grabbed my arm and jerked back a step, but I held my ground. Aren had no reason to kill me, not yet. If I died, Lady Winter intended it to be through my own failures, not by murder.

The seam darkened, then stretched, as if made of shadow, before a glimmering wave spread across the wall, similar to frost patterns across windows.

I blinked, and realised I'd stepped forward, pulling a resistant

Melisande with me.

'This is magic,' she hissed. 'It's not safe.'

'At least you have *some* sense,' Aren remarked blandly, to which Melisande flung her a vicious look.

I ignored them both, stretching out my hand – my fingers ached from the cold; when had I pulled off my glove? – towards the wall.

'Emri, please, don't touch it,' Melisande said, betrayed by a shrill note in her voice. '*Please.*'

I easily ignored her. I had to touch this; I needed to.

The ice in my chest swelled in response to the rising magic, like calling to like. To something familiar, a yawning ache to be reunited.

I should have been afraid, but the cold made all fear dissipate. I should have been afraid, and the magic made it so I wasn't.

My fingertips touched the seam, and the shadows *writhed.* Cold pierced my skin and dug into my bones, crackled around my veins and nerves, arched up my arm.

I opened my mouth, but hadn't time to scream before darkness filled my vision. Melisande's nails dug into my arm, the buffering wind carrying a faint echo of her scream, and then there was nothing but deep silence.

TWENTY-TWO

We landed in a heap, hard, at the foot of steps carved from the rock itself.

Melisande grunted under my weight. 'Haven't they heard of *doors*? If this keeps up, one of us is going to smash our head open and their damned challenge won't matter.'

I huffed out a laugh, pressed my forehead against her shoulder for a moment, and braced myself to move. No amount of jumping off walls or from trees could prepare anyone for gods flinging people through doorways created from nothing. I took a deep breath, then hoisted myself up with a groan.

'You sound like a grandmother,' she grumbled, then let out a similar sound as she rose and brushed her hands against her trousers. 'Right, where are we?'

'As if I know,' I muttered, already digging through my pack. My hands closed around a sheaf of folded parchment, and my heart leapt as I gently pulled it out, but instead of a map, or at least one I expected, it was an inked drawing of spirals and interlocked circles. 'Oh,' I said, glancing up at Melisande, who looked as baffled as I felt. 'I don't suppose you… have any idea—'

'We're lost and going to die,' she said.

'I'd prefer more optimism.'

'What little I had dried up after being kidnapped by shadows with glowing eyes.'

There was little to argue with that. I dug further into my pack – perhaps this was why Aren had chivvied us along, so we wouldn't know the provisions were useless until it was too late – and sighed. 'No compass, either, but it probably wouldn't work with all the magic.'

Melisande peered up. 'No way to see the stars, either.'

Our gazes settled on the steps arching upwards. 'The only way is up, then,' I said, tucking the parchment back into my pack. Perhaps it would be readable in another part of the mountain, or we had to do or get something for it to properly reveal itself.

I waited for Melisande to start up the steps, but she shook her head and gestured me forward. A cynical part of me wondered if she wanted anything unpleasant waiting for us to attack me first, but then, she was equally in danger if something approached from behind.

The steps circled up the centre of the cavern, carved from the same rock that supported their great height. Unlike the previous cavern, the light at the top wasn't as bright, making the open sides around us even more treacherous. After the first few turns, we discovered some steps were unevenly carved after I tripped and almost tumbled over the side.

When she had to lunge for me a second time, Melisande

snapped, '*Be careful.*' We stared at each other for a long moment, and Melisande's annoyance shifted to concern before she let me go. I'd felt no fear, I realised after a few moments, only an empty acceptance. I would have lived, or I would have toppled and plummeted to my death, and that was that. Melisande had likely seen that blank acceptance, instead of the terrified relief she had expected. We might not like each other very much, but even she knew that wasn't right.

An icy burn flared within my ribs.

At the top, we stopped and let out long shaky breaths. Melisande peered over the edge at the distance we'd covered, then immediately drew back, looking peaky. The unsteady light radiated from the jagged ceiling far overhead, similar to the bright veins of the wall that had brought us here.

When Melisande focused on what lay before us, she sighed. 'I knew having no map was a bad sign.'

Before us, the path split in two, one track going further up while the other went down, both areas too dim with shadow to properly make out.

After a long silence, I ventured, 'Up, surely?' In the stories, nothing good happened deep below.

Melisande sighed again. 'Up.'

So we climbed. Several steps onto the higher path, the ceiling shifted above us, brightening as if the mountain possessed its own sun. We flinched at the sudden change. I braced myself, then peered over the edge: the light hadn't penetrated the shadows in the lower path. If anything, they seemed to be growing thicker… and moving.

I glanced at Melisande, who clenched her teeth and said, 'Don't look down again.'

We climbed. Up and up, step by step, until our legs trembled and our breathing grew heavy. A set of winding steps shouldn't have presented such a challenge.

Except they appeared to have no end.

'I need to stop,' Melisande said, already sprawled awkwardly on the steps when I stopped. Her hair was plastered against her forehead, cheeks, and neck, and she heaved for air as if we'd raced during the height of midsummer heat. 'I… can't…'

I peeled my hair off the nape of my neck and grimaced at the dampness. 'We're not walking fast or hard enough to feel like this, even with the packs and clothes. Something's wrong.'

'Wonderful,' Melisande wheezed, before she froze, eyes widening at something further down the steps. 'Pull me up, Emri. Now.'

'What?'

'Pull me up – *now*. We need to run!'

I lunged, glancing down the steps as my fingers closed around her arm. The shadows from the lower path had crept closer and now they rolled up towards us, much faster than we'd walked. As I swallowed, the shadows curled and solidified into the shape of wolves: grey and black fur, lolling red tongues and bared fangs, their coal-fire eyes fixed on us.

Wolves.

The wolf was loyal to Lady Winter, as was the raven.

My heart was worthless if I didn't live for her to control me. But there were many other dangers beyond death.

As I locked eyes with one of the wolves, my breath caught, and every nerve inside me screamed.

Melisande burst into a torrent of swearing, jerked from my grip to grab my arm instead, and took off, heat and exhaustion no barrier to her survival instincts.

We raced up the stairs, Melisande cursing at the air almost as much as me. Her height and longer legs meant there were times where I lost my footing and she literally dragged me along, but I didn't care with the snarls and thumping paws behind us growing closer.

It didn't matter that the steps were uneven and unsafe, that the lack of barriers meant we could plummet to death with a single ill-judged turn. Nothing mattered except outrunning the wolves.

If I'd still had a heart, it would have been hammering against my ribs, but even without it, a roar filled my ears, as I struggled to breathe against the panic tightening my throat. I stumbled and jerked and ran, fighting to keep up with Melisande, who never let go of my arm.

We finally reached the top of the steps – I actually hadn't

believed they would end, that we'd run until we finally dropped from exhaustion and the wolves caught us – and raced across into another cavern. Melisande still dragged me along, flinging us desperately around corners and into smaller, narrower corridors, roughly-hewn from rock, closing in around us –

Until we reached a dead end.

For a moment, we stared, stunned, shaking, our lungs heaving.

Melisande stepped forward and slammed her palms against the rock. Once, twice, three times, before a deep scream ripped from her throat.

The dregs of her scream merged into the eerie sound of a howl, too near and coming closer. Fear rippled through me in a hard shudder. As the howl faded, we glanced at each other, then silently turned to face the mouth of the corridor we'd just run down.

But this couldn't be how it ended. Given provisions, something almost like a map, then killed by Lady Winter's own messengers? Not much of a trial or quest. I'd read stories as a child that were longer than this.

A voice, cool and calm – very like Mother's – said, *Think, Emri. Why send wolves after you?*

I took a deep breath, and another, trying to steady myself as growls and thumping paws drew closer. Melisande grabbed my hand, clinging hard enough to hurt.

She doesn't let go, I thought distantly. *Not when it truly matters.*

Why send wolves after us? We hadn't been going fast enough for Lady Winter's liking – perhaps, but I doubted she'd ever actually taken those stairs herself – or the wolves were trying to ferry us in a particular direction.

Towards a dead end.

Apparently.

I glanced over my shoulder at the wall of uneven rock, splayed with patches of moss and glimmering under a sheen of frost. It appeared extremely solid and extremely inaccessible.

Was I meant to believe otherwise? Convince myself otherwise? Have – and my mouth curled in scorn before I've even finished thinking the word – *faith*?

Faith.

What the gods needed from us, nearly more than we needed them. The belief in something that couldn't be proven, nothing tangible or visible. A hope wrapped in a wish, a prayer for aid: forgiveness, assurance.

Hope.

Shadows trailed on the wall leading into our corridor, accompanied by panting and yipping, low, rumbling growls.

Melisande squeezed my hand even harder, but she seemed frozen, whether in fear or disbelief, all bravado and stubbornness and confidence wilting before the approaching wolves.

Faith. Hope.

I had no faith in Lady Winter – unsurprising, considering her solution to my defiance was to take my heart and threaten my family – and no faith in her messengers. I'd been raised with no religion, that gods and magic were nothing more than myths, a story formed as a sensible explanation for the extraordinary deeds of people from too many centuries ago. Even with Lady Winter proven to exist... I couldn't just immediately believe in her, *trust her*, simply because she insisted upon it.

That wasn't how faith worked.

I knew now, without doubt, that she existed, that she was far more – and worse – than a myth, but that wasn't the belief, the devotion, she wanted from me.

But I believed in my parents. In my family. Even in Isra, though she'd probably keel over if she ever found out.

In the first months after my arrival in Edar, I'd known my parents wanted to keep me safe. We didn't love each other then, not yet, but I knew they loved each other, and they wanted to do their best by me. They introduced me to their families and closest friends, who'd unquestioningly accepted me as their daughter and heir.

And as weeks had passed, months, and slowly years, I knew they loved me, not just because I was a solution to a succession crisis, no matter that I was a living reminder of a usurper. I was their daughter, and their heir, and with every kiss, hug, and morning walk, every evening spent together, in countless small gestures and smiles, they told me there wasn't anything they wouldn't do to keep me safe.

Mama had killed to keep Mother safe, to keep them both safe, so they wouldn't have to live in fear anymore.

And deep down, I suspected they'd both do that and more to keep me safe.

I had no faith in a goddess, but I had faith in my parents, and loved them as deeply and fiercely as they loved me. I had faith that a cranky spymaster, disappointed by life but building one of her own choosing, had done her best to knock as much sense into me as possible, even if facing gods was beyond her list of worst scenarios.

If Lady Winter didn't intend for me to die by her wolves, they could still injure us. They could still maim us, and without the right provisions, such wounds wouldn't heal well. Even if it wasn't her intention, the consequences could still kill us.

If I was meant to end up somewhere else than this corridor, then I'd simply have to believe it was possible. For magic to work, it needed faith.

I took a step back, gently tugging at Melisande's hand. When she frowned at me, I tugged harder.

'Emri, what—'

'Trust me.'

Another step, and another, until my back was pressed against the wall. The chill seeped through my jacket, making me shiver, but I forced the discomfort away.

Right before I closed my eyes, the first wolf padded around the corner. Clouds huffed from its nostrils as it regarded us, coal-bright eyes flickering with embers.

'Emri.' There was no mistaking the stark terror choking up Melisande's voice.

'Trust me.'

I took deep breaths again, counted them for lack of a measuring heartbeat, tried to force my mind to stillness. The wall wasn't solid. It had never been solid, my mind merely insisting that it was so. This wasn't a dead end. This was a way through: a portal, a door to where we were supposed to be.

Portal. Door.

Safety.

Now let us through.

An impatient snarl, followed by paws bounding towards us.

Melisande's scream abruptly cut off, as I toppled backward through the wall, pulling her with me.

My grip on her hand never faltered.

Once, there is a goddess.

And she is alone.

She has the snow at her fingertips, ice in her veins, and the bitter wind for a companion.

She is adored and feared by those who worship her, who beg for a boon, some of which she deigns to grant. Her people are hard as frozen earth, as angry as storms that freeze and kill, and she prefers to encourage such strength so they can solve their problems, rather than pray to her for solutions they can achieve themselves.

But they are only mortal; ambition can only take them so far. She may be a cold goddess, but she is not without pity, despite the steep prices she demands for her aid.

She takes a particular interest in those who take up a sword and seek adventure, or the families who send a child into her service, the harsh life of devotion.

And then there is one who despises both.

She does not notice him at first; there are so many, and their prayers drift upon the air like snowflakes in the wind, building into a swirl of want and desperation, fear and desire. But one day, his prayer reaches her simply due to its vehemence: rage, agony amid a curse.

Lady Winter has always had a fondness for the strong-willed. They remind her of someone, though she can no longer remember who.

He is dying.

She appears close by, easing the snowfall with an imperious wave of her hand, so it drifts into a sprinkle. The storm has already covered some of the red-soaked snow around him, but not all. He should already be dead; whoever, or whatever, abandoned him, assuming he would soon die, clearly underestimated him.

A mortal did this, she decides after further consideration. A predator would not leave flesh behind in a storm like this, during a winter that has been one of the bitterest in mortal memory. She has let the weather continue its course: it will be good for the mortals, she feels, and those who do not survive were unsuited to the North. And those who endure will prepare better for the next winter.

She draws closer, letting her clothing drag against the snow, and his eyes flicker open as she pauses above him.

His skin has a chill to it, mottled with blue and purple, and snowflakes cling to his hair, eyelashes, and mouth. He stares at her blankly for several moments, before his gaze abruptly sharpens.

'You,' he hisses. 'I hoped it would be you.'

Intriguing.

She raises an eyebrow. 'I can summon Lady Death, if you wish for a swifter end.'

The threads of his life are tattered and fraying, barely clinging to his soul, so Lady Death will soon arrive, regardless, but few wish for her to witness their death, not even her most faithful priestesses.

'I curse you,' he says, despite his hitched breathing, the shudders wracking his body, the slowing ebb of crimson from his wounds. 'I curse you, for the life my sister should have lived rather than entering your service, for the life I should have had rather than picking up a sword and enacting your justice. For the fear my family felt for your judgment, which lead to these choices for their only children. I curse you.'

The words, though juddering and weak, are heart-strong. He means them, with every scrap of his remaining life. She respects that.

They are also useless.

Lady Winter frowns, and the storm rises again. She has always respected courage, even if it despised the sword or refused to enter service. She has always favoured those who have followed her favoured paths, but she has never required it. Mortals have so many other roles in life. They could not function with only war and prayer. She has never damned a family who hasn't provided a warrior nor a priestess.

So she kneels beside him, as the wind howls and the snowflakes cradle them in ice, and within that spiral, she turns all silent except their voices.

'Service,' she says, 'is a choice, whether with a sword or within a temple. Not a command. If your family made those choices in fear, it is not of my doing.'

But perhaps she has grown lax towards those in the highest ranks of power and devotion. It has been some time since she has given them cause to fear her.

'It does not change the lives we have been forced to live,' the mortal says.

'No,' she agrees. All colour is gone from him now, given up to the blood-soaked snow, and it is beautiful. He is, she supposes, handsome, in the way of mortals, but that is not why she is on her knees beside him as he draws ever closer to death. The sharpness in his gaze, the stubborn refusal to resign himself to the end of a life not of his choosing, the rage that ripples from him like cold fire – she cannot look away.

And it would be useful, all of it, to her.

She trails a hand down his face. As he shudders, whether from the dark talons or something he cannot admit lies within him, she asks, 'What will you give, for your sister to have the life she wishes instead of one shaped for her?'

He does not answer and, for a moment, she fears the last thread of his soul has snapped. Then he raises a trembling hand to grasp just above her elbow, where a branch bursts from her skin and wraps around her upper arm, before merging with the ruff at her shoulders and neck, and his fingers stroke where flesh and bark meet.

Now it is she who shudders, as his grip falls to her wrist, where he turns her taloned hand and kisses the palm.

So it is.

She leans over him, her raven-wing hair shielding him from the bloodied snow, the branches arching above her head defying the wind and ice, and she kisses him.

Her lips deepen the kiss, coaxing the last of his breath, gusting snow and frost down his throat and into his lungs—

He arches, screams into her mouth, and she takes that, too.

He doesn't notice when her claws slice his skin, gentle as a lover's caress, and slip between his ribs. When they close around his heart, splintering ice deep within the muscle, he arches again, shuddering as the last thread of his soul snaps.

Mine, *Lady Winter thinks, for she is immortal and remembered, with the snow at her fingertips, ice in her veins, but no longer with only the bitter wind for a companion.* Mine.

She pulls back as his eyes darken into a soft blue, the deep glow that devours the last gasp of sunset. As stars blossom and burst within his eyes, and the Tree of Life's power, guided by her desire and rage, begins to reshape him, he reaches up to pull her into his first kiss of eternity.

When Lady Death appears in a ripple of shadow, heralded by

the silence of the grave, the mortal man is no more. A god stands beside Lady Winter, newly-born, with blue-dark eyes, wrapped in stars and cloaked with the first shadows of night.

He claims the twilight as his own.

And Lady Winter adores him.

She is not a kind goddess, but something in him answers to her cruelty, a devotion as fierce and brutal as her own. The twilight is his, and the fox and blackbird especially loyal. He offers his protection to spies, those who deal in secrets and stealth, especially those who avert war and battle. Lovers pray to him, for the unity he represents and the sweetness of his smile. And he is merciless to those who over-reach through his Lady's authority.

After the High Priestess, the Queen, and her general all face Lady Winter's displeasure, his sister is released from service. When her death comes, peaceful and many decades later, Twilight manifests as a hidden witness.

She dies, never knowing what became of her brother.

TWENTY-THREE

We thumped against cold ground, hard enough to wind us.

As we lay there, stunned into silence, I finally ground out, 'If Lady Winter wants us to pass her trials, perhaps she should be more concerned about our skulls being bashed open.'

For a long moment, I stared at Melisande's back. At last, she let out a choking snort that turned into a wheeze, before her shoulders started shaking. When she finally managed to turn around, she'd dissolved into heaving gulps of laughter, even though it made her face twist in pain.

'Also – *doors*,' I continued, spurred on by sheer irritation at Melisande's helpless laughter. 'I know it's a mountain, and carving temples out of solid rock takes significant time and energy, but if we can feel all the magic here, *why can't they make proper doorways?*' Now Melisande had a hand over her face, fruitlessly trying to hide that she was crying from laughter. 'You're not helping! Do you *like* falling through walls?'

'Oh yes,' Melisande finally managed through tears and actual *giggles*, which she was surely too old for. 'This is precisely what my spine needed.' She tried to sit up, let out a strangled cry, and sank back down. 'Just… give me a moment.'

'As if I can get up,' I said.

'I could… uh… help?'

It was miraculous, what your body could do when you realised you weren't alone. Within moments, we'd scrambled to our knees, Melisande trying to yank me behind her. My back screamed, but my survival instincts were screaming harder, and I trusted them more.

A man crouched near us, his hands held out in a calming motion, which would have been more reassuring if he wasn't holding a dagger.

'I'm not going to hurt you. See, I'm putting this down.' While his posture screamed *I'm not a threat*, the man held eye contact as he placed the dagger on the ground, then nudged it away from him. His voice was deep and measured, an Othayrian accent tinged with a southern lilt.

I wracked my brain, trying to figure out how it sounded so familiar, when it abruptly came to me: he sounded like Prince Aubrey, once of Othayria. Even after so many years in Edar, he'd never fully lost his accent, and he sounded like no one else I knew. Everyone had expected Mother to marry him. She had not, obviously, though they still remained friends. Mama tolerated him mostly because she liked Lady Astrii, his wife.

The man was younger than I'd assumed from his voice, likely close to Melisande's age. If my parents were here now, they'd perhaps mistake him for a younger version of Prince Aubrey, though his black hair was cropped shorter, most of his curls falling over his forehead in a tangled swoop. His eyes were larger than Prince Aubrey's, his nose a little bigger, and he sported an untidy beard, but the family resemblance was unmistakeable.

This was Prince Aubrey's nephew: Prince Theobilt of Othayria. And, if my parents managed to finally hammer out an agreement with the Othayrian royal family, my eventual husband.

I gulped.

Melisande's gaze darted between us, but when I remained silent, she asked, 'Who are you?'

Tension eased in his shoulders at her firmness, and he replied, 'I am Prince Theobilt of Othayria. A pleasure to meet you, though I wish it were under better circumstances.' He glanced at me, swallowed, then added, 'Princess Emri.'

I finally managed to pull myself together, and said, 'Your Highness. This is my cousin, Princess Melisande of Farezi.' When in doubt, always retreat to etiquette.

He bowed, which felt ludicrous under the circumstances. We were all royal, but his older sister was the heir, while Melisande and I were both set to inherit our parents' thrones. We were of equal rank, but also not, and since we were technically in Farezi, Melisande had the highest standing between us.

But considering Aren's polite goading, not to mention the immortal, furious presence of Lady Winter, who bowed to no mortal, I suspected protocol wouldn't help any of us much.

'Prince Theobilt, forgive me for my bluntness, but what are you doing here?' Melisande asked.

'We could ask the same of you,' another voice said, and a young woman stepped out from behind him. She scowled at the dagger on the ground, before stooping to pick it up. The young woman glanced at me as she straightened, and I stepped back, startled.

She was near my age; about two years younger, last I'd heard. A little shorter than Isra, she had the same warm brown skin and arched eyebrows pulled into a frown. Her dark eyes were thickly lashed, her mouth firm, and the jut of her pointed chin implied she was in no mood for an argument. Her hair was pulled back into a messy braid, a few small, escaped curls framing her face.

Princess Gabriela: Isra's eldest niece, and the second in line to the Eshvoni throne.

Never mind my parents destroying Melisande if she abandoned me here. If I let her niece perish in this mountain, Isra would do the same to me.

'Princess Gabriela.' I kept my voice soft and respectful. 'Your aunt, Princess Isra, speaks highly of you.'

Something fractured across her face as her mouth tightened. 'Do not speak of *her*,' she spat. 'I have little regard for traitors.' Her sweeping gaze indicated she included Melisande and me, with our shared, murky family history, in that same sentence.

Melisande and I spoke of Rassa in much the same way.

'Gabi,' Prince Theobilt said. 'That is no way to address your peers, particularly in regard to family.' If I'd known him better, I'd have thought there was a mild rebuke within his words, but his tone was otherwise careful, a young man gauging three future Queens and making a snap decision on how to prevent an argument erupting between us.

Perhaps this was how he'd grown up with two older sisters, one the heir and the other intended as her right hand. Or this was how he'd been raised with a royal marriage in mind, trained so he could one day *manage* me, so polite and deferential that I wouldn't realise until it was too late.

Though he used a nickname for the Eshvoni princess, and she didn't seem likely to allow that from someone she didn't respect. Melisande eyed him thoughtfully.

'So,' Princess Gabriela said, 'are you going to answer the question? What are you doing here?'

She sounded so like Isra, only younger, that my shoulders stiffened to attention from sheer instinct.

'We asked first, *Your Highness*,' Melisande replied, 'and with a great deal more courtesy. And since this temple is in *my* country, I should reconsider my tone, if I were you.'

She'd treated Aren with this exact same kind of irritated abrasion, though Melisande had reason for it this time. Princess Gabriela flung a pointed look at me, her contemptuous expression saying a great deal more than any insult: that I, technically, was also an imposter, being the Edaran heir while also very assuredly cut out of the Farezi succession.

If she'd expected her contempt to make me shrink, she would be sorely disappointed. She was part of an old, beloved royal line, set to rule one day, yet she was plain *rude*. Mother would have been secretly appalled, while publicly responding with cool authority, while Mama would have remarked upon the merits of courtiers who hid their steel within silk and velvet.

It absolutely did not matter that she reminded me of Rialla. Or that, more than once, I'd wished for the freedom, and security of self and reputation, to speak like that.

More importantly: if she was going to insult me – or Melisande – she'd address us properly while doing so.

Before I could speak, Melisande stepped forward and said, in a voice that Lady Winter would surely admire, 'I am Princess Melisande, heir to Queen Sabine II of Farezi. This is my cousin, Princess Emri, heir to Their Majesties, Queen Aurelia IV and Queen Xania of Edar, and linked by blood and birth to the Farezi blood royal. And if need be, Your Highness, we will treat you with the precise courtesy you deserve.'

As I searched for the right words to de-escalate this, Prince Theobilt snapped, '*Gabi*,' in a tone that made everyone freeze. He bowed deeply to us, and yanked Princess Gabriela's arm for her to follow suit. 'Please forgive my cousin, Your Royal Highnesses. It's been several weeks since we were wrenched from our homes without warning, through… through…'

'Magic?' I supplied softly, and his gaze snapped up to meet mine.

'Yes,' he said, equally soft, his voice flooding with relief, as if deep down he had feared this situation – this mountain, this kidnapping – to be the construct of an unsteady mind. But I had voiced his other secret fear – that they'd been brought here by magic, trapped within a mountain temple brimming with cold, brutal power – so either my mind was equally unsteady, or this was the truth of a different unpleasant reality. 'We were brought here through shadows, moving in ways they could not – should not – move.'

'Shadows with glowing eyes?' Melisande asked, her mouth twisting in a brittle smile when he nodded.

'As such,' he continued, with admirable calm, 'this is the sort of situation that has significantly dented our good manners. We beseech your forgiveness and beg for a fresh introduction.' He dug an elbow into Princess Gabriela's side, forcing her to let out a grunt that could be taken, with some grace, as reluctant agreement.

After a long moment, Melisande said, clearly impressed, 'Othayria *does* raise their sons well.'

I couldn't stop an aggrieved sigh, which had the unintended consequence of making Princess Gabriela snort while trying not to smile.

The tension in the cavern immediately evaporated.

'You've been here *several weeks*?' I said, unable to hide my dismay. We'd only been here a few hours, and I was already close to simply letting out an endless scream at Lady Winter the next time we crossed paths.

'Regrettably,' Prince Theobilt said, less formal now. My initial shock overcome, I now realised how exhausted he and Princess Gabriela looked. His brown skin had an ashen tinge, and they both looked filthy and bruised, something shared with Melisande and me. Quite possibly they were also in desperate need of doorways rather than being tossed through shadows and walls.

'Come,' Princess Gabriela said, looking as if even this show of courtesy cost her a great deal. 'We have a fire in the next room. If we're about to start explanations, I'd prefer to be sitting down.'

We followed them through to a smaller cavern, with a smaller entrance in the opposite wall, so we weren't trapped if something – or someone – happened upon us.

A small dais took up most of the room, encompassing a little hollow filled with a crackling fire and enough space that we could safely sleep around it. The fire wasn't large enough to fully banish the mountain's chill, but I let out a relieved shudder at the warmth, a more welcome heat than the one that had overtaken Melisande and me before the wolves had surged from the shadows. Until now, I hadn't realised how *cold* the temple was.

Prince Theobilt shot me a sympathetic look. 'It takes a few

days to adjust.'

'Or some of us simply refuse to,' Princess Gabriela said, huddled resentfully in her quilted jacket.

Melisande and I opened our packs to inspect our food rations and compare resources. Princess Gabriela had balanced a large, flat-headed rock close to the fire, warming thin slices of bread upon it. She cast a knowing eye over our stores, pointing out what would last longer, if we were careful, and what would help when we were particularly exhausted and cold, and needed both comfort and nourishment. Melisande looked disappointed at the amount of dried meat and pulses.

Prince Theobilt chimed in: they had passed a river a few days back and filled up their extra flasks. The water was so cold, it hurt their teeth, but it hadn't made them ill. Of us all, he was the only one who had any small experience with mountains, though the Edaran and Farezi ranges were far superior in number and height. The air sickness would hit us, he cautioned, and when it did, we would need to drink to help it pass until we grew accustomed.

Brisk and grimly pragmatic, neither sounded as if they'd been trapped here for only a few weeks. It made my stomach squirm, though I did my best to ignore it.

They had not been at a ball when the shadows came for them. Princess Gabriela had been out riding with her ladies, and Prince Theobilt had been at an aunt's estate, spending time with his cousins before they all returned to Court for the Harvest Festival.

I jerked at that, while Melisande paused with a slice of bread near her mouth. We glanced at each other, barely a flicker, but Princess Gabriela noticed.

'What?' she demanded.

'You've only been here a few weeks, you said?' I began cautiously.

'Yes,' she replied impatiently, 'less than a month.'

Prince Theobilt had gone still, watching us with firelight trembling in his dark eyes.

'Tonight was Midwinter in Edar,' Melisande said, unable or unwilling to soften the blow. 'The Harvest Festival was months ago.'

I thought back to my birthday, then my debut at the Harvest banquet, the last celebrations before Melisande's arrival. Autumn felt like a lifetime ago, before I'd learned the truth of Mama's actions and the far-ranging consequences of Arisane's brutal decisions so many years before. That memory of me already felt like a child.

Princess Gabriela scoffed, but uncertainty bloomed across her face at our silence. Prince Theobilt remained still, save for the firelight moving across his dark brown skin, until he finally said, 'Tonight was Midwinter?'

I nodded. 'We were at my parents' celebration. We stepped out onto a terrace... and the shadows... well.' I didn't speak of Florette, and the strange cadence of her voice, the green glow of her eyes. No point in trying to explain things I didn't understand.

Princess Gabriela took an unsteady breath, before jamming a knuckle into her mouth. She appeared close to tears, and I understood exactly how she felt.

'Then we've been here *months*, while it's felt like only a handful of weeks.'

Enough time for them to develop a slow confidence in themselves as the days passed and they continued to survive, to become more familiar with the temple's maze of paths and corridors, its strangeness. Until our arrival, and the horrific truth we'd brought with us: they'd been gone for months, and their families had no idea where they were or if they were alive, nor – most likely – who had taken them.

They certainly wouldn't have expected them to be kidnapped to a mountain temple in Farezi still loyal to the Edaran patron goddess.

Princess Gabriela had begun to shake. As she clapped her hands over her mouth, Prince Theobilt leaned over and pulled her into a hug. As he coaxed her to take deep breaths, I was aware that Princess Gabriela was the youngest of us here, and keenly aware of how desperately I wanted my parents.

Melisande reached over and squeezed my hand. Perhaps she also wanted someone here who could hug her and tell her what to do.

Trying to hold firm to the last of my calm, I thought back to

Isra's warning before the Midwinter Ball, only hours ago, though it felt like days. The Othayrian and Eshvoni heirs had been watched since the equinox, amid increasing religious tension. She'd been right to be sceptical of the information, but not for the reasons I'd assumed. Prince Theobilt and Princess Gabriela hadn't survived assassination attempts: they'd already been captured at the equinox.

It wasn't surprising that the news had been muddied with false rumours for spies. It was the kind of information that sowed chaos and destabilised countries.

'When you woke up here,' Melisande said, far gentler than I'd expected, 'who greeted you?'

'An acolyte,' Prince Theobilt said. 'I can't remember her name, but she and Gabi irritated each other.'

'Ah,' Melisande said. 'Probably the same one who greeted me when I woke up, then. Were you also offered a challenge, like Emri?'

Uneasiness swirled in my stomach, precluding a swoop of fear and the scorch of ice in my chest.

Lady Winter hadn't manifested in front of any of them – only me.

Here were the mortals referenced in Lady Winter's bargain, since the priestesses and acolytes, like Aren, wouldn't have any intention of leaving the temple. And to win the bargain by escaping the mountain, I'd have to get us all to work together.

Simple, I thought wearily. Herding cats was probably easier than convincing royal heirs to trust each other above duty to our countries.

'No, not a challenge,' he said to Melisande, 'but I presume you were told the same as us. That our gods have no power here.' His gaze shifted to me, and I swallowed. 'And if Princess Emri doesn't lead us out of the mountain before the last full moon of winter… we die, and our sacrifice will free Lady Winter and her companions from the mountain.'

TWENTY-FOUR

Melisande raised her eyebrows. 'Die? I wasn't told that.'

Prince Theobilt's dark eyes never left mine. 'Because of the bargain she made with Lady Winter. To win, we must work together to get out of here. If we don't, we die. Except for Princess Emri, of course.'

'Of course,' Melisande said, so calmly that I knew she would implode the moment her mind caught up with her emotions. 'And why, precisely, is Emri exempt from an untimely death?'

'Because there are worse things than death,' I said bitterly, before I could think better of it. 'If you all don't get out of here but I do, or if we all fail, then my family will be little more than puppet rulers for Lady Winter. I'll wear the crown, but be her mouthpiece. My hand will carry out only her wishes.'

Rage rose within me, struggled against the hoarfrost in my chest. No ruler was perfect, but monarchs were driven by mortal concerns. Lady Winter despised us, and I had little hope that my family being conduits for her hatred would bode well for Edar.

When Melisande's gaze cut to me, I added, 'I wasn't told that anyone would die through my failure,' though it now seemed terribly obvious. They were all bound to other gods, useful to Lady

Winter only as leverage against my conscience. Would I have accepted the bargain if Lady Winter had told me? I couldn't say for certain.

I wasn't really certain of anything about myself anymore, except that I was a princess, not a martyr.

Maybe that's why she had to take your heart, a clipped voice said in my mind, which I viciously ignored.

'I wasn't told any of you would die,' I repeated softly. 'Only that you all had to escape with me.'

'That was stupid of you,' Princess Gabriela said. 'What use would Edar's patron goddess have for us if we remained trapped here?'

Clever, and a brutally pragmatic observation. Isra would be proud of her. I filed it away: Princess Gabriela was annoyed and understandably so, but she wasn't to be underestimated.

'What, you think your gods are still doomed to myth when Edar's has returned?' I countered. 'You think they will take kindly to Lady Winter slaughtering heirs of royal families from whom they expect devotion?'

'I'm not sure I'm the sort of heir La Dame des Fleurs would expect,' Melisande muttered, low enough that I was really the only one intended to hear, but Prince Theobilt glanced away, his mouth twitching.

'Of the entire continent, Edar is the one who fully abandoned religion,' I continued, 'and yet here our gods are, steadily growing in strength. Farezi, Eshvon, and Othayria all kept a stronger faith. Of course yours will return, if they haven't already.' Which begged the question: if the other gods had returned due to stronger faith, where were they and why did no one know about it?

'This is probably what Lady Winter wants,' Melisande remarked. 'Us arguing and blaming each other. It'll make it harder to escape if we can't work together.'

'Princess Melisande is right,' Prince Theobilt said, looking relieved that someone was trying to be reasonable. 'We need to work together and trust each other.'

The doubt in the ensuing silence was thick enough to cut.

'Well,' Melisande finally said, 'the three of us will all be Queens, eventually. And you,' she added at Prince Theobilt, 'will be...' She waved a hand between us, implying our eventual union.

'Married,' I said flatly.

'So we'd all have to trust each other sooner or later,' Melisande continued, her reasonable tone actually bordering on earnestness. 'Otherwise, well, international diplomacy—'

'Would go right back to how it was under your grandparents,' Princess Gabriela said coldly.

Melisande's left eye twitched, but before she could speak, I added, 'It wasn't much improved by the old Edaran King, either.'

'Yes, both your birth *and* adopted heritage are quite inglorious,' Princess Gabriela said, her eyes narrowing when I snapped back, 'As opposed to *your* grandmother's unyielding nature?'

Princess Gabriela's mouth curled in a rising temper, but Theobilt snapped, '*Enough.*' We all flinched except for Melisande, who remained seething.

'Future Queens or not,' he said, breathing hard, seemingly appalled both by our squabbling and his shouting, 'none of your families would stand for this sort of behaviour. Nor would any etiquette tutor, I imagine. We all need to finish eating and *sleep*. Then everything will be easier to deal with.'

'Do we need to stay up in shifts overnight?' Melisande said. 'Well, I'm assuming it's night, but it's hard to tell in here.'

Princess Gabriela shook her head, though she didn't hide her sullen tone. 'Nothing has ever come for us, but we've always slept with a fire. It gets cold.'

'Sensible,' Melisande agreed.

We finished our food in silence, then spread out our bedrolls. I chewed a small stick – the best I could do for cleaning my teeth – and wished vainly for some mint, and tried not to focus on Prince Theobilt as he double-checked the fire. I wanted to ask what he feared might happen if the flames died out overnight, but it already seemed better not to voice such things aloud here – better not to even think of them. He seemed just as reluctant to look at or speak to me; once he was done, he pulled his bedroll around him and turned his back to the fire.

I stared up at the ceiling shrouded in darkness. The fire wasn't enough to penetrate it, so there was no way to tell how high up the chamber stretched. My thoughts raced, my mind having decided it was the perfect time to overthink now that I was trying to sleep.

So I was responsible for them all. A nice sting in Lady Winter's bargain. Of course she had no need for them to remain alive if they didn't escape the mountain with me. Lady Winter had a grudging respect for her opposing force, Aestia, the Eshvoni goddess of summer, and tolerated Hatar, the Othayrian god of autumn. He was the peacemaker between all the highest gods, and oft-times Consort of Aestia. Together, they ensured bountiful harvests so mortals had a better chance of surviving the bitter winters. But Lady Winter's tolerance likely didn't stretch into caring about the consequences of Princess Gabriela and Prince Theobilt dying in one of her temples, or how Aestia and Hatar would react to their deaths.

La Dame des Fleurs... that was another matter. I couldn't say it in front of the others, but I suspected there was a reason why Melisande hadn't been warned that her life depended on my getting her out of the mountain. Lady Winter's loathing of the Farezi goddess, a merry trickster to her stern nature, ran deep in every story about them, and Melisande being trapped within one of Lady Winter's oldest temples, possibly forever, would infuriate La Dame des Fleurs.

To the gods, there were always worse things than death.

Lady Winter had known this, when she'd curled her fingers around my heart. If she wanted to destroy Melisande, and send

La Dame des Fleurs into a rage, the sort that would set Edar and Farezi against each other, trapping Melisande here while I escaped would be an ideal solution.

Melisande kept insisting she'd face dire consequences if she escaped the temple without me, but if the situation were reversed, the same was true for me.

And there was a greater question, one that concerned the entire continent: how were we to live with free gods? How *could* we live alongside them, if this was what they were like? Lady Winter and La Dame des Fleurs had a long history of goading each other: what would that mean for all the diplomatic work my parents and Queen Sabine had done over the years? If our patron gods got into a spat, were we to automatically take sides? Would we be obliged to do so whenever gods valued their squabbles above mortal concerns?

My breathing had sped up until it hurt. I pressed my hands over my eyes and forced myself to take slower breaths, fighting every anxious thought that tried to disrupt my breathing pattern. When my skin no longer felt taut over my bones, I lowered my hands and swallowed hard. There was no point in indulging these thoughts. Everything always felt worse at night, and that was normally in the safety of my own room, with my parents and the palace guards nearby. Nothing could feel all right when I was trapped far from home, at the mercy of a goddess's bitter whims and her loyal followers.

I closed my eyes, continuing to breathe deeply until I was lulled towards sleep. On the brink of slipping into unconsciousness, my mind threw me one last barb:

Instead of warning me the others would die if they didn't escape the mountain with me, maybe Lady Winter had taken my heart because I might not have accepted the bargain to save others beyond my parents, but I would to save myself.

Emri opens her eyes to dusk.

The sky stretches above her, sunset gently fading into twilight. The deep soft blue is a balm, and she lets out a long sigh, following the splashes of orange, yellow, red, and pink as they flee west before the encroaching blues and purple. The clouds drift lazily upon a faint breeze, content to soon be hidden by nightfall.

She lies upon her back on the hard, cold ground. She cannot bring herself to move. If she lies here, and does not move as the day slowly dies, she will be safe. She is alone and here, so close to the beautiful sky, nothing can hurt her.

'Nothing is truly safe.'

The voice is low and deep, ringing with a musical lilt that sounds familiar and yet not.

Emri slowly sits up.

'Forgive me. My Lady does not permit unnecessary kindness even in circumstances such as these.'

Emri looks to her left. A man sits close by, robed in purple and deep blue slashed with black, gripping an immensely tall staff. He meets her gaze and… it is not a man.

A god.

Unlike Lady Winter, whose eyes hold tumbling stars that die and return, over and over, his blaze with the light of a single star, the Evening Star, in place of a mortal's pupil and colour. At first he seems to glow like Lady Winter, but shadows flicker across his skin, similar to clouds tumbling across a full moon.

But where terror rose within her at the sight of Lady Winter, this god envelopes her in a gentle calm. Emri should be afraid, but she can't find it within herself to be… or the god simply does not wish her to be.

'Hello, Lord Twilight,' she says, twitching with the need to bow, though she can't find the strength to stand.

But he shakes his head. 'Only my Lady holds a title. Though I appreciate the gesture, little one.' His voice is soft, but threaded with a firm conviction, and she suddenly realises his lips are blue, the deep shade of twilight. His hair is dark and loosely curled.

'This isn't real,' she says. 'This is a dream.'

'The mountain is real, as is this,' Twilight says, glancing at the sky, 'though we are not strictly here at this precise moment. But my time is short before nightfall.'

Unwilling to meet Twilight's gaze, she looks out towards the horizon instead. The sight drives her up in a sudden burst of strength to stagger towards the edge.

She does not worry about falling, for this is a dream.

She and Twilight stand upon a plateau jutting from the higher reaches of the mountain, surrounded by smaller peaks draped in snow. Emri can make out the ladders linking them, and staircases hewn from the rock itself. They're made tiny by distance, and it should frighten her that she can see everything clearly from so far away, but it does not.

She twists her head to peer up towards the mountain top, but the darkening sky hides it. Behind her, a carved doorway reveals only shadow.

On the mountain, with the endless sky overhead and the calmness in her bones despite the deepening chill, Emri feels, just for a moment, that it will be all right.

'It's beautiful,' she says, and she means it. 'I never thought it would look like this.'

'It is beautiful,' Twilight agrees, 'for a prison.'

The calm briefly fractures.

'My Lady's nature means that she is often harsh when she should be gentle,' Twilight answers. He has not moved from the ground, but even sitting, his frame reveals that he would tower above her, only a little shorter than his staff. 'That is my role, to soothe and encourage those she has chosen for a greater purpose.'

'*She stole my heart.*' The words burst out of her, almost a snarl, her mind scrambling to catch up with her voice. 'There is nothing you can say or do to soothe *that*.'

'Yes, she has your heart,' Twilight says, as calmly as if they were discussing the weather. 'But you can retrieve it. Others have – and succeeded.'

Which means there are likely many who have failed.

'All of their lives depend on me.'

She sucks in a deep breath of cold air that mingles with the frost in her chest, trying to recapture that dissipating sense of calm. 'I don't know what to do,' she finally admits. 'I don't know how to survive this.'

She needs to have faith, Aren has implied as much. But Lady

Winter has given her little to be faithful about, and Emri suspects that her faith in herself will soon run dry.

'I cannot teach you faith,' Twilight says, standing in a fluid motion between one blink to the next, 'but we are here in your dream for a reason. When you stare out at the mountains of our domain and think of the land that stretches south, when you peer up at the sky as daylight succumbs to dusk and then to night... consider how you feel. Consider your insignificance against all that surrounds you, how it has endured beyond the span of countless mortal lives. That is not faith... but it is a start.'

Emri's legs shake, as her mind grapples with irrefutable proof that he can read her thoughts.

'You were thinking very loudly,' he informs her.

He comes to stand beside her; she doesn't even reach his chest. His robes ripple, the streaks of black seeping into the purples and blues, as the shadows flicker across his pale face and her mind revolts against his blue-drowned mouth.

She stares up at him, and repeats, 'Why are you being kind to me?'

His staff disappears. She blinks, and he has cradled her face in his hands. Unlike Lady Winter, it doesn't hurt to look at him, but his divinity is nonetheless unsettling, pricking uncomfortably at her.

'I am kind,' he says, 'because there will be times when I will not be. I am kind because, nevertheless, I want you to remember this moment when I was.'

He leans down and kisses her forehead, like a father. Like the father she should have had, and did not, who would never have been kind to her anyway. He kisses her forehead like Lady Liliene feared to, like Arisane could never bring herself to.

He kisses her on the forehead like Mother and Mama used to, when she was younger.

'Xania Bayonn may not know me,' Twilight says, and too late Emri remembers that he has always favoured spies and their masters, 'but I remember her. And I will be kind to her child.'

With a sweet smile and a gentle shove, he pushes her off the mountain and sends her hurtling awake.

TWENTY-FIVE

I jerked awake, panting. For a moment, I couldn't move, frozen by the memory of plummeting off the mountain. In the dream, there had been hardly any breeze, but the drop had been so swift and sudden, the frozen chill still gripped me.

At last my breathing slowed, and I reminded myself that it was just a dream. I hadn't really been on the mountain top with Twilight – he'd admitted as much – and he hadn't really pushed me off. The gods did this kind of thing in visions to unsettle and hinder those they'd chosen for their quests. You couldn't be a hero if you hadn't earned it.

Except I didn't really want to be a hero. One day, I would be a Queen, and that would be difficult enough.

I sat up, rubbing my eyes, and caught movement at the fire. Prince Theobilt was also awake, hunched over something in his lap. I shifted, disturbing the grit under my bedroll, and he glanced over at me.

'Couldn't sleep either?' he whispered, sounding friendly enough despite being disturbed. 'The first few days are the worst. But nothing short of an attack or the ground disappearing under us could wake Gabi now.'

I hesitated, then crawled out of my bedroll to come sit near him. If we'd met under more normal circumstances, like his arriving on the back of a marriage treaty, no doubt he would be immaculate and pristine, though he was still trying to behave at his best under the circumstances. He didn't look precisely *terrible*, and I was under no illusions that I looked my best, either, but he'd probably hoped to, well, not look like he desperately needed a hairbrush and a bath.

Both of us sank into an uneasy silence, before I glanced at what lay on his lap. 'Oh!' I said, hurriedly softening the word mid-syllable. 'We have one of those! Is it a map? Can you decipher it?'

He shook his head. 'No, it seems... nonsense, really. I also assumed it was a map, but perhaps in a much... *much* older style.'

I leaned forward to touch the parchment. 'It's thinner than ours. Odd.' I stared at it, so hard I could feel the line between my eyebrows, then murmured, 'I wonder... hold on.' I scrambled back to my pack, eased out the parchment – indecipherable or not, I suspected it was old enough that scholars would scream if I accidentally damaged it – and returned. 'Maybe if we...' I rolled out the map, then urged him to lay his on top. The two slotted together, but only seemed to make a denser pattern of spirals and thick lines. 'Oh,' I said, disappointed.

But Prince Theobilt, now frowning hard, turned his intense stare towards the fire. 'Perhaps...' Still frowning, he stoked it into a stronger flame as quietly as possible, then held the two sets of parchment carefully together against the light.

For a moment, as we hardly dared breathe, nothing happened. Then light flared against the parchment, and it *changed*.

A fainter ink appeared, darting between the spirals and lines, intertwining and linking them all together. A neat elaborate script bled onto the edges, flowing beside some of the lines and blooming within the spirals. Prince Theobilt's hands shook, but he didn't drop the parchment – a good thing, since it would have landed in the fire and instantly gone up in flames.

When it finally stopped, we waited a moment, still not speaking, before he lowered the parchment.

The two sheets had joined together, as if melded by the heat, and we now stared at something much closer to what was, perhaps, a map.

I touched it gingerly. 'Do you think it's a map just of the temple, or the entire mountain?'

'I don't know,' he said, suddenly pensive. 'If it even is a map. I know we'll have more time to compare experiences over the next few days—'

My stomach swooped at the idea of being trapped here for that long, but he and Princess Gabriela had been here for *months*, and Melisande and I weren't exactly that special–

Except you are, that cool voice muttered at the back of my mind. *You are Lady Winer's Chosen, and she took your heart to prove it. By her decision, their lives are* your *responsibility.*

'–but the temple has changed around Gabi and me,' Prince Theobilt continued, unaware of the dark turn of my thoughts, 'so it wouldn't surprise me if this changes alongside it.'

'We were chased,' I mused, 'by shadow wolves. I had to convince myself that a dead end wasn't solid and pull Melisande through the wall to escape them. Though… though now I think we weren't exactly chased so much as ferried here, so we could meet you and Princess Gabriela.'

Ferried to a wall I had to convince myself wasn't real, so I could have faith – limited faith, but still – in myself, if it wasn't possible to have faith in Lady Winter and her companions. But what had Twilight's dream visit been, but a chance for him to implore me to have faith in him and to remember his kindness when he later had to be cruel?

Gods were complicated when they weren't being capricious. No wonder Edar had done away with religion. Life was much simpler without them.

Prince Theobilt didn't seem as sceptical of my suggestion as I'd expected, his thoughtful expression returning. 'Well, we wouldn't have this… I suppose it *is* a map… if you hadn't come crashing from thin air.'

'We fell through a wall. Details are important, Prince Theobilt,' I said, mimicking my most stuffy tutor, whom I now missed terribly. The days when I dreaded a full morning session with him now seemed quaint.

'Theo,' he corrected. 'Considering our present situation, titles and honorifics are hardly necessary. But if Theo is far too presumptuous, then you may call me Theobilt, though I'm only called such in public, or when I'm in trouble, or by my least favourite aunt.'

'You seem far too sensible to ever be in trouble,' I said, trying to hide how flustered his intimate, yet kind gesture had made me.

'You'd be surprised,' he said dryly.

'Then… then you must call me Emri,' I replied, inwardly a little satisfied at how he flushed. 'Though I can't speak for Melisande allowing the same, and forgive me if I suspect Princess Gabriela won't be so eager to share your kindness.'

'Your sudden appearance frightened Gabi,' he said frankly, 'though she'll never admit it. And she was already frightened – and angry – with good reason. Despite our… our…'

He gestured awkwardly between us, and I supplied: 'Our potential future marriage?'

'Yes. Ignoring that for a moment, neither Gabi nor myself should be involved in a spat between Edar and its gods,' he said, unwittingly echoing what I'd turned over in my mind while trying to sleep. 'Princess Melisande, I somewhat understand, considering you're cousins, along with the animosity between your patron gods—'

Yes, Lady Winter could never take a joke, I thought viciously, gritting my teeth at a burst of ice in my chest, unconnected to my present motions.

'–but we have nothing to do with this. And I can't say our gods, whether or not they're in a similar fluctuating state as Lady Winter and her companions, will be best pleased if they find out about this. It's unseemly to be another god's bargaining chip.' His assertive, almost annoyed tone spoke of one who had not faced Lady Winter, nor spoken to Twilight in a dream and then been pushed off a mountain.

'Spoken as someone who's only met the acolytes in this temple,' I said, unable to hide the bleakness in my voice. 'That you and Princess Gabriela are involved *is* unfair, and I dread how your gods will react, but this would only be a passing concern if you'd faced Lady Winter when you woke up here, instead of one of her followers.'

He was quiet for several moments, then asked, 'How terrible was it? Hatar is a kind god, as they go, but… you have no faith, don't hold to any religion.'

I closed my eyes, but the memory rose unbidden: being in that frozen room, staring at a Tree of Life rippling in a stained-glass window, my heart thumping as footsteps and dragging skirts came closer and closer. My heart, before I'd lost it.

I opened my eyes again and finally said, 'I can't explain the truth of her.'

A long silence.

'On a better note,' Theobilt finally said, a smile curling his mouth as he gestured at the map, 'we figured this out. Together.'

After a moment, I returned his smile. 'Yes. We did.'

'Figured out what?'

We both jumped as Melisande spoke, a yawn thickening her words. She sat up in her bedroll, rubbing her eyes as she fought another yawn.

Theobilt held up the parchment. 'Our parchments turned out to be parts of a whole. It still doesn't make complete sense, but a bit more than it previously did.'

Melisande brightened. 'How did you manage that?'

'The fire,' I said, and shrugged when confusion flooded her face. 'More magic, I think.'

'Wonderful,' Melisande said, flopping back into her bedroll and yelping when she made contact with the cold, hard ground. 'How are we to succeed if we keep approaching a magic-infused temple with logic?'

'A good question,' Princess Gabriela said from her own bedroll. 'Possibly the smartest thing Her Highness has said since we met.' Melisande glared at her, which she ignored.

There was nothing for it but to get up and eat before moving on, though I suspected none of us had benefited from a restful sleep, and that it was actually still dark outside. But day and night didn't seem to matter much in the temple.

If we were lucky, Theobilt explained, as we chewed on cold bread and dried meat, we'd stumble across a proper waypoint again, where we could boil water for tea and a hot meal and wash up a bit better. They'd found one about a week after their arrival, close to a small river within the temple, so they'd managed to gather more rations, wash their hair and spare clothing, and then had a swift, frigid dunk in the river. Regretfully, they hadn't had room to bring the kettle or other larger cooking implements with them.

Melisande and Princess Gabriela studied the parchment in turns as we tidied up, scrubbing our faces and swishing our mouths with water from the skins. We'd been warned not to overindulge, as Theobilt and Princess Gabriela had often gone days without coming across a fresh water source. Along with the river, there were occasional springs where they found extra skins, could refill theirs, and generally rest a moment before moving on.

'I think this part of the mountain was once a pilgrim route,' Princess Gabriela said, frowning as she absently traced the spirals and circles on the map, trying to decipher them. 'From before your gods were trapped here and magic warped everything. People likely travelled here, maybe in late autumn when Hatar's influence was waning and Lady Winter's was growing towards the peak of her season. They'd arrive, then follow a route within the temple: there's probably an ancient shrine here somewhere to Lady Winter and her companions, where they'd pray and make offerings.'

'What would you pray to Lady Winter for?' I muttered. I'd

intended to keep it low so no one else would hear, my tone fuelled by my less-than-charitable feelings for the goddess, but Princess Gabriela answered anyway, deeply unimpressed.

'A less lethal winter? For friends and families to survive it? If the winter is harsh, for livestock not to be killed by predators? For her storms and floods to be a little kinder?' She frowned at me, baffled. 'For someone with a winter patron goddess, you seem to accept that your terrible winters just… *are*.'

'Edarans probably accepted harsh winters for a long time,' Theobilt pointed out reasonably, 'feeling that Lady Winter considered them a test for her faithful.' He glanced up at the shadowy ceiling, thinking, then said, 'Even so, your winters have been particularly harsh for the last forty years or so, yes, especially in Northern Edar?'

It took me a moment to realise he was speaking to me. 'Oh. Yes.'

'Interesting,' Theobilt remarked. 'The change happened just before Queen Aurelia was born.'

I stared at him for a long moment, then finally managed: 'Are you saying my *mother* is the reason Lady Winter has grown in strength, even trapped here, and made our winters worse?'

'No,' Theobilt said, appearing to be thinking very hard, 'but apart from the first Sionbourne King, she was the one who spent the most time in the North and had the strongest ties, where Lady Winter was always most powerful. Maybe that was the link she needed: Queen Aurelia's love for Northern Edar. When he took the throne, the first King never returned to the North because he had to consolidate and strengthen his power, and he married his brother off to Farezi soon after' – he glanced at Melisande, who shrugged – 'and later Kings didn't spend much time up North, either, preferring Court life. And even if Lady Winter didn't intend to trap your mother here, every choice Queen Aurelia made has led to… well, *you*, Emri.'

I almost didn't catch his use of my name, thinking too hard on his academic conjecture. It made sense: since House Sionbourne had become royal, Mother was considered the first monarch to have properly returned to her roots, before she took the throne anyway. But even now, she was still kept informed of Northern concerns and how the nobles felt about her rule, far more than any of her ancestors had since the first Sionbourne King.

But I didn't like the idea that her deep love for the North had been an indirect force at play for Lady Winter, that Mother had been unconsciously shaped into choices that had her refusing to carry a child and adopt me instead; everything leading to my being trapped in a temple with a vindictive goddess who'd stolen my heart as the price of a challenge.

And yet that was the problem with gods now being involved. We'd never know for certain, not unless Lady Winter or the others confirmed it. We'd never know if every action leading up to my being cold and miserable in a mountain with other royals was the result of a happy twist of fate (for Lady Winter), or if she'd influenced Mother into making the choices that she wanted. If the gods could manipulate free will, even a little… we'd always be questioning if our decisions were our own.

But then, said that cool, nasty voice in my head, *how else would you describe the wolves chasing you to that dead end, but Lady Winter forcing you and Melisande to go where she wanted?*

'I must say,' Melisande remarked, pulling me out of my rising horror, 'you have studied *so hard* to be a future Edaran Consort, *Prince* Theobilt. I'm impressed. Your tutors must be so proud of you.' She'd caught his use of my name, without title nor honorific, and had the speculative expression of someone realising she'd slept through a *very* interesting discussion between us.

Theobilt swallowed and looked away, while I promptly wished for the shadowy ceiling to collapse on Melisande's head.

'As I said to Emri while we were figuring out the parchment,' he said, consciously pulling his shredded dignity around him, 'considering our present situation, it makes little sense for us to constantly address each other by title or honorifics. Temporarily,' he added hastily at Princess Gabriela's outraged expression, 'until we're out of the mountain, and then we can return to etiquette. But…' he faltered, then took a deep breath and continued, 'but we'll have to depend on each other to survive here. And to not let this place – and these gods – wear us down into hopelessness. And we can't do that if we're constantly focused on rank and power.'

'I agree,' I said into the silence that followed. 'Even if just until we're free and safe.' I didn't want to admit a lurking fear within me: that this place could fundamentally alter us all. In the future, when we became Queens and most probably a Consort, when we accepted the responsibility and power that awaited us, only we four would truly understand what we'd been through here.

That was a topic for much later, if we could even speak of it.

Princess Gabriela twisted her mouth, wrestling with the stubborn pride that dominated the Eshvoni royal line. 'Very well,' she finally agreed, reluctantly. 'But only until we're free of the mountain.'

'I concur,' Melisande drawled. 'But I want none of you to forget that we're currently in *my* country.'

TWENTYSIX

We all agreed that trying to keep going upwards was the best course of action, sharing an unspoken fear about going deeper into the mountain. Since the map – if that was what it was; Theobilt's certainty kept wavering – was unhelpful about where any of the mountain entrances actually *were*, we had no choice but to keep going up.

'What if we follow the river?' Melisande asked, which in other circumstances would have been a sensible question.

'And if the river is shaped by magic?' Gabriela countered.

'If it's a magic river, it still has to start somewhere.'

'It disappears,' Theobilt said, 'sometimes.'

Melisande let out a long sigh, drew in a deep breath, then cursed in a stream of Farezinne, Edaran, Othayrian, *and* Eshvoni, with a sprinkling of Riija thrown in for good measure (the last, at least, would have impressed Mama and Grandmama Kierth).

'You're good at languages,' Gabriela said flatly, when Melisande paused for breath. 'Congratulations.'

Melisande immediately called her something uncomplimentary in Farezinne slang. Theobilt and I glanced at each other and, in perfect harmony, swooped into the brittle pause before insults or fists could start flying.

It was, I realised later, a look I'd often seen my parents share in similar situations, and I tucked that realisation away for further examination in less life-threatening circumstances.

Our parents would probably have been appalled that we could so easily bicker and annoy each other. But if we didn't, the sheer enormity of what we faced pressed upon us until we fell silent, trapped within panic and fear. And if we succumbed to panic and fear, we'd never work together or keep going.

As the days passed, to my great relief, we found ourselves in a better part of the temple. Better rather than pleasant, because it was still cold during the day, and bitter when we stopped to eat and sleep, assuming we still went by the pattern of day and night. Melisande held out hope that we'd find windows, or a viewing plateau, to orient ourselves and see if there was a safe way to get down outside the mountain, but no one really entertained it. Our provisions didn't extend to surviving outside the mountain in deep winter, and no one really thought Lady Winter would make it that easy.

How I'd already changed, that I now considered surviving outside a mountain in winter as *easy*.

In the stories, the quests had seemed straightforward. You walked, you ate, you slept, you defeated monsters along the way with a powerful weapon. Then you reached the end, and even if you died at the last moment through a hidden twist or miscalculation, your memory endured. It all seemed linear and sensible when written down.

The stories seemed to have been condensed a little.

Having found Theobilt and Gabriela, Melisande and I now encountered far more archways and a lot less falling through walls and shadows, for which our bodies were grateful. But the walking was endless, and we sometimes kept to our own thoughts because there was little to say that wasn't complaining or talking about something that seemed frivolous.

I found myself thinking about how devastated I'd felt over Rialla's rejection, and how silly it now seemed. More and more, I desperately wished Micah were here, who would have soothed fears, and petty annoyances, and the irritation we spiked within each other with ease. If they ever met, he and Theobilt would like each other. Rialla would be wary of Theobilt because I suspected she'd always feel like she had a prior claim over me, no matter how it had ended between us. But I also sometimes wished she were here, if only because she would have refused to let me give up or sink into despair, which was as important as Micah's diplomacy.

The caverns and corridors no longer appeared roughly hewn, the walls smooth and carefully shaped. As we made our way up, slow and twisted, possibly in the right direction or merely in circles, some of the floors were tiled in neat patterns.

'Do Lady Winter and her companions have specific colours?'

Theobilt asked me, as he studied a pattern of white and blue tiles, with dashes of grey that were perhaps meant to resemble silver, before infinite centuries of dirt had accumulated.

'Night has black, obviously,' I said, 'and Twilight has deep blue and purple. The Edaran colours – royal blue and silver – are thought to be Lady Winter's. We just adopted them.'

'Maybe there were paths for each god,' Gabriela suggested, who had thus far revealed a staggering amount of pilgrimage knowledge.

I resisted the urge to eyeroll, then immediately felt guilty, but Gabriela's levels of piety were sometimes difficult to take seriously. Melisande didn't even try to hide her scorn.

No matter our scepticism, Gabriela remained convinced that Lady Winter's challenge had a deeper meaning than simply proving my worth. 'Maybe this is a pilgrimage, Emri,' she'd said one afternoon, while we crept along a rope-and-wood bridge that lurched and swayed over a chasm full of shadows, 'for you to regain faith in the gods.'

She was still prickly about addressing Melisande and me without titles, but Theobilt had made a point of doing so until Melisande had calmly said that if he used her name *one more time*, she'd break his nose and not feel a drop of remorse. I'd then said that if she punched him, I'd tell her mother, to which she had grumbled and scowled at Theobilt as if it was all his fault.

I was starting to realise it was a good thing that Melisande intended to never have a husband.

Slightly warmer rooms and brighter floors didn't change that it was still miserable. Now numbering four, we were able to bring things with us that made our lives easier: more tinder, extra water skins, dried rations that we used to bulk up our sufficient, but otherwise uninspiring meals. Between us, we did the best we could, but only Theobilt had a basic knowledge of cooking. And even with his best efforts, thanks to scant resources, our meals were edible and little else. I longed for coffee, fresh meat, and soft, warm bread. I dreamed about breakfast with my parents, and dinners with Rialla and Micah, sharing tart wine and desserts.

If my heart were still within my chest, it would have ached. As it was, I woke up dissatisfied and tired, the tolerable food and terrible sleep beginning to catch up with me.

Neither Lady Winter nor Twilight visited me in my dreams. It didn't feel like a reprieve so much as patiently waiting for the jaws of a trap to finally spring around me.

On our eighth day, after breakfast, I pulled everything out of my pack to better rearrange it before we moved on. My hand closed around a bulky bag of thin cloth that had been squashed into a bottom corner, and I hefted it curiously. Tugging it open, a cascade of small, round polished stones spilled onto the ground: blue, white, black, and purple, engraved with small trees, snowflakes, and an arch of stars.

I held one between my thumb and forefinger, baffled.

'Boon stones,' Gabriela said, who I hadn't realised was watching. 'Or prayer stones. Different places have different names, but the purpose is the same. You bring them to a temple to pray with an offering.'

'For what?'

She shrugged. 'Mercy. Good weather. Forgiveness. War. Bountiful harvests. Peace. Help. Everything, anything, nothing.'

'But what if the gods don't answer?'

Gabriela shrugged again. 'That's the point. You never know for certain. But you hope they will, and do the best you can so they'll consider you worthy to grant their aid. You have faith.'

Faith.

Everything came back to that.

I thought back to my dream with Twilight. How he couldn't teach me faith, but encouraged me to think about how being one person on a mountain above an endless sky had made me feel. How everything I had faith in – my parents, books, my friends, sometimes myself – was something solid. *Real.*

How could you beg for help, with nothing more than an offering and a polished stone, and hope it would be answered? It made no sense. And if Edar had once had faith, it was long gone, hidden in the faint ruins barely visible within all that had been built around and above them. Faith belonged to a different people, in a different country, from an older time.

It had no place here now.

I scooped the stones up and tucked them back into the bag. 'I'll think about it,' I told Gabriela, who rolled her eyes.

When we set off, it looked to be yet another day of uneventful walking, though we desperately hoped to find the river to wash our clothing and ourselves. After eight days of only scrubbing our faces and digging water into our scalps, none of us looked even remotely at our best. I'd wrapped my curls up in my spare shirt to avoid thinking about how they looked, while the others had tied or braided their hair back.

We left the cavern and faced a set of thick steps roughly gouged out of a piece of rock large enough for us to walk on.

'That wasn't there last night,' Theobilt said.

'The last time we went up a set of stairs like this,' Melisande said unhappily, 'we were chased by shadow wolves. I may be prejudiced, but I don't like it.'

Inwardly, I agreed, but the wall behind the steps was smooth – and striking in its lack of doorway. This time, if I tried to convince myself to pass through, I suspected it wouldn't work.

'If we ignore the stairs,' I said, 'do you think something terrible will happen?'

'Undoubtedly,' Gabriela said.

After a long moment of silence, she heaved a breath and approached the steps. 'The sooner we get this over with, the sooner we might end up in a room with warm baths.'

'She makes a compelling point,' Melisande remarked. 'I don't believe it'll happen, but I suppose it's a good excuse to work on the concept of faith because I'm *extremely* devoted to hot water.'

I took a step forward, then glanced at Theobilt, who was contemplating the stairs with deep foreboding, a line creased between his eyebrows. He was still the peacemaker in our group, but he struggled with Gabriela and I being younger, and didn't really know how to balance a sense of authority with Melisande, who was two months older than him and acted like it was two years on good days and twenty on bad ones.

'I don't think we have much choice,' I said gently, though winding stairs appearing out of nowhere was never a good omen in this place.

'I know,' he said. 'I just have a terrible feeling.'

'I think we all do,' I said, already walking away and forcing him to follow.

The steps were as treacherous as the ones Melisande and I had climbed, but somehow seemed safer with four of us. This time I didn't flirt with the concept of tumbling towards my death, and none of us started gasping and sweating as if we'd been running underneath the noonday sun.

At the top, we stared down a long, wide hall. 'Well, that was easy,' Melisande said, apparently disappointed. 'Almost too easy.' Then she squinted and added, in a flatter tone, 'Oh, that explains why.'

At the end of the windowless hall was a set of double doors

made from unremarkable wood. An emblem glowed in the left door, as if rippling with fire embers – which *was* remarkable – one that we all recognised: a stylised flame with three stars arched over it. Eshvon's official flag.

Gabriela made an odd sound deep in her throat.

As we watched, a second symbol flickered into existence on the other door: a stylised pomegranate. I faced it on every door belonging to Isra: it was the royal family's personal emblem, which also doubled as an Eshvoni symbol, depending on the context, similar to the Edaran rose briar.

'Oh no,' Theobilt said, as Gabriela strode forward. 'Gabi, wait, this could be a trap!'

'Oh, this is absolutely a trap,' Melisande said. 'And we'll have to spring it because the stairs are gone.'

I whirled. The stairs *were* gone, replaced by a smooth wall that radiated an impenetrable air.

I cursed under my breath, then glared as Melisande and Theobilt absently said, 'Language,' in unison.

'This is all starting to feel distinctly unfair.'

Melisande raised her eyebrows at me. 'Eight days, and you're only starting to think this now?'

Theobilt had already run after Gabriela. The walls were dark, smooth and polished, and resembled nothing we'd seen in the temple so far. I couldn't look at them for long, my gaze slipping and sliding away like rain down windows.

My skin prickled, and it had nothing to do with the cold air.

We caught up with Gabriela and Theobilt at the doors, who were in the middle of an argument in hushed Eshvoni. I was close to fluent thanks to Isra, but they were speaking faster than I could manage, flinging slang and half-bitten words at each other like snowballs, sometimes descending into a mesh of Eshvoni and Othayrian.

It was impossible to ignore the dark shadows under Gabriela's eyes, and her strained tautness as she glared at Theobilt. Sometimes, late at night when sleep eluded me, I wondered if Lady Winter's true test was simply to see how long we could survive on poor sleep and pitiful food before we collapsed or turned on each other. Despite their affectionate nicknames, Theobilt and Gabriela didn't know each other as well as Isra and Prince Aubrey had growing up, and with each passing day, their differences became more pronounced than their intertwined family history.

'Gabi, *why* would there be Eshvoni symbols here?' Theobilt demanded. 'Of course it's a trap or some kind of test!'

'Then what do you suggest?' she snapped back, her eyes flashing as she squared up to him. 'Wait here until we drop dead? There's no other way left except through the doors!'

'Ouch,' Melisande murmured. 'I forgot how brutal sixteen-year-olds are when they know they're right.'

Theobilt flashed us a beseeching look, but Melisande shook her head as I shrugged. Gabriela was right. There was no way back and no other way forward except the doors.

Gabriela turned back, still scowling, as the emblems rippled like glowing embers, then pushed the doors open and stepped inside.

We had no choice but to follow.

They step out onto a terrace.

The air is cool and sweet, late spring teetering on the cusp of summer, too hot for the clothing that keeps them from dying in the mountain, so they're sweating and uncomfortable within moments.

Emri pulls a deep breath into her lungs. Some of the scents are familiar, but most are not. It doesn't matter: the entangled riot of smells is intoxicating, underlaid with the tang of grass.

A pale blue swathe arches overhead, a kinder colour than the mountain sky in her dream with Twilight. Two birds spiral overhead, spinning and trilling.

Before them, terrace steps descend into a patchwork of lawns and gardens, a careful construction made to appear artful. The trees are already thick with fruit blossoms: a source of the beautiful smells. She hasn't much of a knack for gardening, despite Grandpapa Kierth's best efforts, but some of the planting makes her suspect these are working gardens more than a casual stroller would realise.

To her right, Melisande has been drawn to where rose bushes crowd a higher terrace and twist up the arches around tables and seats. It's probably lovely to look at, but Emri couldn't drink or eat with the scent of roses so thick on her tongue.

To their left, the terrace turns into a cloistered walk, arched on both sides, a cooler way to admire everything in sunny weather. Emri turns, and can't stop herself from gawking at the immense three-tiered fountain stretching towards the building beyond them.

A marble statue stands within the main bowl, braced against those of the smaller tiers, her hair tumbling over her shoulders and down her back, her dress billowing from an invisible wind. She seems both delicate and strong, graceful and stern, her grip tight on a golden jug from which water gushes back into the bowl she stands in. The fountain is made from pale stone and marble, gleaming in the sunlight, but the only colour is in the jug, a trio of golden stars painted across the lady's forehead, and the flame cupped in her other outstretched hand.

Aestia: Lady of Flame and Stars, goddess of Eshvon.

Emri looks behind her to stare up, up, up at the immense building made from pale marble, the spirals of its towers capped in gilt.

Yes, the Eshvon emblems on the doors were a trap – specifically for Gabriela.

They're at the royal palace in Eshvon's capital, the seat of the ruling family for centuries.

Emri whirls back around to look at Gabriela, who has turned ashen. She turns from side to side, as if searching for something... or someone.

As they stand on the terrace, there's a strange tug in the air. Emri winces, before the scene blurs and drags around them, and resettles with them inside the palace.

Gabriela lets out a sound that could, charitably, be called a whimper.

Inside is blissfully cool. The walls stretch towards arched ceilings; Melisande, entranced by the intricately painted moulding, almost walks face-first into a door. The hall is small, away from the main thoroughfares, the windows flung open to let in the sweet air and views of the gardens below. The decoration is tasteful, and just out-dated enough that they're probably in the family wing.

Ahead, they catch snatches of raised voices.

Gabriela's forehead gleams with sweat unconnected to the weather. 'No,' she whispers, though Emri probably isn't supposed to hear. 'No, not this one, please, whoever's listening. *Please*,' just before she breaks into a run.

They stare, mouths agape, before Emri takes after her, Theobilt and a grumbling Melisande fast behind her a moment later.

The hallway is long and quiet, apart from the sound of distant arguing. They're definitely in the royal wing; Emri recognises the serene quiet, free from the buzzing chatter of courtiers and ministers that usually fills a palace.

Gabriela abruptly turns into a room, upsetting the double doors left ajar, though no one inside seems to notice. She stops suddenly enough that Emri narrowly avoids smashing into her back.

Two women and a girl stand before them, trapped within a tableau spun tight with tension, and it occurs to Emri that this could be a memory, not a dream. And they shouldn't be witness to it.

The room is large and bright, the ceiling scrolled with elaborate moulding overhead where it meets the walls. The cream and gold walls are subtle enough to make the space seem even larger. A fire-place dominates, but the grate is clean and empty. A large portrait of a crowned couple hangs over it. Even if she didn't know that Eshvon is a queendom, Emri would know the woman was the more powerful: the eye is drawn to her, as much for the striking presence captured in oils as the rich trappings and symbolism of her station.

It must be Queen Juliaane in her younger years: Isra's mother and Gabriela's grandmother. The resemblance is strong, though everyone who describes Isra's resting expression as *consistently ready to knife someone* has never met the Eshvon Queen. Juliaane wears her disdain as easily as the ancient crown upon her head.

Gabriela now appears ready to vomit. Theobilt takes a step towards her, as if to offer comfort though Emri doesn't know what he could offer in a situation like this, but Gabriela flinches away from him.

At the further end of the room sits a large desk, stained dark from time. Emri's parents and Isra all subscribe to the idea of organised chaos in their private workspaces, compared to the bland neatness of their public studies, and it's the familiar tilting stacks of paperwork that convince Emri this is Queen Juliaane's private study. Her suspicion is backed up by the Queen sitting easily at the desk, and the two others – one older, one younger – seeming very much *ill* at ease.

The woman frowning behind the desk has the same brown skin as the younger one in the portrait, her dark hair now streaked with silver and grey. Juliaane may have been touched by forty years since the painting, but her dark eyes are still sharp, her demeanour still imperiously stiff.

Standing before the desk, Princess Lucia is Gabriela's mother and Queen Juliaane's heir. She was not, however, the firstborn daughter. Her older sister had died in a riding accident years ago that was, eventually, deemed not to be foul play. Soon after, her older brother had misjudged the depth of a river, drowned before anyone could reach him, and Lucia, already the heir, now found herself the head of her generation in the family.

Isra had not returned to Eshvon for any of the funerals, nor had Queen Juliaane requested her presence. But she had written, to her father and the siblings she was closest to, and worn Eshvoni mourning colours. And throughout, she had calculated the political repercussions from the unexpected deaths because not even grief could stop Isra's mind from tick-tick-ticking away.

Gabriela is Lucia's eldest daughter, but her third child, and as such, her birth was greeted with a significant amount of relief. It had been generations since a daughter was born so late in the succession. Emri's tutor had considered it the great flaw of Eshvon's matrilineal succession, rather than the absolute primogeniture of Edar, Farezi, and Othayria, but had known better than to say so in Isra's hearing.

Eshvon's royal colours are red and gold, the deep colours of a flame. Unlike in Edar, they are sported both by the Queen and her heir, and Lucia wears them splendidly. At first glance, she appears eerily similar to Isra, despite the five years between them, but as they draw closer, Emri can pick out subtle differences. Lucia is taller; Isra curvier; Lucia's nose is longer.

Despite being the youngest of her siblings, Isra has always been intense about her responsibilities. But now, as Emri considers the way Lucia holds herself, the dignity with which she controls her breathing, expression, and body, Isra seems positively light-hearted.

And the last person is… is Gabriela.

Not the one standing beside them, trembling from trying to keep her furious tears in check. A younger one, a little shorter – Gabriela will, like so many others, tower over Emri in a few years – dressed in a light, sleeveless tunic and leggings with thin leather slippers. Her hair is tightly braided back from her face, hanging down her back in a thick rope. Her features are a little softer than her grandmother's, but she holds herself with brittle stiffness, poised on the brink of her temper exploding.

This is a memory, not a dream.

They've walked into the middle of an argument. The silence between the three is thick with a rising tension about to turn into angry words that can't be unsaid.

Gabriela's mouth has tightened to a thin line, but her expression is resigned, as if this scene is familiar, a reoccurrence. Emri has never liked Isra being angry enough to upbraid her in Their Majesties' presence, but it has never felt like this, not once. Her parents simply wouldn't allow Isra that level of control.

'I don't know why I'm surprised' – Queen Juliaane breaks the silence with cold, precise words – 'considering your past behaviour.' Her glance flicks to Princess Lucia, who appears to subtly brace herself. 'I have warned you before, Lucia: all in the direct line of succession must uphold the behaviour expected of an heir.'

Lucia starts to sigh, then catches herself. 'Mother, Gabriela is aware—'

'No, she is not, or she wouldn't so strongly resemble your traitor of a sister.'

Theobilt sucks in a shocked breath, while Emri jerks as if a bucket

311

of frigid water has been dumped down her back. Melisande looks distressed, but mostly confused; unlike Theobilt or Emri, she would not know the fraught history of the Edaran spymaster.

Gabriela stiffens hard enough to injure herself, but otherwise refuses to betray any further reaction.

'*Mother,*' Princess Lucia snaps. 'That was uncalled for!' Others possibly easily wilt at the look Queen Juliaane flings her, but Lucia merely accepts it, unflinching. Perhaps she would have been cowed, once, before her sister and brother died and she had to shoulder far more responsibility than had ever been expected of her.

'The truth is never uncalled for,' Queen Juliaane replies, ice in her tone, and fixes an equally cold look on the memory-Gabriela. 'You are no longer a child, and I will not suffer another disappointment in this family. If you cannot uphold the standards expected of you as heir, then I suggest writing to your traitor aunt and have her beseech the godless Edaran Queens for asylum on your behalf.'

As Princess Lucia lets out a horrified gasp, the memory-Gabriela turns and bolts from the room without a word.

'Gabriela!' Princess Lucia calls, but she doesn't slow, the tails of her sleeveless outer robe billowing like frail wings behind her.

Before her grandmother and mother say anything else, Gabriela turns and runs after the shade of her memory.

In the distance, Gabriela's coltish height is obvious, her long legs propelling her through the palace towards the outside doors, which she bursts through and bounds down the terrace steps, her speed hardly faltering for safety. They follow her across the lawns to a part of the gardens that is a bit wilder, more unkempt, and thick with orange trees.

A gentle breeze tugs through Emri's hair. As she pants, the scent of oranges bursts upon her tongue. It reminds her of early summer: sitting with her parents in their favourite garden, dozing in the warmth, orange rind trapped under her nails as they sipped icy cordial and nibbled from platters. It is a beautiful day, and something terrible has just happened.

The leaves flutter around them as they make their way towards Gabriela's memory self. *Their* Gabriela has wrapped her arms around herself, skin taut over her knuckles, her mouth drawn into a hard line. Her dark eyes reflect almost no light. Her memory is sitting under an orange tree, arms clenched tight around her legs. Pulling in around herself so she takes up as little room as possible.

Emri squints at her, recognises the anger simmering across the memory's face. She's not making herself small against the world; she's restraining her temper from exploding.

More footsteps.

Lucia stands over her daughter, who is determinedly not looking at her, and sighs.

'Gabriela,' she says. 'Her Majesty didn't mean it. It was spoken in a moment of anger fuelled by you both.'

Gabriela still won't look at her, pointedly grinding her jaw from side to side. 'I would never be like her,' she finally bursts out. '*Never.* I'd never be a traitor to Eshvon, or to the gods!'

Emri abruptly remembers her first conversation with Gabriela, so many days before, and her stomach drops. So much makes more sense now, including why Gabriela had felt Emri's parents had done much to modernise Edar, but insisted their lack of faith and Lady Winter's innate nature were deficiencies in the national character.

Lucia sighs again, and kneels to sit beside her. 'No one thinks you're a traitor, my dear. If a temper implied treason, Mother would have been exiled as a child.' She does her best at glibness, deflating a little when Gabriela refuses to go along with it. 'My dear, please. This will pass.' There is no mention of an apology, which doesn't surprise Emri: from what they've just seen, Queen Juliaane isn't the type to apologise, even within her own family. 'And Isra... Isra's situation has always been complicated, even before she left for Edar.'

All anyone knows about Isra's feelings towards her family and home country is what she lets them think, and a significant portion of that is speculation, which she carefully manipulates. Emri suspects, though no one will probably ever admit it, that even her mothers don't know the full truth behind Isra's reasons for accompanying her brother to Edar almost twenty years ago to help him win a Queen's hand.

There have been letters, sent direct when the family is on good terms and filtered through the embassies when the family is not. Choosing to remain in Edar wasn't treason, but Isra becoming the royal spymaster very much *was*, no matter the attempted justification.

Sometimes Emri wonders if her parents offered Isra the role so she'd never be forced to return. She wonders if Isra's family thinks the same, and how that would make them feel.

'It's not complicated,' the memory-Gabriela snaps, glaring at her mother. 'It's perfectly simple. What she did – what she *does* – is treason. She turned away from us and Aestia's eternal flame!'

What Isra currently *does* is keep Emri and her parents alive. But to Eshvon, of course it would seem like treason. Emri glances at their Gabriela, who refuses to meet her eye. Does she regret her outburst or that other people have now witnessed it? Which does she consider worse: that Isra rejected her family or rejected being one of Aestia's living mouthpieces? Or does rejecting one automatically mean she rejected both?

Lucia sighs. 'Gabi.' In that moment, they are mother and daughter, not two royals waiting to succeed a ruler with a forceful personality. 'One day… one day, I fear, you'll learn that life is not so stark as you insist it is. If not, you'll find being my heir – and eventually, Queen yourself – terribly difficult.'

Gabriela raises her eyebrows. 'Grandmother doesn't appear to share your views.'

Her mother raises her eyebrows in return. 'And you know I disagree with many of hers.'

Gabriela retreats to silence. It deepens, until her mother presses her lips tight and stands. 'If that is how you feel. You'll be expected for the evening m—'

'*Enough.*'

They all jump as Gabriela – *their* Gabriela – shouts, interrupting the memory, which continues around them, unheeding and unaware, as Lucia finishes gently berating her daughter and turns to leave.

'Gabi—' Theobilt attempts, but falters. Whatever comfort and reassurance he thought to offer, Gabriela wants none of it. She is fury wound tight within a cage of flesh and bone, ready to lash out.

Her privacy has been breached, by the magic of the temple or Lady Winter herself, and she is in no mood to forgive nor understand why. The Gabriela of memory, meanwhile, has been left to stew in her bitterness. Her posture is a little looser, but her hands are balled into fists against her knees.

Gabriela tips her face back to the sky and once more screams, '*Enough.*' Her voice bounces against the glorious blue, freezing everyone in place except for her memory, who still steeps in her unhappiness. 'No wonder Edar is a backwater if this is the kind of test their gods would consider a trial!'

Theobilt and Melisande stiffen. They know, as Emri does, that goading a god in one of their oldest temples is the quickest way to die – or something far worse.

Emri appreciates that Gabriela had the decency not to call the *people* of Edar backward, at least, but it is poor comfort.

'Not the wisest thing to say,' she remarks.

Gabriela spins to face her, eyes blazing, mouth peeling back to snap and deflect her rage and embarrassment, but before she can speak, the gardens blur and shift around them, a nauseating swirl of colour and shift in temperature.

They blink, and find themselves in a bathing room. Having never stepped foot in Eshvon, Emri has no idea if they're now within the palace, but if she were to imagine an Eshvoni bathing room, this is close to what she'd conjure from what she knows of the style. Isra has great disdain for what Edarans consider acceptable bathing facilities.

The floors are polished stone, engraved in swirling patterns to prevent anyone slipping in the damp. One wall has windows high above, flung open to let in the brightness of early summer. The walls are tiled in gold and sea-green, shining as brilliantly as the sun. They face a large communal bath and three smaller ones, and a door nearby that Emri assumes leads to a steam room.

Her forehead and hairline break out in a sweat. The curls of heat twisting up from the largest bath make her want to weep. It's been so long since she felt clean.

'I want to marry this room,' Melisande says with great and deep sincerity. Theobilt looks overwhelmed at the prospect of scrubbing off several layers of dirt.

'No,' Gabriela snaps, and scowls at the painted ceiling. A stylised wave dominates over them, tugging at Emri's memory until she remembers it's the symbol of one of Aestia's sisters, who rules over water and healing, beloved of physicians and fishing communities. In the stories, Aestia and her sister love each other deeply while often at odds.

'No,' Gabriela repeats. With scorching rage in her voice, she sounds far older than sixteen. 'No, I *won't* accept this after what you've done. I don't value myself so little. You can't show a memory that should be *mine*, and private, and think I'll accept a bath as a peace offering, on my behalf or anyone else's. I—'

But they don't know what else she intends to say, or threaten, or shout because the temperature abruptly plummets.

Oh no, Emri thinks, because she has been robbed of the breath to say it aloud. Hoarfrost prickles in her chest, creeps towards her throat, and she shivers uncontrollably. Ice stretches across the windows, the sun lost behind sudden cloud, and the damp floor turns treacherous.

Protect her, Emri thinks, and she doesn't know if she can actually speak, or if Theobilt had a similar instinct, because he's already reached Gabriela, ignoring her protests as he wraps his arms around her.

Good. He is right to fear a goddess's displeasure.

So be it. The voice is familiar: the baying of a winter storm, the howling of wolves, the deep quiet as snow settles upon you, gently guiding you towards a cold death. *Aestia has always favoured weakness.*

Shadows burst from the walls and roll towards them. Pressure grows until Emri's ears threaten to burst. The last thing she feels is her and Melisande grappling for each other's hands, their grip clammy, as the memory shatters and there is only darkness.

TWENTY-SEVEN

When the world remade itself, we found ourselves back in that strange corridor, the double doors now sealed shut and the Eshvon emblems gone.

I rolled onto my side, resisting a strained yelp as my ribs tried to scrape against each other. I thought longingly of the warm baths, rejected by Gabriela because of her embarrassment, and wanted to shake her. Then I wanted to weep for the lost chance to scrub my hair and sink up to my shoulders in hot water.

Of course, with my current run of luck, I would have drowned just after getting to properly wash for the first time since arriving at the temple.

But there had been the chance for a moment of calm. And it was snatched away from us, because the gods knew Gabriela could never abide comfort for the price of us knowing something so intimate about her, and she had walked straight into their trap.

And that familiar, terrible voice, dripping with scorn… yes, that had been Lady Winter. I'd never thought she would stoop to pettiness, but if I'd been trapped here for countless centuries, I probably wouldn't behave much better.

Melisande lay nearby, still but conscious. She met my eyes and said, 'I *will* get up, I just need a moment.'

I shrugged; it didn't look like we'd be leaving the corridor any time soon.

Theobilt was struggling to sit up near us, and suddenly swore. 'We never looked at the map!'

I blinked. The map had been the last thing on my mind while we were in Gabriela's memory, and I didn't know what that said about me – or him, for that matter, since seeing the map under the blatant influence of magic would have been extremely useful, if only for gathering knowledge on how it worked.

I snapped my head towards the sound of a moan bitten off into a gasp, and the lurching footsteps of someone forcing themselves to stand. Gabriela wobbled, gritted her teeth, and limped back down the corridor. Her intentions were clear: we either followed her, or she'd leave us all behind.

Ignoring every screaming instinct in my body, I stood and went after her.

We found ourselves back in the landing, the stairs still gone, and nothing else changed. Nothing we could use as a fire pit, no alcoves to wrap ourselves in. Just a landing that led nowhere and a corridor that led to a set of double doors we could no longer open.

Gabriela dropped onto the ground and covered her mouth just before a scream ripped from her throat.

I knelt near her, and yanked my pack from my shoulders to dig through it. I hadn't the faintest hint what I was looking for –

some instinct had taken over, convinced I could find something to make Gabriela feel better, as if anything could – but I paused when my fingers closed over the pouch of boon stones.

I teased open the string, pulled one out between two fingers, and cupped it in my palm.

Gabriela and Theobilt kept trying to explain prayer and faith to me, amused and exasperated at the reality of Edar so thoroughly abandoning religion. They were both deeply unimpressed with Melisande, who didn't bother hiding how little she cared about the gods and religion compared to the rest of her family, whose prevailing opinion was *believe just in case*.

I tightened my hand around the boon stone. Gabriela and Theobilt kept insisting prayer wasn't a barter system – 'That's not the point of *faith*, Emri,' he'd repeat wearily, pinching his nose and trying to find a better way to explain – but right now, it felt like someone owed Gabriela after Lady Winter's humiliation. I knew better than to seek anything resembling kindness from her; she'd insist that learning from this would only make Gabriela stronger. Humiliation hardened you up; kindness as an apology would only make her demand it again.

So Twilight it was.

The least you can do is give us hot water and a way out, I thought. *Showing us Gabriela's memory was cruel; what use do we have for knowing her secrets?*

For a moment, there was only pounding anger in my head.

Then calm washed over me, a gentle wave like I'd felt on the mountain with Twilight, staring up at the sky and the peaks around me, feeling insignificant in a large, ancient world. Peace spread throughout my blood and bones, lowered my shoulders.

You should go to her, Twilight advised, his voice echoing softly in my mind. *The memory was not only for her. My Lady's methods are her own.*

I sincerely doubted it, but now wasn't the time to pick a fight with said Lady's consort.

A bout of shivers rippled through me, before a mild rebuke: *You are lucky I find you amusing.*

Perhaps I needed to take my own advice about not goading the gods.

I wavered for a moment – I felt too sore and tired to manage Gabriela's (somewhat justified) temper – but I'd flung a demand at Twilight, not a prayer, so it made sense that he'd have conditions of his own attached.

Besides, she was sixteen and had just had something embarrassing happen to her. We couldn't pretend otherwise. Because if Lady Winter had done this to her, it would happen to the rest of us soon enough.

As I approached, Gabriela spat, 'Go *away*.'

'Too bad,' I said, lowering myself gingerly to the ground beside her. 'There's nowhere else to go. Do you want to talk about it?'

I probably could have been more subtle, but more than anything, I wanted a bath and a clean bed – and neither of those things was likely, thanks to Gabriela's temper. I wanted to be kind, but my patience was also in short supply. If she wasn't careful, I was in the mood where it would be much easier to lose my temper back at her than be kind.

Her lip curled, her eyes gleaming with disgusted rage. 'What a *charming* princess you are.'

I leaned my weight back against my arms, trying to ignore how my shoulders protested. 'You should be cleverer with your insults. No one has ever called me charming, not even my parents.'

'Which ones—' she started bitterly, and my patience immediately snapped.

'Let me make one thing perfectly clear,' I said, injecting Mother's cold regality and Mama's iron will into my voice. 'What Lady Winter just did to you was humiliating. But that does *not* give you an excuse to be cruel. And if you *ever* try to use my parents or family history against me, I will abandon you here, no matter the consequences for Melisande and Theobilt, no matter how your goddess will retaliate against me. I won't help someone who knows they're being cruel and continues anyway.'

I would not help anyone who acted like Rassa, no matter the circumstances they claimed as justification.

She was sixteen, and had grown up with such a domineering Queen for a grandmother that she'd become convinced that honouring Aestia was to twist her pride and anger into a weapon.

No wonder she sneered at me and my parents, no wonder she rejected any link with Isra. In becoming my parents' spymaster, Isra had lost her family, her place in the succession, and – worse, in Gabriela's eyes – the favour of their goddess, who entrusted them as her mortal representatives.

I'd never had a younger sister, not like Rialla or Micah, whose family dynamics were delightfully strange to me. (They'd know if this urge to grab Gabriela by the shoulders and shake her, screaming, '*We could have had hot water if not for you*,' was a normal reaction to a petulant, embarrassed sixteen-year-old.) But I could try.

I pulled my knees up against my chest, and wrapped my arms around them. Took a deep breath and let it out slowly, tamping down on the urge to scream and shake her. 'They let Isra keep the Eshvon pomegranate on her doors, you know.'

Gabriela blinked. 'Who?'

'My parents. On the doors to her study,' I continued. 'On one side is the Edaran rose briar. And on the other is the Eshvoni pomegranate. Isra might be an Edaran Duchess, but she's still a Princess of Eshvon, part of the Blood Royal. She's loyal to Edar and gives her service – and she's loved in Edar – but her roots will always belong to Eshvon. My parents allowed her to show that, so no one can ever forget.'

Gabriela didn't reply, but picked at the skin around her fingernails. This didn't align with her idea of Isra as a ruthless traitor to her family and country.

'I'm not sure why they allowed it,' I admitted. 'Sometimes I think it was too lenient. A spymaster shouldn't show a scrap of loyalty to anywhere else, no matter their past. But my parents and Isra have known each other for almost twenty years. I don't think I'll ever understand everything that happened between them, but I trust that my parents had their reasons for allowing it.'

Gabriela still didn't say anything, but I ventured, 'If your mother says things are complicated with Isra and to be kinder about her… maybe it's worth trusting her?'

Gabriela ripped off a piece of skin as I finished speaking, then hissed as blood gushed and she had to stick her finger into her mouth.

I waited with as much patience as I could dredge up from within myself. After a few moments, Gabriela lowered her hand to study the bleeding, then asked in a small voice, 'Does Aunt Isra ever talk about me?'

'No,' I replied. As her shoulders slumped, I added, 'The only person she ever talks about Eshvon and her family with is Prince Aubrey, whenever he's back at Court. Maybe with my parents, sometimes, or my aunt.' Now wasn't the time to try and explain the complicated relationship Isra and Aunt Zola had built between themselves over the last fifteen years or so. 'She never speaks of it around me. I think… I think she feels talking about everything – and everyone – she left behind is a weakness she can't allow herself as Whispers.'

Gabriela's mouth trembled with misery. 'I've always been compared to her, since I was young. She was very like me, apparently: *headstrong and scholarly.*' Her tone shifted in the last few words, and within it, I heard Queen Juliaane's scorn. 'Not as religious, though, even before she left for Edar, but everyone seems to forget that when it's convenient,' she added, almost pitifully. I was overwhelmed with the urge to hug her, even though she'd probably try and scratch my eyes out if I tried.

Before this had happened, as Gabriela had slowly lowered her guard around Melisande and me, I'd started to form an impression of her. She was the most fluent in languages, and knew the most mythology out of us all, including from the other countries. If she managed to control her temper, and Queen Juliaane didn't grind her into suppressed bitterness before Princess Lucia took the throne, I suspected Gabriela would be an extremely sharp, clever Queen: a force to reckon with in her own right.

If Isra lived to see it, she'd be outrageously proud of her, even if it made her life as Whispers difficult.

'But Isra, she…' I twisted my lips, debating whether to continue, but it could hardly make our general situation worse; it might even help. 'She mentioned you, a few hours before Melisande and I were kidnapped. She'd heard worrying things out of Othayria and Eshvon – clearly smokescreens to hide that you and Theobilt had *disappeared* – but she said she wasn't worried about you because you were sensible.'

Gabriela raised her eyebrows doubtfully. 'Sensible?'

'She's never called me sensible once in my life.'

Gabriela still appeared dubious, but a little calmer. 'Grandmother still hates her.'

'But your mother doesn't,' I pointed out, swallowing my instinctive answer: *Queen Juliaane hates everyone she can't control.* 'Doesn't her opinion also matter?'

This time Gabriela's silence appeared less fraught. 'Maybe,' she finally said.

A chime note shimmered in the air, then slowly faded. In a stretch of wall opposite us, the outline of a doorway flickered into existence.

I glanced over at Theobilt and Melisande, who were hovering where the corridor met the landing. Then a deep, prevailing sense of calm drifted upon us like a gentle weight. Twilight's calm.

The memory was not only for her, he'd said.

This was still manipulation of a sort: a god encouraging us towards strengthened bonds, either for a greater purpose or through impatience at mortal stubbornness. But he was kinder than Lady Winter – for now.

And Gabriela had endured Lady Winter's memory, even if her mortification had made it backfire on all of us, and I had obeyed Twilight's *suggestion* to offer her kindness when I could have simply bellowed at her. I had not given him a prayer, offered him no faith, but we had managed it all nonetheless, and now we would all be rewarded.

I stood, and held out a hand to help Gabriela up, which she accepted. She didn't let it go once standing, and I raised an eyebrow, more curious than unnerved. Emotions flickered across her face, an internal war raging within, before she finally said, 'Gabi. Theobilt is allowed to call me such, and now so are you.'

I nodded, and tried not to laugh when Gabriela scowled towards Melisande and added, 'But not her, not yet.'

'Melisande has gone to great efforts to keep you alive,' I said. *And knows all too well what having a domineering grandmother is like*, I added silently.

Ignoring my gentle rebuke, Gabriela leaned close and added conspiratorially, 'Theo would rather fling himself off the mountain than admit it, but he'd prefer you to call him by his nickname. All his family do in private, and well, you *will* be married, after all.'

'Nothing has been confirmed,' I reminded her, ignoring the sharp twist in my stomach. 'We haven't signed a binding contract.' It didn't matter: she ignored me just as assuredly as she'd ignored my efforts to bolster her opinion of Melisande.

Through the doorway, we found ourselves in a warm cavern, the closest to a proper room I'd experienced since arriving here. The walls were smooth polished stone, emanating a soft, wavering light. A large fire pit stood in the middle of the room, surrounded by a dais where we could sleep. Wool mattresses were neatly rolled and stacked in a corner, along with firewood, cooking utensils, and what I hoped were foodstuffs sealed in boxes. The river churned to our right, arching in a deep curve away from us.

'We can boil water,' Theobilt said, relieved, but Melisande was striding towards a smaller archway that had already caught my attention, filled with light from torches high up in the walls that emanated no smoke.

She let out a sound somewhere between a yell and strangled sob. '*Baths.*'

We froze, then nearly knocked each other over as we charged through the archway.

A small snarl of the river coursed through this room, filling a deep pool with a continuous churn as it surged back out to meet the main current. But what stunned us all into silence was the steam curling up from the pool. It was, in all respects, a heated bath.

Before anyone could stop me, I went to the edge, dropped to my knees, and dipped my hand into the water before it entered the pool. Icy; true mountain water caught in the grasp of winter. I studied the steaming water only a few feet away, frowned, then shook my head and gave up.

Perhaps there was a thermal spring deep in the rock; perhaps it was magic carefully shaped by Twilight in an unspoken apology for his Lady's actions. Regardless: for one night, we had an interlude. We could clean ourselves, eat reasonably well, and sleep soundly, as warmly as the mountain would allow.

I would accept the reward, even if I chafed at how we'd received it.

Everyone was too tired and filthy to protest that this could be a trap; if the unseen jaws closed around us, so be it. Theobilt bathed first, having been nominated for cooking duty and also because, having the shortest hair, it would take the least amount of time to clean and detangle. While he washed, the three of us rolled out the wool mattresses, which were more battered on closer inspection but still functioning, on the dais and arranged our bedrolls. We sorted through our clothing, trying to find the cleanest things to wear and what we could wash after we'd all bathed. Gabi and Melisande studied the firewood pile, discussing whether they could assemble something for the clothes to dry on overnight.

Theobilt returned soon enough, his hair still dripping, but looking the most cheerful since I'd met him. He all but shoved us into the bathing room, rolling his eyes at Melisande when she threatened dire things if she caught him watching us.

'Gabi's my cousin,' he snapped. 'And you'd gut me, and Emri is—' He cut off, as I tried to ignore the heat that flooded my cheeks. No one finished his sentence as to what I *was* to him, exactly.

The pool was just big enough for us to bathe together. We scrubbed ourselves until Melisande turned red, and I felt like I'd scoured a layer of skin off. It took three lathers before my hair squeaked.

Melisande dug out combs that looked suspiciously like they were carved from bone, and we each worked on the other's hair. As she tackled Gabi's knots, Melisande calmly told her every terrible thing Arisane had ever said or done to her, as emotionless as if she were reciting the previous week's weather.

I sank up to my shoulders, unsure what expression was twitching over my face. We'd never really spoken about Melisande's experiences with Arisane after I'd left for Edar, or my experiences at Saphirun that I didn't remember or my memory had blocked. Melisande spoke of petty criticisms to harsher punishments and arguments, none of which I felt could have been sanctioned by Queen Sabine.

But from what I knew about Arisane, and the brief flashes of memory that abruptly resurfaced both when I was awake and dreaming, everything Melisande spoke of sounded true. She was the heir Arisane had wanted to shape into a true Queen, and she had made the experience terrible and lonely.

What sort of person had Melisande returned as to her mother's Court? Had she retained any resemblance to the child who'd been sent to live with me?

'And Arisane is *her* grandmother, too,' Melisande said briskly, inclining her head towards me. 'Both of us know what it's like to have grandmothers who demand too much and give too little in return. You are not alone.'

It was possibly the kindest thing she'd said to Gabi since we'd met her. And she meant every word.

Gabi didn't say anything in response, but as Melisande's hair, though thick, was longer and finer than ours, we worked through it together, and Gabi tried her best to be gentle whenever her comb caught on a snarl.

It was impossible to ignore that Melisande had lost weight since we'd arrived here, and Gabi was too thin for a girl still growing. Free of the layers that kept me alive in the mountain cold, my hips were already less curved, and my shape was different. We ate less well here, and the days of long walking weren't helping. Hopefully Twilight had given us the means for Theobilt to cook a decent meal.

After getting out, we rubbed ourselves dry and dressed in the cleanest clothes we had left, then sorted through the bathing creams and lathers, debating whether we could rearrange the packs so one person could carry most of it without anything leaking onto food.

As the last of the meal cooked, Melisande and I hauled everyone's clothing into the room to wash. Theobilt had looked momentarily aghast, until Melisande said she already thought little of him as a man, so his dirty clothing was hardly going to make her insufficient opinion any worse. In response, he'd threatened to give her no meat, but by now, it felt more like good-natured teasing than the spiky tension of dislike.

It took longer than planned – Melisande and I had assumed the mystical art of laundry would unveil before us like an unlocked instinct, which it did *not* – but we did the best we could, then arranged everything on the structure Gabriela had created from a thin rope, stacks of wood, and a great deal of hope. It stayed upright, and that was enough.

Theobilt had fared much better with the meal: he'd uncovered fresh strips of meat tucked away in the coldest part of the room, which he'd fried with fat, and chopped up vegetables and simmered them with barley in a flavoured broth he suspected came from fowl bones.

Melisande stared at her plate, took a bite and chewed carefully, then frowned at him. 'How can a *prince* cook this well?'

I paused mid-chew, suddenly realising that I'd never questioned the fairly decent job he always managed. In contrast, last week I'd finally managed to avoid boiling vegetables into mush. He preferred to cook with Gabi, who mostly followed his instructions. Melisande cooked the least of us, treating it all with regal scorn, despite the fact that she very much liked – and *needed* – to eat.

Theobilt shrugged. 'Every summer, we stay at one of the family estates and go into the woods. When we're old enough to ride and track with the adults, we're taught how to skin and gut our game – and cook it. If something ever goes wrong outdoors, or we get separated and lost in the forest, a servant won't always be there to keep us alive.'

Othayria was heavily forested and only fools underestimated the dense woods from which their older, crueller myths had been born. It made sense that even the Othayrian royal family would teach their children to respect and survive within them.

In comparison, I'd never felt more useless, but then, my parents didn't encourage me to wander into forests, and the one outside our capital was practically tame compared to the ancient Othayrian forests.

'Oh,' Melisande said, after some consideration. 'Well, if we survive this, please pass my compliments to your family.'

'I'll be sure to,' he replied dryly. 'Shall I brew tea next?'

It didn't take long for exhaustion to dig its claws into Melisande after we finished eating, and she crawled into her bedroll with a mumbled thanks to Theobilt and, to all appearances, immediately passed out. Her bleeding had started two days ago, and it was getting harder for her to ignore the pain and cramping. We'd had to wash the used cloths together, a traumatic experience that had possibly done more for improving relations between our countries than any diplomat could have managed.

The rest of us sat up, talking quietly and finishing our tea, then banked the fire and buried into our own bedrolls. The wool mattress felt like luxury against the ground. I snorted to myself: how quickly my standards had changed.

I was on the cusp of drifting off, a great wave gently tugging me towards soft oblivion, when Melisande shifted and whispered, 'Emri?'

I kept my eyes closed. 'Mmm?'

'We've been here ten days,' she said.

'Mmm,' I repeated.

'I can't stop wondering how long it's been outside the mountain since we disappeared. And what our families are going through. Whether they think we're dead.'

My stomach had dropped at her words, and now it felt full of old iron, the weight pinning me against the earth, forcing me wide awake. I had no answer for her, no useless reassurance.

We lay beside each other in our bedrolls, silent and afraid. As the night deepened around us, hints of firelight flickered under the banked embers, only a pittance of the time lost to us outside the mountain.

Once, there is the night.

And no god holds dominion over it.

A mortal is once again given a choice and the power of the Tree of Life plunged into their heart to reshape them into divinity. But this time Lady Winter wraps the night chill under their skin and within their bones, and Twilight traps darkness in their eyes and stars in their hair. In their voice, they twine the long silence of a still night and the terror of the deepest moment before dawn.

The god's reach stretches far beyond mortal borders. The owl and all cats come at their call. But Night's loyalty is to Lady Winter and Twilight. There is no choice, for both had a part in their creation.

Where Lady Winter is brutal, and Twilight coldly kind, Night keeps their distance from mortals at first Even so, their worship grows, for the night is long and dark and, no matter their bravado, mortals fear it.

The three gods – Lady Winter, the highest of all; Twilight, her Consort; and Night – become a triumvirate of harsh worship. It makes for a hard people with fierce pride, who learn when to bend but not to break.

But the night is long and deep. And faced with Lady Winter

and Twilight's fierce devotion for each other, Night is alone.

Temples are built in their name, swollen with ranks of faithful. Night is beseeched to keep loved ones safe from danger and to keep them alive during war. They are prayed to, and begged, and sworn at, and people prostate before their statues, begging for aid and love and forgiveness and mercy and revenge and hope, an end to suffering and life and death, and within it all, the agony and pettiness and adoration of mortals, Night feels only an eternal loneliness.

And within the safety of nightfall, mortals dream.

Night becomes witness to their dreams and nightmares, chaotic spinnings of the mind that often defy logic and reason. They defy Night's loneliness, a little, with brash colours and looming fears, as they watch mortals try to unravel the effects of living: the glorious, bizarre wonder of it all; the boredom and pain, the bravery in living a short life with such joy.

The night is long, and the stars follow in its wake, and yet — and yet...

As sunset falls to dusk and then to twilight, and the stars tumble and scatter across the sky, Night sweeps over all. The sky is deep and dark, and beneath it, mortals plot and scheme and kill and slumber and love and dream.

Night sits in judgement over it all.

Alone.

In the darkest part of night, when everything is soft and still and waiting, two former spymasters meet.

The tent is constructed on the eastern side of a field that is, according to the most up-to-date map, precisely on the border between Edar and Farezi and belongs to neither. Neutral ground.

As a distraction against the roiling terror that threatens each passing day to overwhelm her, Xania looked into the potential tax ramifications for the farmer, but it appears an ancestor saw the potential headache coming and decided an orphaned field was better than paying taxes to two different monarchs. A small mountain of paperwork was also probably involved. Bureaucracy at its finest.

Xania would deal with triple paperwork every day for the rest of her life if it meant Emri was returned to them by dawn, as emotionally or physically unharmed as possible under the circumstances.

Until over a month ago, almost losing Lia to abduction was one of the worst periods of Xania's life. Now that the same has happened to their daughter, Xania doubts either of them will sleep through the night again if – *when* – they find her. Alive.

Emri has to be alive. The cynical part of Xania – from when she was a spymaster and moved the chess pieces of people's fates and lives, from when she played the game and lost, from when she won a Queen's heart and *killed* in retribution – the part she has kept close because being Queen means gauging the poorest choice out of many – insists their daughter has to be alive, because she is more valuable alive than dead. An heir only has potential when they can be manipulated, and Edar, being a country that remembers a winter goddess best, does not hold well with martyrs.

It is too easy to die from the cold.

It was only later, when years of marriage meant cultivating an interest in the myths Lia loved so dearly, that Xania began to understand a fundamental part of her wife in a way she couldn't when they were younger. Lia's ancestors were noble before they were royal, and their roots in the North stretch back to the Second Empire and likely beyond to the First Empire and older, even if Lia is sceptical of that long-held family belief because the records are long gone. But House Sionbourne's power and influence in the North is still considerable, even if it has changed as each subsequent generation dwindled and their power shifted to the capital down south.

Lady Winter has been Edar's patron goddess for as long as her myth has endured, and the North has always held her closest, the frozen heart around which they built their lives and survived the harshest season in their harsh lands. It is less faith than an understanding long maintained by Northern Edarans.

Someone can't survive a Northern winter by being unnecessarily soft, by giving too much so that they doom their own survival, by failing to prepare or consider the worst-case scenario. When Xania first met Lia, she had assumed it was simply her personality, a consequence of her lonely upbringing. But when she travelled up North with Lia, as her closest companion and then later as her wife and fellow ruler, and met the people that Lia had grown up with, who served her as she protected them, met the other noble families of the

Northern bloc, she realises these characteristics are simply *Northern*. Their pride is only surpassed by their stubbornness, their deep, cold rage, and the unyielding determination and respect they have for the harsh land they hold so beloved.

In this, the people of Northern Edar are a true manifestation of their brutal goddess.

Emri doesn't have the same demeanour. But Xania can see the parts that she's absorbed, unconsciously or otherwise. Her careful consideration before coming to a decision; her study of the Edaran triumvirate; the stubbornness; and the depths of her rage and fear, which she tries to hide from them all.

She wishes she could make it better for Emri, but it is beyond her capabilities, except to love her. To regret her past actions only in how they affected their daughter, but never regret doing them. They are a family, and they all carry their own hidden wounds.

The tent flap opens. Neither Xania nor her guards flinch. They are too well-trained, and she has not been a spymaster for many years, but she can still tell the absence of sound from the careful removal of it.

The heavily cloaked figure stops before her, and inclines into a bow, just short of the respect owed a foreign monarch.

Xania raises an eyebrow. 'Still the same games, I see.' Without looking away from the cloaked figure, she flicks a hand: her guards leave the tent and take up their stations around it. 'We'll be overheard, I'm afraid, but I handpicked these guards. They know the consequences of a loose tongue.'

The cloaked figure removes his hood and regards her with a faint smile. 'What a fierce Queen you grew up to be, little spider.'

She can't help smiling back. 'Hello, Truth. Or have you changed names since our last correspondence?'

'Truth will suffice, Your Majesty. Only for you, of course, you understand.'

'How flattering,' she replies dryly.

His hair, once black as pitch, is now almost fully white with streaks of silver and grey, but his dark eyes are the same, as are his soft smile and careful stride. He still radiates the promise of a death, slow or otherwise. He is very old for a spymaster who never quite retired. Xania is convinced his successors must be aware of his existence, just as she is convinced that he terrifies them all and they decided that keeping an eye on him is safer than ever coming face-to-face.

If they had met under different circumstances – and this is the first time they have met since she left Farezi with Lia – Xania would probably indulge him with more sly talk and veiled references. She imagines it's very lonely to be one of the most feared people in Farezi, even if he isn't in favour with the ruling monarch.

But her daughter is missing and no one – absolutely *no one* – has any idea where she is, and so Xania turned to her final, desperate measure, a man who anticipates the worst and always has three contingency plans prepared.

Lia doesn't know she is here, because it would give her hope, which Xania can't afford because if it turns out to be in vain, it will likely break her. Every suppressed nightmare from Goldenmarch, every terrible impulse, has resurfaced in Lia; her biggest setback since Xania pulled her out of that white nightmare years ago. She hasn't slept well since Emri's disappearance, and the shadow of Goldenmarch is so heavy upon her that it's all Xania can do to keep up a brave face, and then safely weep alone in private.

She already has a wife who has never been the same after the terrible things she endured. She doesn't know if she can bear to see the same in their daughter.

(The first night after Emri arrived, they had sat outside her bedroom door after she'd finally managed to fall asleep, their gowns pooling around them on the floor as they gripped the other's hand.

'How did our mothers *do* this?' Lia had asked, panic threaded thick in her voice.

'I don't know,' Xania had replied, knowing the real question, since they had both lost their fathers young, was how had their mothers done this *alone*?)

Xania raises her face, firms her jaw, and says, 'Where are Emri and Melisande?'

For a long moment, Truth does not speak, merely watches her with that deep, implacable gaze. The lamplight washes over them in a thin, golden glow, suffusing his pale skin with warmth he desperately needs.

He takes the chair opposite her, and the silence continues.

She waits. She is Queen Xania of Edar, once Xania Bayonn, and she has learned how to be patient.

Finally, he says, 'I am uncertain. The traces are faint, and almost feel like misdirection.'

'Deliberate evasion or accidental foolishness?'

'Both. Neither. Perhaps.'

'That is unhelpful,' she says.

'I myself do not enjoy being toyed with,' he replies through gritted teeth.

Others would probably laugh at his annoyance. But Xania has known him only a little less long than she has known her Queen, and his show of irritation is dangerous and worrying. You don't survive decades as a spymaster and a murderer without learning how to shield your emotions from others. Xania learned this, eventually: at heart, being a ruler and being a spymaster are not so very different.

'Is it Farezi?' she asks.

It must involve Farezi. Isra suspects so because she's practically ripped Edar apart looking for the two young women, and she now suspects the stories of the Othayrian and Eshvoni royal children being watched are smokescreens against their own disappearances. Isra is too grim and too cynical – very like Truth, in some respects, though she wouldn't appreciate the comparison – for Xania not to believe her.

'If your Queen is involved—'

'The Queen is not involved,' Truth says tightly. 'She wants her heir back.'

The Queen, Xania notes. Not *my* Queen.

Truth's use of *heir* and not *daughter* is likely his own.

'As do we,' she says, because arguing with him on semantics is a terrific waste of her time.

There is also the matter of Princess Melisande being with Emri when she disappeared, her whereabouts also unknown. Their initial fears that Melisande was behind the disappearance, that Farezi had waited patiently to enact vengeance, were mollified by Queen Sabine sending a missive with three different layers of encryption that essentially amounted to: *Where is my daughter? Find her.* If Queen Sabine had actually marched to Edar and straight into the palace, Xania suspects she would have punched them or tried to throttle them, perhaps both.

Melisande is not Sabine's only child, but she is her oldest and threats involving heirs are significant and pointed.

It has been over a month, and there's not a whisper of them. Every day the shadows deepen under Lia's eyes as she grows thinner, and every morning Xania loses a little more of her stubborn hope that they are *alive*, both of them. They must be, because they are more valuable alive than dead.

Another tense silence, and then she says, 'Please tell me something useful.' She can't keep the exhaustion out of her voice, and Truth twitches in something that might be considered sympathy in anyone else. 'Are they at Goldenmarch?'

The estate where Lia was held captive, that white, silent nightmare, was shuttered up soon after Rassa's death and has never, to their knowledge, been reopened.

Truth shakes his head. 'I've been there. They should rip it down, brick by brick, and let it fade from memory.'

'Then *where*?' Xania demands. 'Where are they?'

He swallows, something odd flickering across his face. If she didn't know any better, she'd describe it as *nervousness*. But Truth does not get nervous. Truth does not allow himself to be gripped by fear.

'There are rumours,' he murmurs, 'of an ancient temple deep in the Farezi mountains, primarily dedicated to Lady Winter. There are whispers that there are still devoted followers within the temple, that strange things happen there.'

She frowns. 'Be serious, Truth.'

He shrugs, but the movement is uneasy. Truth is a man of sense and logic. But it seems his logic does not extend to openly dismissing the gods. 'They say the temple was where the gods retreated as their power diminished. That the place is brimming with magic and those who journey there do not return.'

'The gods aren't real,' Xania says with full conviction because though she loves her wife, and suffers through her love of myths, she does not adore them even half as much and doesn't believe them. Perhaps people existed, once, who became Lady Winter, Twilight, and Night: legends who became stories who became myth.

She does not believe in the gods, and she is not someone they would favour.

'So this is all you have for me,' she says bitterly. 'Speculation.'

He watches her, perfectly calm and serious, and she wishes she wasn't so exhausted, so ground down by her terror, that she could truly mock him. 'If there is any shred of yourself willing to entertain gods and religion,' he says. 'I would use it to pray, Your Majesty. Even if the gods are not involved, that both heirs have disappeared without any ransom nor boast should worry you enough. We are up against someone clever – perhaps several clever people – and it does no good to underestimate people like that.'

She shakes her head and gestures that the meeting is finished. She rises to leave, when Truth suddenly asks, 'Did your daughter find out?'

Xania allows a furrow of confusion to crease between her eyebrows.

'About the bargain you struck so many years ago?'

She stiffens; she can't help it.

'She did,' Xania admits, because they both know this is a leading question.

'Ah.' She can practically see the gears clicking in Truth's mind: Melisande likely being the one to tell Emri, who confronted Xania, and the inevitable consequences that had ensued. And she can see the same bafflement that has plagued her for weeks, as she's rerun the same sequence in her mind, over and over, because it's *something* but it doesn't easily fit as an explanation. If there are supporters of Rassa still in Edar and Farezi – and Sabine has *thoroughly* rooted them out, keeping those she couldn't execute under her eye, while Xania and Lia have destroyed Rassa's memory in Edar – they have little to gain by staying quiet about abducting both heirs.

'She will understand,' Truth finally says. 'Eventually.'

Xania twists her mouth into a semblance of a smile. 'You think so?'

Truth tilts his head, his expression turning thoughtful. It puts her to mind of a wolf considering the deer it has been stalking for some time. 'Yes. If the gods are involved – *if* – then it is likely your daughter will have to make difficult decisions of her own. They are not known for their kindness in any of the stories. Even those involving their chosen.'

Xania lets out a bark of laughter. 'You truly believe Emri is a god's chosen?'

Truth shrugs. 'Perhaps. Perhaps not. But I am very good at what I do, and I have not survived this long by being careless—'

She spares a thought for any of the guards outside foolish enough to ever repeat any of this conversation.

'—If there is no trace, and what remains is deliberate obstruction… the hand of the gods upon her is a *possibility*.'

A chill runs down Xania's spine. The gods. Chosen. Magic. Stories. Myth.

But in every myth, there is a seed of truth.

Perhaps they've all just misinterpreted what, precisely, the seed is.

There are many arguments they are still readying themselves to have with Emri. That she is likely to marry the Othayrian prince, unless his character proves terrible. That she must, if possible, have several children, because the family has only had one heir for two generations now, and – putting aside Rassa's efforts for a moment – it's generally a miracle that neither of them has succumbed to illness nor assassins. The succession can never be vulnerable like this again, even if putting that pressure on Emri keeps Lia up at night.

But she is a Queen, and so will Emri be, one day. Lia followed her heart and suffered the consequences. Neither of them knows the answer to the impossible problem: break their daughter's heart, or ignore a future crisis that was within their power to stop.

But this... the gods... there is nothing they can do to stop this, if they are truly real. If they were always real, and waiting.

Except hope.

And perhaps—

'We would be grateful, Master Truth,' Xania says, regal and cold, 'if you would spare a moment to pray for our daughter's safety, and that of the Farezi heir.'

TWENTY-EIGHT

The next morning, we lingered over a warm breakfast, packed up our mostly dry clothes and whatever new provisions we could stuff into our packs, and continued on.

Three days later, my bleeding started, and it was my turn to grit my teeth and trudge through the discomfort and pain, the craving for sweet things. At night, I stared at the ceiling, internally arguing with myself about wasting a boon stone to bargain for a cake with Twilight. I wasn't certain I could survive Gabi's scorn if one actually manifested, and I had to explain why.

Everyone took turns brewing their versions of a tea that would make me feel better, including Theobilt, who insisted his sister and younger brother swore by a sharp-smelling one. The underscent reminded me of loamy earth after a sudden, heavy rainfall.

It tasted similar – as much as I could tell, having never tasted earth – and I couldn't stop myself from gagging.

'I told you,' Melisande muttered to me, and arched an eyebrow at Theobilt. 'I think your siblings played a joke on you.' When Gabi, sceptical, took a sip and promptly spat it out, Theobilt's shoulders drooped.

'Don't worry,' Melisande continued, her tone generously cheerful, 'you're still the best cook. Just don't make any teas to help when our insides want to bleed out and grind our bones to dust all at the same time.'

For one long moment, Theobilt's expression was clear: *I am so utterly relieved to not be marrying* you.

It was my worst bleeding in years, and I slept little and badly. One early morning, with both of us unable to get back to sleep, Melisande had asked my opinion on an Edaran writer who'd had a longstanding rivalry (and potentially a decades-long secret relationship, or affair, depending on who you asked) with a writer in Farezi. Within minutes, we were mired in a whispered argument, unaware that anyone else was awake until Gabi, with perfect timing, had mentioned the name of the *Eshvoni* writer who'd married the Farezi writer and stoked the rivalry even further (or been a front or willing participant in the secret relationship, or affair, depending on who you asked).

Theobilt had woken to metaphorical books at dawn.

Throughout my bleeding, the temple began to change again around us, as if Gabi's test had been an unknown lock that set us on a new path, perhaps the correct one. Theobilt refused to let the map out of his sight, determined to see if it changed when we faced someone else's memory, though it was still essentially just a decorated piece of parchment and little else. The temple turned warmer around us, more modern, the walls and floors smoother and polished. In some rooms, we found the battered remains of tapestries or faded paintings on the walls.

Some of them made little sense: battles or marches, with figures none of us recognised at the front of the columns, circles of flaking gilt surrounding their heads like halos in the depictions of the patron gods in older manuscripts. Having seen Lady Winter and Twilight in their true guises, I knew the illustrations didn't match their actual likeness.

Theobilt began to hope we were steadily making our way upwards, and possibly getting close to chambers that led to outside. The idea of fresh air and a glimpse of the sky was incredible, unless we turned out to be greeted by a blizzard. But our improved surroundings – and improved sleep – buoyed our mood. We decided to risk the prospect of hope.

The day after my bleeding finished, we came to another room that made our risk of hope seem utterly foolish.

The hall leading to it appeared normal, the walls painted deep, forest green, with a topiary of trees, vines, and flowers picked out in pleasant colours. The open doorway also appeared normal, and to compensate for the lack of windows, the room was filled with candles, flooding the room with golden light. Our hearts sank – it was the very opposite of the view of daylight we'd hoped for.

Melisande side-eyed Theobilt. 'Getting close to the outside, hm?'

He glared at her.

What I assumed was something like a low altar stood in the

centre of a room. Plain, unadorned, empty apart from two lamps at either end, and three vials and a shallow dish in the centre.

We circled the altar, trying to find a note or any indication as to what we were meant to do, but there were only the vials and dish.

Melisande finally lost patience and unstoppered one to sniff. She jerked back, coughing with streaming eyes. The vial slipped from her hand, but she managed to catch it mid-drop before it hit the altar.

'That's foul,' she spluttered, replacing the stopper and stepping back to wipe at her eyes. 'I think it's poison.'

'Poison,' I repeated blankly, then whirled back in the direction we'd come. I knew one of the flowers had looked familiar: its pollen could be dissolved in warm liquid, then decanted into food and drink as a tasteless poison. It was slow-acting, designed to deflect suspicion, and resulted in a quick, agonising death a few hours later. All the topiary we'd passed on the walls was likely related to poison: a subtle hint we'd all missed.

There was nothing in the room to suggest who had set this trial.

'Which of the gods did poisoners pray to?' Melisande asked.

I thought furiously. It was probably a toss-up between Twilight and Night; Twilight favoured spies, who often used poison, while Night oversaw all that happened in the dark hours, and poison often lurked in an evening glass or meal. 'They probably prayed to Twilight or Night,' I finally decided, 'depending on where their devotion already lay.'

'That's not helpful,' Melisande muttered, stepping back up to the altar to unstopper a second bottle to sniff. She frowned, but there was no coughing or watering eyes this time. The third made her flinch as she inhaled, but didn't appear as astringent as the first.

'I think at least one is poison,' she finally said. 'Maybe two. And the third is a decoy.'

I stepped up to examine them myself. The first smelled strongest, and the after scent lingered on my tongue and made me frantically – and uselessly – swallow to clear it. The second was a poison made from the flower I'd recognised, with no taste or smell. It reacted particularly well in sweet things, and was usually hidden in the dessert course. The clear liquid in third vial had a strong scent and was either a lethal poison or a pretender to make us second guess ourselves.

If only Isra were here to witness me finally put all her drilling and preparation into use.

'So… what?' I finally asked. 'We guess the one that's not a poison to make a doorway appear?'

Melisande's frown deepened. 'I think one of us also has to drink it.'

Ghastly silence greeted her words. I swallowed, hard. If I'd still had my heart, it would have begun pounding in staccato time.

'I'll do it, of course,' she said decisively, then blinked when I snapped, 'Of course not!'

She arched her eyebrows, which would have been more impressive if she was dressed and held herself like the Melisande I'd known in Edar. 'Emri, must I remind you that my family has a long and inglorious attachment to poisons? I'm sure Isra has given you a thorough education in how to survive them, but I hazard she's never taught you how to *make* them.'

I swallowed again, harder this time. A princess with an in-depth knowledge of poisons would be a lethal Queen, if her darker impulses ever led her down a dangerous path.

I thought fast. No matter Melisande's knowledge and confidence, she could just as easily make an error or second-guess herself. And Theobilt had been clear: the rest of them were vulnerable to death in a way that I wasn't. Their lives were dependant on the outcome of my bargain with Lady Winter, while my heart and free will were under threat. Both were terrible outcomes, but only one was truly fatal.

'And if you guess wrong?' I asked. 'And drop dead? How am I to explain that to Queen Sabine? Or my parents?'

Melisande's eyes narrowed. 'Your parents will kill me if I let you die.'

'There's a very good chance Aunt Sabine will raise an army for the first time in nearly five hundred years if I let *you* die!'

'I have siblings!' Melisande snarled. 'You are the last direct

Edaran heir, and our parents have not done all this work just for Edar to plunge back into a succession crisis!'

'Edar is *not your problem!*'

'*You* are my cousin, and my future pain in the neck as Queen, and therefore very much *my problem!*' Melisande yelled back.

Both of us fell silent, save for our heavy breathing.

'If we don't solve the poison problem,' Gabi said into the quiet, 'none of that will matter as we'll be stuck in this room.' Her words were followed by a furious squawk; Theobilt had clapped a hand over her mouth, looping his other arm around her waist. They struggled for a few moments, then he let go with an outraged yell of: '*Don't lick my palm!*'

I snorted before I could stop myself, as Melisande's mouth twitched.

'We have to make certain which isn't the poison first,' I admitted. 'Then we can decide who'll drink it.'

Melisande nodded firmly: we were back in the safer area of solving a problem. As Mother often said, ruling was mostly figuring out solutions to a series of ever-shifting problems.

Theobilt stayed out of our discussion, keenly aware of the sharp undercurrents in our muttered debating, and forced Gabi to also keep quiet.

For two hours, we went in circles, zeroing in on one of the three, then backtracking, unable to prevent ourselves from skidding on doubt. In truth: all three could have been poisons, and this was a trap we could never win. But that would be a poor end to Lady Winter's bargain, which made us convinced that one, at least, was safe. But again and again, for all our combined knowledge, we kept returning to *which one?*

At last, we were caught between the second one and the third vial. The first I'd insisted was too obvious, a clever ruse, though Melisande still remained doubtful.

It took another hour to debate between those two; Theobilt and Gabi sat on the floor and chewed on dried strips of meat. She finally took a nap, with a folded tunic on Theobilt's lap as a pillow. Melisande and I had ignored all suggestions of stopping for food, facing each other on either end of the altar, our patience worn down to fraying threads.

Melisande finally picked up the first vial. 'Yes, I think you're right: it's too obvious to be poison.'

I scoffed. 'And it only took two hours for you to believe me!'

Theobilt rubbed his face and sighed, perhaps louder than he'd intended, and jumped at our swift glares. Still asleep on his lap, Gabi muttered and shifted.

'Why must you be the one to drink it?' I demanded, returning to the other argument we'd spun between us. 'Do you think courting death like this will make up for our childhood in Saphirun?'

She jerked back, two spots of colour blooming on her pale face. I'd unintentionally hit a nerve – the right one.

'You think yourself a martyr of old?' The force of my shouting surprised even myself; Gabi woke up so fast that she smacked her head against Theobilt's chin, sending him reeling. Melisande's eyes widened until white showed all around, but she raised her chin and straightened her shoulders, settling herself to weather the storm of my rage.

I slammed my hands against the altar, so hard that Melisande flinched. 'You don't get to decide to be the sacrifice! You don't get to decide what your actions will atone for! Your dying won't change Saphirun. It won't scour away everything you said or did – or worse, everything you *should* have done or said!'

This time Melisande's stubbornness faltered. 'I'm sorry,' she whispered, too low for the others to hear.

'It doesn't matter!' I yelled. 'Whatever nightmares I still had about Saphirun, they've been replaced by everything happening here. And if you're not able to forget, that's your guilt not mine. A bargain with Lady Winter is not how we'll settle everything between us,' I added, lowering my voice and trying to project a pretence of calm that I absolutely didn't feel.

Theobilt and Gabi watched us in stunned silence, though he was clearly spinning political calculations in his head. He likely knew about Saphirun, however little and however it had been changed in the telling.

And it made me furious.

I knew the anger that lurked within me. I buried it beneath the worry and fear that were my constant companions, the fear that I would never be good enough, that I would never fulfil my parents' legacy; that no matter how I was raised or how much I was loved, at heart I was only a usurper's daughter and no better than his treason.

But I could never truly show the rage that rippled like embers within me.

For all that Lady Winter had ripped out my heart with blood-ied claws and replaced it with brittle-burning ice, the flame was still familiar to me.

And now I set it free.

My breath in scorched, as if I was forcing ice-fire down my throat alongside the air. For a moment, I stood still, cradling the heat in my lungs, then balled my hands into fists and slammed them against the altar.

Frost crackled on the impact, snapping and spiralling across the altar. Melisande scrambled back, sickly pale. Theobilt surged to his feet and grabbed Gabi around the waist to drag her back.

I slammed my fists on the altar again and again, spirals of ice and frost layering upon the altar, and finally let out a shriek from deep in my stomach. The echoes rang in my ears, then slowly faded into a dreadful silence.

Caught up in my terrible rage, I gasped for breath and locked eyes with Melisande.

Without a word, I grabbed the second vial, the one I'd guessed was a tasteless poison, thumbed the stopper off, and tipped it into my mouth.

'*No!*'

I hadn't known Melisande could make such a sound, as she practically flung herself over the altar towards me. Speed didn't matter. The empty vial slipped from my already numb fingers to smash against the altar.

I opened my mouth to – fling insults? Beg forgiveness? Weep to be remembered? – and there was only the sudden taste of cherries and redcurrant as the poison reacted with my saliva. The candle flames flared, higher and higher, until the brightness forced me to close my eyes.

Emri opens her eyes.

She is home, and it is impossible.

She gets up from the floor, which she recognises for all the times she has strode and stormed and run along it, and stands in a corridor of the royal wing, which she also recognises.

But – she tilts her head – it is not quite the same.

The carpet is threadbare in the farthest corners, hideously old-fashioned. The paintings on the walls are not to her parents' tastes, and the portraits are not of ancestors they prefer to memorialise in close quarters. The skeleton of the space is the same, but it is not the right… time?

Careful footsteps sink into the carpet behind her. She turns, and comes face to face with her mama.

It is Xania Bayonn, and she is not yet a Queen.

She looks about Emri's age, tense and watchful with dark, wary eyes. She moves stiffly, ungainly, like she doesn't belong here, as if the observing portraits have found her wanting. Her walk barely resembles the authoritative, measured stride of Emri's mama.

But in her narrowed eyes, her firm mouth, and the defiant tilt of her chin, Emri recognises her. Recognises glimpses of the woman she'll become.

Spymaster. Murderer. Queen. Mama.

Xania Bayonn slinks along the carpet, and her daughter, not yet born, follows her. They pause at a corner, and ahead of them a set of doors open.

Matthias, Baron Farhallow, steps out, closes the doors behind him, and sighs.

Like Xania, he is younger, similar to the man Emri has grown up with and yet not: he's grimmer, harder, exhausted, his edges sharp enough to cut. A young man on the cusp of crumbling at the edges, who has held on to a staggering duty in secret for too long.

She knows that he recommended Xania Bayonn to be Mother's spymaster. That he introduced them.

But she has never learned how it happened.

Something cold and brittle snaps into shards in her stomach.

She does not want to see. She does not want to know.

'You have no choice,' Twilight says from beside her.

She whirls, and a hand slaps over her mouth before she can scream.

'I do not allow unnecessary disruptions,' Twilight says, his voice primed with disapproval. It is his voice, and his eyes, glowing with the Evening Star, but the body he wears is Mama's. A similar-yet-different version to the one standing near them, watching Matthias just around the corner: her face is thinner, dark brown skin stretched tight against her bones, and the shape of her mouth is cruel. Her posture is stiff, aloof, her demeanour as distant as the winter wind howling from the mountaintops.

Apart from appearance, Twilight's manifestation is nothing at all like Emri's mama. And yet, hope rises at the sight of her anyway.

As they watch, Xania Bayonn stiffens and reaches into her skirts. Withdraws a worn, well-loved dagger and tightens her grip on the hilt, almost in reassurance.

The walls blur around Emri, pinned by a nauseous twist in her stomach, and when everything settles, she watches Xania Bayonn confront Matthias and brandish her dagger at him.

Everything goes still, their loud voices plummeting into a silence strained enough to snap.

And then the doors are flung open and Mother – Queen Aurelia IV – stands before them in the doorway, her annoyed bewilderment spinning into anger.

The walls melt once more, and Emri grabs hold of Twilight-as-Xania-Bayonn for support before she can think better of it.

In the study, her parents square off on either side of the desk, while Matthias seethes in embarrassment, a peculiar mesh of emotions that Emri has never witnessed in him. A back and forth begins, a sharp negotiation of wits. And simmering underneath their wariness, suspicion, and fear, Emri can sense something else rising between them, a potential for something greater.

This was when the seeds of their choices were sown. Without this moment, they would never have met, never fallen in love and risked everything for each other. Without this moment, she would likely have never been born, a traitor's daughter adopted by two Queens to avert a succession crisis. Adopted by two Queens and loved as their daughter and heir.

Without this moment, Xania Bayonn would never have had to murder Rassa.

'Murder was already in her heart,' Twilight remarks, seemingly oblivious to how his words make Emri feel like the walls are closing in around her. 'Her father was killed, and before she met her Queen, she desired nothing greater than to bury a dagger between his murderer's ribs.'

Her parents freeze, still wary, still cautious and brittle-sharp, and then something in her mother's – no, the *Queen's* – face shifts. Something tiny, but the swoop in Emri's stomach fears that it was important and that, for something so small, it will have a fundamental impact.

Something, too, changes in Xania Bayonn's face: the guttering fade of hope.

'No,' Emri says in a trembling voice, right before the room churns around them. It snaps back into place in a small palace courtyard. Emri scrabbles to place it in her memories, settling on a corridor hidden behind a row of windows overhead, a corridor that links to a solar used in Mother's grandmother's time and a small library that one of her tutors was occasionally forced to hunt through for obscure volumes related to their research interests. It's a quiet, forgotten part of the palace, just like the courtyard it overlooks.

Above, clouds swirl and skitter across a blue sky solid enough to break. Time coils around them, tighter and tighter, even as Emri feels like if she stops thinking – stops being *frantic* – for a moment, it will spin completely out of her control.

A small dais and scaffold have been hastily constructed out of rickety, rough-hewn wood. It looks ready to collapse under the first authoritative stride up the steps.

Her mama – no, this is *Xania Bayonn*, not her mama, the difference as thin as a strand of hair and as immense as the sky – is led onto the dais. Her back is straight, as much from feigned bravery as the wrists bound behind her. Her steps are even and steady, but fear rolls off her like smoke.

There is no crowd, only three people as witnesses:

The executioner, the Master of Justice, and Matthias.

Xania Bayonn and Matthias, Baron Farhallow, lock eyes for a single moment. While she refuses to let terror crack across her expression, his face is pale and bleak. He regrets. He fears.

As Emri wonders where the rest of the family are, the knowledge blooms inside her mind, as the way in all dreams: Xania Bayonn's mother and sister are locked in prison, her stepfather bound to his rooms, all accused as accessories to her murderous intent.

'No,' Emri repeats.

Right before the blindfold is tied around her head, Xania Bayonn allows herself to shed a single tear.

The executioner is professional: the beheading is swift and clean. Her blood drips and spatters red, just like everyone else's. Just like a Queen's.

It is a dream, a vision. Not a memory. None of this happened, but the sound that rips from Matthias's throat will nevertheless haunt Emri until she dies. She simply doesn't know it yet.

'*No*,' Emri says for a third time. 'This didn't happen. This is a bad dream, a horror to frighten little girls in their sleep.'

'It was a potential consequence,' Twilight corrects her, still in the guise of a Xania Bayonn in possession of her life and head. 'Neither trusted the other; both young women trusted very few people, in fact.

Both were young and alone, even in the company of those who loved them. And Xania Bayonn held murder in her heart. If Queen Aurelia had been less determined, had refused to recognise the spark between them, if she had chosen caution over her self-made duty, she would have kept Lord Vigrante as an ally and disposed of the woman she would eventually marry. And in doing so, shatter the love and trust between her and the boy she once saved from drowning.'

He must mean Matthias. She has never heard anything about Mother saving him from drowning, though she has also never heard of Mama wanting to kill Lord Vigrante, a man Emri *does* know was a traitor to Edar, murdered by Rassa when his usefulness ran out.

'But Mother didn't,' Emri retorts.

'She didn't,' Twilight agrees. 'But there was a moment when, facing Xania Bayonn across her desk, she considered it, unknowing, in her heart.'

Emri rounds on him, refusing to acknowledge the strange lurch of losing her temper at the woman who is, and is not, her mama. 'Is this my test, then?' she demands. 'My version of what Gabriela faced, but only myself as witness? You show my parents' past, then the worst-case scenarios that *could* have occurred? Drip secrets in my ear that they never intended for me to know? And for what – that I'll question everything I know about them? Question their love for me? Question, question, and question, until I can no longer decipher truth from lies? Give up and let Lady Winter keep my heart and rob me of my will?' She comes closer and closer, each step loud in the silence pressing around them. 'Is that what you want? Is that the truth behind your smiles and apologies for your Lady's cruelty?'

A shadow slides across his face; starlight flares in his eyes. 'Gabi,' he says silkily, 'not Gabriela. She gave you permission to use her nickname.'

Emri stops, and belatedly realises that Twilight has stepped back as she has come towards him. She stops, and does not speak, allowing the hideous silence to deepen.

'I told you that I would not always be kind,' he finally says.

'If Mama knew you were real,' Emri replies, 'I know that she would worship you for the rest of her days to keep me safe.'

Twilight's form ripples, the flesh and bones of a harder, crueller Xania Bayonn sliding away until the god of dusk, of change, protector of spies, with his starlight eyes and blue lips, stands before her in all his great height.

His smile is kind, sharp-edged, and regretful. 'Night is coming for you, my dear.'

TWENTY-NINE

For three days, Theobilt prayed to Twilight for the means to keep Melisande and me alive.

While darkness took my mind, and the poison tried to take everything else, I dropped to the ground, foaming at the mouth and convulsing, and then disappeared. Before anyone could stop her, Melisande's panic convinced her that the only way to find me was also through poison. She unstoppered the third vial and swallowed the contents in a single gulp.

Both were poison. Both made us disappear.

Now alone, and understandably terrified, Theobilt and Gabi waited for us to return. When that didn't happen, they waited for someone to lose patience and present them with forceful, omniscient instructions. None came.

At last, after two days of fitful sleep and subsisting on bread and a water-skin, Gabi wore Theobilt down: the way forward for them was surely the last vial, which at this point was poison… or not. So they unstoppered the third vial, measured half into the cap of the now-empty water skin, held hands, and swallowed it together.

The magic spat them into an opulent, beautiful bedchamber,

where they found Melisande and I lying on two beds, well into the business of dying.

For three days, they battled to keep us alive, trying to break the fevers that dragged their claws through us. Theobilt dumped out the entirety of our stores, trying to find anything that resembled any sort of antidote he knew. Nothing helped, but neither did we tip over into death. They bathed us, wiped our sweat and our tears, unknowingly shed from the nightmares and hallucinations, the fever and the pains. They dribbled water down our throats, just enough, Theobilt reasoned, fearfully, to keep us alive.

Nothing helped. But we did not yet die. We refused to succumb to the fever's claws.

That was when they turned to prayer.

Theobilt prayed to Twilight mostly because he was too frightened to draw Lady Winter's attention upon us. He prayed for help, for the necessary knowledge, the necessary ingredients, to make an antidote. In his worst moments, he prayed for the antidote to simply appear.

He beseeched Twilight, once known as the kindest of the Edaran triumvirate, to remember the daughter of two Queens who had served him faithfully despite their ignorance of his existence. The Queen who had once been a spymaster and had stopped a usurper. And the Queen who had been forced into terrible choices and yet chosen love A mortal love almost as great as his for Lady Winter, though it could only be a shade against the adoration gods held for each other.

He went through boon stone after boon stone, beseeching, begging. Pleading. Weeping.

And Twilight, as he presented me with Xania Bayonn's execution, took pity on Theobilt. He was not Edaran – not yet, anyway, perhaps – but Twilight and Hatar had always been on pleasant terms, despite their differences.

On the second night, Twilight visited Theobilt in a dream. He opened his eyes to the same mountain top where I had met Twilight, with the same beautiful sky, surrounded by the same peaks. Twilight and I stood before Theobilt, having our same twisting conversation. And as Twilight pushed me off the mountain and I fell, he shoved the knowledge of the poison antidotes into Theobilt's mind with the force of a battering ram, hard enough to slam him back awake with a choked scream.

While he had slept, and Gabi had dozed for a moment, the ingredients for the antidotes of both poisons had appeared on a table. The recipes flared in Theobilt's mind like ember sparks, spinning, floating, dancing within his mind, threatening to scatter just out of reach if he thought about them too hard. He let his eyes drift out of focus, hands moving to shred and measure and pound ingredients into dust. If he did not act fast, he had the terrible horror that we would not survive a third night.

By the afternoon of the third day, they poured the mixtures down our throats and then collapsed into a dreamless sleep beyond their control. By sundown, towards the height of Twilight's power, my fever broke.

Soon after, Melisande's fever broke. But she took longer to awaken.

Within a day, we all knew something terrible had happened to her.

I was able to keep water and food down, though my legs trembled when I tried to walk. Even so, the fever didn't return, and despite the sheer amount of proper sleep I now needed, it was likely that I would recover.

Melisande took longer. Much, much longer. Food made her nauseous, water just about all she could keep down without gagging. Her eyes were glassy, no matter the broken fever, and the first time she tried to get off the bed, she collapsed. Theobilt barely managed to catch her in time.

I lay on my bed, and behind my closed eyes, I replayed our argument, the rage scorching through me, and my foolish decision to take the poison. If I hadn't done so, Melisande wouldn't have taken the second poison and ended up like this.

Wouldn't she? that cold, cynical voice murmured at the back of my mind. *She intended to take the risk anyway to assuage her guilt. And what would* you *have done then, if she had disappeared?*

I would have gone after her, too. No matter our childhood, no matter her guilt and my festering anger, one of us wasn't leaving the mountain without the other. It was an unspoken promise.

It was, I decided, better to ignore that voice.

Twilight's mercy to Theobilt seemed sincere: every morning we woke to fresh food and supplies, so he and Gabi could focus on keeping themselves – and us – alive.

One evening, as Gabi dozed beside a sleeping Melisande on her bed, Theobilt sat near mine, pretending to read while I kept my eyes closed and listened to my breathing. Now that our fevers had broken, Gabi insisted on stoking the fires to keep us warm, no matter that it plastered her and Theobilt in sweat, while Melisande and I appeared unaffected. It also kept the hoarfrost in my chest under control, and it was pleasant to breathe without the prickle of cold or scorch of rage in my throat.

'He pushed you off the mountain,' Theobilt finally said. 'Under a sunset sky, surrounded by mountain peaks.'

'Yes,' I said, my eyes still closed. 'I think he meant it as a joke. A clever trick.'

There was far more we needed to say to each other, but he wouldn't tell me everything he and Gabi had done to save us. As it was, Theobilt's sunken eyes and the skin stretched across his cheekbones hinted that he'd reached the limits of politeness and civil feeling, and so we didn't talk about it.

Gabi's animosity towards Melisande faded like snowmelt under a bright spring sun; it would have been childish pettiness to nurture it in the face of Melisande being so undeniably *unwell*. There was also now the matter of time inside the mountain: had

Theobilt and I dreamt of Twilight at the same time, even though mine had occurred soon after we'd all first met? Could Twilight exist within my execution nightmare while at the same time showing Theobilt my fall off the mountain?

Where did the power of gods end, even between themselves? Was it because so much magic had seeped into the mountain over centuries that Twilight could manipulate dreams as easily as Night, who had always held dominion over mortal dreams and nightmares?

To Gabi and Theobilt's significant relief, connecting doors to other rooms had opened soon after Melisande had awakened, so the four of us were no longer crammed into one room with two beds. While Theobilt watched us, Gabi cautiously explored the hallways to try to gauge the best way forward, inching her way further along each day without taking unnecessary risks.

While it was obvious that we'd have to move on (Theobilt was anxiously awaiting the morning when Twilight's patience ran out), no one wanted to admit it out loud, but we feared Melisande would simply not survive if we continued through the temple.

She'd taken on a ghastly tinge, thick slabs of shadows under her eyes as decent sleep eluded her. On the sixth day after we received the antidote, she'd finally been able to eat most of a meal, though her hands shook too much to hold a plate and bowl. To her great humiliation, Gabi had fed her, slow and patiently, reciting the story of how sparks from Aestia's eternal flame had shot into the sky to become the first stars; how later she had gifted the Eshvoni with a sliver of her flame so they could keep warm and protect themselves against predators.

I tried not to watch when Gabi was effectively Melisande's nurse, but I listened to the stories. When Gabi became so wrapped up in the rhythm and cadence of the words, I once again saw the glimpses of the Queen she could one day become. Theobilt and I never spoke of the change between our group, but more than once I caught him studying the two of them thoughtfully, as if he'd noticed the same.

In the end, it was Melisande who insisted we had to move on because, in her own words, she'd *burn this bed down if I have to spend another night in it*. Melisande didn't have the strength or finger co-ordination to even light a taper to set the bed on fire, but we all recognised the tone that warned us she'd make a good attempt at it, even if it resulted in the flames taking us all.

So we repacked our packs, which took three attempts because Theobilt refused to leave anything behind that could potentially be eaten or useful, though Melisande and mine's packs were noticeably lighter than the other two. I braced myself for an amount of walking I privately wasn't certain I could manage.

A walking stick, made from mahogany, polished and elaborately carved with a wreath of lilies climbing up to the top, appeared at the end of Melisande's bed. What little colour in her face retreated like the morning tide. I didn't know which was worse: the way she stared at it, aghast, or the resignation with which she picked it up.

Before, we'd walked mostly in single file, occasionally walking beside someone to talk, but usually we'd bounced conversations between ourselves as Theobilt stayed in front. Now, that all changed. Theobilt was still in front, but he insisted I stay with him in case I needed his help or support, while Gabi walked beside Melisande and dared her to protest about it.

The mood was subdued. Despite the cold, the discomfort and the fear, the poor food, the lurking threat of Lady Winter had now become all too real. While Theobilt had invoked Twilight's aid in pulling us back from death, my return to health was still slow and Melisande's appeared overwhelming in how far she still had to go.

After everything Theobilt had done to keep us alive, it made a horrific kind of irony that our way became blocked by a set of sealed double doors marked with the fir tree of Othayria.

Theobilt stopped. 'So this is how your god rewards me for my prayer.'

'He is the kindest of the three,' I replied sadly, as a sudden tangle of nerves hardened in my stomach, 'but even his kindness still has limits.'

'No offence,' Melisande piped up, a shadow of her snide drawl in the rasp of her voice, 'but I cannot wait to revel in your embarrassment, Theobilt.'

I didn't feel the same. For better or worse, Theobilt would likely be my future husband, and whatever lay beyond these doors, whether humiliation or arrogance, or simply a secret, it was something he had never intended to share.

'You know,' I said, trying my best to sound light hearted, 'if we survive and they manage to get through all the negotiations' – he stared at me with wide eyes; neither of us had directly referenced our potential marriage until now – 'this experience should form a solid base for a long and successful marriage.'

He only looked more terrified.

'… or not,' I concluded.

'If this is your attempt at flirting,' Melisande groused, 'then I shall have no choice but to beseech Twilight for whatever liquor they keep hidden in this place.'

I closed my eyes. 'Melisande, I am beginning to regret, *just a little*, that Theobilt managed to save you.'

'Good. If you regret my survival, then I'm making you feel something,' she retorted. 'And I simply couldn't bear it if my continued existence made you feel nothing at all.'

In a flash, I remembered her brisk, sharp response to my letter all those months ago: *as for my continued existence, you may conjecture similar from this missive.*

I smiled.

Theobilt, however, was not smiling. 'Let's just get it over with,' he declared. 'Whatever is behind those doors.'

Before any of us could speak, or second-guess ourselves, he strode forward and shoved them open.

They find themselves in the centre of a lush field.

'Oh,' Melisande says.

Theobilt shades his eyes with a hand, squinting at the dark line of a forest that stretches up the side of a valley and keeps going, then up at the sky. He takes a deep breath, as if the precise chilliness of the air will jog his memory as to what awaits them.

The summer air holds a refreshing crispness, a hint of the harvests to come. It makes Emri think of long golden days of picking and shearing, salting and pickling and preserving, building the stores to survive the months of Lady Winter's brutal cold and Night's encroachment upon daylight.

No matter the decay and the cold, the bitterness, rebirth always comes. Night always retreats to day, and so the cycle continues.

The field is lush, the forest a smudge in the distance, and Othayria— Othayria feels like... hope, in a way that home and Farezi do not. Here, Emri is known only as a future Queen that Theobilt will likely marry. Her family history is known, but in considering a marriage with her, the Othayrian royal family is looking to the future and not dwelling on the past.

She is still the daughter of a usurper. But, more importantly, she is the heir of two Queens and that will shape her as a ruler more.

'It's beautiful,' she says.

'Yes,' Theobilt says, his voice thick with longing, 'it is.'

For all that she has worried about her eventual marriage, Emri has not given much thought to what *he* will have to give up by coming to Edar. It's no different to the choice that Isra and Prince Aubrey made in staying in Edar, or the choice that was made for Emri when the adoption was finalised, but it's easier to dismiss the gravity of such a choice when viewing it from the perspective of a success. Even if that includes herself.

Before she can doubt, Emri reaches across and squeezes his hand, flashing a smile.

He stares at her, shocked, even though courtly manners have given way to cautious familiarity between them after weeks in the mountain. Approaching hoofbeats save him from responding.

Six riders crest a gentle hill, mid-race, skirts and riding jackets flapping behind them as they call out and jeer at each other. Two are in the lead, only a few paces between them, the coats of their swift, white-socked bays gleaming in the sunlight.

Much like Gabi had in her memory, Theobilt turns ashen. He flings a pleading look at Emri, but then, oddly, it lingers on Melisande, who raises her eyebrows and would seem more imposing if she didn't also look green around the gills.

The race is over, the bottom of the hill apparently the finish line, and the riders coax their horses into an easy walk to cool down, gathering close to laugh or sulk, commiserate and tease. Emri squints, and the horizon suddenly tugs towards them, a similar sensation from her vision with Twilight. Bile rises in her throat before the riders settle again.

They're now close enough to see that Theobilt is the rider who came second. His teeth flash in an easy grin as one of the two ladies riding with them teases him for losing. 'I let Eadric win, obviously!'

Eadric huffs, but there's no true venom in his scowl. 'Your horse wanted to gallop,' he retorts, 'and you wouldn't let him. You won't succeed by restraining yourself, Theo.'

Theo. Once again, the familiarity of a nickname, which Emri will not use, not yet.

One of the riders hoots from further back. 'Theo has no choice but to restrain himself. His wife will be a Queen: all his power will be within the limits *she* imposes.'

The woman in the riding skirts shoots him a filthy look. 'Tell that to your mama, and see how she responds.'

Theobilt told them, while justifying his cooking, that he spent his summers at family estates and learned how to survive in their forests. Emri's gaze drifts towards the distant forest, then looks back at the riders. It's hard to tell on horseback, but there's enough family resemblance that Theobilt is most likely with some of his younger siblings and cousins.

'Princess Emri has been raised by two formidable women,' another rider says in a deep, thoughtful burr, 'who successfully pulled Edar back from ruin. I would not be so quick to judge her.'

'Sensible,' Melisande remarks.

Emri jumps, having forgotten that they can speak and the riders will not hear them.

'Conrad has always been sensible,' Theobilt says softly. 'In another time, he would have been a monarch's general, their right hand.' As Conrad is built with the bulk and muscles to rival a bear, no one disagrees.

The woman sniffs, returning her attention to the rider who scorned Emri. 'This is why your parents are so reluctant to marry you off. You won't go far by insulting future rulers.'

'*Ada.*' Theobilt doesn't raise his voice, but the edge is unmistakeable and he looks unhappy. 'We are honoured guests at our aunt's home. Remember your manners.'

Eadric nudges his horse closer. 'It'll be all right, Theo. The princess is clever and raised to respect her duty.'

'Her mother refused to marry Uncle Aubrey,' Theobilt replies stiffly.

Emri and Theobilt wince in unison.

'That was different,' Eadric says with an easy shrug. 'Queen Aurelia did not wish for a husband. And Queens who follow their heart often face the consequences of their actions, and can't allow their children to do the same.'

Eadric is also exceedingly sensible, Emri thinks sourly.

'Besides,' Eadric continues brightly, 'Uncle Aubrey is happy now. He often writes to remind our grandparents of that. You won't be alone over there.'

Theobilt sighs and shifts in the saddle; his horse grumbles. Petting his gelding's neck, he mutters, 'I don't even know her. We're not far enough in negotiations that we can write to each other.'

'They're saying you can start writing to her from next spring,' Eadric says, 'once the snows clear and post resumes. So you can think of her at Midwinter, dancing, and write something sufficiently effusive and romantic so she can be open to the concept of being *wooed*.'

'How do you know this?' Theobilt asks, appalled. 'And what do you know about wooing anyone?'

'Unlike you, I eavesdrop in the right places,' Eadric replies dryly. 'You can ask Conrad, if you prefer: he certainly enjoyed being wooed by you.'

Beside Emri, Theobilt covers his face with his hands and lets out a tortured groan. Behind them, Melisande lets out something that can only be described as a cackle.

Emri swallows, aware of heat crashing over her like a wave. Not quite embarrassment; not quite anger. Indirect mortification, as if Theobilt's humiliation is spreading to her like a spark after handling wool.

On closer examination, Conrad shares none of the bone structure and family resemblance of the others. Eadric is broad-shouldered, but nothing compared to Conrad, who looks like he could punch a wolf in the face, but is gentle with his horse. He's not like other young men who've occasionally caught Emri's eye, but he's not unattractive.

His seat is excellent, Emri thinks distantly, knowing she's shying away from Conrad being mentioned in the context of Theobilt wooing someone.

And while she has devoted a not inconsiderable length of time to considering her future marriage, especially after things soured between her and Rialla, Emri has not actually spent a lot of time thinking about *Theobilt*.

Of course he would have been sceptical and afraid. Theobilt knew nothing about her, really, except for the portrait the diplomats had sent, along with a list of her interests and more flattering personality traits. Even now, they still don't know much about each other, not in the way of betrothed couples doling out morsels of knowledge and secrets in correspondence. Because in the mountain, they are only two people trying to stay alive who *may* end up marrying each other. What is the point of sitting beside the fire and hammering out their own sort of terms if one, or both, of them does not survive?

It still doesn't make witnessing this any easier.

'It's reasonable to be worried, Theo,' Ada says, guiding her mount to his other side, and probably meaning to be more reassuring than she sounds. 'And you won't be alone. I've decided that I shall travel to Edar and visit you as often as I'm able.'

'Along with your future wife?' Eadric asks, failing to hide a smile.

Ada sniffs. 'My future wife will also want to travel, *obviously*. Besides, you're not the only who eavesdrops on the family. They decided I shall visit you all regularly and remind you of your family obligations, regardless of who you marry.'

In the strange way of these memories, without having to ask Theobilt, Emri knows this is a reasonable conjecture and likely true. Theobilt's oldest sister will be Queen, eventually, and his next oldest sister will remain as her indomitable support. He will marry to secure Edar as an ally, and Eadric will marry into a high-ranking Eshvoni family, because the royal blood ties won't be distant enough for marriage for another generation or two. Which leaves Ada and his youngest sister.

Ada has always been curious about the world: to have her visit her siblings and remind them they are still Othayrian and represent the family is politically smart and subtle enough not to irritate other monarchs.

'Am I the only one who doesn't eavesdrop?' Theobilt demands, exasperated.

'Considering you're being married off,' Eadric points out, 'you should have been doing so once Edar rekindled their interest. This contract should have been agreed upon years ago, even if you're not signing it for another few years, and the Edaran Queens have been remarkably cagey about why the negotiations temporarily lapsed.'

Rialla, Emri thinks, and if she'd still had her heart, it would have dropped straight into her stomach. The negotiations had lapsed because Isra had found out about Rialla, and Emri had convinced her parents – begged, really, if she were being honest with herself – for time to prove their love was true and there would be no need for Emri to marry a prince.

It was the closest she'd ever come to a full-blown argument with them, and she and Isra had descended into a vicious one. She'd used her parents' own history against them, shamefully; Isra had stayed silent, twitching with rage, and Emri had known she'd just lost what little respect Isra had held for her.

At the time, she had thought it exceedingly cruel of her parents, that they would deny her something they had refused to deny themselves. Now, she realised they had all known that Rialla would not make a suitable Queen... and that Rialla would also soon realise the same.

Rialla had loved Emri, of that she was certain, but not enough to sit on a throne beside her. Not enough to rule a country and do right by its people.

But now. Glancing at Theobilt – and how laughable that even in the midst of *his* excruciating memory, she ended up thinking about her lost first love – she reconsiders. She doesn't yet know all of the little details that make him a person, not like she does with Rialla and Micah, but she has never had to survive something like this with her friends. And while Theobilt is enduring and keeping the rest of them alive, she can't say whether Micah and Rialla, if they were here, would be able to do the same with such calm.

That is, perhaps, a start. Assuming they both survive the mountain and the gods.

Assuming he can ever again look her in the eye after this.

'What if she doesn't like me?' Theobilt asks, momentarily distracted by his fidgeting horse, as if he can sense his rider's anxiety. His question is soft enough that those behind can't hear it. 'What if she refuses to let me have *any* power? What if the marriage turns terrible and it affects our children? What if—'

'What if none of that happens?' Eadric asks gently, and Ada nods in firm agreement. 'What if you meet, and it goes well, and after a few years, you realise you've fallen terribly and madly in love with each other? What if you are precisely the kind of support she needs?'

A moment's thought, and then Theobilt declares, 'You're far too optimistic.'

'No, you simply think too much,' Ada replies.

'You do,' Melisande tells Theobilt, thoughtfully.

'Shut up,' Emri tells her, and hates the strain in her voice.

'Besides,' Ada says, a wicked little smile lighting up her face as she reaches over to Theobilt's saddlebags, 'you can just show her *this*.' She tugs the closest one open and pulls out a battered sketchbook, ignoring his outraged cry.

'Ada—'

'*No*,' both Theobilts yelp in unison, though it upsets the horses.

She flips the sketchbook open, pages of sketches of people, flowers, and landscapes fluttering under her fingers to stop on one of–

Emri.

He's used her miniature for guidance, so it lacks the warmth and vitality of drawing her in person, but the likeness is still astonishing. There's a terrible intimacy to it, the idea that he's sketched her hair, eyes, and mouth in charcoal, all while never actually having met her.

It's both flattering and uncomfortable.

Without Ada realising, the rider who scorned Emri earlier has come up behind her horse and reaches over to snatch the sketchbook out of her hands. As she lets out an outraged yelp, he tosses it towards Conrad, who shows remarkable reflexes in catching it without startling his horse.

He considers the sketch of Emri thoughtfully, then glances at Theobilt, who's noticeably flushed and won't meet his gaze. Conrad's dark eyes are sad, but filled with a deep affection that's almost painful to see. As he examines the page further, everyone else falls into a hideous silence.

'I don't know if it will be a good match,' Conrad finally says, 'but I hope she'll make you happy.'

It is this, apparently, that forces Theobilt to tip his head to the sky and bellow, '*Enough.*'

Maybe that's how we get out of the mountain, Emri thinks blankly, just scream *enough* at the ceiling. None of this business with maps and tests and humiliation. Though knowing their luck, the ceiling would simply cave in on them.

The field starts to quiver and shudder, the sky rushing up to meet them and spiral away at the same time, a nauseating miasma that Emri's mind refuses to comprehend.

'*Enough,*' Theobilt yells again, hoarser this time, and despite everything that has happened since they've met him, Emri now realises what the last of his fraying patience sounds like.

But this time, unlike what happened during Gabi's memory, Emri swears that Ada frowns and glances in their direction, just before the memory breaks.

THIRTY

We came to facing another set of sealed, empty doors, and Theobilt wouldn't speak to anyone.

As with Gabi's memory, I'd expected us to be back where we'd found the Othayrian doors, but we were somewhere overlooking a plummeting waterfall. There had been no indication that a waterfall could exist within the mountain.

Gabi sat close to the edge, transfixed. As the water toppled over the upper edge, it partially froze close to our hollow in the rock. Parts of the spray turned into snowflakes that danced, suspended, upon the air, before the magic wavered and the water melted to smash into the river below.

The river below was shrouded in mist. We seemed part of a stack of tunnels and caverns that all peered out upon the waterfall, almost like we were in a courtyard.

I frowned, peered over the edge again, then looked around for Theobilt. This was such a distinctive layout, it had to be on the map so we could orientate ourselves.

He'd tucked himself into a small jut of rock overlooking the waterfall. I sighed, then jumped as Gabi tugged at my sleeve.

'Be kind to him,' she said.

The sound of the roaring water muffled my footsteps, but Theobilt betrayed himself by shifting away as I drew close. I didn't take it personally: it was no different from when Gabi had lost her temper after she'd flung us out of her memory. No one wanted to be watched as they wrestled with humiliation.

'I apologise for what you had to observe,' he said. His formality would have sounded better if he hadn't had to shout over the water.

'Maybe we should move away from—' I gestured towards the cascading waterfall '—this?'

He froze, as if I'd just suggested he fling himself over the edge, and looked so frustrated and terrified that I had to struggle not to laugh. Then he nodded, and forced his shoulders to relax.

We moved towards a corner as far away from the others as possible. Melisande opened her mouth, clearly ready to tease him, no matter that she still looked wretched herself, but I pinned her with a hard look.

Theobilt pressed against the wall again, dragged his hands irritably through his hair, and refused to look at me. I knelt a few feet away, crossed my legs, and tried to get into a comfortable position. When we were younger, Rialla had often resorted to sulking when she was angry or upset, while Micah had preferred nothing better than a long, comfortable silence. If Theobilt thought he could wait me out, it would take a while.

'I again apologise for… that,' he finally said.

I tilted my head, grimacing as my neck crunched. 'For what? Expressing worry about marrying me? Why should you apologise for that?'

'Because it wasn't... it wasn't polite!'

'Theobilt, under normal circumstances, would we ever discuss what conversations we had with others about our potential marriage?'

He shook his head.

'Precisely. If not for the gods, I'd never have known what you said during that ride. I'd never have known about Conrad unless you'd mentioned him. No more than you ever finding out about my discussions with my parents about marriage.'

'Was I discussed?' he asked, apparently genuinely curious.

'Wait until we reach a set of doors with the Edaran rose briar,' I said dryly. 'I'm sure you'll find out then.'

'Melisande will be intolerable,' he muttered.

'Melisande will do whatever helps her forget how ill she is,' I said, 'whether or not it's kind.'

Theobilt tilted his head back against the wall, took a deep breath, and attempted a rakish smile. It would have been more impressive if he hadn't looked exhausted and damp from the waterfall spray. 'Astonishing how much people keep bringing up our potential marriage when negotiations aren't even complete.'

'That depends.' I planted my hands against the ground and stretched my legs out. 'There won't be any need for a marriage contract if both of us don't make it out of here alive.'

'That sounded more like a threat than you perhaps realised.'

I smiled, and needed no mirror to know it was sharp and unpleasant. My patience with our situation was swiftly dwindling.

We lapsed into silence, but this time it seemed more comfortable. The sound of the waterfall somehow turned into a soothing background noise.

Finally, I asked, 'Who was Conrad?'

Theobilt closed his eyes, resigned. 'A friend. His grandfather got the family banished from Court before Conrad was born, but my grandmother extended them an invitation to return when Conrad was ten. They still weren't fully back in favour, but we became friends and then, well... it felt natural, when it changed between us.'

I clearly remembered the painful swell of affection in Conrad's eyes as he'd gazed at Theobilt. 'And did he... know that you were intended for a marriage alliance?'

'Oh, yes,' Theobilt said, startled. 'My parents don't encourage gossip—'

I snorted: no Court could effectively function without gossip.

'—but they felt it was prudent that their children's futures be known, so... so...' His face twisted. 'So the nobles knew which of us would stay in Othayria and could plan accordingly.'

I sighed. 'They probably all have copies of the family trees to compare everyone's ages and where we rank in power.'

It was Theobilt's turn to snort. 'You will all be Queens one day. Your value on the marriage market is clear.'

My smile sharpened again. 'I'm a complicated offer.'

'Only if you consider yourself to be,' he countered, and I had to drop my eyes against his apparent sincerity.

'Was there anyone else?' I asked, not so much because I needed to know whoever he'd cared for – or still did – but because this similarity between us was oddly comforting. It was an arranged marriage, at its heart, even if trying to survive the mountain wasn't the sort of courtship anyone had intended for us, but knowing we cared for other people, had loved them, perhaps meant we could also eventually care for each other.

'Roan,' Theobilt said, a faint smile curling his mouth. 'The son of one of my aunt's neighbours. Second son, so he wouldn't be inheriting the estate or title. I… it was every summer, and we had no illusions that it would ever last.'

'Women?'

He shook his head. 'There were some I found attractive, and it was lethal when they were also clever, but they knew I was bound for a foreign marriage and didn't want the complications. Roan wanted to know what it was like being with a prince, and Conrad… well, I should have stopped that when I realised how serious it was becoming to him.'

How had Theobilt found this so easy? To love and move on, knowing it couldn't last, that neither of them had intended it to, even at the beginning with Conrad? How had he fallen in love and not fought against it ending?

'They had their own lives,' Theobilt continued, as if he could guess my thoughts from my expression, 'their own duties and plans. A prince didn't fit into them so well, even if they sometimes wished otherwise.'

'Oh,' I said, despising the flush that scorched across my face. And here it was again: Theobilt's self-awareness, not just for his own situation, but also for those he'd fallen for. When I'd been with Rialla, I'd been so focused on *me*, on the duty that awaited me, the pressure and expectations, that I'd forgotten about *her*. Even though we'd been childhood friends, and I'd grown up listening to her hopes and dreams, no matter how wild and impractical, when we returned each other's feelings, I'd pushed it all aside, so convinced that we too were destined for a great romance.

I'd never stopped and thought about what *Rialla* wanted, and I'd certainly never asked her. And if I'd caught a hint that she regretted declaring ourselves before our families and Isra, that she'd later realised the enormity of what was involved in loving me, I'd done my best to ignore it.

The realisation hit almost like a physical blow, as shame-sweat broke out under my arms.

I had, indeed, been the spoilt, selfish princess Rialla had accused me of: the final insult she'd hurled at me during the argument that had destroyed everything between us. And no wonder she'd lashed out so harshly: I'd reacted with stubborn disbelief, convinced that she was utterly wrong when she'd said our relationship had to end.

Or maybe, offered that sly, cynical voice inside me, *you were simply terrified that you would lose someone else you loved. If Rialla could love you, and then pull away like it was nothing, then perhaps Arisane was right about you all along. And if Arisane was right about you, then perhaps your parents' love was conditional on being their heir, no matter what they said or did otherwise.*

Maybe you simply have a limited capacity for being hurt.

'Emri,' Theobilt said cautiously. 'Are you all right?' He shifted closer, the familiar guise of the concerned prince settling back on his features, banishing the mortified young man – the *real* Theobilt that perhaps only his family ever saw.

'No, of course you're not all right,' he said immediately, berating himself. 'None of us is all right. But... did you... did you have someone...?'

I hadn't wanted to have this conversation with him. It was *never* the conversation I'd wanted to have with him. But if negotiations concluded, and he came to Edar and we *were* married, he was astute enough that he'd guess from one interaction with Rialla who she'd been to me, once.

'One,' I finally said, moving so I could lean against the wall and tip my head back, wishing that we'd stayed closer to the roaring water after all. 'One more than my parents wanted, really. There were other flirtations, occasionally, but they were never serious.'

Theobilt nodded. 'Your mother was careful before she met Queen Xania. But she came to power in a far more precarious political situation.'

I laughed, not caring how bitter it sounded. 'Really? Because sometimes it still feels like people are waiting for me to make a very large mistake, so they can claim I'm truly a usurper's daughter and blood will always out.'

'Queen Aurelia was also distantly related to that usurper,' he said mildly.

'They tend to be hard of hearing around that reminder.'

'Who was she?'

'Rialla. Her family is politically terrifying and were *deeply* unhappy that she'd fallen for me. They don't believe in interfering with a monarch's plans for their child's alliance.'

A tear slid down my cheek. 'Rialla was my first true friend in Edar, and I thought I'd make her my Queen.'

After a long moment, broken only by the roaring of the water, Theobilt ventured, 'But?'

'But she was cleverer than me.' I closed my eyes. 'She saw what I refused to acknowledge: that loving me ultimately led to a crown and a throne. It led to duty and a responsibility heavier than most could imagine. Before my parents, most of the Edaran Kings weren't good rulers. They lived in comfort and shunted their responsibilities to politicians with their own agendas. But being Queen isn't a ceremonial thing. I've never questioned it, because I've always known it's my duty, but I never thought about how *Rialla* would see it.'

Theobilt's eyebrows made interesting movements towards his hairline.

I shook my head. 'She didn't reject all responsibility like you're imagining. There's a difference between being a good courtier or advisor and being a Queen. They're different kinds of power.'

I rubbed my eyes. 'Rialla was raised to be an advisor, eventually, and she will serve me extremely well as one. But she was not raised to be a Queen and she didn't want to be one. And neither of us is to blame. Well, I'm a bit to blame, because I ignored everyone when they tried to warn me. I even ignored Rialla's heavy hints every time I waxed lyrical about our future. So, really, there's no one to blame but myself.'

'You were in love,' Theobilt said softly. 'You can't blame yourself for that.'

'I can blame myself for being stupid.'

We lapsed into silence, and watched the waterfall cascade, freeze midway for a few heartbeats, then crash into the river. Frozen snowflakes danced between tendrils of mist. Sometime during our awkward conversation, I'd stopped being afraid of the waterfall and could admire it now that we were safely away from the edge.

'Do you think we'd be happy together, if we married?' he asked.

I gave the question the careful consideration it deserved. 'I don't know,' I finally answered. 'My parents once told me that it's very easy to be dramatically romantic, and a lot harder to build a life together.'

'I don't think I'm a dramatic person,' Theobilt said.

I raised my eyebrows. 'Theo, you just yelled at a god in a vision. I think some might call that dramatic, even just a little.'

His face lit up with a grin. 'You called me Theo.'

'Well,' I reasoned, trying for dignity, 'I just learned that you sketched me. It's the least I can do.'

He laughed, a light sound that I hadn't heard from him before, yet clapped a hand over his face in embarrassment.

'Don't worry,' I added. 'It's a beautiful sketch.'

'Thank you,' he said ruefully.

'Have you always drawn?'

He shrugged. 'Since I was a child. It's soothing, and mostly for myself. My sisters like it when I sketch them, but there's not much use for a prince who can sketch and paint.'

I thought of Aunt Zola, who had caught Isra's attention so many years ago through her viola playing. 'Not necessarily.' I worked my bottom lip between my teeth, then asked, 'Have you sketched me while we've been here?' I'd seen him sometimes at the fire with a stick of diminishing charcoal and a little notebook, but I'd always assumed he was making notes or trying to decipher the parchment.

'Of course not!' he said, appalled. 'Sketching you from your miniature is one thing. Sketching you here, without your knowledge, is quite another!'

I laughed, overtaken with a rush of warmth towards him. 'Well, if you ever want to sketch me, consider my permission granted.' I paused, then touched my hair self-consciously. 'Though, perhaps you should wait until I look less... less...'

'Like you're on a quest in a mountain temple?' Theo suggested with a crooked grin.

I snorted. This time, our silence was much more comfortable.

'But doesn't it bother you sometimes?' I finally asked, genuinely curious. 'That our choices can never truly be our own?'

His expression turned thoughtful. 'I've always known my future lay in a marriage alliance,' he said at last. 'When my youngest sister was born, my parents started to decide how best useful the youngest four of us would be, politically, depending on our strengths and personalities. Othayria has always pushed for peace the most, and never shied away from using marriage to achieve that aim. You can't grow up in my family and think you can shirk your duty.'

'I know some of the other monarchs judged Mother, privately,' I said. 'For choosing love over duty. It was always in what their diplomats *didn't* say.'

'I'm only a little older than when Queen Aurelia took the throne,' Theo said. 'I don't think my choices would have been much better.'

Peace was such a fragile thing. Easier to destroy than to maintain. It often seemed like it was upheld solely through the sheer force of will of my parents, the other monarchs, and Rijaan's High Council, underpinned by trade, commerce, and marriage alliances.

'I hope we can be happy,' I said, betrayed by the thread of wistfulness in my voice.

Theo knew exactly who I meant by *we*. Realistically, if we survived this, how could we refuse a marriage? He would be one of only three people on the entire continent who would truly understand what we'd experienced here.

'Well,' he said reasonably. 'You said Rialla was your oldest friend before your feelings for each other… expanded. Isn't this what we're doing here? Becoming friends? Isn't that a start?'

He was right. If we managed to survive this, we'd have a strangely solid foundation for a state marriage.

'Tell the diplomats to send books rather than flower seedlings,' I said. 'And if they insist on flowers, don't send roses.'

'They're Edar's national symbol,' he said blankly.

I shrugged. 'The *briar* is, technically. Roses upset Mama, though she never shows it in public.'

Worry rippled across his face.

'My parents will also require you to visit before I sign the marriage contract,' I added.

'*Visit?*' Theo sputtered, understandably. Suitors didn't visit prior to signing a contract unless there was demand for a monarch's hand, such as when my mother took the throne. Isra had championed Theo as the best suitor for me since I was young, backed by Prince Aubrey. Theo had very little to prove, except against my parents' expectations.

'So they can judge you, of course,' I explained, fighting not to smile as his eyes widened. There were politicians who'd do everything possible not to face the Edaran Queens, never mind a prince being considered for their daughter's hand.

THIRTY-ONE

I finally took pity on Theo and declared we needed to find somewhere better for the night. Because no one, no matter how much they loved waterfalls, delighted in sleeping beside one.

But when we turned back to Melisande and Gabi, they were already asleep. I understood Melisande passing out: she needed more rest than we could reasonably give her right now. Gabi, however, was in as good health as months trapped in the mountain could allow. Perhaps she was also reaching the limits of how much more she could withstand.

'We can't keep this up for much longer,' I murmured.

Theo nodded grimly.

I tucked Melisande's bedroll around her and rolled up the wool mattress to ease it under her head as a makeshift pillow, trying not to wake her, as Theo did the same for Gabi. But as I lay down beside Melisande, keeping close for warmth, she opened her eyes.

'Was that a hint of personality I heard from Theo?'

I rolled my eyes, then smiled and leaned in conspiratorially. 'Perhaps.'

She mock-gasped. 'How scandalous!'

Before I could help it, relief and... *happiness* burst inside me, like I'd drank a glass of expensive Othayrian wine too fast. I started laughing, almost to the point of tears, thankfully almost fully drowned out by the waterfall.

Melisande smiled and reached over to squeeze my shoulder.

Then: a slow, cracking sound, loud enough to jolt Theo and Gabi awake. I followed the sound until my gaze landed on the waterfall, which was freezing–

Upwards.

'Oh, no.' My words were low with dawning horror.

The waterfall froze in jagged chunks, the ice stretching towards the river drop high above. A groaning rumble, followed by a deep roar.

Lady Winter howled in our minds, as terrifying as an oncoming avalanche: *You dared to* aid *them?*

The waterfall exploded, raining jagged chunks of frozen ice, as the ground crumbled under us and pitched us towards the churning river below.

The plummet was almost gentle, despite the frigid air screaming around me, because for a short moment, my mind was unable to catch up with what was actually happening. Instinct forced me out of the bedroll, knowing what my eyes couldn't yet see: we were about to hit the water.

My body spasmed from the shock when I plunged through. It was so cold, I didn't even have the breath to scream.

For a long moment, all was peaceful. We'd tumbled down through darkness, but the water was somehow bright, speckled with glimmering snowflakes. Chunks of the frozen waterfall slammed into the pool, disturbing the water around me, but none hit me: a stroke of divine luck, certainly.

I sank slowly, my hair snapped from its tie to spool around me. There was no fear, no rage, only the slow sink deeper into the depths.

Then the pain started.

First at my fingertips, a burning prickle like whenever I foolishly went into the cold without gloves. It twined up my arms and gouged against my ribs; down my legs to stab into my feet. I shuddered, fighting against the water now suddenly pressed against me, trying to keep me down, so different from before.

It punched against the hoarfrost in my chest, and I screamed, and choked against a mouthful of icy water, and kicked upwards until I broke through the surface, spluttering and gasping.

We'd fallen into a pool below the waterfall and river, deep and dark and still. As I treaded water, blinking to clear my eyes and coughing furiously, the only light was the pinprick bursts in the water itself, and a rippling glimmer in the walls: the same wavering brightness I'd seen in the walls when Melisande and I had woken up in the mountain.

The water was so horrifically cold.

'Emri!'

Theo's shout bounced against the walls. I flinched, whipping my head around to find him pulling a shivering, coughing Melisande out of the water. Gabi was huddled against the ground behind him, soaked and spluttering.

'Come closer so I can get you out!' He looked as bedraggled as the others, his hair dripping into his eyes and his clothes plastered against him. Melisande, now out of the water, was so wracked by coughing that she sounded close to gagging or passing out.

My clothes seemed heavier than my most elaborate Court dress, clinging to my arms and legs like chains, but I forced one arm up and then another, a pitiful attempt at swimming, but enough to get me close to Theo so he could reach me.

He grabbed the back of my jacket and hauled me out. I managed only a few crawling steps on my knees before I collapsed onto my side, hacking water out of my lungs. Theo sprawled beside me, as if his strength had immediately abandoned him now that we were all out of the water, even if not necessarily safe.

'That was awful,' Theo finally wheezed. 'Why would Twilight do that after helping us?'

I shook my head. 'That was Lady Winter, probably *because* he helped us.'

'A marital spat. Wonderful.'

Yes, Lady Winter and Twilight being at odds over our progression was *just* what we needed.

After a while, when all of us – except Melisande – had finally managed to stop coughing, I said, 'We need to try and warm up and see what supplies we have left. And figure out where we are.'

Theo closed his eyes, resigned, but got up after what I suspected was a stern mental talking to.

It was grim. Our supplies had tumbled into the water with us, and while Gabi and Theo had managed to fish them out, a lot had been destroyed, save what had been carefully wrapped in Theo's precious leftover wax paper.

Most of the dry food was now inedible, our spare clothing sodden. I pressed the heels of my hands against my eyes, hard enough that spots danced in my vision, fighting the wave of despair threatening to drag me under. Doing so was exactly what Lady Winter wanted, to prove me unworthy of winning her challenge.

The sound of chattering teeth made me pull my hands away. Melisande was curled up around herself, shivering hard. Her hair was plastered to her skull and cheeks like rills of ink.

Theo and I locked gazes and came to a silent agreement.

'Gabi, try and find something to start a fire,' I said, flinging up a desperate plea to Twilight for scraps of dry(ish) kindling. 'Theo, help me with Melisande. We need to try and warm her up, quickly.'

As I reached for her, I let out a sudden, sharp sneeze.

For three days, Lady Winter made us pay for Twilight's foolish kindness.

Gabi and Theo managed to wrangle a pitiful fire together, while I yanked Melisande's heavy jacket off, wrung out a blanket as best I could, and got her as close to the fire as possible without her accidentally going up in flames. But the consequences of damp clothes and bedrolls, ineffectual flames, and our fall into frigid water hit us all.

For three days, we were felled by chills, sneezing, and a hacking cough that clawed deep into our chests. Apart from sipping water, all of us (other than Melisande, who was struck harder with her existing ill-health) could only keep the fire from going out, then collapse back into feverish dreams.

No god answered our prayers.

No god seemed to remember us at all.

On the fourth day, as far as I could reckon it, Gabi appeared over the worst and Theo was able to mostly sit upright and stay there. She revived the fire, while he rooted through our remaining supplies to find something that he could fling into a boiling pot and reasonably brew into a tea to soothe our throats and aching heads.

I tried to tell myself that Lady Winter could do far worse to us than horrific colds, but the blitheness didn't hold up against Melisande's worsening state.

She'd improved the least, lapsing back into feverish restless sleep as we pulled free of the worst of our symptoms. Theo focused on drying her spare clothes and blankets to help keep her warm, while I tried to break the fever with little success. With our old supplies, we could have kept ourselves reasonably well fed while taking care of her, but now…

After some hissed arguments that Gabi pretended she couldn't hear, Theo and I sent her to explore the nearby tunnels with the (still mostly indecipherable) map and stern instructions that she be careful and not go far at first. We debated my going with her, but Melisande had developed an alarming rattle in her chest.

Gabi looked pleased, if mildly overwhelmed, at the trust we were placing in her, particularly with the map, which Theo had become attached to and was loath to let out of his sight. She did as we ordered, inching along the tunnel, memorising her turns and the shape of the spreading tunnels, until she finally arrived back and asked Theo if she could borrow his notebook and charcoal to help her keep track.

While the map had been saved thanks to the wax paper, Theo's notebook had been in one of his pockets and hadn't fared so well. The charcoal, slowly diminished to a nub, had recovered after time beside the fire, but the notebook had dried into a crinkle of stained pages. His log of days was practically indecipherable, and it was this, the loss of proof at how long he and Gabi had spent here, that had driven him almost to hopelessness.

'I don't think it's going to be much use,' he said, and Gabi seemed equally dubious as she poked a finger at a crinkled, water stained blank page, but it was all the paper we had left and the map didn't show the tunnel in detail. The alternative was for her to get lost.

While we tried to get Melisande to keep down water and break her fever, Gabi grew bolder in her explorations and started bringing back things she found in alcoves and corners.

'I think this was a pilgrim path,' she said, when she returned with a wrapped parcel of cured meat, still somehow edible. (I claimed magic, while Theo pointed out the temperature plummeted the moment we stepped out of the fire's range.) 'A really old one.'

'Unsurprising,' Theo muttered, 'if we had to go under the river to reach it.'

But we began to believe her when she kept coming back with what appeared to be offerings: preserved food, jewellery that I decided to keep in case we needed bribes for aid once we got outside the mountain, and spices that could only have been found outside Farezi. When Gabi retrieved a wedge of ginger that Theo carefully pared to make into a tea, I frowned into the fire until she asked me what was wrong.

'Ginger is native to the Sekran Empire,' I said. 'How could it have ended up here, as an offering to Lady Winter?' The Sekran Empire was to the north-east of Othayria, and most of Edar's contact consisted of an embassy and a diplomat whose primary concern was keeping the trade agreements intact.

'We were all trading since before the First Empire,' Gabi said pragmatically. 'Someone probably bought it as a fancy offering to soften the blow of asking Lady Winter for aid.'

'Maybe not Lady Winter,' Theo said. 'Could have been Twilight or Night.' He hefted the lump of ginger in his hand. 'We all share the same sky, after all. Some of the gods were worshipped across borders.'

He was right. Most of the temples were long gone or in ruin, but smaller ones had existed for gods in other countries, like the goddess of day and her twin sister, who had once held dominion over the sun, both answerable to Aestia.

The ginger tea wasn't as strong as Theo had wanted, but it felt as good as a proper meal, and revived us in mind as well as spirit. It also eased the terrible cough in Melisande's chest, which convinced Theo that I should now accompany Gabi to find as many new provisions as possible and get a better sense of how we'd start to recover the vast progress we'd lost.

Now without Theo's makeshift calendar, from which we'd been trying to guess the difference between the passage of time within and outside the mountain, we'd also lost anything resembling a guess of how long we had left until Lady Winter's deadline: the last full moon of winter. The calendar hadn't been very helpful, but better than nothing, and without it, we were practically wandering in the dark in terms of time.

Despite being under the river, the tunnels themselves were cold, but not damp, which made sense if this had been a pilgrim path. Lady Winter might have disagreed, but it wouldn't have been good business for the temple if pilgrims had sickened or died from damp seeping into their lungs. Gabi walked briskly, confident in the progress she'd already made, and briefly explained why some tunnels were useless as we passed by; blocked by rockfall, or suffused with an unsettling feeling that we both agreed was best to avoid. In such a place, this far deep, it was best not to ignore one's instincts.

We took turns sketching each turn we took, trying to guess which direction would lead upwards. The offerings varied from the practical, similar to what Gabi had already found, to the poignant – decayed remnants of what I suspected were dolls, stuffed toys, and baby blankets – to the ornate. Gabi lingered over an elaborate candelabra made of what we suspected was gold, while a set of dusty crystal drinking glasses caught my eye, carved with images of stylised snowflakes and forests.

Here, on the pilgrim path, it didn't matter how wealthy or high-ranked someone was. They'd all finally come north, journeying through the cold and deep into the mountain, to beg the gods for help.

What could that kind of power do to a god? And how would they react when a mortal then tried to defy them?

'Will Melisande get better?' Gabi asked abruptly.

It was our third day exploring the tunnels together. After studying our notes, we'd decided to try the last remaining route, which we hoped would lead to an incline or staircase, and had lapsed into silence as we walked.

'I don't know,' I finally said, because there was no sense in pretending or lying to her.

What food provisions we found, most of them went by unspoken agreement to Melisande, who still look haggard, even though her appetite wasn't improving and Gabi's stomach often complained. (To her embarrassment, Melisande would silently hold out the rest of her meal for Gabi to finish.) Theo wasn't certain if it was the drop into the water that had exacerbated Melisande's already poor constitution, or that it had taken him longer to brew Melisande's antidote than mine. (I suspected the latter, but was stern at Theo whenever he brooded on it.)

Gabi made a troubled noise. 'But surely when we're free of the mountain, the physicians will know what to do?'

'I don't know,' I repeated. Knowing how frustrating that probably sounded, I added, 'The physicians are familiar with mortal ailments. Not with anything related to magic, not for a long time.'

It was another thing to add to my ever-growing list of concerns about how we'd function with gods and magic returned to our world. Would healers now have to work alongside physicians? Would physicians without magic still be considered as important? How could we even train healers, except to beseech help from the gods or accept the potential tragedy of mistakes – which made my stomach drop, both as a person and a princess – while healers trained themselves?

'It's very harsh of Lady Winter,' Gabi said, still sounding troubled, 'since she isn't even Melisande's patron goddess.'

'Our families are linked a few generations back,' I reminded her, 'and the borders were different, once.' Which still didn't matter much, since the Farezi royal roots were primarily in Southern Farezi, the domain of La Dame des Fleurs.

Who was going to be *extremely unhappy* when she learned Lady Winter had poisoned Melisande.

Yet another problem to add to my list of concerns.

'Oh,' Gabi said, as we turned a corner and found ourselves facing an archway leading into a cavern. 'A dead end.'

But we both paused instead of turning back. A strange feeling radiated from the cavern; I shuddered as my skin prickled, trying to step back and unable to.

'I… I…' Gabi swallowed, her forehead slick with sweat. 'I think we have to go inside.'

A blink, and for a sickening moment, the blurred movement of time in the visions happened to us in reality. We found ourselves in the cavern, unsure how we'd got inside, shivering hard enough to make our teeth chatter.

'A grotto,' Gabi breathed, sounding enchanted despite her uneasiness.

The cavern was small, the curved walls smooth and polished. With candles or lamps, it might have appeared comforting, cosy, even. Lit by the rippling glow in the walls, four ancient statues stood in the centre.

All at once, it came to me: this glow in the mountain walls was the same as in the passages at home, the secret pathways known to my parents, Isra, and myself.

Magic. All this time, magic had existed for centuries in the palace, and we'd never realised.

I recognised the tallest statue immediately. They were all ancient, weathered unlike the offerings we'd discovered, but the branches bursting from her skin were unmistakeable: Lady Winter. I peered up, trying to swallow against sudden fear in my stomach.

The frost in place of my heart throbbed, almost like a heartbeat in itself.

The resemblance was close to the actual deity, so she had likely manifested here before waning faith had trapped her within the mountain. The folds of the dress looked the same, as was her bearing and the proud tilt of her chin. While her features were blurred, I could practically sense her icy disdain.

Twilight stood to her right, discernible by his height and staff, with a third god at her left: Night, I presumed. Weathered like the other statues, there was a sense of sturdy armour over flowing fabric, and hair even longer than Melisande's.

A fourth statue stood behind them, weathered beyond all description, a god lost to time. I froze, frowning. There was no fourth god on par with the Edaran triumvirate. There had *never* been a fourth god. The statue was closest to the wall, and I squinted at a set of carvings above their head.

It was quiet, like the eerie stillness when I'd been floating in the pool, but there was no relief this time. Instead, something skittered up my spine, splintered over my back and wound around my ribs, a more unsettling sensation than the hoarfrost Lady Winter had burned into my chest.

We weren't welcome here.

Even so, we'd been compelled to enter. I clenched my teeth and approached the fourth statue, trying to get a better look at the carvings. For a moment, the circles and half-circles made no sense, symbols of a language beyond my understanding, and I struggled against a sudden wave of panic that the mountain had started to take even my intelligence from me.

Then Gabi came up beside me, narrowed her eyes, and asked, 'Is that a full moon at the bottom?'

Immediately, it all made sense: the phases of the moon, from new to full.

I frowned, trying to bully my mind into working, and a phase kept returning to me: *the last full moon of winter*. When we had to have escaped the mountain to win Lady Winter's bargain.

'Gabi,' I said, 'please sketch this.'

As she did, she kept glancing back towards the statue of Lady Winter. 'Edarans still make no sense.'

'Hm?'

She gestured at the statue with the charcoal stub. 'To have sculpted your gods in such a way, more monster than magnificent.'

None of them had seen her, or the other gods. They had no idea that this statute, bound in branches and hate, was the closest to Lady Winter's actual appearance.

The cavern had already been cold, but now the temperature plummeted. Ice thickened on the statues, cracked against the walls, turned the ground lethal.

Fear spasmed across Gabi's face.

I blinked, and in a flash of brightness, Lady Winter loomed before me, terrifyingly real. Another blink, and another, and she slammed her nails into my neck, curled them into my throat, and lifted me up by my flesh.

My blood pooled down her hand, spiralled down her arm, soaked into the sleeve of her ice shard glittering gown. It flooded my mouth and surged down my throat. So much of it, pooling into my lungs.

The stars had extinguished in her eyes. Darkness seeped into her face, stained her lips. She opened her mouth, and her teeth were bloody.

The blood kept pouring from me, so thick it was as dark as Lady Winter's starless eyes, so hot it scorched the frost in my chest. There was so much of it, and I couldn't breathe, *I couldn't breathe*–

'Emri!'

I opened my eyes, and I was huddled on my knees, my chin tucked tight against my chest to protect my neck. Gabi kneeled beside me, ashen, tugging at my arm. 'What's wrong?'

My hand flew to my neck: unblemished. No gouging, no blood.

'We…' My voice rasped, as if something had happened to my throat. I cleared it wincing, and tried again. 'We should get back to the others. We're not welcome here.'

I loosened my arms, realising I'd crushed the useless map against my chest, and Gabi let out a sharp cry as the parchment hit the ground and unfurled.

In the rippling light, the thick lines and spirals rearranged into the pattern of the moon phases we'd seen above the fourth statue.

The moon, from new to full, was a passage of time in itself.

Ink spread across the phases, marking the days we'd already lost. And how little time we had left to escape the mountain.

THIRTY-TWO

It had never been a map.

A paper hourglass, ink bleeding over the parchment until only the last full moon of winter remained untouched. If we'd realised sooner, walked faster, forced ourselves onwards through poor sleep and fear, ignored the pain as it embedded into our muscles…

If. If. If.

If was an unspoken wish, never proven true.

When we returned to the others and showed Theo what the parchment had turned into after we'd found the grotto, he was so horrified he couldn't speak for several moments. He held the parchment in trembling hands, then laid it flat on the ground and traced over the moon phases already filled with ink, pausing at where it was only partially full. He seemed to be counting in his head, eyebrows furrowed as he mouthed calculations to himself.

When he finally looked up, his face was grim and tight. 'If I have my numbers right…' He glanced at the parchment again, his throat working furiously. 'We have days left, if that, before the last full moon of winter.'

Days left to escape the mountain. And if we failed, they would all die, and my parents and I would become Lady Winter's puppet Queens when she was free of the temple.

Days left. And the mountain was wearing us down, and Melisande was on the cusp of illness I feared couldn't be cured without divine intervention, if it could be cured at all.

Days, and we were now deep in the lower bowels, all our progress lost.

'You said the parchment changed after Lady Winter appeared to you,' Melisande said abruptly.

My hand pressed against my throat, remembering the sensation of her claws plunging into my flesh, her strength as she raised me off the ground, how my blood had spilled down her hands and my skin and pooled into my lungs, trying to choke me, trying to drown me.

I swallowed. 'Yes.'

'So she was... she was trying to help us?' Melisande ventured, her eyes full of troubled doubt.

I thought. 'Yes and no,' I finally said. 'I think she was tired of nudging us along, or furious at Twilight and trying to make a point. We know exactly how much time we've left, now, but it's a curse and a worry as much as a blessing. Whatever else, now she wants us to be afraid.'

And in that, she'd succeeded; Gabi had been on the verge of tears since we'd fled the grotto, and nothing Theo had said, belatedly trying to show reassurance, had made her look any less terrified.

Theo frowned. 'Why would she aid us even by forcing you into the grotto to trigger the parchment changing? Without our deaths, it'll take much longer for her to gain the power to free herself from the temple.'

I thought of the fourth statue, weathered beyond recognition, of a god that none of us could remember, crowned by the moon phases that had appeared on the parchment. We were missing something, something that was the key to all of this—

—but we didn't have enough *time* to figure it out.

'Well,' Melisande said, trying to wrap shreds of authority into her voice, 'if we don't start moving, then we'll have definitely failed. And no offence, Emri, but I don't intend on dying so you can be Lady Winter's mouthpiece.' The shadows were thick under her eyes, and she was shockingly pale, but her smile was dangerously sharp, and her expression dared us to contradict her.

We couldn't, so Theo stayed with Melisande to help build up her strength so she wouldn't collapse on us, while Gabi and I resumed searching for a way out. Panic made Gabi fret and foolishly rush, and I wasted more time trying to keep her calm and think logically while holding my own growing fear at arm's length.

Finally, two days later, we found a wide staircase and returned to the others. Theo was reluctant, but Melisande was resolute: we had to move on and if we didn't, we risked Lady Winter's interference again.

So we gathered our meagre supplies, Theo and Melisande argued over whether she needed help to walk, and we started our slow journey through the tunnels towards the staircase.

Melisande slept poorly and walked slowly. One day, she was in so much pain that Theo finally went against his better judgment and offered to carry her for a while.

Melisande calmly, pleasantly, told Theo exactly what she'd do to him if he tried to carry her.

Then she stumbled for the fifth time that morning and, for a terrifying moment, looked like she was about to cry.

'Perhaps we should stop for a while,' I suggested tactfully, though we all knew we no longer had time to waste.

Even so, Gabi immediately dropped her pack where we stood. Melisande sank to her knees in stubborn, teary silence. No one spoke as we chewed mouthfuls of stale bread and refused to look at each other.

Melisande reached over and clutched my hand hard enough that my bones hurt.

It was easier at night, when we stopped and made camp. Theo, Gabi, and I had reorganised the work between ourselves – none of us could bear the idea of Melisande using what remained of her limited energy beyond keeping up with us every day – which Melisande chafed at, both because she couldn't argue against it and because I suspected she resented our kindness.

As we ate, she kept up the majority of the discussion, even if we were too tired and wanted to eat and clean up quickly before falling asleep. Since Gabi had spent months trapped in a mountain, Melisande had decided it was no reason for her education to suffer and became her new tutor, much to Gabi's appalled disbelief. Theo and I tried not to laugh and supplemented Melisande's teaching where possible.

Tonight, she was drilling Gabi on the treaty terms the newly sovereign nations had hammered out between themselves in the collapse of the Second Empire. She didn't seem perturbed that since Farezi had built the Second Empire, she was criticising her own ancestors' greed and folly.

Our ancestors' greed and folly.

'This happened over four hundred years ago!' Gabi finally burst out. 'It's not necessary.'

Despite her exhaustion, Melisande stared Gabi down. 'You will be Queen someday,' she said coldly, 'ruling in your own right. And unless our parents completely destroy the peace they're trying to build, we'll still be keeping to it. What you consider *unnecessary* is why we can't just invade each other's countries without a damn good reason.'

The terms of that treaty were why Rassa usurping Mother's throne would have always failed, one way or the other.

From the twisted, conflicted expression on Melisande's face, and the brief eye flicker towards me, I suspected she was thinking the same thing. But neither of us said anything. I didn't have the energy, and even Melisande's pride likely had limits.

Deciding to change the subject, I asked Gabi, genuinely curious: 'Eshvon is a queendom, but what would happen if a future ruler decided they didn't want to be known as a Queen?'

'It's already been discussed,' she replied, her expression making it clear she was deliberately accepting the topic change. 'One of my younger siblings decided if they were heir, they wouldn't want to be known as King *or* Queen, but as a Sovereign.' She shrugged. 'They're third in the succession after me, so it's unlikely to happen in this generation, but Eshvon would remain, just no longer as a queendom. It wouldn't change our duty to our people.'

I sat in thought, as Melisande said dryly, 'I suppose Queen Juliaane is thrilled about that.'

Gabi's face hardened. 'She hates all the changes Mother will bring in as Queen more than whatever will change long after her death.'

The lesson ended soon after when Theo declared the food was ready, and we descended into our usual tired attempts at a polite dinner conversation. (Sometimes, I ruefully wished we could tell our etiquette teachers, who would have been so proud.)

Tonight, Gabi had managed to spark something in Melisande, possibly the unpleasant memory of Rassa, as she kept talking to me after everyone else was asleep. I was about to finally admit that I couldn't keep my eyes open, when she mentioned her diminishing health, something she'd twisted herself into knots to avoid admitting until now, and I snapped my mouth shut.

Of course, she then sprinkled salt into the wound by going the way of grim humour.

'I don't think you understand,' she said, 'just how much I hate all of this. Our family has no use for *weakness*.' Her bitterness didn't surprise me; Arisane's poison ran deep in us both.

'Oh no,' I replied tartly before I could stop myself. 'No one else currently in existence could gauge exactly *how much* you despise this experience.' I rubbed my eyes, then knuckled above them where the beginnings of a headache threatened. 'No, that was unkind. We haven't been affected by poison like you have.' I let out a long sigh, then added, 'My position hasn't changed. I'm not leaving you behind, even if the illness means we're making slower progress.'

'You need to get out of here by the last full moon,' Melisande reminded me.

'And we're not leaving you behind.'

Melisande didn't reply for several moments, then said, 'I know I should thank you, but mostly I hate what they've done to me. At the beginning, I only knew I couldn't leave *you* behind. The others… perhaps, back then. If I escaped without you, your parents would declare war on Farezi in a heartbeat, no matter our lofty assertions of a *new peace*. Or whatever counts as war these days, since we don't have standing armies anymore.'

I took a moment to consider, then agreed, 'War isn't like what it used to be.'

My brain flicked through different potentials and scenarios, sinking into the familiar patterns of solving a hypothetical situation or problem. 'My parents would banish your ambassador and shutter your embassy, and recall ours. All trade and diplomatic agreements would immediately cease. Merchants would be reluctant to trade with you, which would convince the Rijaan banks that Farezi was a bad investment and strain your credit lines. Othayria and Eshvon would agree with Rijaan, perhaps simply to bide time, so your economy and free movement would come under strain.

'Not one threat of an invading force, and my parents would strip Farezi right back to the instability after Rassa's death.'

A terrible silence descended between us.

'Then they'd probably have you assassinated,' I added generously, 'just in case their feelings weren't fully understood.'

'I've changed my mind,' Melisande said. 'Just leave me behind to die.'

I snorted and settled into my bedroll. But sleep eluded me, as it did Melisande, judging by her restless, pained shifting.

'Things seemed to have improved between you and Theobilt,' she said, just as I was beginning to teeter on the cusp of sleep.

I sighed. Of course Melisande would return to this. 'It seemed only fair after we all witnessed his memory.'

'Foolish boy,' Melisande said, almost fondly, as if Theo were years younger than her instead of two months.

'I keep waiting for his niceness to be a disguise,' I admitted. This wasn't exactly a secret; Melisande had practically made goading his patience into sport, thrilled when he refused to rise to her bait. I felt intensely sorry for her younger siblings, none of whom I'd met.

'Just… no one can truly be that nice,' I continued. 'He makes even my *grandpapa* seem terrible by comparison.' And Grandpapa Kierth was one of the nicest people in the world.

Melisande shrugged. 'Othayria raises their younger sons for marriage. Prince Aubrey was the same, from what I've heard. My parents were a love match, but Arisane considered one of his sisters for… *him*' – the choked-out word could only refer to Rassa – 'so she kept an eye on them all.'

She was right about Prince Aubrey, who was still considered the ideal prince. Whenever he returned to Court, it was impossible to ignore his impeccable manners and warm demeanour. It didn't matter that he and Lady Astrii had been married for years; he was still buried in invitations before they returned to the country. People simply wanted to *be* in his presence.

'I mean, let's be logical,' Melisande said, suddenly in remarkably fine spirits for someone who could hardly keep her eyes open while we ate. 'Your families have been considering you for a state marriage since you were children, even if they moved *very* slowly about it.' She made a hand motion that possibly meant she understood Rialla had been the reason behind the slow pace, though initially Mother had wanted to be certain I was open to the idea of the marriage and didn't prefer only women, like her. 'So Theobilt's been raised with the assumption that he'll marry you, a princess who will one day rule in her own right. He's marrying *in*, and there's no guarantee you'll elevate him to rule beside you. I'm sure his family hopes so, but if they're smart, they've also hedged their bets, so he's *also* grown up knowing he may simply be your Consort. And if Theo ever tries to overreach through you, he'll not only have to answer to your parents, but also his own grandmother and mother.'

She raised her eyebrows. 'And speaking for myself, those are four women I would absolutely *not* want to anger.'

There was also a fifth woman Theo should fear angering: me.

I opened my mouth, but before I could speak, Gabi did.

'Theo *is* that nice,' she said reproachfully. 'One of my younger aunts married into a high-ranked family who've been loyal to the Othayrian royal family for generations. I grew up hearing about him, years before we were encouraged to exchange letters. It's not just how he was raised. He's simply... *good*, and kind and sensible. If you marry, he'll want to help you become the best Queen possible, whether as your Consort or King.' Her eyes gleamed in disdainful judgement from the firelight, before she rolled away onto her other side. 'You could be doing far worse than marrying him.'

'Indeed,' Melisande said. 'You could be marrying Gabriela instead.' She ducked as Gabi sat up in a blur; a rock sailed over her head to smash against the wall behind us.

'You deserved that,' I informed her.

'I did,' Melisande agreed cheerfully.

'Is this a good time to admit I'm awake and can hear you?' Theo ventured.

Every drop of blood instantly withered in my veins. It must have dried up, because that was the only possible explanation for the excruciating pain coursing through me. Melisande's cough sounded suspiciously like a concealed laugh, while Gabi muttered, still turned away, 'I'm going to sleep.'

It didn't even matter that, unlike anyone else who'd have overheard two princesses discussing them as marriage potential, Theo sounded as mortified as I felt, instead of smug or confident, as if he too wished to sink into the ground and be welcomed into its eternal embrace.

After she'd managed to compose herself, though her shoulders still shook a little, Melisande said, 'You know, maybe I can somehow dump the succession onto my brother and become the Edaran ambassador, so I can watch your courtship and laugh the entire time.'

'Not part of a diplomat's job,' I said through gritted teeth.

'Oh, I'm sure I can make it the new fashion – ' Melisande pulled her bedroll over her head with admirable reflexes as I, in turn, fired a rock towards her, then peeked back out. 'Violence is never the answer.'

I glared at her. 'One day, you might fall in love, sudden and violently. It will consume you and be everything you mock, and I will ensure that a junior diplomat follows you around to laugh on my behalf.'

'That is *absolutely* not part of their job,' Melisande retorted primly.

'*I will pay them out of my own purse.*'

'Will both of you,' Gabi snapped, '*shut up.*'

I finally managed to sleep, but only after an hour's fitful wishing (which may have been prayers, of the desperate sort) for the ground to swallow me up, or for a god to take pity on me and wipe the conversation from everyone's memories.

But as much as the Edaran gods wanted to be worshipped, they seemed to consider the consequences of mortal humiliation to be character building.

Emri opens her eyes to the tang of leather and metal on her tongue. The scent of impending death drifts upon the air.

She stands on a cliff bluff, gazing down at an army readying for a battle charge. The plain below throngs with people and horses roiling into a tense boil. Sunlight bounces off blades and buckles, warms leather into a supple glow, makes skin gleam with sweat and scorched flesh. It is too hot. There is no chance of rain.

She is too far away, strictly, to see all of this, but in the dream – in the memory? – her eyes are eagle-sharp, her nose wolf-keen. Just as she knows that by nightfall, most of the people lining up on the plain, trying to get horses and chariots in line, angling their shields and swords and spears into a semblance of order, bracing their grip on bows, will be injured or slaughtered.

Emri is no god. But here, watching a battle before the charge, she is in possession of a god's infinite wisdom for inevitable sorrow.

The banner emblems are different, but the dominant colours are familiar: what she recognises as Edaran blue and Farezi green. The symbols will change, but the colours will endure.

Her gaze focuses on two women: one, her blue cloak pinned against burnished, well-maintained armour. A helm topped in blue is cradled against her thigh. No matter that Emri has never led an army on horseback and is unlikely to do so: she thinks, instinctively: *She should already be wearing that helmet.* Strands of the woman's brown-black hair have escaped from her tight braid, plastered against her temples and cheeks. Her grey eyes, darker than Mother's, are narrowed. Her gaze is cold enough to freeze, no matter the simmering heat.

The woman's eyes and frigid gaze tug at Emri: an ancestor of Mother's, perhaps? Nothing she knows of the family tree matches a Queen who rode into battle, but Emri suspects this woman, with a small crown engraved on her helm and embroidered on her cloak, is not part of the historical record.

No. This is all much, much older.

Emri doesn't recognise the woman in Farezi green, flame-red hair visible under her helm, shoulder and arm muscles bunching and tensing as she guides her horse forward. The worn grip on her broadsword hints at much use, and her gaze is equally cold, equally merciless. Her commanders follow on horseback and in ancient fighting chariots. Further behind, soldiers and archers march in perfect formation.

A faint breeze stirs the feathers and dyed horsehair on top of helms, scant relief from the heat shimmering upon the air.

Emri blinks, and a figure stands before the Queen-in-green, striding forward with easy confidence. She is not equipped for battle: no helm, no armour, no weapon. A dress of forest green linen, hemmed in thick bands of gold, wraps around the curves of her tall figure. Even from a distance, this is no mortal. As she moves, her dress shifts, revealing glimpses of vines crawling up her thighs, similar to those spiralling up her arms to encircle her neck. Flowers bud, bloom, and die against her skin, over and over, and without doubt, thorns lurk within the vines.

The figure's hair is unbound, loose against her shoulders and back, moving in a breeze no one else can feel. The colour shifts with each step: blonde, red, brown, black, grey, and silver; shades between that Emri has never seen before. Her pale skin is tinged with gold, as if rewarded by a day in summer sunlight, but a green glow spills from her eyes.

Goddess.

La Dame des Fleurs.

Farezi's patron deity leads her people towards a death she will never experience, an immortal general who will never raise a blade against another to grant the kiss of ending.

La Dame des Fleurs stops suddenly, but the Queen continues on, unaware of the goddess's presence. She reaches forward to brush her hand against the horse's neck as they pass, her voice warm with a blessing.

Another blink: now the goddess sidles between the soldiers, or stands still while they move around her, unknowing, bestowing blessings upon favoured mortals almost like prayers. A benediction, a hope for survival or – more likely – confirmation of glorious deeds that will lead to a glorious death: memory into legend into myth.

Except myth fades, eventually, into a mist of faint reminiscence. It only remains if it is truly remembered.

Something wrenches Emri's attention towards the army in blue, and she immediately recoils. Lady Winter stands at the front of the mortal army. She should seem ridiculous, a winter goddess in such heat, but the branches bulging under her skin and bursting from her shoulders only reinforce her monstrosity, the icy rage radiating from her nothing more than an insult to the sun.

Her dark eyes, full of stars spinning between life and death, fix on La Dame des Fleurs, and Lady Winter *hates*. Even on the bluff, Emri can't stop a shudder at the sight of such hatred.

While La Dame des Fleurs softens her divinity with beauty and warmth, her thorns hidden, Lady Winter scorns such things, refuses to conceal the truth of her immortality. Spring can delight and caress; winter endures and waits, stark in its bleak beauty.

The Queen-in-blue, now wearing her helm, rides forward, also unaware of her patron goddess. But this time, there is no acknowledgement. There is no blessing.

There is only abandonment.

Lady Winter turns away from the Queen in silence, and strides through the soldier ranks. Unlike La Dame des Fleurs, these soldiers flinch and shiver, as if surprised by a cold breeze or an icy touch, the source of which they cannot see.

In the distance, Twilight waits for his companion, his demeanour stiff, his eyes fathomless. If he's gripped by rage, like Lady Winter, or a similar grief to that wracking Emri, he keeps it hidden tight and deep within.

La Dame des Fleurs watches Lady Winter retreat, her hair and dress tossed by the wind felt by no one else. The vines twist along her skin and, in the span of a moment − a blink, a heartbeat − every bloom upon her skin dies together. Her mouth jerks, but Emri can't tell whether in fury or triumph, and she doesn't know which would be better − or worse.

As the buds bloom once more, the drums beat, the horns sing −

The green army charges.

Watching the two armies crash together in a scream of horses and ringing steel, Emri wishes the songs, and sagas, and poems had written and sung of this. Of the scorched earth soaking up life blood, the moans and weeping of the dying, the twitching limbs of fallen horses.

The stench of death thickens upon her tongue until Emri reels away to retch, her gorge as vile as the stench surrounding her.

'It does not get easier,' a soft voice says, shimmering with grief.

Emri blinks; now it is night. The fighting has paused upon the encroachment of darkness, and death has begun in earnest. It is easier for the final strands of life to fray and snap when there is no hope.

She will wake, and the sounds, the weeping, the begging prayers of the dying will haunt her. Awake or sleeping, it will make no difference. They will tuck themselves into the deepest part of her memory, enfold within her ever-present shadow, and sometimes when she closes her eyes she will hear them again, as if for the first time.

She turns, trembling as she wipes her mouth.

A god sits on top of a boulder that wasn't there when she turned away, a divine witness to the slaughter below, and this god is all too familiar and yet a stranger.

Her Midwinter costume was almost correct and yet, somehow, terribly wrong.

They are tall, their skin as brown as Emri's. Their eyes are fully black, as deep as a silent night promising a lonely death, and their long hair is the gleaming ripple of a raven's wing, much like Lady Winter's – yet stars are trapped within the black tresses, hundreds of them, twinkling as if Emri were on her back, staring up at the sky and tracing constellations with a finger.

Their nose is straight and proud, their bone structure clear and strong. Their mouth curves in a pout, but their lips gleam as red as freshly spilled blood. Emri glances back at the battlefield carnage and wonders – wildly, irrationally – if blood appeared on Night's lips with every life wound, every death. Night and Lady Death have always had an uneasy bargain that no story has ever fully explained, and faced with a god whose reach spans as wide as the sky, sharp-edged with black eyes and a cruel, bloody mouth, something small and *mortal* flares within Emri, a deep-rooted instinct as ancient as the one shrieking for her to flee.

And yet–

Night sprawls upon the boulder, their dark leather armour bound in silver, sweeps of black linen melding with the shadows and the fall of their hair, and – there is grief in the line of their shoulders, in the bow of their head as they look away from the weeping, pleading swell of mortality below.

Night is cruel, and brimming with sorrow.

Now, faced with their star-speckled, looming presence, Emri thinks the Eshvoni goddess of the day must have been brave indeed to not only set limits upon Night's power but also enforce them.

She does not think she would have been so brave.

'Hello,' Emri finally says, because she doesn't know what else to say to a grieving god.

'I wanted no war. So much wasted life,' Night says, their voice echoing with an eternal grief, their gaze fixed on the fires and the battlefield. 'So many hopes and dreams, snuffed out in a moment. Mortal lives are so short, and their threads have been cut too soon. And so it goes, always.'

She hovers near the boulder, feeling she should be polite, but leery of coming too close. 'We don't tend to think that way, I'm afraid, we mortals. Or we'd simply never be able to get up and, well... *live*.'

They do not answer, and a strange scent fills the air below them, stronger than the blood and the dying.

A lady prowls through the battlefield, hooded and cloaked, shadows spooling around her. A lantern guides her way, floating in the air, and she holds a tall staff from which a thurible swings, emitting a strange smelling smoke that floods the battlefield, drifting over the dead and the dying. Two wolves accompany her: one dark, wavering with shadows and glimpses of bones under the flesh; the other pale as snow, tinged with flames along its back and tail.

In their wake, silence falls. The dead have already lost their voices, and the dying need cry out no more.

A chill wracks down Emri's spine, and she takes a step back before she can stick her courage firm.

An imperious trill draws her attention back to Night, as a shadow slinks from their linen folds. A black cat trots towards her, their tail waving lazily in the air, and stops before her with a chirp. Like Night, their dark fur is dappled with tiny stars. Large golden eyes regard her, before the cat rises on their hind legs and bats their front paws at her.

Emri picks the cat up without thinking, and they climb up her chest to burrow against her neck, whiskers tickling her skin. They press their nose into her ear, making her giggle, the sound of loud purring revibrating against her. She immediately relaxes, finding strength to keep watching from the warm, soft weight in her arms.

Lady Death stops before the Edaran Queen, her skirts and shadows pooling around them, and a flash of brightness upon one of the opposite bluffs catches Emri's eye.

A lady in shining white, as pale and stunning as moonlight upon fresh snow, watches over the battlefield. She strikes a serene figure, but something in her demeanour is stiff, furious, braced on a knife-edge of violence. In one hand, she holds a spear, its tip gleaming just as bright, honed by a bitter truth.

The wind shifts direction, taking the stink of death away from them, and the lady's stance changes, as does her gaze.

Emri follows it, and finds Lady Winter on one of the other cliffs.

She and the pale lady lock gazes.

Emri draws closer to Night, still holding their purring cat. Night drapes one of the upper folds of their clothing around her in an attempt at comfort. 'You need not fear,' they say. 'You are not their pressing concern.'

But even from here, Emri can feel the hatred Lady Winter and the pale lady hold for each other. And she fears for what has happened and what is to come.

THIRTY-THREE

We should have seen the pattern sooner: that every time we communicated properly, offered comfort or understanding to each other, the gods were waiting to inflict another strike against the strengthening bonds between us.

And despite everything that had happened to Melisande and me already, our tests were still to come.

Melisande did finally improve, a little, and the collapse we were all expecting never fully materialised. True, the amount she could walk dwindled a little more each evening. Sleep became so non-existent that she was never warm, even when she sat beside the fire, huddled under Theo's spare lined jacket. The smudges under her eyes became worse, her face turning tight and angled as her bones strained against her skin.

We stopped trying to hide our worry. Melisande kept pretending nothing was wrong, except for the nights when the hunger – though food was impossible – and exhaustion – though it seemed like the gods intended for her to never sleep again – grew too much, and she sobbed until her throat was raw.

Theo would sit beside her, and silently wrap his arms around her until she was weeping into his chest. There was no teasing, no arguments.

From that night on, Night appeared to take pity on her and granted her sleep when she could cry no more. We took turns to walk beside Melisande, keeping an eye on her labouring pace and taking on her weight, as much as possible, when her energy inevitably began to dwindle.

And every night, more ink filled the moon phases on the parchment as our pace didn't improve, and we tried to hide our growing dread from each other.

One late morning, we reached a hewn stone bridge stretching across a river far below, the current turned violent from the waterfall a few feet away, which had somehow returned, though we were in a completely different part of the mountain from where we'd last seen it.

I'd given up trying to make any sense of it. There was too much magic seeped into the temple and the mountain, too vast and strange for a mortal to comprehend.

I was also secretly certain that one of the gods just liked waterfalls.

It was my turn to walk beside Melisande, so I didn't immediately realise that Theo had ground to a halt, not until Gabi yelped as she slammed into his back. When I glanced up he was staring out at the bridge, frozen.

'Theo?'

He looked back at me over his shoulder, his eyes wide. 'Emri…

Melisande— I…'

Melisande frowned. 'What?' It had taken three stops over an hour for her to sip enough water to ease her cracked lips, so her irritation was warranted, and whenever we stopped, it was harder for her to get back up. The rest of us had taken to eating what we could hold as we walked.

Then she looked beyond him, and her breath stuttered.

Halfway across the water, a set of double doors spanned the width of the bridge. They stood there, alone, attached to no walls.

On the left door, the golden Farezi lily glinted, as if it had been painted during sunrise. On the right door, the silver Edaran rose briar twined around a sword, capped by a crown, glowing as if surrounded by moonlight.

Two symbols.

'Oh, no,' I said.

'Oh, yes,' Melisande replied flatly.

'Is it for one of you?' Gabi asked, perplexed. 'Or both?'

Melisande and I exchanged a look. Technically, we both had Edaran and Farezi lineage, thanks to Lord Erik's marriage generations before, so the door could have been for either of us. But Melisande and I were linked far closer than a strategic marriage from over a century ago. We'd been brought here together, and had vowed to leave the mountain together. It was a terrible kind of logic that we'd need to go through the doors together.

I sighed. 'Both, I think.'

The river roared below as we approached the bridge, and the spray dampened my face as we made our way across, step by cautious step. Theo and Gabi followed close behind, Theo almost thrumming with anxiety in case we'd slip.

When we stopped before the doors, we were pressed so tightly against each other that I could feel Melisande trembling. She was now a shadow of the sly, accomplished courtier who'd arrived in Edar months ago.

Maybe this was the point of Lady Winter's trials, the unspoken truth hidden in the myths and sagas. That to be a hero was to face the worst about ourselves, to be ground down until only a shell remained, a brittle hollow that we had to fill with our own strength, our own rage, our own stubbornness to endure. Perhaps to be a hero meant being remade into a new version of ourselves, and knowing that over time, others would remake it further, beyond mortal understanding.

Heroes could only be legendary if everyone else felt they couldn't be one.

I swallowed and squeezed her hand. 'We've been through worse,' I whispered, low enough that only she could hear me over the waterfall and river. 'Gabi and Theo both managed to get through their memories. So will we.'

Melisande's laugh was rough with self-loathing. 'I think I've done far more hurtful things than them – and you.'

I remembered being in a shadow-soaked room with Mama,

as she confirmed the worst thing I could have imagined about her, as she acknowledged the far-reaching consequences of her actions so many years ago – how those consequences had affected *me* – and how, when I'd pressed her, she'd admitted that she would do it all again.

All my pain, all my rage.

Flung right back at her.

'Everyone is hurtful to others at some point,' I said.

Melisande arched an eyebrow, a familiar shade of her old self, and I was taken aback by the stab of relief. If she could still look at me like that, then she was not fully gone. There was still a chance for her to survive the poison.

To survive the gods. To survive all of this.

'We should probably stop dithering and just go through the doors.'

'Just remember, afterwards, that you like me,' she replied.

We pushed the doors open together.

For a long, hopeful moment, Emri thinks it will be all right.

Bearable.

Then she opens her eyes, and she has returned to Saphirun.

Every part of her revolts.

A blink, and she is on her knees, arms wrapped tight around herself, shaking, teeth chattering, eyes squeezed shut because she cannot face it, she can't be back, she can't do it—

'Emri. *Look at me.*'

Melisande is beside her on the ground, legs akimbo, as if she promptly dropped the moment Emri let her go. Her hands are pressed against Emri's cheeks, fingertips lightly digging against her temples, and her mouth is clenched into a snarl.

'You are not alone,' she hisses, fear and fury tangled in her voice, glaring at Emri with a feverish light. 'We go through this together.'

They stare at each other, knowing what they're about to face will reopen old wounds and half-healed hurts anew. It will change how Gabi and Theo regard them.

But there is no way forward but to endure it.

A hero does not give up if they want to be remembered.

Emri nods. Drags a hand down her face, then shakes her head. She gets up, holds out a hand to Melisande, and pulls her up when she takes it after a flicker of hesitation.

There is no way out but through.

The memory is of Saphirun at its best: high summer, the sun burning, the glorious blue of the sky reflected in the large river that gave the estate its name. They're all standing within the orchard, where Emri remembers climbing to pick apples, the crisp skin giving easily under her teeth, the fruit tart or sweet by turns. She remembers the scrapes and scratches when she misjudged the climb or descent, how the staff would attempt to clean them, and Arisane punishing her if they weren't successful at hiding the physical consequences of her climbing.

When she came to Edar, it was easier to tell Micah that she didn't know how to climb trees. Easier to pretend ignorance. Micah had taught her to climb, anyway, and with him, she never feared falling or scrapes. If she'd ever given herself away, he kept quiet.

In the distance, the manor looms.

Melisande swallows. Emri knows that Melisande had an easier time (and even comparisons like that are mostly useless, because *easier* does not mean *kind*), but she also knows Melisande has no fond memories of this place. And yet, a small, spiteful part of Emri hopes whichever of Melisande's memories are about to be revealed, it is a terrible one instead of embarrassing.

'Where are we?' Theo asks. His voice is soft, careful, as if he can not only sense whatever complicated history is radiating from Melisande and Emri, but that they're simmering towards an eruption.

'Saphirun,' Melisande says flatly.

'The estate of the Dowager Queen, Arisane. Our grandmother,' Emri clarifies, her voice starting flat and turning bleak. 'We lived here when we were younger. Before I left for Edar and Melisande was summoned back to her mother's Court.'

'Oh,' Gabi says, brightening, as if seeing the place with fresh eyes. She probably had an easier time away from Court and assumes the same of everyone else. Emri regrets what she's about to witness; they may have no hint of what this memory is, but the odds are extremely unlikely it will be pleasant.

Another blink, and they find themselves within the manor.

It is high summer, and Melisande and Emri's younger selves are not speaking to each other.

This is not particularly unusual, and happened often, making it harder to pinpoint when exactly this summer was. Melisande openly squints as they study the younger versions of themselves. Both have their hair pulled back – the staff was instructed to be merciless if they tangled their hair, Emri remembers suddenly, no matter that their waves and curls tangled if a branch so much as came within a foot of their heads. She was terribly anxious about her hair when she came to Edar, until she realised the staff, who had first learned under Mama's tight curls, was expected to treat her hair with care.

She had sat in stiff silence the first few nights, while the servants had vainly tried to relax her with a burble of soft chatter. The staff was often encouraged into conversation in Edar, another thing that had confused her. Arisane had shaped her ideal of a Queen, and she'd never met Aunt Sabine, so she had assumed that all Queens were like her grandmother: seeking strength through power and succumbing to bitterness when it was taken from them.

It wasn't until many years later that Emri had wondered why, exactly, Arisane had been banished from her daughter's Court.

Emri's bottom lip trembles, to her horror. She must not – *cannot* – cry during this. She simply will not allow it.

Even so, a tear drips down her cheek, and she swipes it away before anyone can see.

The vision shudders; the corridor changes around them.

There is, Emri slowly realises, as they wander through the halls and rooms of Saphirun, no precise memory, not like what they witnessed with Gabi and Theo. No pinpoint of hurt or humiliation. Just the oppressive silence, the hushed whispers of the staff as they move about their work. There is no sound of two girls barrelling through the house, chattering and laughing. No play between them, except for when they're on good terms with each other, and only then when they are outside, far away from the windows where Arisane can see them.

Though young, they are already thrown into a rigorous education, Melisande because she is her mother's heir and Emri because she will be the heir of other Queens, and Arisane's pride overrules the bitterness for the second grandchild in her care. She will *not* have the Edaran Queens criticise Emri's education.

So they read, and study, and recite, and debate with their shared tutors whose lessons they attend separately. Never together, on Arisane's decree, and on the days neither likes the other, their own incentive.

It is a lonely life. As they walk, Gabi and Theo, who grew up in loving homes despite the pressures of expectation and duty, can't hide their horror and pity.

The pity is worse. After years spent with her parents, Emri also feels the true horror of it, no matter how much she tried to bury it in the deepest parts of her memory.

But the further they go, Melisande becomes increasingly furious.

Emri finds this almost brave, considering at least one god is waiting for them to break, but whichever one it is apparently feels insulted that Melisande has the gall to be angry rather than embarrassed at their sad, lonely childhoods being revealed, and so the memory turns pointed.

Melisande would have preferred to be stabbed in the liver.

Every slight, every petty argument, every jab flickers around them, blurring and slowing at different speeds, as Emri watches their terrible relationship play out.

None of it is the worst she has ever experienced. In the beginning, some of her parents' courtiers were far cleverer and cutting than Melisande, by far, though Rialla and then Micah were buffers against them. But it is constant and relentless, and Emri watches how it shapes her through the weeks and months at Saphirun. How she rarely speaks without first being spoken to, how she is soft-footed and cautious, never making unnecessary noise. How her eyes are downcast, her shoulders curled in. She could never see the effects so clearly, and witnessing them now makes her feel terribly grateful for that.

She cannot believe that Arisane would shape Melisande to be so cruel. She cannot believe that Aunt Sabine would have allowed it and then never seen shadows of it in Melisande when she returned to Court.

And now that she knows what to look for, she sees similar things manifest in Melisande: her caustic defensiveness, the dark humour she turns into a shield. The deep, corrosive need for Arisane's approval, even though she knows it will never come.

The one servant foolish enough to utter Rassa's name is flogged and thrown out without a reference. It does more to solidify Melisande and Emri's terror of Arisane than any implied threat. A threat can be withheld upon proof of continued good behaviour; a public flogging before the household is an all-too clear warning.

Emri swallows. Closes her eyes. And thinks, because she cannot say it: *Yes, I can see why Mama killed Rassa. What drove her to it, why she will never truly regret it, even if the consequences hurt me.*

She will never kill Arisane. But there is a small part of her, that she goads the watching gods to reveal to everyone else, that wishes she could.

It would not be pleasant for Arisane.

And Emri knows that Mama would warn her that it wouldn't be pleasant either, no matter how much she wants it.

They're watching a younger Emri silently struggle though a brick of a history tome, alone, when the room swirls around them and reshapes into Arisane's private study.

Unlike Isra's study, Arisane's is not a guarded trap. It is cold, even in high summer, and stripped down to basic needs. Even in the memory, Emri remembers how the room's chill sank into her bones and nothing could warm her up for hours after she escaped.

She and Melisande are seated on the other side of Arisane's desk. Emri notices their clothing and stiffens, recognition rolling over her in a terrible burst. Beside her, Melisande swears under her breath, then braces herself.

'The adoption papers have been signed and sealed,' Arisane says briskly. Her expression is, as usual, cool and indifferent. Emri is the grandchild whose departure she has been waiting for. 'You will depart in two weeks.'

There is no sadness at her impending departure. Arisane is stern, resolute, warns her that though she will now be the Edaran heir, her actions will still reflect upon the family she was born into. Melisande is a stiff figure in the chair beside Emri's, her gaze focused on a painting behind Arisane to the right.

She is not spoken to, and does not speak. She is the Farezi heir, and she knows precisely what kind of relationship she and Emri will have in the future: that of rival Queens.

She is silent when they are dismissed, and silent as they leave. Silent as they walk to the end of Arisane's corridor and pause, only for a moment, before they prepare to go in opposite directions.

'I'm glad you're leaving,' Melisande says abruptly. Her tone is cold, the words sharpened so they will hurt. 'You do not belong here, nor in this family. The Edaran Queens are foolish if they believe a traitor's daughter will make a good heir.'

Emri doesn't see Melisande's expression as she speaks, nor the expression of her younger self as she absorbs the words, because her own eyes are already closed. She knew they were coming. She knew exactly what Melisande would say. And yet… yet, there was no way for her to prepare.

She opens her eyes at a soft thump, followed by retching. Melisande is on her knees, turned away as she vomits.

Instinct overtakes Emri: she kneels and gathers Melisande's hair back from her face. Something dark and foul gushes from Melisande's stomach, resembling nothing that they've eaten. The sight makes Emri inwardly recoil: yet more evidence that whatever Melisande is suffering from, it isn't natural.

It gleams like ink, thick enough to resemble the night sky but without stars.

Melisande wipes her mouth with shaking fingers. They both gaze at what she's thrown up, then share an uneasy glance. This isn't good. Whatever else is waiting for them, they are all tired, and ground down, their bonds still too fragile to withstand whatever else the gods will throw at them.

'You shouldn't be kind to me,' Melisande mutters. 'I don't deserve it.'

'You don't have the right,' Emri counters, 'to tell me what I can and cannot do.'

Once again, she stands and holds out a hand to help Melisande up. But this time, she refuses it, even though it feels wretched to watch Melisande slowly, painfully, force herself to stand. Once they realised they were in Arisane's study, and unlike every other time they've been in a dangerous situation, or Melisande has been afraid but unable to say it aloud, she hasn't reached for her hand.

Emri is glad, since she doesn't think she'd be able to take it.

But this is only Melisande's humiliation.

Hers is still to come.

The vision begins to shift again, and they silently continue down the hall.

Scenes unfold, flutter, rip apart around them:

Melisande watches Emri being helped into the carriage that will take her to Edar. As the carriage clatters down the drive, she keeps watching until the faint speck is out of sight.

Melisande being ushered into her mother's presence upon her return to Court. The polite, stifled conversation between them that stretches and swerves around the topics they cannot address: *why did you leave me with Grandmother; didn't you miss me; why have you summoned me back; what person has my mother turned you into; what do you expect of me?*

Emri walking into a room to face two young women. One looks more like her than the other, but neither can hide the uncertainty in their smiles. Emri curtseys, her eyes downcast as she was taught, and waits to be spoken to.

Instead, there are footsteps and a rustle of skirts. Warm hands take hers, and Emri's gaze flies up to find both women crouched so they can look her in the eye. Their smiles are still nervous, but also kind.

'Hello, Emri,' says the pale lady with the storm-cloud eyes.

'We've been waiting for you,' adds the second lady, whose skin is brown, like Emri's, and her eyes large and dark.

In that moment, a tiny part of Emri allows herself to hope that this will be different. A fresh start.

Melisande inherits the height of both her parents, and the dark swirling mane that her mother keeps pinned up. She has the hazel eyes common to the Farezi royal family, the ones that Emri hasn't inherited, and the same cunning and intelligence.

The Farezi Court does not reward good people, so as she grows older, Melisande builds her armour efficiently: her wit, her blackmail, the fine art of manipulation. She hones her smiles, her lips, her beauty, and her flirting into coy weapons, but only unleashes them on young women strong enough to respond in kind.

She will not break hearts, as her grandmother and mother have already broken her own.

But plenty of young women are willing to see if she can try anyway.

Melisande treats them well, binds the relationships with firm conditions, and when they end – as they always do, because she will not marry, not yet – they part as allies.

She does not allow herself to have friends.

She's uncertain if she'll even marry. If instead, she and her brother will actually go through with their agreement that one of his future children will be her heir, since Queen Aurelia in Edar has proven it's possible to prefer women, rule, *and* provide a child. Even so, Melisande doubts that if she marries, she'll allow her wife any further power than Consort. That would involve a level of trust she can't afford in this Court that she'll inherit. Queen Sabine has done much to drain the poison, but some still lingers in dark corners.

Saphirun is a thread in her shadow that Melisande cannot unravel, no matter how hard she tries.

Emri grows, shaped by love and kindness and duty, choosing to bury her fears and past deep within herself until she has almost convinced herself that they were never real. She has friends, and reluctant allies, taught to survive Court by a grim spymaster who always seems to find her irritating. Her mothers' families welcome her, and love her as their granddaughter and niece.

It is a good life. A safe one, stitched together with love and affection and bickering and loyalty. It is a good life.

And yet Saphirun remains a stain in her shadow.

Emri swallows, again and again, watching the glimpses of her and Melisande's past blur in the wavering corridor. The urge to acknowledge Melisande, even to reach out for her, is strong, but a looming sense of dread stays her hand, that the worst is still to come.

Gabi and Theo are still silent. When Emri glances at them, Gabi is pressed against his side, unnerved, his arm wrapped tight around her. He meets Emri's gaze gravely, but says nothing. There is nothing he could say that could make this better, not even a little bit.

These memories feel different to Gabi and Theo's: darker, unsettling, on the knife edge of loathing and rage. The air feels taut, ready to snap and unleash a storm.

Two memories appear and mesh together. Both recognise them and flinch.

For Emri, it is midwinter over a year ago. She and her parents had an early meal together before they went to get ready for the ball, Emri trailing in their wake to watch their transformation into Lady Winter and Twilight, trying to hide how wistful it makes her feel. But by next winter, she will have gained her majority. By next winter, she will accompany them as Night.

After her parents have left, Rialla and Micah are ushered into Emri's quarters, their families also attending the Ball. Emri and Micah are in good spirits, chattering and laughing with mugs of spiced cider – Micah has swiped a small bottle of snow liquor for them all to share later – but Rialla is uncharacteristically withdrawn.

As the hours trickle by, Emri and Micah can no longer ignore her quietness, and their exchanged glances grow longer. By the time they've shared the snow liquor between them – an icy burn down Emri's throat that warns of danger if she's not careful with it – Micah feigns an exaggerated yawn and bids them a sleepy goodnight, with warm hugs and kisses on their cheeks.

When they are alone, Emri shivers despite the fire, unsure if it's from the liquor or a warning of what's to come–

–Melisande stands in the Night Room, chin raised, shoulders squared, legs planted for balance, seven years old with her eyes fixed on Arisane.

Arisane, who holds a candle flame. Arisane, who blocks the doorway.

The similarities are striking. The same nose, long-lashed hazel eyes, and strong cheekbones. A mouth made for stubbornness and strength, a gaze meant to pin any unfortunate enemy into stillness.

In her defiant stance, Melisande already seems to know that she has lost.

'When you return to your mother,' Arisane says, her glass-sharp accent a torment to Emri, her tone cool, almost indifferent but for the intensity of her glare, 'you will not be a disappointment to me. I have already been disappointed by my dead son and his daughter—'

Behind them, Gabi sucks in a gasp and Theo murmurs her into silence.

' —and I will *not* allow the future Queen of this disgraced country to follow the same path.' The candle flame dances in Arisane's eyes, her mouth flattening into a thin line before she continues, 'Perhaps I let you get away with too much while your cousin was here. My failing, perhaps, not to be sterner with you.'

In the way of all these visions and memories, Emri knows that what Arisane considers familial love is mere tolerance to how the other royal families treat their children and grandchildren. A royal family must always consider their duty, but they do not always have to be cruel.

Arisane's failure is not that she wasn't stern enough with Melisande. It's that she refused to show her even a façade of affection, never mind respect, from a Dowager Queen to a future monarch.

Melisande does not speak. She does not scream. She does not shout. She does not argue.

As Arisane turns away and takes the candle with her, Melisande stands in silence, enveloped in shuttered darkness as the lock snaps into place—

—Emri attempts a smile, because it is Midwinter and she and Rialla are alone, a thing that doesn't happen as often as they would like. She smiles because it is Midwinter, which is for families and for lovers, and she has the love of all the most important people in her life.

She smiles.

Rialla does not smile back.

Later, Emri will wonder why Rialla wasn't kinder about it, before more time will pass and she will realise that being kind was the absolute worst thing she could have been.

Rialla somehow knew the exact amount of force to place upon a heart to break it.

—Melisande sits under the largest set of locked shutters in the Night Room, her legs drawn up to her chest, her arms wrapped tightly around her knees. There is a bed, but she will not flee to it. She could hide her face against her legs, but it is darkness upon darkness and makes no difference.

She will face the reality of the Night Room exactly as expected: back straight and eyes open.

And if her arms hurt from how tightly they're wrapped around her knees, no one will ever know.

—When her candles are flickering out, hours after she should have been asleep, Emri hears soft murmurs outside her door. The servants have, presumably, informed her parents that something happened while they were at the Midwinter Ball and their daughter has been weeping alone for hours.

The door doesn't creak as it opens. Only the rustling of their skirts gives them away.

Emri folds tighter upon herself, keeps her face buried in the pillows. Gentle weight as they sit on either side of her, fingers delicately brushing curls back from her face; a hand rubbing her upper arm in comfort, coaxing her to roll over and look at them.

Two Queens gaze down upon her, glimmering in bone-white and twilight-blue silks, diamonds and sapphires blazing at their throats and in their hair. Her mothers' faces are concerned and grave, resolutely set, as if they know what Emri is about to tell them, as if they predicted what Rialla was going to say and do months before and were simply waiting for the inevitable.

But their eyes and smiles are full of love: for her.

Midwinter is for families and lovers.

Midwinter is for love.

'I didn't know she locked you in the Night Room,' Emri says.

'It was always going to be me,' Melisande replies, 'that she'd actually carry out the threat on. She couldn't have you going to Edar terrified of the dark.'

Emri thinks back to how intently Melisande has always stared into the fire. How she struggled to sleep even before the poison.

One of them locked in the Night Room, the other threatened with it, and both afraid of the dark. Until now.

'That doesn't mean you deserved it,' Emri says, because she doesn't know what else to say.

Melisande only shrugs. 'It doesn't seem fair that I knew you had your heart broken.'

'I never told you that,' Emri says, struggling not to frown.

She shrugs again. 'I could see it, in both of you, and how Micah was a buffer. I know what a broken heart looks like.' Her mouth twists, viciously. 'More than one woman has hoped she will be my exception, like Queen Xania was for your mother, and one day sit beside me on a throne.'

They stare at each other, refusing to look at Gabi and Theo, neither willing to face pity nor shock. They are too fragile, their half-healed cracks threatening to shatter them beyond all hope.

The air suddenly freezes, the temperature plummeting so fast that Emri's skin almost vibrates as her teeth throb.

She almost expects to see snowflakes and ice shards floating around them.

Midwinter, Lady Winter howls, and Emri can tell by everyone's wide eyes that they can all hear her, *is not for love.*

The rippling corridor explodes with darkness, and Emri grabs for Melisande's hand, gripping it tight as her eyes try to adjust. After a long moment, a pinprick of light appears, growing until it bursts; they blink and find themselves in a room full of golden sunlight.

The room is narrow and long, one wall filled with large windows that present a view of a perfect summer sky. Emri peers out: this side of the palace overlooks some of the public gardens. Beyond, she catches a glimpse of the palace walls, strong and resolute.

Yes, this is the palace. Home. Though the room doesn't seem familiar, it still tugs at her memory. The colours are cool for a room with such generous sunlight, and there's a curiously empty feeling to it.

Brisk, light footsteps approach. Emri turns and watches herself stride down the room, flanked by two young women around the same age. Her double seems an exact replica, yet there are subtle differences. The cut of her dress is far more traditional than anything Emri has seen at Court, even in paintings from her great-grandparents' and grandparents' time, the fabric stiff and constraining against the swift pace her double has nevertheless set. Her hair is tucked into a bright net kept in place with pearl-topped pins, a style brought into fashion by Mama with her cloud of curls, but only for social occasions and not everyday use. Even her walk is puzzling, until Emri realises it's all grace and little authority.

A princess must walk with both.

Emri's double brushes by her with no indication that she can see or sense anyone else. No pause, no flinch, no flicker of her eyelashes.

Melisande, still looking shaken from the memories just revealed, says: 'That isn't you.'

Up until Midwinter, up until this nightmare, Emri would have laughed at the idea of Melisande being able to recognise her stride, her habits, her mannerisms, and tell her apart from a version of herself that never existed.

But not now. They have spent too much time together, seen each other at their worst. Their shared past is still a painful horror, but it's no longer the only barbed thread linking them.

'This isn't a memory,' Emri says, amazed that she can sound so calm as a sense of foreboding deepens within her.

They follow Emri's double around corners and down halls, everything familiar and just a little strange. Gabi and Theo seem curious about their surroundings – Theo perhaps using this as a chance to familiarise himself with his potential future home – but they also appear to have picked up on Emri's unease.

When they reach the entrance to the Royal Wing, the only odd thing appears to be that Emri doesn't recognise the guards on duty. But when they slip by them, unseen, and Emri glances up at the portraits out of habit, she stumbles to a stop.

Every portrait of the former Edaran monarchs, their Consorts, and the other close family members that warranted remembrance upon the walls, are gone. Melisande, who dutifully suffered through a tour of the Portrait Gallery, realises this only a few moments after and her sickly pale face turns ghastly.

She shares a resemblance with many of the portraits, some stronger than others: the shape of her nose, the familiar long-lashed hazel eyes, the deep-set eyes that stare out of the frame in silent challenge. The same resemblance Emri would have, if she took after Rassa more than Lady Liliene.

The portraits are all from the Farezi royal family.

There's only one reason why they would have a strong presence here.

Emri's stomach drops. 'No,' she whispers, and breaks into a run.

Melisande curses and follows her, beginning to wheeze after only a few steps. So different from the cousin who bolted through the temple alongside her as they fled from shadow wolves.

Emri catches up with her double quickly, and the further she gets into the wing, the more wrong everything appears.

They stop outside a door that Emri has walked by several times but never entered because her family is small enough that this part of the wing is used for storage. Her double smooths down the front of her gown, subtly, making it seem like an absent-minded habit rather than a sign of nerves or stalling, and nods at the guards on either side of the doors.

They are announced.

The solar is tastefully decorated in shades of cream, lilac, and egg-shell blue, but the sun isn't strong enough to stop the room from feeling cold. It feels like a place to be on one's guard, not to relax or laugh, or even smile.

Lady Liliene sits in the centre, surrounded by a small court of her ladies, and Emri's foreboding explodes within her stomach.

This is no memory.

This is what might have been.

It's especially worse because Lady Liliene is *smiling* and *happy*. Emri has no doubt that some of these ladies are spies, and others serve her birth mother because ambition rises in every royal Court, but from the way Lady Liliene – *Queen* Liliene – interacts with those sitting closest to her, they appear to be true and loyal companions.

It doesn't seem fair that for her birth mother to be happy, so much else has to have gone wrong.

Her face lights up at the sight of Emri, which hurts because her actual last memory of Lady Liliene is the broken shell she'd become, trapped within despair and weeping. 'My darling!' she says, holding out her arms, and Emri's double goes to her mother and kisses her cheeks. The princess's own ladies are abuzz to be around such esteemed company; Emri's own ladies don't often spend time with her parents.

But then, the Edaran Queens do not spend their days in a solar, surrounded by music and ladies reading aloud, needlepoint and gossip. There are other women in Court who do such things, and Their Majesties deeply respect them, for their own needlepoint is not especially impressive and they appreciate the information passed to them or Isra from such gatherings.

The scene is light-hearted and cheerful and utterly *wrong*. Emri struggles to pinpoint what has caused the hairs on the back of her neck to stand on end, what has set her spine to crawling, and finally, she realises: this is not her. This is not who she is.

This Emri smiles easily, and does not have the shadow of Saphirun trailing her, but something feels… off. This version of Emri doesn't have shadows clinging to her, but she feels… underwhelming.

Emri circles around her double and Queen Liliene, her frown deepening at their conversation. Flippant, superficial, focusing on her marriage…

…to a high-ranking Farezi noble.

There is no mention of Rialla. No mention of Micah.

But then, their families were fiercely loyal to the *true* Queen.

The foreboding in her stomach twists into spikes that dig mercilessly into tender flesh.

And she realises: this Emri doesn't speak of her education, of any awareness of Parliament's actions or plans, to any unusual undercurrents within Court. She appears to have no knowledge of the capital nor wider Edar, whether their people are well.

This Emri shows none of her knowledge, her logic, nor her ability to tease through problems.

This version of her has not been raised to be a Queen. She has been raised to sit upon a throne while others wield power on her behalf.

Emri steps back, aghast, and locks eyes on Melisande, whose mouth has flattened to a grim line. Theo and Gabi, now close enough to hear the conversation, don't look much better.

Before Emri can do or say anything, the door opens.

A women with ash-blonde hair approaches Queen Liliene and

curtseys. 'Your Majesty,' she says. 'Your Highness.' Her voice is light, cultured, but something in her tone puts Emri on her guard, as if this lady publicly respects Queen Liliene but scorns her behind closed doors. 'I came as soon as I heard.'

Queen Liliene puts aside her glass of summer wine. 'Lady Terize, welcome. What news?'

Lady Terize sinks into the seat indicated and leans conspiratorially close. 'Her Former Majesty, Queen Aurelia, is dead. Xania Bayonn was captured soon after, Your Majesty, and is being returned here to await your husband's pleasure.'

To await your husband's pleasure is a lovely, cautious phrase, but Emri knows the true meaning lurking underneath: Xania Bayonn is being returned to face public execution.

'And the baron, Farhallow?' Queen Liliene enquiries.

'Also dead in the attack. They were fed false information by Queen Arisane and thought the guards at Goldenmarch would aid them in freeing Queen Aurelia. They walked straight into an ambush.'

Everything in Emri turns to ice.

No. *No.*

'Xania Bayonn's family will witness the consequences, of course,' Queen Liliene says thoughtfully. 'Including the Kierth. The younger girl lacks her sister's treachery, from what I've heard. A suitable match to ensure her loyalty would not go amiss.'

'Miss Bayonn is a beauty and a wit,' Lady Terize agrees, her eyes sharp and her hands folded demurely upon her lap. 'I'm sure she would be *most gratified* to accept what marriage is offered to protect her family from any further... consequences. One that keeps her in the country, perhaps?' Something vile taints her voice in that last sentence, barbed like a poison-tipped briar.

Emri stumbles back, revolted, so violently that she trips, caught before she can smack against the floor. Theo holds her firmly. 'This isn't real,' he rasps. 'None of this happened. None of this *can* happen. Rassa is dead, and your parents live. Your aunt lives a life of her own choosing.'

He's right. Emri knows this, and yet something dark and snarling claws up her throat, threatening to erupt in a howl. Instead, she clings to an irrefutable fact, a snowflake of cold logic: she wasn't born when Mama and Matthias fled to Farezi to rescue Mother, declared traitors by Rassa. She was not born when they found her, tortured into silence in Goldenmarch.

Even if this had happened, even if Arisane had betrayed them, and Rassa kept the throne and Emri was raised as *this* heir of Edar, she would not have been this vacant husk of a princess, listening with wide eyes as Queen Liliene and Lady Terize calmly discuss a true Queen's murder, the execution of her beloved, and a young woman being orchestrated into a loveless marriage. She wouldn't be denied knowledge and curiosity, wouldn't be so *untrained*, so— so— lacking in imagination. In *spirit*.

So ignorant of the cruelty around her, accepting the small world and ambition granted to her by her usurper father. A hollow King.

Emri wrenches herself out of Theo's arms. '*No*,' she says, but it's a hoarse cry with little rage. 'This didn't happen. It never happened.

Even if we escape this mountain, it can never happen. He is dead. He is *dead*, and rotted in an unloved grave!'

Her voice gains strength as she speaks, but the fake memory doesn't waver like in Gabi and Theo's memories. Something has changed for herself and Melisande. Yelling is not going to force the gods to end this test.

Emri's gaze spins around the room, enraged and frantic, and focuses on two things: a long mirror on one of the walls, immense enough that she dare not calculate the cost, and an empty innocuous chair close by.

As she storms towards it, her body knows what she's about to do before her mind has caught up.

Her grip is tight and certain on the back of the chair. There is no doubt.

Melisande stutters out a faint curse, moments before Theo yelps in comprehension. But of the two, Melisande has always been closer to embracing violence. Perhaps it's a rotten seed within them common to the Farezi royal family.

Emri braces her legs, lifts the chair, and swings it against the mirror with the full might of her shoulders and hips.

'*Enough.*'

The smash is a shouted curse in the gentle atmosphere of the Queen's solar and, for a moment, silence falls. The women stare around, unable to see what has been smashed or who has done it.

But Emri's double stiffens and turns towards the mirror.

They stare at each other.

Then the windows explode inward, followed by screams as shards scour the air, slicing through fabric and flesh. The floorboards warp and buckle as deep cracks gouge up the walls and across the ceiling, raining down plaster dust in warning.

Emri gazes at her double, and her double gazes back, and the room lurches and spins into a swirl of snowflakes as darkness envelopes them.

THIRTY-FOUR

I landed on my knees on the mountain top where I first met Twilight, overlooking the peaks and the distant hint of wider Farezi.

Of course. I was always going to return here. He had warned me, as much as a god could.

I forced myself to stand, my knees throbbing from the impact, but after everything I'd gone through, physically and in my mind, it seemed like only a small hurt.

Twilight was waiting, seated upon his boulder, gripping his staff.

I met his starry gaze, and it was kind and sorrowful, but deep within, I caught a trace of cruelty. His demeanour was stiffer this time, rigid: he was in the full guise of Twilight, Lady Winter's Consort.

He had warned me that he would not always be kind – and he and Lady Winter had already quarrelled over us.

I bowed. 'Lord Twilight,' I said. 'A pleasure to cross paths with you again.' This didn't seem like a vision, not least because I hurt too much.

A chorus of gasps rang out behind me, as the others faced a

god for the first time.

The wind was brisk this high up, heavy with the threat of snow. The sky barrelled and rolled overhead, a clash of blues, purples, and greys. A storm was rolling in.

Twilight smiled. 'Emri.' He spoke with deep affection, and part of me couldn't help but be pleased. 'Welcome.' His gaze shifted to the others in turn. 'And to you all, of course.'

'I don't apologise for breaking the mirror,' I said. 'It was a petty kind of test, taunting me with something that never happened.'

'Yet necessary,' he replied, his blue lips shaping the words carefully, 'for someone who will not face her past.'

Melisande hissed out a breath.

Theo stepped forward, for once grim rather than alarmed, if you ignored the whites showing full around his eyes. 'With respect, my Lord Twilight, that is not fair, considering what we all just saw. How was that not Emri and Melisande acknowledging… prior events?'

Twilight regarded him, amused. 'You will make a fine Consort. When you marry, I suggest you remember me.'

As Theo gulped, I muttered, 'I think you should leave the talking to me.'

'Gladly,' he replied, somewhat strangled, and shut his mouth.

Twilight was a strange balance: a kind expression against his looming height and broad shoulders. His glowing eyes and blue lips didn't seem so strange now, simply an unalterable part of his divinity.

There was no doorway back into the mountain. Something stirred in my stomach, another swirl of premonition, but I stayed silent. I wouldn't fulfil his intentions by speaking them into existence; whatever he had planned for us, he'd have to guide us there himself.

Except—

'There's no way back into the mountain,' Gabi said.

—I'd forgotten the others hadn't faced the gods before.

As Melisande and Theo muttered, my eyes flickered towards the edge and the deep plummet towards the lower peaks. When I looked back, Twilight held my gaze for a long moment.

He had said there would times when he could not be kind.

In the dream, he'd thrown me off the mountain.

And there was no way for us to go…

…but down.

Very good, little one. His voice in my mind held a hint of an evening wind, remote and cutting in its chill. *I wish we could say that we tried to convince my Lady otherwise, Night and I, but this was always woven into the threads of your life.*

Or perhaps this is what you'd say to try and take every choice from me, I thought back furiously, and to add insult to indignity, he laughed.

That is for us to know, he replied, *and for you to endlessly wonder.*

If I live to do so, I shot back, and this time there was no answer.

I would not be frightened. I thought this to myself, over and over, as I moved closer to the edge. The others were wandering around the plateau, exclaiming at the sky. Theo simply watched Twilight, apparently torn between curiosity and terror. A future companion to a Queen looking at the Consort to a winter goddess, perhaps gauging how strong his worth would have to be.

I wanted to be brave about this, but if I couldn't be brave, then I would be practical. Lady Winter's warning remained: that without me, the rest of them wouldn't survive this. *Will they be all right?* I asked, *if this is the wrong choice? Can you and Night protect them from Lady Winter's consequences?*

No answer.

Coward, I flung out, but there was no answer to that, either.

Whatever was to come, it hinged on me.

Near the edge, the wind picked up, snapping my curls back from my face, plucking at my clothes. Overhead, the sky churned like a choppy sea. Once again, I was greeted by the vista of the surrounding peaks, marked here and there by snowdrifts and caps, and the enticing hint of the country stretching further south.

I'd never seen much of Edar. Saphirun was my earliest memories, and smouldering panic had turned the route I'd taken to Edar into a blur of roads and fields.

I'd seen so little of Farezi, too. A country whose roots and culture and hopes meant little to me, no matter the lineage I came from.

I'd seen so little of it all.

It took several moments of swallowing and sternly reminding myself that I was *not* afraid until I finally managed to look down – and promptly wished I hadn't.

The drop was steep and wreathed in shadows.

Everything returned to darkness here.

My first thought was *my parents were never afraid*, but now I knew that was surely wrong. They'd been afraid, for themselves and for each other, and doubted themselves and each other at times.

But they'd still done their duty. They'd still done what was right.

They had not let their fear rule them.

I took a slow breath, first through my nose and then deep into my throat. Closed my eyes. Willed my body, which seemed to know what I intended to do and wasn't in favour, to calm down.

If I'd still had my heart, no amount of calm would have slowed it.

I swept my gaze back towards the others, as if I could imprint their memory upon my mind. Melisande and Theo met my look, only briefly, but whatever my expression, however I held my body so close to the edge, they both realised what I meant to do.

If the only way for us to move on was down–

Then I'd open the door for them.

'Emri, *no!*'

Under the circumstances, Theo was faster than Melisande as he flung himself towards me.

But not fast enough.

I closed my eyes and flung myself off the mountain edge.

Once, there is a princess.

And she jumps off a mountain to open a door.

It feels like flying.

Except it's falling.

THIRTY-FIVE

I opened my eyes to a starry sky on the cusp of twilight succumbing to nightfall. Pinpricks of light upon a fall of deepening dark velvet.

It was very quiet.

I felt very calm.

I blinked, and realised I was floating upon a lake so still and clear, it felt like I was drifting through the sky itself.

There was no cold and no warmth. Just the gentle lap of water against my arms and legs, the sensation of my hair unfurling underwater, and the calm certainty that I was not alone.

'You are not,' a voice agreed.

Night.

I forced my legs underwater so I could tread in place. They sat upon a rock overhanging the lake, the long dark folds of their gown disappearing into the lake. Their hair hung down around their face, the longest ends dipping into the water – stars meeting stars. There was no sign of their cat.

I didn't speak. At last, they looked up and across the lake towards me, and the terrible sorrow etched upon their face made the water seem cold.

'So you accepted the fall,' they said. 'Twilight was certain you would. I was not so sure.'

'I suppose I have no pride left,' I said, because it was easier than admitting I didn't know how much more of this I could take. I was exhausted bone-deep and sucked dry of hope. I'd accepted the fall, with no certainty if it would help, and there didn't seem much admirable about it.

'You are so close,' Night said.

'I want to go home,' I said. The starry waters and the lake's gentle push and pull had detached me from my responsibilities, ever so subtly. It no longer mattered about keeping Gabi safe, or my history with Melisande, or the marriage I might have with Theo. I was tired, and I wanted to go home.

'The way to leave is under the lake,' Night said, leaning down to trail a hand through the water. 'You should be proud of yourself. So few people have ever been in this part of the mountain. It is my domain, not Lady Winter nor Twilight's.'

The serenity was making me consider the logistics of devoting myself to Night for the rest of my life, however long or short, if praying to them would bestow this sort of calm upon me.

Night's lips quirked into a smile. 'Perhaps. I shall think on it.'

I kept treading, absently aware I should have started to feel tired by now, and that my clothing had changed since I'd jumped off the mountain: the fabric was thinner, somehow not soaking up water, though I should have been fighting not to sink.

A terrible chill crawled up my neck. Was that how I reached under the lake? By letting myself drown?

Night scoffed. 'I have no time for such dramatics, not when the solution is much simpler.' Their dark eyes were intense, as if they could see into my soul. 'Simply give me a memory that you could not bear to lose. What absence in your mind and life will be a hollow you can never explain?'

The gods had stolen me from my home and ripped out my heart. They had set me on a quest through a bargain I couldn't refuse. They had chased me, hurt me, presented me with others' humiliation, and tried to grind me down with my own memories and the worst things that could have come to pass if others had made different choices.

Now they were asking me to give up a cherished memory.

And I was so very tired.

'You ask too much of me,' I said.

Night raised an eyebrow. 'You accepted Lady Winter's bargain. This is one of the conditions, the same as everything else you've survived to get thus far. Will you really stop now, so close to your goal?'

'So you say.' I limited my irritation to a hand swipe underneath the water. 'After everything I've survived to get thus far, as you've said, forgive me for not believing I'm so close to the end.'

Night's face abruptly shuttered, becoming as still as a winter's night. 'It will end, one way or another. What will you choose?'

I spread my arms, closed my eyes, and let myself float on my back again. The memory would come. I was at the end of my limits, my nerves frayed to breaking: the ideal conditions for a reassuring memory to resurface, something that would make me long for a time in my life that I could no longer return to.

In the darkness, a window slowly began to take shape, and then, around the edges of the closed drapes – a flash of lightning, followed by the grumble of thunder.

I'd been in Edar for a month, and it was the first proper storm since my arrival.

And I could not sleep.

Pressed against the headrest of my bed, I'd curled into a tight ball. Even though I couldn't see the lightning with the blanket tossed over my head, I could hear the thunder, and each time it seemed to be coming closer.

The palace was the tallest building in the city, situated on one of the hills, and I was convinced we were all going to die.

Another boom of thunder, and I buried deeper into the bed, trying to pull a pillow over my head, too afraid to whimper or cry.

As the thunder faded, my door opened, followed by light footsteps. A hand pressed lightly against my back.

'Emri,' Mother whispered. 'Emri, darling, it's just a storm. It can't hurt you.'

I couldn't remember how long it took her to coax me out from under the pillow, but her lamp had filled the room with golden light, making everything seem less frightening. At another flash and burst of thunder, she pulled me close.

'It's all right,' she said, rocking me against her. 'It's all right. Come on, now, up.'

Clinging tightly to Sheep (a little stuffed sheep knitted for me by the Essinfall steward's wife, and which I still had in a closet years later, threadbare and much-mended), I gripped Mother's hand and followed her down the hall and into their apartments. Through their sitting room and into their bedroom.

To my astonishment, Mama was fast asleep, her hair tucked into a silk cap, the blankets pulled up to her chin.

Mother smiled at me. 'Storms don't scare her,' she explained.

'Do they scare you?' I asked.

'I have a healthy respect for them.'

She lifted me into the centre of the bed, between them, and tucked the blankets around me after she had climbed in on the other side. Unlike the thunder and lightning, *this* woke up Mama, who turned around, mumbling sleepily.

'She couldn't sleep because of the storm,' Mother whispered. 'I thought it best for her not to be alone.'

Mama leaned over to kiss my forehead. 'Storm won't hurt you, Emri. We won't allow it. Now, you and Sheep need to sleep.' She wrapped an arm around me, and I breathed in the familiar scents of her soap and hair cream. Behind me, Mother buried into her pillows and rubbed my shoulder.

Soon, their warmth and the soft sound of Mama's breathing lulled me into sleep. Their very presence seemed to make the lightning less intense, the thunder quieter. I held Sheep tight, safe in the knowledge that I wasn't alone and my parents had said they would protect me.

In the morning, the storm had blown itself out, and the sky was a cloud-tossed blue with pale sunlight. The only reminder of what had happened was that I'd woken up in my parents' bed.

When I opened my eyes, I realised my tears were sliding from the edges of my eyes into the lake. And with each falling tear, the memory of that night – the fear, the thunder, Mother's gentleness, the warmth of my parents' safety – faded and drained away, until the lake had taken it all.

My parents' love that night.

Their promise of safety.

The knowledge, that night, that I was loved and protected.

For a moment, there was only the sound of water lapping against me.

Then Night said: 'You loved them, and they loved you. They kept you safe.'

'I love them,' I replied, 'and they love me. They have always kept me safe, as much as they can.'

Even through killing Rassa, Mama had averted the potential of my growing up in Edar under his rule: constrained, underestimated, poorly equipped to be a monarch in power.

'But that night,' I said, staring up at the sky, overcome with longing for a memory that was already drifting away in wisps, 'it was special. I didn't fully trust them yet. They were still figuring out how to be parents – *my* parents.'

Later, I'd learned that storms had still kept Mother awake then because of Goldenmarch, and she had gone to my room on a hunch that I also wouldn't be able to sleep. My governess had slept through it all, and her reassurances while putting me to bed hadn't been enough to quell my fears.

'When you reach the final domain,' Night finally said. 'I urge you to make the correct choice.'

As they spoke, the lake changed around me: the lapping turned stronger, the water grew heavier, or perhaps it was my waterlogged clothing now gaining weight.

'Whose domain is it?' I asked. 'Yours or Twilight's?'

'Neither,' they replied.

I took a deep breath, as the water crept towards my chin.

'It is my beloved's,' Night said, their voice trembling with sorrow. 'And I have not seen her in some time.'

As I sank under the water, I caught a glimpse of a full moon rising overhead.

O nce, there are two gods.

And in their adoration, they have a daughter.

And from her birth, the moon is drawn to her.

But this time, the mortals give her a name: Selene.

Like her mother, she is pale, but her beauty glimmers, soft where her mother's is sharp, and she has her father's grave demeanour but less of his kindness.

And like the moon, Night is also drawn to her.

Between the wax and wane of Twilight's hours, Selene and Night control the long dark hours. But her love is fickle, as are her whims, and she often flees from Night's embrace in the sky.

Of them all, her parents and Night, it is she who loves mortals most.

And they return it with their own devotion.

At first, her parents consider this a good thing. For mortals, the triumvirate can be difficult to worship: Lady Winter too brutal; Twilight too distant; Night too aware of their secret fears and nightmares to offer hope. But Selene is a young goddess, and the moon is reassuring to night-time travellers and those whom sleep evades, a source of beauty in darkness.

But Lady Winter was the first of them, and as mortals begin to turn towards her daughter, her jealousy grows. And lingers.

And waits.

And as devotion wanes, and the threat of war looms, Lady Winter turns from them, offers no help, and refuses to allow the others to grant their unasked-for aid.

Like her beloved, Selene wants no war, and in desperation against the slaughter to come, she disobeys her mother and strikes a bargain to stop it.

But she is tricked, and the war is fought and lost and won. The spilt blood runs deep into the earth.

And when magic wanes from lost devotion, and they have no choice but to retreat to the oldest temple, Lady Winter turns on her daughter for her treachery.

Her vengeance is as her nature dictates: brutal and merciless.

With the dregs of her magic, Lady Winter binds her daughter in the deepest bowels of the temple, hidden under a lake that only the bravest can discover. Her mother's curse wipes her from mortal memory and myth, her existence stripped from every story.

And within her binding, she holds a dangerous choice. Within her binding, she waits to be freed.

THIRTY-SIX

As the lake depths withdrew, I found myself surrounded by glowing frost.

Ice shards surrounded me, like a maze of interwoven branches made from snow. I drew in a breath, crisp and clear, that burned down my throat, oddly replenishing.

A little of my despair lifted.

I seemed alone, and there was no blatant path ahead. The ground was frozen solid, ridged so I wouldn't slip. Finally, I shrugged and started forward. Nothing would change by my standing here and doing nothing.

I hoped.

It felt like making my way through the oldest parts of the royal forest by foot: slow, careful, frustrating. I pulled myself over the rippling, twisting branches of ice, crawled under them, ducked, backtracked, wished for a sword so I could try and hack at them. It didn't seem like a good idea – there was a curious, charged feel to the air, as if it were waiting for me to make a wrong decision – but it was still a little comforting, as if I was actually a hero in a story, brandishing her weapon as she reached the crux of her quest.

I actually stopped to laugh. I was many things, but not a glorious hero of old. They'd find me pitiable indeed.

With no idea if I was going in the right direction, I pinned my hopes on the odd charge in the air growing steadily stronger. There was nothing for it but to keep walking.

At last, after one more duck under a low hanging branch, and cautiously pulling myself over a large one half-melted into the ground, I stood at the edge of a frozen lake. Like the place where I'd met Night, this seemed outside the mountain: overhead, a large full moon glowed… in a starless sky.

'So you made the choice,' a voice said, chiming like bells, as delicate as spinning snowflakes upon the air, as clear as the sky after a heavy snowfall.

In the centre of the frozen lake, a woman sat trapped within a frozen sphere.

She was pale as snow, her lips stained a light blue. Unlike the other gods, there were no stars in her eyes: they were silvery-grey, glowing like moonlight behind a storm cloud. Her hair was silver and white; short ringlets framed her face, the rest perfectly straight and spilling onto the ground. She wore a white robe, edged in light blue with a light grey sash, the folds billowing around her.

She watched me approach.

If I were to imagine a moon goddess, this would be who I'd imagine.

I stopped a few paces away and stared, then looked up at the moon and back at her again.

Her pale blue lips curved in a smile.

We had no god or goddess of the moon.

Why didn't we have one? Why had I never questioned it until now – why had no one ever questioned it?

In all the stories, the gods held dominion over winter, snow and ice, the twilight hours, and the night and its countless stars – but the moon was barely mentioned, an unacknowledged part of the sky unclaimed by Night.

Because it had been claimed by another god who had been forgotten. The fourth statue of a god in the grotto, the phases of the moon carved above her head.

I walked closer, until we were only separated by the frozen sphere.

In her, I saw Lady Winter's brutal nature, but softened, and Twilight's distant compassion, though tempered less by kindness. She was regal, a goddess to be admired and feared, yet still loved. Even as I looked at her, something within me yearned to be closer to her, to be *seen*, acknowledged; loved.

'My mother has underestimated you since the beginning,' the goddess remarked, 'as my father warned her. She scorns your bravery and determination, but more than that, she scorns your cleverness. It will be her undoing perhaps, one day. Or perhaps not.'

'Who are you?' I whispered. My knees shook, but didn't threaten to give up on me. But unlike Twilight and Night, this goddess had a strain of Lady Winter's brightness that made me want to look away and kneel in wonder.

But only a little. And I was no longer in awe of gods as when I'd first met Lady Winter.

She smiled. 'Selene, Lady of the Moon, daughter of Lady Winter and Twilight. And I can see why my father likes you. He always preferred the mortals who were too brave – or simply, perhaps, too stupid – to stand on ceremony.'

I raised an eyebrow. 'And you, my lady?' Like her mother, the use of a title seemed abundantly wise.

'I am trapped within my mother's binding,' Selene said. 'It makes little difference what I think or want.'

'Hardly,' I replied. 'Or I wouldn't be here.'

Her smile turned sly. 'Very true.'

I reached up to rub my face, then dropped my arms back to my sides. No point showing weakness before a god, even a trapped one. 'You have the choice.'

'I do,' she agreed.

I braced myself.

'When I was born,' Selene said, 'the moon could not help but be drawn to me, and so I became her mistress. And over time, mortals could not help but be drawn to me; my mother could no longer contain her jealousy, even knowing that my nature was simply less brutal than hers. Mortals retained their devotion to her; I was simply a safer goddess to ask for aid.'

Her beautiful voice rose and fell with a lilting musicality. I found myself swaying, lulled into complacency.

'But even so,' she continued, 'their worship dwindled, and so did our power, and magic began to fade from the land. And a war broke out, which held the potential for slaughter and devastation to heights mortals had never reached before, with magic no longer a balancing force. I could not allow it.

'But my mother turned her favour from those whose ancestors had ceased to worship her. And she ordered the rest of us to also withhold our aid.'

The war that had been the beginning of the end for the First Empire. The war that I'd seen in the vision, with the Blue and Green Queens, where Lady Winter had turned from her army and La Dame des Fleurs had strode out onto the battlefield at the head of hers. The vision where I'd seen a lady in white gazing upon the fires and smoke and blood, a cat with star-strewn fur purring in my ear, the air laced with the moans and weeping of the dying. She'd held a silver-tipped spear, radiating the grief I'd heard in Night's voice as we gazed upon the wounded and the dying.

'You were the goddess in the battle vision,' I whispered.

Her smile turned grim. 'I was. And I was foolish, as my mother has often reminded me since: I disobeyed her and made a bargain, born out of desperation, in an effort to stop the war. And I was tricked. Betrayed.'

Rage flooded her eyes. 'That war was our downfall. What little faith remained died in the aftermath, and all that was left for us was this temple. And when my mother discovered what I had done, and that it had been in vain… well, you know her nature. She is not known for her mercy nor her forgiveness.'

Selene swept a hand around us. 'This is what remains of the magic in the world, binding me in a frozen prison. The icy heart of the temple. Along with my mother's fury, and the sorrow of my father and my beloved, it's transformed the temple into a pilgrim's maze. And after my mother imprisoned me here, deep in the temple, she wiped me from all mortal memory and record.'

We were right. The temple had been corrupted by magic. No wonder nothing had made sense.

Something spiked in the charged air – no, the *magic* – around us, forcing me warily to my feet.

Selene rose, too. Upright, the full dignity of her presence was unmistakeable: she was distant and as unknowable as the moon itself, a source of mystery and wonder to everyone who had ever looked up into the sky and thought *how?* and *why?*

I should have been terrified of her, as I was wisely terrified of all the gods, even a little. And part of me was, but it was far lesser to the rest of me which was exhausted and growing weary of my constant pain, who wanted her heart back and to go home and hug her parents and cry into their shoulders like I was a child again.

Instead of admitting any of this, I asked, 'What is the choice?'

'If you wish to meet the final challenge,' Selene said, and her voice had changed, deepening like the vibration of a large bell, 'then you must face the last obstacle which, if you surmount, you will be free of the mountain: you must break the sphere and free me.'

'Is that all?'

It seemed a natural choice: to free the Lady of the Moon, to have her in the myths and stories again, the daughter of Lady Winter and Twilight. How was it a difficult choice?

'But there is a price,' she added. 'In freeing me, you release the trapped magic back into the world. And it has been a long time since the world remembered how to live with power such as ours; the balance is unchecked. The times ahead will be difficult for mortals.'

She paused, her glowing storm cloud gaze – which vividly reminded me of Mother's eyes – boring into me, and then she whispered, 'And if you free magic back into the world, you also release *us*.'

And if the world no longer remembered how to live with magic, it absolutely didn't remember how to live with gods.

I hesitated.

If I didn't break the sphere, I was dooming Melisande, Theo, and Gabi to death, and myself to a life devoid of choice and free will. Yet based on everything we'd gone through so far, was it really fair to return magic and gods to a world that had moved on?

But had we been right to force them away? Would returning magic to the world keep it in balance? Would someone like Rassa have tried to steal a crown and usurp a rightful Queen, with the threat of magic and the gods to deter him?

I'd never know.

But perhaps I could stop the next person like him from trying.

And the strength of the power here... I'd no doubt that Lady Winter's rage would only keep rising, year after year, unknowingly empowered by small, unknowing acts of devotion like the Midwinter Ball. Even if the others perished here, and I became Lady Winter's future puppet ruler, she would return to the world in strength and *fury*. Better for all of us to escape so we could educate and warn the world.

If we had to live alongside gods, I'd prepare my parents as best I could so Edar would survive it.

For a long moment, I gazed at the goddess within the sphere, trapped by her mistakes and her mother's rage, and felt a faint twinge of sympathy. I knew all too well what it was to suffer the consequences of someone else's actions.

'Why me?' I asked. 'Why has no one else been able to break the sphere? Twilight, Night – not even Lady Winter herself?'

Selene's mouth twisted into a sharp, bitter smile. 'When my mother trapped me here, so strong was her fury, so deep her loathing for me, that she also trapped part of her own magic in the sphere,' she told me, soft and vicious. 'She cannot break it, for it would mean attacking part of herself, and my father and my beloved were never strong enough. No patron god can step upon another's sacred ground. It was always to be one of my mother's Chosen.'

The enraged sound that burst from me was nothing less than a mortal show of weak fury. It had never been about escaping the mountain, not as Lady Winter had originally presented the terms. It was always going to end up here, if I made it this far, in a frozen lake deep in the forgotten bowels of the mountain, faced with a terrible, impossible choice. In my winning the bargain, Lady Winter would also win.

She had played the game so skillfully, her true intent hidden by her all-too-real anger towards mortals.

With difficulty, I forced myself to calm. Swallowed. Closed my eyes. Hoped – *prayed*, I supposed, to whichever god was willing to listen, even the one standing trapped before me – that I wasn't about to make a choice I'd regret for the rest of my life.

'I break the sphere?' I asked.

'Break the sphere,' Selene confirmed.

I took a deep breath. Loosened my shoulders. Stepped back and readied my posture.

Curled my gloved hand – *please, please let me be able to do this with gloves* – into a fist, exactly as Mama had taught me.

I swung back, steadied myself, and smashed my fist into the ice with the full force of my shoulder.

The pain came slowly.

But it came.

Alongside the cracks in the sphere.

The gloves only delayed the inevitable: the cracks frayed the material, and when the frayed threads were gone, my skin was next. My hands grew warm from the blood before it smeared and pooled, cooling.

Selene gave me no gratitude, no encouragement, not that I had really expected any from her. This was not a rescue. This was the fulfilment of a condition to a bargain that involved her.

I doubted if there had ever been much love between her and Lady Winter. Certainly, if my parents had ever trapped me like this, in such a manner, I wouldn't have remembered them well. The next time we argued, perhaps I'd manage to remember that it could always be worse.

So I hit. And kept hitting. And screamed. And cursed.

And eventually, I began to weep.

If I failed, Melisande, Theo, and Gabi would die.

If I failed, my parents wouldn't be prepared for Lady Winter's return.

If I failed, I lost a life of my own choosing, in so much as duty would allow.

I could not fail.

But if I won, magic would return to the world.

I hit. And I punched.

And I screamed.

When the smash came, I wasn't ready.

I wasn't ready at all.

I'd forgotten that Selene, Lady of the Moon, had her own power also trapped within the sphere. As it shattered, a gale blew me back against the ice, hard enough that I almost expected it to crack underneath me. For a moment, as the back of my head throbbed, I saw stars amid an edge of darkness.

When I was finally steady enough to get to my knees, Selene had stepped daintily over the ruined shards of her prison. Power spun around her, tossing and plucking at her hair and robe.

She approached me slowly, gracefully, as if we had all the time in the world.

For a god, perhaps we had.

'You chose, mortal.' Now free of the sphere, her entire demeanour had changed. A goddess stood before me, stern and remote, vast and unknowable in her divinity.

She was free, and no longer had need of me.

'I did.' The reedy tone of my voice should have worried me, but I had little worry left at this point. It was simply one foot in front of the other, move from one choice to the next, until I won my freedom and everyone else's.

One choice made, and now on to the next.

Selene gestured. I blinked and found myself upright, but without a gift of fresh strength or energy. But still, I was standing, which had previously been beyond me.

Another blink, and she was before me, her pale, cool hands gripping my face.

She kissed my forehead.

'This will grant you passage to the final challenge,' she said, as I shuddered from the cool power coursing through me, similar to the hoarfrost burn from when Lady Winter had ripped out my heart, though not as brutal. 'And this will give you the courage to take back your heart from my mother.'

She kissed me, expelling a burst of frigid air into my mouth.

I gagged, and it coursed down my throat.

And the hoarfrost, the ice that could never be my heart, *burned*.

THIRTY-SEVEN

I opened my eyes to a pinprick of light far above.

I sat up, wheezing against the cold. I was in a smooth dark tower of brick, with no way out apart from a small grid set into the wall near me. Other than that, it was row upon row of neat bricks stretching towards a scrap of sky.

If I managed to survive this, I was never going near a mountain again.

Never. It didn't matter who I offended, not even Lady Winter. I would laugh in her face, then try and run her through with the nearest blade simply for my own satisfaction, since it wouldn't even *kill* her.

None of us should ever be so lucky.

I lay on my back, contemplating the dull throbbing in my skull, the creak of ice in my bones, and slowly realised I was crying.

They weren't dramatic tears. I didn't have the will or even the *heart* for those. As they trickled from my eyes and into my hair, I felt nothing except a bone-deep exhaustion. Emptiness.

Hopelessness.

But to feel hopeless meant I'd felt hope at some point through this wretched ordeal, and really – had I ever felt hopeful that I'd succeed?

I'd accepted the bargain, even if Lady Winter had made it so it was never really a choice. I'd worked with Melisande, Theo, and Gabi, trying to coax us into a semblance of a team so we could work together for our freedom. I'd started to trust them.

And for what?

I had no idea where any of them were. If they were alive, if they were searching for me, if they'd made their own desperate bargains with Twilight or Night after I'd jumped off the mountain.

Now I lay at the bottom of a tower with no way out, staring at the sky, and there was nothing left to try, short of growing wings, and that happened in none of the stories.

We could do many things, with the aid of gods and magic, but we could not fly. No god had ever given that gift.

I'd die here. I'd never get my heart back.

But I wouldn't live without it, as a puppet of Lady Winter, forever cut off from my true feelings.

I took another breath, and gagged against the chill at the back of my throat. A gift, Selene had called it, so I could face her mother and win my heart back.

But I was so tired.

Yet… yet. If I let myself die here, if I gave up, then I was abandoning everyone – the entire known world – to the return of gods and magic; unprepared, unaware. Defenceless. My parents, my family, my friends. Even my blood kin in Farezi, who'd never know what had happened to Melisande if she perished here in the mountain. Princess Lucia, who loved her daughter even as they both struggled within the confines of duty. And Theo would never again see any of his rambunctious, teasing family, who loved him and would mourn him.

I was a princess. I had been raised to fulfil my duty and to eventually rule well. And one aspect of ruling well was to do what was right, what was best for my people, and to take responsibility for the consequences of terrible decisions when those two things didn't align.

I had to get up.

'Good. That was how we raised you.'

Mama's voice was crisp and no-nonsense, exactly her tone whenever I took too long to come round to her (correct) opinion of a situation. I knew this wasn't real, that she was a figment of my mind. She hadn't been there a moment ago, and she certainly wouldn't have been so calm while impeccably dressed in Court finery in an enclosed tower room.

But her dark eyes pinned me in place, her chin tilted back in authoritative defiance. I was her daughter, and while they hadn't raised me in preparation for this exact situation, they had given me the tools to navigate it.

And yet.

I choked out a sob from my ice-ridden throat. 'I miss you. I miss you both, so much. And I'm so scared.'

Mama's expression softened. 'I know. We love you, and we've been trying to find you.'

Before my mind could caution me to stop, before I could be disappointed by an illusion, I flung myself into her arms, and she was *solid*. She was warm, and the silk of her dress slipped under my hands, and the familiar scents of her soap and hair cream engulfed me.

I cried until my throat made it impossible to do so.

Rocking me in her arms as I wept, she hummed an old lullaby she'd sung to me when I was a child, the same one her own mama had sung to her. I hadn't thought about it for years. If this was magic, if this moment was Twilight or Night taking pity on me one last time and not just my own desperate mind, then I would gladly accept.

I shuddered, coughing, instinctively trying to clear the ice at the back of my throat. 'I have to climb.'

'Yes,' Mama said. 'You must.' She looked me in the eyes and added, 'So get up.'

The climb was monstrous.

Selene's gift shifted from a scrape and prickle in my throat to a frostbitten burn through my entire body. The magic scorched like ice in my veins, cracked into my bones, sent my nerves juddering to numbness.

It forced me up. It forced me to climb.

I don't know how I managed to dig my fingernails in between the bricks to hoist myself up, but the magic insisted I do so and I could no longer fight it. I was a hollow, exhausted shell, and the power filled me, overflowing, urging me *forward, forward, up, up*.

So I climbed. The magic helped my boots find purchase, and I dug my fingernails between the bricks and even when they snapped and turned bloody, the magic wouldn't let me stop.

When my fingers were bloody and numb, I started smashing the wall to get a handhold.

In each punch, frost crackled across the marks, gouging into my skin and knuckles as I hit and punched and hit until I could grip and force myself upward.

And with each hit, a vision flashed across my eyes:

On the mountaintop, Gabi sits at a table, the winds snapping her curls like a banner. Her hair and face are clean, and she wears a crimson Eshvoni long tunic, stiff-collared, over trousers, golden embroidered flames twining down her arms. Her hands are neatly folded on the table. Her face betrays nothing but calm serenity against the winds and the grumble of thunder overhead. Every royal is taught this public mask from a young age, but it is imperative for heirs within the direct succession.

The Eshvoni expect their Queen and her daughter to embody Aestia, their Lady of Fire and Stars. They do not want them to show their true selves.

Gabi has grown up to show no fear, to be stubborn and merciless and heed no one but the Queen, who wears the crown, and her own mother, who is expected to rule before her. But her rage, her secrets, her vulnerability; that has all been kept secret, private and safe, for she will one day take the throne as a living embodiment of a goddess, and a goddess has no weakness and answers to no one.

And Gabriela, granddaughter of a Queen, daughter of an heir, has always dreaded the day the crown will settle upon her head. Now she dreads it even more because one day, soon, Aestia will return and her family *will* have to answer to a higher power which, though kind, has always had limits to the mercy extended to mortals.

Night sits on the opposite side of the table.

Between them lies a board set up with Root and Fang. The squares are red and gold, the figures carved from dark marble with touches of gilt.

Through Gabi's eyes, Night's expression is sly, each movement coiled like a snake waiting to strike. 'Shall we begin?' they ask.

'You are not my god,' says Gabi, who will one day rule the queendom of Eshvon, who is the granddaughter of a Queen and daughter of a Queen-to-be. 'This is not your game. I do not fear you.'

Night smiles, sharp enough to cut, and there is no kindness in their dark eyes. 'You should,' they say, 'for night falls in Eshvon, too.'

For Gabi to show her temper moments after first meeting us, I now realised, was an act of great trust. She was raised not to show her true self, and this temple, this mountain, had pushed her until she could do little else.

If Gabi could take on a god's game, then I could keep climbing.

With every punch, flashes of moving pieces, fanned cards, a furious, polite battle played out on a board, flickered across my eyes. The hoarfrost crackled in my chest, gouged between my ribs, pricked against my lungs. My body – my weak, mortal body, cradled by bones and protected by fragile skin – couldn't last much longer.

If the magic would kill me, so be it. But I would not die easily, not anymore.

'This game is pointless,' Gabi says, affecting boredom, while her gaze twitches back to her winged horse, whose defence is threatened by her poor hand. 'Your lady was clear in her intentions. Without Emri, we die in this wretched mountain.'

'This game is not for your freedom,' Night replies. The wind does not sway their hair or clothes; they do not flinch at the growling thunder overhead.

A third of the way from the top, I began to cough. Snowflakes tumbled from my mouth as I spat out ice shards. I pulled myself up, up, up, as numbness crawled down my arms, tried to lock my shoulders.

Through the game, Gabi keeps her expression as blank as a perfect card sharp. Night underestimates it, proving there is a little folly in them, until she lays down a hand that wipes two of their army off the board. They hiss, their face twisting for a moment, before they pull their dignified mask back into place.

Gabi's face twitches, as if she's fighting a scowl. 'Then what is the purpose of this game?' she asks, prickly with irritation.

Night's gaze freezes her in place, like prey aware that there is no escape from the monster who has pinned her in their sights. 'Buying time,' they say. 'For Emri. And my beloved.'

So close to the top, I started to cry. My tears froze upon my cheeks.

Gabi purses her mouth, studying the board, then flicks her gaze up to contemplate Night. Despite the wind and the tossing clouds and groaning thunder, for a long moment, both mortal and god appear unnaturally still.

At last Gabi reaches out, moves a single piece, and wins the game.

'Then we should play again,' she says.

At the top of the tower, I rolled onto my back, spluttering, wheezing against the chill wracking me and the ice clogging my throat. A dying sunset stretched overhead: a brief moment of doomed serenity.

I closed my eyes.

Theo is still within the mountain, slumped against a wall, staring at the parchment in his trembling hands. The ink has stretched across most of it, leaving only a sliver of a waxing moon unfilled. In the centre, the final full moon of winter is the only remaining thing untouched by ink.

We are so close.

And so very far from freedom.

His mouth moves silently in a desperate prayer, over and over: 'Please help us, grant me what I need to help us succeed, please help us, please help us. I want to live; I want us *all* to live—'

An abrupt wave of familiar calm envelopes me – *Twilight* – as Theo lets out a terrified sob, almost of relief, and–

'My Emri,' a familiar voice said.

My eyes snapped open, and I sat up so fast my head spun.

Mother sat nearby, her arms wrapped loosely around her knees. Like Mama, she was dressed in Court finery, ludicrous against our surroundings, and I knew this wasn't real because her hair drifted in the breeze, and save the servants who helped dress her, Mama was the only other person who saw Mother's unbound hair.

She smiled at me, stunningly bright, warm and kind and sorrowful, full of *love*. And for an isolated moment, a fleeting breath, it felt like everything was possible and everything would be all right.

I reached for her, and from one moment to the next, Mother was gone.

I sucked in an agonised breath, struggled to my feet, and turned to face Lady Winter.

But it wasn't her.

THIRTY-EIGHT

Rassa stood before me.

'No,' I said stupidly. 'You're dead.'

Growing up, I had always felt – had always been told – that I resembled Lady Liliene more than him. I had seen his portrait before I'd left for Edar and imprinted his face upon my memory, as if by refusing to forget, I would stop myself from resembling him as I grew older.

But perhaps the image locked in my memory had begun to fade. Perhaps I'd simply forgotten, lulled by slow changes that I didn't recognise, a faint resemblance that my parents couldn't bear to acknowledge.

Perhaps the resemblance had always been there, and no one wanted to admit it.

Unlike Lady Liliene, it was not a striking similarity. Rassa tilted his head in thought as I did, braced his shoulders and hips like when I needed to steady myself, along with some other traits of the Farezi royal family that I had also inherited.

Where I had glorified in sharing my mothers' mannerisms and habits; these... these I wanted to shuck from me immediately, as if I could reach inside and claw them out.

I wanted nothing more from this man than what I already had to suffer.

His gaze flicked me up and down, considering, and his slow smile had an edge of cruelty. 'So. You're the daughter, all grown up.'

The daughter; not *my* daughter, or even my name. I was a thing, a symbol of his legacy, nothing more.

Well. Then the board was set.

'You're dead,' I told him, 'and no one speaks your name. Your portraits are covered, and dust gathers on them with each passing year. Your name is stricken from the family record, your followers dead, imprisoned, or scattered with no hope. Your sister rules as Queen Sabine II, and her reign will be remembered. And I am the heir of the Queen you tried to destroy.'

Rassa's mouth curled, and I moved with him as he circled me with lazy strides. 'Of course Lia would adopt you, so she could have an heir *and* marry that viper.'

'They love me,' I told him, proud of the strength in my voice. 'They love me better than you ever could, and they deserve their happiness ten times more than you.'

He laughed, flicking a hand as if my words were nothing more than a mild irritant buzzing around his face.

'They may love you,' he said, 'but that didn't protect you from the gods.'

'And you would have, if you had remained King?'

'I would have immediately bent the knee and hammered out an understanding,' he replied promptly. 'There's nothing to be gained by defiance towards gods.'

I sneered, unable to help myself. 'So you'd give up your ability to choose – as a ruler *and* yourself? No wonder you won't be remembered.'

He raised an eyebrow. 'And yet here you are, without a heart and facing your own loss of choice. And your path has been far more arduous than my solution would have been.'

I pulled myself up to my full height. 'I am the daughter and heir of two Queens who have never given up, and nor will I.'

He smiled faintly. 'You may be their daughter... but it's *my* blood. When they look at you, no matter whose heir you are, no matter what future ruler they try and shape you into, they still see *me*.'

'No,' I said, but my voice wavered, just for a moment, just for long enough.

He resumed pacing, his smile broadening as he prowled around me. 'Now, if I had kept the throne,' he continued, 'your suitability would never have been in question. No one would have ever doubted your position, your capabilities, as heir. None of this... *speculation.*'

'Hardly,' I scoffed, moving with him again, keeping my gaze locked on him. Arrogance suffused his every footstep, the swagger in his hips. 'I've seen what kind of life I'd have had as your heir:

constrained, unchallenged, untrained. Taught to unquestioningly accept the limits placed upon my power. No life at all, really.'

He stopped, forcing me to stop with him. 'And what makes you think you deserve the life those Queens have given you?' he asked, utterly serious.

I swallowed as the barb struck home, a jolt of disquiet spreading through me. I knew it was foolish. I knew it was lies, that he was nothing more than an illusion.

And yet. And yet–

Something glimmered just beyond Rassa. Lady Winter appeared, tall and imposing, regal in her brutal satisfaction. Of course this was her doing. Of all the gods, it would be her who'd fling the harshest truth and lies at me when I was, according to Night and Selene, so close to freedom.

Her eyes, where stars were born and died, the branches that bulged under her skin and arched around her head like a monstrous crown, her pale skin and crimson mouth. An ice goddess for a hard people, who fought and endured the bitter cold with stubborn pride, nobles who had created some of the most ancient lineages in Edar, stretching back before the gods and magic had begun to decline.

What was I to her, but a puny mortal easily shaped to her will?

'I understand, now, why Mother was so pleased at your death.'

I jumped, turning as Melisande appeared, half-flung and half-staggered, from a mass of shadows. Her hair was in tangled disarray, her eyes half-wild and shining like she was gripped by a fever, and her hands shook as they gripped a sword.

A sword.

It gleamed like moonlight, a wavering shine rippling down the blade, a sign of master craft. The hilt was black, and even though Melisande looked, frankly, half-dead, she held it as if she knew how to use it.

Stopping beside me, she looked Rassa up and down with a sneer. 'What a vainglorious peacock you are.'

'How did you get here?' I muttered. 'Why do you have a sword?'

She eyed me grimly. 'You're not the only one who can make bargains with gods that you'll later regret.'

'But you can't use a sword!'

She hefted it. 'Yes, I can. Normally better, when I don't have one foot in the grave.' She smiled crookedly at my astonishment. 'Challenging someone to a duel at the Edaran Court would have *absolutely* counted as a diplomatic incident, so it was decided I'd be quiet about it.'

Lady Winter, however, was focused on Melisande's sword. 'So. One of you freed my daughter. A pity. I had thought Night's devotion to her would have waned by now, and yet here you stand with the sword they forged together for their Chosen.'

Melisande shrugged. 'You are not my gods. I'm not particularly thrilled about it, but needs must. You understand.'

I'd given up every pretence of understanding what was going on.

Rassa attempted to recover himself. 'So, here stands my sister's arrogant daughter—'

'Oh, shut up,' Melisande snapped. 'I don't care about your insults, or having your respect. I also don't care about your existence and certainly not your death.'

Before I could help myself, I laughed. A burst of joy, the kind of sound I thought Lady Winter and the mountain had robbed from me.

Melisande spun to face me. 'We swore we'd leave the mountain together. That we wouldn't leave each other behind. I'm getting out of here, and I'm dragging you with me. No theatrical sacrifices necessary, thank you. Mother would never forgive me, and your parents would… well, let's not finish that sentence in front of *her*, shall we?'

A sound like water hitting a hot pan erupted from Lady Winter.

And snow began to fall around us.

'How?' I asked, hating the exhausted despair in my voice. 'We can't kill a god.'

'No,' Melisande said thoughtfully, adjusting her grip on the sword hilt. 'But we can kill *him*. Again. Probably, with a divine sword.'

The snow transformed into a freezing gale. Flurries whirled around us, freezing and blinding.

'He died once, he can die here again. History repeating itself.'

Melisande fumbled for my hand in the storm, pressing close to shout in my ear: 'Do you trust me?'

Did I trust her?

The part of me still buried deep and small from childhood said: *No.*

The part of me that had grown up in Edar said, *Yes*, because she knew her duty lay in peaceful relations with Farezi.

The rest of me that had been brought here, and lost her heart, and run with Melisande and pulled her through walls, and coaxed her along when she no longer had the strength, and who had vowed that she would not leave the mountain without her said: *Yes.*

'Yes,' I shouted back, flinging it out in defiance to the gods. 'I trust you!'

'On three, run with me: one.' Melisande pressed me against her. 'Two.' She gripped one of my hands around hers on the hilt, then wrapped her other one around my waist. 'Three!' She charged forward, and I ran with her, our hands around the hilt, and somehow, whether through Melisande's instincts, or the sword guiding us—

—we ran Rassa through.

His disbelieving scream was terrible, and I relished none of it. The sound rose higher and higher, blending with the howling wind, and when I took a deep breath, snowflakes flooded my throat, whirled into my lungs, and burst against the hoarfrost in my heart—

I screamed, and screamed, and screamed as the snow and ice cut through me, until there was only merciful darkness.

I am back at Essinfall, and it is a beautiful summer's day. Aestia's time.

While the North has a reputation for brutal winters, the summers are occasionally wonderful. The first time my parents brought me here, we were lucky: the sun blazed in a glorious sky, and I ran through Essinfall's gardens and fields with Rialla and Micah during days that never seemed to end.

This is not that time.

My parents stand nearby, only a few years older than me. There's no trace of the lines and weariness on their faces, so familiar to me, from their years of ruling. They walk arm in arm, but something is different about them, something fragile, cautious. But I recognise the haunted look in Mother's eyes: Goldenmarch.

This is sometime after their return, when Mother had regained the throne, but before they married, before Mama also became Queen.

I walk towards them, trying to decipher their soft words and laughter. Despite caution, they shine in each other's presence, pressing as close as they dare, their shared smiles warm and secret.

They are two women in love, whose feelings for each other surpassed duty, treason, and vengeance. Two women who came to love me as their daughter.

The depth of how much I love and miss them almost makes me stagger. I will free myself of the mountain. I will return to them.

'Flatterer,' Mother laughs, and she tucks a stray curl behind Mama's ear.

'It's not flattery,' Mama insists, 'if it's true.'

'To you, perhaps.'

Mama stops suddenly, her skirts settling around her. 'You are the most beautiful woman in Edar,' she says, tugging Mother's hand for her to stop. 'And the cleverest. Maybe not the most cunning—'

'That's you,' Mother says, smiling, but her eyes are serious. She has gone utterly still.

'—and a Queen who will drag Edar back into prosperity. Damn your ancestors, Lia. *You* will be the Sionbourne monarch remembered throughout history.'

'Perhaps,' Mother says. 'But I don't intend to rule alone.'

Now Mama turns still; she swallows hard. A long moment of silence, and then she places Mother's hand over her heart. 'I know you love me,' Mama says, the words deliberate and careful, 'and I know a part of your heart will always belong to Edar and your people, because you were raised to be Queen and I expect nothing less. But…'

She trails off, and Mother finally coaxes, 'But?' There is something terrified and hopeful in her eyes.

'But you will always have my heart,' Mama finally says. 'All of it. It has always been yours.'

Mother attempts a trembling smile, then cups Mama's face and pulls her into a kiss.

In a blink, they are gone, and Lady Winter stands before me, baleful and bitter.

'You didn't need to give me the worst scenarios that could have been,' I tell her. 'I could always have imagined worse.'

'So you say.'

'Was that the final choice?' It hurts my neck to look up at her, but I refuse to break eye contact. 'To run my birth father through, the source of so much anguish, to prove that I would no longer listen to the worst of what people thought of me?'

She tilts her head, considering me.

'I must say,' I add, exhaustion turning my voice careless, 'I didn't expect a vision of hope this late in our bargain.'

'That was not a vision,' Lady Winter says. 'That was a memory — but not one of yours.'

I pause, then whisper: 'I'm glad.'

She stretches an arm towards me, and I flinch. She does not care and does not pause. Her ink-dark claws slice easily through my clothing, my skin, and slip between my ribs to the hoarfrost where once I had a heart.

A twist, and the frost is gone. My heartbeat thumps once more.

'The terms of the bargain are fulfilled,' Lady Winter says. 'You are free to leave the mountain. But this is not the end.'

Around us, growing stronger with each moment, pressing against the edges of the vision, magic looms.

As Lady Winter's claws squeeze around my heart, briefly, perhaps out of unthinking instinct, I smile up at her.

'Your daughter is coming for you,' I say.

SPRING

THIRTY-NINE

Later, they told me that I fell into the grip of a sudden fever, that Theo had to carry me out of the mountain with the last of his strength.

('Very dashing,' Melisande remarked.

'We thought you were dying,' Gabi said, much less amused.)

Theo had to carry me because the mountain had started shaking and was giving the distinct impression that it was about to come down around us. A powerful force propelled them forward – magic, I knew, but I didn't know how to explain it, not yet – refused to let them lag or slow, and when they thought all was doomed, they scrambled through an opening in a wall and found themselves blinking in pale sunlight, somehow at the foot of the mountains, well away from the one that hid the temple.

Magic. Or simply the power of the gods.

That was, it turned out, only the beginning of an entirely new set of problems. They were free of the mountains, but still in Northern Farezi, not exactly a well-populated part of the country. They had no map, no decent provisions, no horses, and I was still caught in the delusions of fever.

Melisande, no longer appearing so close to her death throes, glared up to the sky and screamed for one of the gods to help them, since after everything they'd done so far, it was the *least* they could do now.

With no answer, they finally decided to start walking, and worry about nightfall when it was closer.

Theo kept carrying me. When I pointed out, later, that I was not a light person, he heavily implied that while Gabi had bought time with Night and Melisande bargained with Selene for her sword, he had beseeched Twilight for the endurance and strength necessary to keep us all alive after we were free of the mountain. Within a few hours, they'd stumbled across an outpost of the northern garrison, which maintained support and order for the towns and villages clustered this far north.

Melisande had promptly walked up, despite appearing half-dead and not having seen the good side of a warm washcloth in several days, and demanded to speak to the highest authority in the building.

('And it worked?' I asked, disbelieving. 'You just told them who you were, that you were the missing princess, and they simply *believed* you?'

'I mean, I look *very* like my mother,' Melisande pointed out. 'And all our descriptions had been circulated around the country. And we *do* all sound like royals who've grown up expecting people to do what we say.'

'That's not very flattering,' I replied.

'It's not meant to be. The accents also helped.')

Messengers were immediately dispatched south, while we were brought inside and given food, a change of clothes, and hot water. I was placed in a bed where I sweated and raved. The others couldn't explain what had happened to me, nor why nothing the physician did had any sort of effect, but they told her it would pass, hopefully, and took turns staying with me in the room.

On the morning of the second day after we'd reached the garrison, my fever broke and I woke.

Upon seeing Melisande sitting beside my bed, working slowly through an uninspiring pottage, I said, 'Magic is back in the world.'

'That explains the strange feeling in the air, then,' she replied, unruffled.

A full moon had risen in the sky the previous night. We'd made Lady Winter's deadline... barely.

'I brought it back,' I said bleakly, the words tumbling out of me, as if I were now the one close to death. 'That was the final choice to reach Lady Winter. I had to free her daughter, Selene, from the prison Lady Winter trapped her in so long ago, but to do so, I had to release magic back into the world. Have you never wondered why the moon isn't divine in any of the stories? Why it never had a god or goddess?'

'Selene is the Lady of the Moon,' Melisande said, then paused, flabbergasted. 'Wait, what on—'

'Exactly,' I said. 'We never knew of her existence. When Lady Winter trapped her, she wiped her from all mortal memory, all the stories. But if I wanted to win the bargain and get my heart back—' I clamped my mouth shut, too late.

'I *knew* there was something else,' Melisande muttered. 'The bargain was too simple if all you lost was your freedom to choose. They could simply grind you down until it was easier to give up.'

There was wetness on my cheeks; I'd begun crying without realising, tears sliding down my face. 'She took my heart.' I could hardly get the words out around stifled gasps. 'She reached into my chest and *took my heart* and put hoarfrost in its place. Every time I felt something, it burned.'

'So it would be easier simply to feel nothing at all.'

'It hurt,' I sobbed. 'It hurt so much all the time.'

Melisande gathered me in her arms, shushing and rocking me gently. 'Yes,' she said sadly. 'It always hurts to heal.'

'We killed him,' I said, muffled in her shoulder.

'Yes,' she repeated. 'We did. I haven't decided yet what kind of people that makes us.'

I thought for a moment. 'Like our parents, I suppose.'

'Mmm. Then perhaps we should be kinder to them.'

The day after my fever broke, I was deemed conscious enough to travel. I wasn't necessarily strong enough for the journey – none of us was, really, and Melisande was not as recovered as I'd thought when I woke up – but messengers had galloped down and then back up the country and Queen Sabine's orders were clear: get her daughter, niece, and the Othayrian and Eshvoni royals down south *immediately*.

Our families, we were delicately informed, had been frantic – as much as royals could publicly allow themselves to be – but we all understood the implicit meaning:

We were going home.

We'd been gone for about six weeks. Once Melisande and I had arrived, the magic within the mountain had realigned the passage of time with outside, perhaps because it no longer had to fool Theo and Gabi about how long they'd been trapped. We were now on the cusp between winter and spring; Lady Winter diminishing as the land awakened from its slumber, coaxed by La Dame des Fleurs' growing power.

Melisande and I, as the most ill of the group, were watched carefully on the journey. Once, it was suggested that we should be tied to the saddles and accompanied by experienced riders, a suggestion swiftly abandoned when Melisande asked if the person who'd made it enjoyed retaining their position. I could understand her reaction, as the idea was humiliating, but there were also times when my horse did all the work because I hadn't the strength to firmly hold the reins or properly guide him with my legs.

After a week of riding, the pace pushed as much as Melisande and I could stand – the guards lived in terror that we would relapse – we drew near to where Queen Sabine and a retinue were to meet us. Theo and Gabi would be brought back to the palace, where diplomats would arrange their return to their own countries and Queen Sabine could personally reassure the monarchs that their children were safe, while I would turn west towards the Edaran border.

A strange hush fell over us when we realised that our time together was almost done, and that we would likely never again be together like this. The terrifying adventure was over, and our usual lives would soon consume us once more. And as much as we'd frustrated and irritated each other in the mountain, for weeks we had been each other's constant companions and hope. Necessity had turned into a fierce bond, and we weren't ready for it to be over.

'We could write,' Gabi suggested. She had blossomed this week, to everyone's amusement: the guards had taken to her as a prickly mascot, and she'd revelled in people who accepted her without requiring her to change. I was half-contemplating writing to Princess Lucia and suggesting that time with the palace guard would do Gabi a world of good in terms of accepting herself, especially the parts that weren't considered suitable for a princess. 'I mean, we couldn't mention anything that could be considered… well—'

'Treasonous?' Melisande supplied.

Each day we drew farther from the mountains, the healthier Melisande became. Her cheeks, while still painfully tight, now had some colour, and she seemed less likely to topple off her horse. I suspected her steady recovery was linked to whatever bargain she'd made with Selene to find me, but I couldn't bring myself to ask. We were all entitled to our secrets, even if the gods felt otherwise.

Gabi rolled her eyes. 'I suppose. But we could still write as friends.' She glanced between Theo and me. 'Or whatever you two will be to each other.'

'Please,' Theo said, closing his eyes. 'Spare me.'

'Never,' Gabi replied affectionately.

When I'd first seen him after my fever had broken, I'd mortified myself by feeling *flustered*. Someone had found spare clothes for him, even if they were a little too big, and he'd scrubbed himself and dunked his hair into a bucket of hot water, and taken a razor to his beard in favour of the clean-shaven look preferred by Othayrians. It was distressingly similar to how I'd felt around Rialla when I'd started to fall for her.

He still looked like the Theo I knew, but now he resembled a prince, how he'd have looked if we'd met under normal circumstances. A *dashing* one.

Melisande, who'd immediately realised why I was suddenly

flushed and tongue-tied, had hissed in my ear, 'I insist on a wedding invitation. *Someone* needs to heckle you.'

'I wasn't joking about hiring that junior diplomat to follow you around and laugh on my behalf,' I'd hissed back.

Things had been... better wasn't the right word. We were easier around each other now. Melisande had regained some of her good form, and the guards accompanying us had swiftly developed a healthy respect towards her. For her part, she was friendly, albeit in a regally distant sort of way. I suspected at least three had fallen for her, even though she was also dressed in a set of spare clothes cobbled together and we'd spent half an hour brushing out the knots and tangles in her hair, while she contemplated finding a dagger to chop half it off.

When we reached the clearing near the crossroads, and everyone dismounted to set up camp, there was a mild tizzy over how we could be presented to the Queen in our current state, since no one helpfully had a trunk of suitable clothing for meeting a monarch. Melisande finally said, tiredly, that someone in her mother's party probably had a trunk with them if Her Majesty insisted on ceremony, but since we were in the middle of the countryside and the Queen was likely to be more relieved that we were all alive, it was a needless concern.

It didn't help that as we grew closer to Queen Sabine's arrival, my nerves grew. I had never met my aunt before, and this was not the situation I'd imagined.

Theo sat down beside me. 'It'll be fine.'

'What will?' I asked absently, still caught up in my worries.

'Meeting your aunt.'

I glanced at him, startled. 'How did you know?'

'You've been fidgeting all morning, especially when someone mentioned her,' he said. 'Your horse doesn't like it.'

'Oh.' After a moment, I added, 'You'd have made a good spy.'

He shook his head. 'Too much stress. I just know horses.'

We lapsed into silence, but these days it wasn't so uncomfortable. As with Melisande, things were easier between us now. It didn't feel like love – knowing how someone reacted under the worst, most stressful circumstances surely wasn't love – but we had to start somewhere. It could *be* something, eventually, given time and fewer interfering gods.

'What are you going to do first when you reach home?' I asked.

'Go for a long bath,' he said fervently.

I half-covered a smile. 'I think Queen Sabine will allow you the use of her baths.'

'Yes, but they're not the ones at *home*.' After a moment, he added, more seriously, 'Hug my parents, and whichever of my siblings are with them. Sleep for about a month. Take my horse out. Spend a week in the library. Never go near a mountain again.'

'I don't think any of us will be going near mountains again.'

He snorted. 'What about you?'

I thought for a moment. 'Get yelled at by my parents' spymaster for being foolish, probably, if she isn't at the border with them. Spend the day with my family. Hug my friends and spend a day with them. Probably start digging out every book I can find on the gods and magic. Probably make the academics and clergy cry by having to tell them it's all real.'

'I was just going to read,' Theo admitted.

I raised an eyebrow. 'Hatar will be resurrecting soon, once Lady Winter and the others are free. Your god is coming back, Theo, and you can't ignore it.'

He sighed. 'I know.' He hesitated, then asked, 'What about the marriage negotiations?'

'They'll resume, I suppose. I wasn't joking when I said you'd have to visit so my parents can judge you.' He shuddered, and I laughed. 'Mother will summon your uncle back to the Court, so you can meet him, too. He's always championed you.'

'I'd like that,' Theo said wistfully. 'I've heard so much about him, and letters just aren't the same.'

At the distant sound of trumpets and drumbeats, we rose. 'Here we go,' Theo said, rolling back his shoulders. 'Time to explain ourselves to the Farezi Queen.'

'Theo?' When he glanced down, I went on tiptoe to kiss his cheek. Though his skin was too dark to show a blush, his eyes went wide. I smiled at him. 'Thank you for stopping us from killing each other, and feeding us so we wouldn't starve. I'd very much like to get to know you better when we're not trapped in a mountain and terrified about dying.'

I walked away before he could respond, suddenly embarrassed, but stopped when he shouted my name and rushed after me.

'If we do end up marrying,' he said, thankfully in a lower voice, 'you should know that I'll do my best to support you and your parents' legacy. I mean it. Whatever I have to do, however much or little power you decide to give me.'

It was endearing, and terrifying, and utterly too serious in the aftermath of everything that had just happened, when we were all still reeling from our unexpected freedom. Yet I took his words in the full spirit he intended, because I knew he meant them.

'That was horrifically earnest,' I said, returning his abashed smile. 'But if you say that around my parents, they may come to love you more than me.'

'That will absolutely never happen,' he replied, squeezing my hands before I walked away properly this time.

Melisande was sitting under a tree nearby, peacefully watching the camp scramble as her mother's entourage drew closer. 'That was utterly revolting,' she said.

'Did you overhear the entire thing?' I demanded, my hands on my hips.

'Every word,' she said cheerfully. 'If you two had wanted privacy, you should have chosen better.'

I huffed, then joined her on the grass as she added, 'He'll make a wonderful husband. And Consort or King, however much power you decide to give him. He doesn't really know it himself, I think, but he wants to leave his own legacy, too, and he knows that'll only happen through the strength of your rule.'

'Perhaps,' I said. 'We'll see.'

We turned quiet as we gazed up at the sky through the leaves.

While Melisande had improved the further we'd travelled from the mountain, no one could pretend that her health hadn't been significantly altered. The witty princess who'd arrived in Edar had never had to stop for breath, or consider whether she had the necessary strength and stamina to accomplish something. Theo had quietly procured a staff for her from the guards so she could move around without help.

She'd whirled it experimentally. 'Maybe I'll take up the staff alongside the sword,' she'd said, with a heroic attempt at cheerfulness.

Theo immediately looked like he regretted his kindness.

No one knew if she'd ever make a full recovery. If this was her life now, the map of her future. Maybe there would be a cure, or they'd figure out ways to help her manage her new life. For now, she appeared resigned, if not fully accepting, that the mountain had left its mark on her. It had done so to us all, in different ways.

'There was one time you stuck up for me in Saphirun,' I said quietly. 'Remember the hot chocolate?' Her silence told me she didn't, so I continued, 'The thick hot chocolate they added flavours to? It was my favourite, and you forced yourself to like it because if I had something, you immediately wanted it.'

'Oh, for—' Melisande slapped a hand over her eyes. 'I should have asked Night to scrub away every single memory from when I was a child.'

I snorted. 'But I couldn't ask for it often, as the staff couldn't be seen to favour me, so you started asking once you realised. It was…' I paused, realising how pitiful the rest of the sentence was, but after the last few weeks – after facing down gods and surviving – we could surely acknowledge the shameful parts of our shared childhood more easily. 'It was the nicest thing you did for me at Saphirun.'

Another long silence, then Melisande said, her voice thick with regret, 'I'm so very sorry for how I treated you. If demanding your favourite drink is the nicest thing you remember of me, then I was terrible indeed.'

I attempted a shrug. 'You were a child.'

'So were you.'

'And then… I think it was a few months before I left, we had that cook arrive to be trained up for the palace. And he was convinced everything he'd heard about me was true.' Now, years later, I realised the horror of it: adults gossiping about a child banished to the care of a diminished, bitter Dowager Queen. The cruelty of a man so willing to believe the rumours. 'And once he realised you were asking for the chocolate on my behalf, he refused to make it.'

'Was he the one with the straw-like hair?' I could hear the frown in Melisande's voice. 'Never tidy, no matter how Cook yelled at him? I never liked him. I— *oh*.'

'Yes.' The laugh tore from my throat. 'Once you realised, you threw an absolute strop, so bad that they summoned Arisane, and you—'

'I got him dismissed.' Melisande sat bolt upright and turned to face me, her eyes wide. 'I *lied*.'

Her voice, strident, imperious even though she hadn't yet turned seven, echoed in my mind, as she insisted he'd tried to serve us candied walnuts from his own stores. Walnuts were forbidden in Saphirun, after the one and only time Melisande had tasted them: she'd broken out in a rash and her throat had prickled, strong enough that she'd struggled to breathe for several minutes.

There were, of course, no walnuts. The young apprentice cook would have been warned not to bring any, even for his own use. But the kitchens were thrown into disarray at even the accusation, and Arisane had flown into a rage. He was dismissed on the spot before he could even protest or beg for his ingredients to be inspected.

That evening, before bed, we'd had hot chocolate heated with mint. I'd never known if they'd served it on Arisane's orders, quietly resentful; or if the kitchen staff had also realised why he'd refused to make it and were torn between pride at Melisande's anger, or fear at how swiftly – how easily – she'd had one of them dismissed.

Her face was bleak with horror. 'I mean, that was dreadful of him, but – how could I *do* that? What positions would have been open to him after being dismissed from royal service?'

'They made it for me, you know,' I said, because I couldn't answer that for her. It was something she'd have to figure out alone, by examining the sharper, crueller parts of herself, even if it hurt. 'My parents. When they figured out I liked it.'

'They… made it for you.' Something strange twisted in Melisande's voice, and I deliberately didn't focus on it.

'Yes. I mean, the cooks had to figure it out and then teach *them*, and considering neither of them could boil water, it was probably a small miracle they didn't burn the palace down. But on the last night of Midwinter, when entering the kitchens was no longer a terrifying prospect, they made it and we sat on my bed and drank it together.'

My throat swelled, as it always did when I remembered something lovely from my childhood, more painful because it was from when I was young and even if we did it now, it wouldn't be the same.

A short, strangled sound came from Melisande's direction, repeated then quickly stifled. It took several moments, far too long, for me to realise she'd started crying.

'*Melisande*,' I said, horrified.

'Please ignore me,' she said, now openly weeping. 'I just need a moment.' She fished for a handkerchief, remembered she was wearing borrowed clothes and cursed, then wiped at her eyes with her sleeve and sniffed hard, while I politely looked away and waited.

She finally nudged my arm. I gripped her hand, and she squeezed it tightly.

'Our parents have made a decent start,' Melisande said quietly. 'The wounds between Edar and Farezi are healing, even if the gods and magic returning will throw everything into turmoil.'

None of us had dared speculate on how long it would take for gods and magic to seem normal again, or how many would suddenly find themselves with magic, or how we'd train them so they didn't hurt themselves or anyone else, how the return of mages would upset the delicate balance of power. None of us could contemplate it for longer than a few moments without wanting to scream into a cushion.

'But we'll take their decent start and *run*,' Melisande continued, utterly serious. 'We'll learn from them, and we'll learn from their mistakes, and we'll improve on both.

'We'll be Queens, who once looked gods in the eye and lived. Our names will survive in the histories, and they'll call our reigns golden.'

I wasn't prepared for Queen Sabine, my aunt, to look like Rassa, though I should have expected it: the traits of the Farezi royal family ran strong. The same hazel eyes and long eyelashes, the same nose and jawline, though it was all softer on Queen Sabine. But where Arisane and Rassa had been sharp-edged, honed to viciousness, my aunt was shorter, her frame delicate yet assured. When she invited us to rise from our courtesies, I knew from one glance that, like my parents, she was not someone to underestimate. Unlike her mother and brother, she had kept a firm grip on her power and was reshaping Farezi for the better.

'Melisande,' she said, low and calm, 'I am immensely pleased to find you safe.' She reached out her hands, and Melisande took them as they kissed cheeks. 'We will speak in private before we begin our journey. Your Highness— Emri—' She surprised me with a small smile. 'We are pleased to finally meet you, niece. We always regretted that We were never able to meet before you left for Edar.'

You could have summoned me to Court along the way, I thought, catching the switch to the royal We, but bowed again and murmured polite greetings.

Her eyes flickered to Theo and Gabi. 'Your Royal Highnesses, Prince Theobilt and Princess Gabriela. We confess that We never expected to make your acquaintance, but We apparently now live in interesting times.' She gestured, and a servant slipped out of the tent. 'We will be eating a midmorning meal here, before our departure, and would be very much obliged for an explanation as to how you all ended up in the Farezi mountains.'

With the tea and meal set out – Melisande went straight for a small cake, which convinced me that she was finally starting to improve – Queen Sabine abandoned the formality, and turned fiercely attentive as we struggled to explain all that had happened. Now she reminded me more of my parents, being only a little older than them, and I saw much of Melisande's intelligence in her.

Though she grew paler the more we spoke, she didn't outwardly succumb to panic or bewilderment. There were some things we kept vague; all she needed to know was that they had happened, not the specifics. We didn't owe her our humiliations and fears.

'So,' she said, when we finally stopped, 'the gods and magic are real. It was always a possibility, though a dim one. The temple in the mountains is one of the oldest on the continent, and was always Lady Winter's from before the borders changed after the First Empire collapsed. But I never thought she could actually *be* in there.' She thought for a moment. 'La Dame des Fleurs is strongest in the south, so it makes sense, especially since Edar forswore religion so strongly.' She glanced at me. 'Your parents will have a hard time ahead, I'm afraid.'

'We'll *all* have a hard time ahead,' Gabi corrected her politely, the only one of us who would have dared. 'None of our countries has been truly as faithful to the gods as we should have been.'

'Wise,' Queen Sabine remarked, and Gabi looked away, fighting to hide her pleased expression. 'I think your families will be better informed from you all,' she added, 'rather than my sending word ahead of your arrival. They'll likely refuse to believe me, whereas… even when you were all explaining it, I broke out in shivers. Something in me knew you were being truthful. The mark of the gods, and the temple, is upon you all.'

It didn't feel as reassuring as she probably meant it to be, and everyone looked at her in dismay. We'd all been so focused on getting out of the mountain, we hadn't given much thought to the fact that the memories wouldn't leave us so easily.

Just as my parents, especially Mother, had been haunted by Goldenmarch. In this, I'd never wanted to be like them.

Eventually, she rose, and we rose with her. 'We'll be departing soon, so you should ready yourselves,' she said, as if any of us had belongings other than those the guards had gifted us. Everything – every scrap of food, every offering, including the parchment, which had bitterly disappointed Theo – had disintegrated outside the mountain. All that was left was Theo's destroyed notebook. 'Melisande, Princess Emri, please stay a moment.'

For a moment, the three of us simply stood, gazing at each other. Then Queen Sabine stepped forward, clasped my hands, and kissed me on both cheeks.

'Oh, my dear,' she said. 'I can't begin to express my relief that you're safe. That you *both* are,' she added, glancing at Melisande with the same smile.

'Congratulations,' Melisande told me. 'I think she prefers you to me, her own daughter.'

'Hush,' Queen Sabine retorted, and my shock only increased at the easiness between them. I'd assumed Melisande had inherited her sense of humour and timing from her father. 'I've been worried sick, as has your father, since Edar informed me that you'd both disappeared at Midwinter. As have your parents, too, Emri.'

I swallowed, hard, afraid to speak in case my desperate longing for my parents erupted in a wail.

'I shall be introducing you to the party that will accompany you to the border,' Queen Sabine continued, 'where your parents are anxiously waiting. And if anything happens to you – if there's another *disappearance* – those guards know they must answer to me.'

I wanted to tell her that there was nothing she could do if the gods wanted me to disappear again, but I stayed quiet. Eventually, we'd all learn to factor in such thinking.

'And please,' she added, squeezing my hands again, 'I know I don't deserve it, but I hope one day that I will deserve your forgiveness.' At my blank expression, she continued, more quietly, 'For sending you to Arisane at Saphirun. I had… expected better of my mother. Hoped for it, even. I underestimated her bitterness, or that she'd think it appropriate to take it out on you. I am deeply sorry, though I know apologies won't change what has already happened.'

I stared at her, shocked and silent. I didn't know what to say, whether *anything* I could say could portray the full extent of Saphirun, how it had changed me, how I still struggled with the invisible wounds it had inflicted upon me.

Finally, I said, 'Your Majesty honours me,' and hoped Queen Sabine would understand why I hid behind a veil of formality.

Perhaps she did: she smiled, a little more sadly this time, then asked if she could hug me. I allowed it, mostly because I desper-- ately longed for a hug and my parents were still far away.

She smelled of jasmine and lily of the valley. It suited her.

FORTY

It was my turn to hug Gabi as we said our goodbyes before we went in different directions. They would all continue south, while my small party would turn west towards Edar – towards home.

Farezi, for better or worse, would never be home, even if I now had family there.

Gabi wrapped her arms tight around me, and I could tell by her breathing that she was close to tears.

'Remember what I suggested,' I murmured, low enough for only her to hear. 'Talk to your mother. Alone. Definitely not around Queen Juliaane, and no one that could take your conversation back to her. Ask if you could write to Isra. Something mild, polite, courteous. Nothing that anyone could later claim was treacherous in Isra's hands.'

Gabi rubbed her face, hard. 'I will. Do you think Mother and Aunt Isra already write to each other in secret?'

'I don't know,' I admitted. 'Probably not.' Princess Lucia was the heir to the Eshvoni throne, and her sister was another country's spymaster. Anything Lucia said to her could be a potential risk. 'But I think Isra would like to write to you. And I think there are things she could teach you.'

'Write to me,' Gabi said miserably. 'Please. I'm going to miss you, and it horrifies me a little.'

I laughed. 'So will I, though it doesn't horrify me at all. And I will write, once you write back.' I stepped back, smiling, so she could mount her horse and salvage her dignity.

Theo and I smiled at each other and formally clasped hands.

'I look forward to your visit,' I murmured.

'I look forward to your parents terrifying me,' he replied, then surprised me with a kiss on my cheek. I stared at him, wide-eyed, while Gabi rolled her eyes and Melisande cackled.

But when it was just us, she turned serious again, and we pulled each other into a hug, something I couldn't have imagined we'd have meant sincerely a few months ago.

'Our reigns will be golden,' she whispered into my ear. 'Remember that.'

'I'll write soon,' I said, pulling back. 'And this time you *will* reply honestly.'

She smiled, a little shakily. 'I will. I might even visit again just to trounce you at chess – if Mother lets me leave the country in the next twenty years.'

It didn't hurt until an hour into the ride, when I realised it was well and truly over. The adventure had been terrible, frankly, and nothing like as glorious as in the stories, but I didn't know what to do now that I was no longer with them. And except for Theo, there was a good chance I'd never see Melisande or Gabi again.

I swallowed, and bit my lip to stop the tears from falling. If some dripped down my cheeks anyway, the guards pretended not to notice.

We were two days out from the Edaran border, and we rode far into the evening and early in the morning to get there faster. A few hours after dawn on the third day, we officially crossed the border into Edar.

I was back.

I was home.

An hour's ride away from the border, my parents' camp was waiting. My heart swelled at the sight of the familiar Edaran flag, silver on blue, the rose briar wrapped around a sword, the crown above both. And then, as our horn call was answered, another flag rose: similar to my parents', silver on blue, with the briar and the sword, but a snowflake instead of the crown.

The flag of the Edaran heir, with the Sionbourne snowflake.

Lady Winter's snowflake.

I was led to my parents' tent; the heir always came to the monarchs, and they could ill-afford a show of deep emotion in public. Even so, my palms were clammy, my heart racing, as I ducked through the tent flap and found them standing, waiting for me.

They were dressed in riding leathers, rather than finery, with the Edaran emblem worked into the clothing. Their demeanour appeared unchanged before the guards, but I caught the shift in their postures, the way their shoulders eased, and their expressions lightened. I was their only daughter, their sole heir, and I was finally returned.

'Leave us,' Mother said, nodding at the guards.

Moments after the tent flap closed, I found myself enveloped by my parents, hugged tight enough that I almost couldn't breathe.

'Emri,' Mother said, strained and trembling. 'Oh, Emri. *Emri.*'

Mama didn't speak, only clung to me and wept.

I breathed in the scent of their soap, faint underneath their riding leathers and the smell of horse, and hugged them back just as tight. I was suddenly shaking, and it was beyond me to stop, and I knew it was everything from the last few weeks – no, *months* – crashing down on me, and yet it also felt like I was simply falling apart.

When they finally let me go – minutes or hours later, I didn't know and didn't want to – I was once again shocked into silence. The regal masks they'd worn around the guards had collapsed, and now I saw the deep shadows under their eyes, their haggard expressions, the lines around their eyes that had only grown deeper.

My disappearance had left its mark upon them.

I burst into tears.

They pulled me close again, but the tears keep coming. My shoulders kept shaking, and I struggled to breathe in between sobs.

'Emri,' Mama said, an edge of panic in her voice that I hadn't heard in years. 'Emri, please, take a breath. *Breathe.*'

'The gods are back,' I wept. 'Lady Winter is back. Magic is returning to the world.'

In their stunned silence, it seemed like the world as we knew it tilted, a faint crack spidering through it, forever altered and never to be the same again.

'*What?*' Mother finally said, aghast.

'The gods took us to the mountain. Melisande and me.' Now that I was actually with them again, the words couldn't come easily, a jumble that started and stuttered. 'Theobilt and Gabriela had already been there for months, though time runs differently in the temple, and…'

On and on, I went: now that I'd started explaining, I couldn't stop. I told them everything: Lady Winter, the other gods, the bargain, my heart. The temple. Everything we'd gone through, save for the specifics of Theo and Gabi's memories; those deserved to be kept secret, especially Theo's since he'd eventually have to win over my parents. But I told them about Melisande's, as hers was intertwined with mine and always would be. When I told them the visions that hadn't come to pass, my parents held each other's hands tightly. Selene, and my choice to release the magic. And then: Rassa.

Mother sucked in a harsh breath, while Mama's expression briefly shuttered as she avoided my eye.

And I remembered what we'd last argued about, right before the shadows took me to the mountain.

We'd talk about it, eventually: not right now, when I had just returned, with too many guards around, still so close to the border and far from the capital. They'd give me time to sleep and adjust to being back again.

But Mama would want to talk about the argument, eventually, and I'd want – *need* – to talk to her about Rassa, and perhaps we'd be able to come to an understanding somewhere in the middle.

I couldn't talk about it now, but that didn't mean I didn't have to acknowledge it.

I stepped up to Mama and wrapped my arms around her, burying my face in her shoulder. 'I understand why you did it, now, a little more than I did before,' I whispered, and she kissed my hair gently.

Mother came up and wrapped her arms around us both. We stood there, wrapped in each other's love, and for a moment, it was enough.

Moments later, the tent flap flew open. I pulled away from my parents and turned as Rialla and Micah stumbled into the tent.

I glanced back at my parents, wide-eyed, who were unsuccessfully fighting smiles.

'Of course we brought them,' Mother said. 'Otherwise, they would have followed us.'

For a moment, we simply stared at each other. Micah looked astonishingly weary, his eyes sunken and shadow stained. Rialla also looked paler than usual, her mouth trembling, until I remembered that I probably looked worse than them both. Better than I had, after days of improved rest and food, not to mention a good wash, but I hardly resembled the person they remembered.

Then Rialla let out a sob, and they both flung themselves at me.

Wrapped up in an embrace hard enough to knock the air from me, I closed my eyes and finally let my shoulders drop. The hug was familiar, though not quite the same and not normally so desperate.

'We were so worried,' Rialla whispered.

Micah didn't speak, only gripped us both tighter.

As I pulled back and attempted a smile, they watched me, uneasy and guarded. Even now, faced with Rialla after our arguments and bitterness, there was no pained twinge. The hurt was gone. She'd never be my Queen, had never *wanted* to be, but she was my friend and unshakeably loyal, and I'd need both of them in the difficult weeks, months, and years ahead.

'It's been…' I attempted, then stopped and tried again. 'It was…'

But where explaining it all to my parents had felt like a duty expected of me as an heir, an obligation that had let me keep some distance so I could get it all out, it wasn't so easy with my friends. They'd be horrified, and afraid, and I wasn't ready to deal with it, not yet.

'It's all right,' Micah said, his instincts correct as always. 'You don't have to tell us anything until you're ready – or never, if you don't want to. We're just' – he faltered, and I glimpsed the anguished worry he'd been trying so hard to hide – 'we're just very glad that you're alive and safe.'

They'd find out, eventually, about the return of the gods and magic. They'd have to adjust, like everyone else would. But not right now. I'd let them keep their ignorance for a while longer.

I smiled again, steadier this time. 'I'm never going near a mountain again.'

This time, when I leaned in to hug them, it felt right.

FORTY-ONE

My parents debated staying in the camp overnight, fretting over whether I was strong enough to immediately return to the capital. But we were closer to the border than everyone liked, and now that I was back in Edar, I wanted to be in my own bed when everything inevitably caught up with me, including the exhaustion I'd badly kept at bay.

As the camp was packed away, I sat under a tree to keep out of everyone's way before it was time to depart. It felt strange not to have the others with me, and I was already missing Melisande's barbed wit, Theo's peace-making skills, and Gabi's spiky retorts.

A guard trailed me – I had no doubt that I would always have at least one guard with me for the foreseeable future – and stood nearby, watchful and silent. Micah had recognised that I needed to be alone and had stopped Rialla from following me. She seemed loath to let me out of her sight, not that I could blame her.

I rubbed my eyes and sighed. It was smarter to start travelling now, but part of me still desperately wanted to lie down and close my eyes, to let myself sleep for as long as I needed to recover from it all. Even the parts that wouldn't be so easy to recover from.

Now I had my own Goldenmarch.

You are still my Chosen. The icy voice, rough and chilly as tree bark enduring a bitter winter, slid through my mind, incongruous in the early afternoon sunlight. *Don't think you can escape me.*

Yes. I knew. Though we'd only spoken of it to Queen Sabine so far, and my parents. I thought back, equally furious and cold, *Our bargain is done, no matter that you weren't truthful about the terms.*

The end would always be the same, whether the others escaped from the mountain with you or not, Lady Winter replied. *You were always going to have to choose whether to unleash magic back into the world by releasing my daughter. You were never going to be fully free of me. Were you so foolish to think so?*

Had I been so foolish to *hope* so? The implication was brutally clear.

I had my heart back. My parents wouldn't be Lady Winter's puppet rulers, and nor would I, whenever I took the throne. But she was Edar's patron goddess, and Twilight and Night belonged to the land, as did Selene. Their return was inevitable, even if it would be slower because Melisande and the others hadn't perished in the mountain.

Magic would force belief.

But that didn't mean they held all the power. Mortals had co-existed with them, peacefully or otherwise, for a long time. The gods needed us, perhaps far more than we needed them, to ensure their continued existence.

And I was *tired* of being afraid, of being injured, of worrying. I was tired of trying to anticipate the gods' next move, or how they'd react to something, or how they'd punish me or anyone else.

Lady Winter was silent, but I knew she was waiting for an answer. She had endless time at her disposal, after all.

You think I'm foolish for hoping to be free of you, I finally said. *But for once, I'd like a reason as to why I should believe in you. Why should I offer my hope to you?*

More silence. But this time I knew, deep in my heart and bones, it was because this was the last thing, after all my rage and fighting and despair, that Lady Winter had expected from me.

If the gods were to return and endure, they'd have to remember they also had a part to play in encouraging worship. I suspected Twilight and Night still remembered, as did Selene, even if her kindness had sharp edges.

But Lady Winter was older than them all, perhaps the oldest of the patron deities. She'd been so deeply shaped by what she had become, driven for so long by what her nature demanded, that she likely no longer remembered what she needed to be for mortals.

There must have been good reasons why Edar had worshipped a stern, cruel goddess for so long. It was understandable in the past, but it didn't explain why worship of her had continued even to my time, diluted and wrapped in myth as it was. There would have been easier ways to remember a goddess of deep snows and dark forests.

No matter how brutal winter could be, there were still moments of calm and beauty. A quiet joy in the crunch of fresh snow underfoot. The icy burn of a deep breath into the lungs.

The gods could be terrible, but they could also bring out the best in us, just as easily as the worst.

And Lady Winter needed to remember that.

Silence, on and on and on, until I thought she'd actually retreated–

I do not retreat. A burst of coldness in my mind, like eating a shaved ice too quickly, a flare of pain that swiftly receded. *But we will speak again.* I flinched at the sensation of a snowflake against my forehead, but it was gentle, like a kiss from one of my mothers.

Lady Winter's presence withdrew, and I was once again surrounded only by mortals.

I took a deep breath, unable to suppress a shudder. Something had changed between us, something that perhaps could have been achieved without a dreadful bargain involving my heart and courage. But it was possibly a sign of better things to come, if I could hold my nerve and sometimes tell gods what they didn't want to hear.

More than one monarch had fallen in history because people had thought the gods had turned from them. We'd have to be careful of whatever new form the religious orders took – like droll, self-assured Aren – but the gods needed the monarchs just as much, living symbols of faith as they were in the old days. Lady Winter wouldn't have gone to all this trouble otherwise.

I can be your blade. I flung the thought out as a vicious prayer and warning. It would reach Lady Winter, even if she was no longer near me. *But be careful I'm not double-edged.*

'Oh, you *are* good,' a familiar voice said beside me. 'I almost wish I could fully claim you, but my own princess will have to do.'

I jumped; Florette Sigrath sat beside me, smiling. As I was about to scream – in alarm, for help, *something* – she grabbed my arm and locked eyes with me. They flared green, just like when she'd forced me to drop the poison pen and the shadows had taken me.

'Haven't you guessed yet?' she asked, as the scent of fresh flowers rose around us. It was milder in this part of eastern Edar, but spring's grip was not yet so strong.

I blinked, and La Dame des Fleurs sat beside me, in the same forest green linen edged in gold from the battle vision. Her hair was a deep auburn, loose around her shoulders, and her eyes glowed that strange green.

'Hello, Emri,' she said, a strange deepness in her voice. 'We finally meet in truth.'

I whirled to look for the guard, and she added blithely, 'Oh, he can't see this, or hear us. To him, you're having a nice quiet think under a very good tree.' She patted the trunk affectionately.

Perhaps I'd simply reached my limits with gods. Or perhaps I was too exhausted to care. 'If you're about to send me on another quest,' I said, 'I'm afraid I'm not currently at my best.'

She laughed, a sound that reminded me of the sparkle of sunlight on water, the satisfaction of a garden in full bloom. 'No, no. I am much kinder than Lady Winter, in that respect. I don't believe in challenging my Chosen until they're close to dropping dead.'

'Melisande will be thrilled,' I said dryly.

'Mmm.' La Dame des Fleurs' smile turned wicked. 'I do hope she'll enjoy my upcoming manifestation.'

There was probably no warning letter I could send that would be faster than a goddess's intentions.

'Did Florette Sigrath ever exist?' I asked.

'She died when she was almost thirteen,' La Dame des Fleurs said, without pity nor remorse. 'A misjudged step that turned into a nasty fall. And from her last breath to the next, there I was. It was miserable being a mortal girl, I don't recommend it—'

'I'm aware,' I said.

'—but the course was set, and she suited my purpose.'

'And now?'

'She is no longer useful. So the threads of the past will restitch, and she will be the poor girl dead at thirteen as she was meant to be.' La Dame des Fleurs shrugged; her matter of fact tone chilling as she so easily spoke of reshaping mortal deaths into lives never meant to be.

'Lady Death must despise you for interfering.'

The goddess flinched. 'We have an understanding,' she said, her tone implying it was less an understanding than a long-standing feud.

It was too much to comprehend as a mortal, so I switched topics. 'And the Mizyr?'

'Oh!' She laughed again, once more in good humour. 'A means to an end, nothing more. I needed you to *notice* me, just enough that my presence would become familiar, that you'd have to watch me.'

I rubbed my face. 'It would have been so much easier if you were really just a silly girl dabbling at politics.'

She beamed. 'Alas, I am not.'

'Why did you even get involved in this at all? The Edaran gods are not your concern.'

'I'm afraid they very much are, especially since Lady Winter and her daughter don't remember me well.'

I went still. Overhead, a breeze rustled the treetops.

'Who else was at the battle?' asked La Dame des Fleurs, as if we were discussing an evening at the opera.

'Night.' When she shook her head, I paused, then added slowly, fearfully, 'And Selene.'

The goddess smiled, thin and sharp. 'Very good.'

'*You* were the one Selene struck the bargain with,' I said, feeling sick as several things suddenly made sense all at once. 'To stop the war. But Farezi won. You betrayed her.'

'Whatever about Lady Winter,' she said, 'never make a bargain with a trickster.'

'Selene was imprisoned by her own *mother* because of your deceit,' I burst out, yanking my arm out of her grip. 'Trapped, *alone*—'

'Selene made her own choices,' La Dame des Fleurs said coldly. 'She is not so pitiful as you think. More to the point: did you never consider why a child from each of the four countries was pulled into an Edaran godly spat? I mean, *yes*, you're a child of Farezi and now the Edaran heir. But the Eshvoni heir? The Othayrian prince?'

Something dropped in my stomach, heavy and hard, threatening to sprout barbs and pierce the tender parts of me.

'All four of us rule the seasons: a full year. Without one of us, all is unbalanced and we are not at full power.' La Dame des Fleurs' smile turned bitter. 'Forced to bide our time by stealing mortal lives, for example. With the Edaran gods trapped because of Selene's foolishness and Lady Winter's fury, the rest of us couldn't properly manifest. Magic faded because of lack of belief, fuelled by magic fading through the imbalance: a dreadful cycle we couldn't stop. Only one of Lady Winter's Chosen could fix it, of course, as none of us can set foot within another's sacred space. But we could send *help* to aid you in your quest.'

It was becoming hard to breathe, like the snowflakes and ice were choking me again, as if the cold was raging through my body until there was nothing left but to wait for death.

'You,' I said, too small, too soft, too weak. 'You're why Theo and Gabi were taken to the mountain.'

'It was Hatar and Aestia actually,' La Dame des Fleurs said. 'I chose Melisande, for you were cousins and had unfinished business anyway. Hatar decided on Theo because he'll marry you, eventually, and supporting you was good practice for him. Aestia took the most convincing: her hatred of Lady Winter runs deep, enough to spite herself.' A faint smile curled her mouth, as if imagining such a thing brought her great joy. 'But she's *very* impressed with how much you've all improved her heir in such a short amount of time.'

She sighed and shook out her hair. 'But it took me a bit longer to have you and Melisande sent to the mountain. I'd miscalculated, and now you were *so very* suspicious of me as Florette Sigrath. But I'd agreed to do it, since I owed Selene a debt because the trick's consequences were a little unfair—'

'That wasn't a trick, letting Farezi win the war was a betrayal!'

'And you're simply *no fun*,' La Dame des Fleurs chided me. 'But the threads of your fate soon became clear to us all, even those within the temple. If you led our Chosen through the mountain, growing in confidence as you did so, then you'd have the strength to free Selene – and Lady Winter's trapped magic. But without *our* Chosen, you wouldn't succeed. Mother and daughter still very much hate each other, mind you – the mountain almost collapsing around you was Selene making her feelings on her imprisonment *exceedingly clear* – but we agreed that working together for a common cause would benefit us all.'

I closed my eyes, but the darkness couldn't hide the inevitable truth. 'To bring magic back into the world. So you could manifest again.'

'Precisely. You *are* clever,' she reassured me. 'You just need to learn to never trust a god, and I think you're already partway there.' She patted my arm with only a little condescension. 'It's always a difficult lesson for mortals to learn.'

I gritted my teeth. 'Why are *you* not trapped in a temple somewhere?'

La Dame des Fleurs flashed me a smile as she crossed her legs. A fold of her dress fell away to reveal a vine winding up her thigh. 'It's always easier to keep faith with a trickster spring goddess than a brutal lady of deep snow and dark forests. I was never in danger of fading. I've also never lost my temper to the extent that I bound my own power within my daughter's prison.'

I pressed my lips together, hard, as there were many things I wanted to say and few were good or advisable.

La Dame des Fleurs' expression abruptly hardened, as a shadow passed over her eyes. 'And since, unlike Lady Winter, a trickster must occasionally explain her sleight of hand: I, too, paid the price of Farezi winning the war. I thought I'd convinced the Queen and her generals, in dreams and visions, that reshaping mortal borders was foolishness, but they wanted to punish Edar by taking the mountains that held Lady Winter's oldest temples. Spite, nothing more.'

A frown dragged down her mouth, marred her dewy, fresh beauty. 'The mountains were never mine; I had no affinity with them. But the lands in the south now given to Edar *were* mine, and my dominion over them necessary, as the mortals soon realised. *I* manipulated the storms to prevent flooding in the west. *I* convinced the winds to carry the rains to the south and the east where they were better needed. *I* coaxed the eastern river into the sea. Thanks to long-dead mortal spite, the southern lands were unnecessarily afflicted by flood and drought.'

I grew still, even as my mind reeled. The floods and droughts La Dame des Fleurs had described were recurring problems that Mother had been dealing with almost every year since she'd taken the throne; they stretched back long in the written record. It didn't matter how much money was funnelled into the problem, nor what new initiatives were considered: nothing fixed the repeated problem of the western storms never reaching the south and south-east of Edar. No one understood why the eastern river had gone underground, the subterranean water never benefiting the far south-east, which was mostly faded estates and towns chiefly comprised of rocks and goats, and little else.

Brutal winters and ineffectual springs, threatened harvests; all due to divine rage and mortal spite centuries ago.

'If I were you, I'd make sure my parents never learned that,' I finally managed. 'Especially Mother. It won't matter that you're a goddess. She'll find whatever ruined temple you still have in Southern Edar, march straight into it, and scream at you for hours.'

'Oh, I should like to see *that*,' La Dame des Fleurs drawled. 'Queen Aurelia may have frost under her skin and snow packed into her bones, but one can always appreciate her stubbornness.

'But come now,' she declared, and my eyes narrowed at her sudden enthusiasm, 'you're about to have a time of it! So even though you're technically not one of mine anymore, I feel you should have some help anyway. Just a small gift.'

'Thank you, but I must regretfully decline,' I said, drawing on my best regal air. 'I find the generosity of gods beyond the scope of mortal understanding and best left alone.'

Her eyes gleamed. 'Don't worry. You'll keep your heart. I have no need of it.'

Before I could once again decline, she kissed me.

Unlike Selene, this kiss was full of the warmth of a promising spring day, the pleasantness of new flowers, the serenity of sitting in a garden by a trickling stream. And without thinking, I kissed her back.

My mind, thankfully, caught up with my mouth a few moments

later, and I jerked away.

'*How dare you—*'

La Dame des Fleurs kissed her fingertips, then pressed them against my mouth, stopping me mid-sentence. 'Lady Winter is back, my dear, and she was never a kind goddess. You're going to need every possible advantage to navigate all that is to come.

'It was going to happen eventually,' she added, sounding mildly resentful that I'd reacted so poorly to her *gift*. 'I merely… hurried it along.'

I blinked, outrage surging in my throat, and she was gone. All that remained was the fading strains of her mocking laughter.

Something flared on my upper arm, hot and sharp. Before I could think better of it, I'd tugged my shirt sleeve up close to my shoulder.

A mark had appeared on my upper arm. A tree: the same one from the stained-glass window, showing all the seasons at once.

Against my dark skin, the tree's colours were startlingly bright. The stark branches of winter. The fragile buds of spring, the burst of verdant leaves before they drifted to the ground in red, brown, gold, and russet.

Something was stuck in my throat, large and heavy, ready to spike with panic. Something that would turn into a scream if I let it out.

The tree rippled, and the leaves rustled in an invisible breeze before they fell to the ground in their last moments of life.

And deep in my chest, curled around my heart, where the hoarfrost of Lady Winter's rage had once prickled, I felt the stretch of power.

My magic.

Awake, and reaching for me.

*O*nce, *there is a princess.*

And she lives.

But not without a price.

ACKNOWLEDGEMENTS

With only a few exceptions, every writer I know has said the second published book is difficult. I went in knowing this, and yet was still unprepared. Much like Emri against her parents, writing *Daughter of Winter and Twilight* was much different to her predecessor.

Thank you to my agent, Eric Smith, for the encouragement when I said I wanted to return to this world, loving Micah best, and your confidence that I'd make it to the end. Thank you for believing in me. Sorry for tricking you with a prologue and an accidental doorstopper. I'll probably do it again.

My editor, Helen Carr, for only expressing mild concern when I admitted the wordcount had gone beyond even my expectations and for reading the (long) drafts while figuring out how to make them better. Thank you for loving this world, helping me improve, and guiding me away from my impulse to go on plot detours.

Thank you to everyone at The O'Brien Press for wanting to do another book! Special thanks to Aoife and Kasandra for reading an edited draft and providing invaluable feedback, Emma Byrne for the stunning cover, and Bex Sheridan for the fantastic map and family trees. Thanks also to Ivan and Kunak, Brenda and Elena in Sales, Ruth and Chloe in Marketing and Publicity, and everyone else I don't directly interact with, but who helped get the books published. Gratitude must also, of course, go to Michael O'Brien, who sadly won't get to see this book published.

To Gabbie Pop and David R. Slayton: thank you for listening to me agonise about this book for three years and holding my hand through my (frequent) doubts. David, thank you for over a decade of believing in me. Gabbie, thank you for going above and beyond the expectations of friendship. Sorry about the three versions of Chapter Six that never made it through edits and the 5am voice notes as I figured out plot problems against deadlines.

Thank you to my writer friends, who listened and commiserated as I wrote and edited this book, and provide friendship and support as we navigate this industry. Special thanks to those who debuted with me in 2020.

Thank you to Eden for eleventh hour advice on beard growth, and to Lyra for being the real-life inspiration for Night's cat. Best cat (don't tell your sister).

Due to the nature of publishing, things often happen after the acknowledgements are written. So: thank you to Bolinda and Anna Popplewell for making a fantastic audiobook of *Queen of Coin and Whispers*, and to Casemate and Upstart Distribution for helping my books succeed beyond Ireland and the U.K. Thanks also to Samantha Shannon for her kind words and support for *Queen of Coin and Whispers*, and to C.L. Clark for their kind words for *Daughter of Winter and Twilight*.

To continue my tradition of thanking inanimate objects, this time the honour goes to my tiny IKEA desk where I wrote and drafted this book through the pandemic. I wish you were bigger and had storage, but we made it through anyway.

Thank you to all the booksellers, bloggers, and reviewers who championed *Queen of Coin and Whispers* before and during the pandemic, and still do years later. It was a stressful, uncertain time to debut, and you helped make *Queen* a success despite the sudden wobbly odds. I appreciate it so much.

And lastly, thank you to everyone who bought and read *Queen of Coin and Whispers.* You are why I got to return to this world and reveal another side to it. Lia and Xania mean a great deal to me, and I was incredibly touched by everyone who reached out to tell me they felt the same about them. If this is your first time here, I hope you love Emri and her companions. If you've followed me from *Queen,* I hope you love her as much as Lia and Xania.

Read an extract from
Helen Corcoran's
stunning debut novel

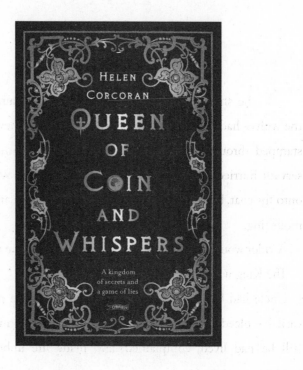

CHAPTER ONE

LIA

The sheep were undeniably dead. As I examined what the wolves had left behind, and tried not to panic, new footsteps stamped through the frozen grass. I rose, stiff with cold, as a servant hurried a rider towards me. The royal sigil was stitched onto his coat, but I focused on his sleeve: no purple armband for mourning.

A rider would race here in late winter for only one reason.

The King wasn't dead, but he *was* dying.

Uncle had been clinging to life for months. The reports had varied – bleeding, vomiting, recovery, bleeding, vomiting – but still he had lived, complained, and made life unbearable for everyone.

And now –

My aunt had given me enough warning, at least. I'd worried that she wouldn't.

'Your Highness.' The servant bowed and the rider sank to

his knees, sweating, and held out a letter. I cracked the seal, tucked the smaller hidden note into my glove, and scanned the expected words.

... no longer eating, can't keep water down, preparations are under-way ...

I'd waited years for this. I'd expected to feel delight, maybe even relief. My uncle was dying. The throne would finally be mine.

Panic bristled in my throat again. I lowered the note.

Father, please give me the courage to do this well.

'You've made a difficult journey,' I told the rider. 'Please take the time to regain your strength here.'

'The pleasure is mine, Your Highness.' The rider trembled, as if the shadow of my uncle's impending death had hounded him north. He'd probably expected to meet me in a drawing room, not in a field examining slaughtered sheep.

They left me, and I staggered towards a tree and leaned against the trunk. The bark pressed against my coat, reassuringly familiar. The air scraped my nose and throat as I took deep, shaky breaths. I fished the second note out of my glove. Matthias had written two words in a version of our childhood code:

No delays.

No delays. Our phrase for when Uncle's death was imminent and I was to *get down here now*.

Matthias hated that I went north every winter when Uncle could no longer stand the sight of me. I was one of the few nobles who did. 'It's ridiculous,' he'd fume. 'You're up there, freezing and alone, while the Court gets drunk and eats too much.'

'I'm with my people,' I always replied.

'You're the heir. Your people are the entire country, not just your estate tenants.'

We'd argued before I'd left Court in late summer. Matthias had suspected – correctly – that Uncle's health was beyond help and I should stay, while I didn't want to resemble a princess hovering over the crown like a scavenger bird. The throne would be mine whether or not I stayed in Arkaala.

I broke into a run, swearing under my breath, and hurried back towards the manor. We'd have to travel quickly. Uncle must have declined suddenly, or Matthias would have sent more warning to prepare for the trip.

I should have listened to him.

As I approached, the doors leading to the gardens burst open. Mother rushed down the steps. 'Lia!'

The house staff were probably huddled at every window facing us. They'd all heard her improper glee.

I stopped. Stayed silent. Everyone at the windows would slink away; only the bravest would eavesdrop. The sun was still pale, the gardens still bright with winter roses. Everything looked the same as when I'd woken up. But nothing would be the same after this.

'Lia, you will be *Queen*.'

If only Mother's joy was entirely for me. She'd locked horns with Uncle long before marrying my father, their disagreements blooming into steady loathing. At least social propriety would get her into mourning dress. Uncle's death would give her back a decade, where Father's had threaded silver in her brown hair, deepened the wrinkles around her mouth.

I slipped by her and up the steps.

'We need to discuss –'

'We leave for Arkaala as soon as possible,' I said. 'There is little to discuss until we see Uncle.' There was, in fact, plenty to discuss before I saw him. There was much to do and decide. But Uncle wasn't dead yet. He still deserved my respect, even if he'd done little to earn it, and I couldn't act otherwise if I wanted to win over his allies as Queen.

I was being unfair to Mother, to both of us – we'd dreamed of this moment for so long. I'd spent years frustrated by Uncle's inept rule, knowing I could do better but powerless until I inherited.

We were so close.

But I could never publicly rejoice at his demise, and I wouldn't allow Mother to relish hers.

She sputtered as I went through the doors.

I strode down the hall, already imagining the Court bowing and curtseying. A hard bud slowly unfurled inside me, releasing not just relief but anticipation. I'd waited years, biding my time, treading the stormy waves of family hatred to reach the other side mostly unscathed.

Now, I was Queen, a wolf in my own right. I held the chess pieces.

It was time to use them.

♀ ♀ ♀

In a moment of decency, Uncle was dying as winter finally lost its grip. Travel would be as swift as the time of year would allow.

As the carriage thundered along the road, the grief finally hit. My chest ached as if someone had dumped cold water over me. I'd spent ten years in my family's estate – too cold in winter, too warm in summer – learning how to be Queen. I'd grown up commanding imaginary armies against Matthias, my oldest friend. We'd wandered through every stream, climbed every tree, and planned our futures lying on summer grass.

Father had died there.

Now the estate would continue without me.

The poor autumn and winter had made food prices soar. About a third of my tenants couldn't afford enough to last them through winter. We'd raided the estate's food stores to keep them alive. Everyone we saw on the road was too thin, and too resigned about it. I'd known Uncle had ignored his duties in favour of the next meal, the next drink, the next entertainment, but it wasn't the same as seeing it.

I worried, even though I tried not to. If I couldn't keep sheep alive, how could I rule Edar?

Bad roads delayed us after several days of rain, so we arrived at Arkaala, the capital, in early afternoon, instead of late at night as planned. My heart still lifted at the crumbling remnants of Empire architecture, surrounded by layers of winding streets sprawling towards the docks.

Then the bells started.

We were too late.

Uncle was dead.

And I was Queen.